The Empty

Jude LaHaye

A Wings ePress, Inc.
Science Fiction Novel

Wings ePress, Inc.

Edited by: Jeanne Smith
Copy Edited by: Dorothy Bodoin
Executive Editor: Jeanne Smith
Cover Artist: Trisha FitzGerald-Jung

Wings ePress Books
www.wingsepress.com

Copyright © 2020 by: Jude LaHaye
ISBN-13: 978-1-61309-561-4
ISBN-10: 1-61309-561-9

Published In the United States Of America

Wings ePress Inc.
3000 N. Rock Road
Newton, KS 67114

Dedication

To William, the number one fan of the Solar System

BOOK ONE: 115 DEGREES

Preface

I have to trust that this document can be read.

I put my story—and the stories of the others involved in this great endeavor—into our version of "writing" and then I ran it through a Universal Translator designed and developed by one of my other selves. If that sounds strange, hopefully you will find understanding as you read what I have written.

Hundreds of thousands of years in humanity's future, marks on pages are no longer used to communicate or to tell stories. We still use visual means to record thoughts and events, but you people of the remote past would recognize them as "streams" of video, audio, and holograph rather than discrete letters combined into words—and then further combined into complete ideas. "Sentences," I think you call them.

So I cannot make any sense of the result of this conversion: the document looks indecipherable to me, an enormous volume of marks. Yes, they are digitized, but they still look like a crazy collection of black marks on a white surface. How odd! No color, no movement, no audio effects. How the people of your time dealt with communications using this method is beyond me.

I have to trust that you can read this because it is vitally important that you do so. You must understand what happened in your future so you can enact laws and develop enforcement to prevent these things from ever happening in the first place.

Do not pursue science to violate the membrane between parallel universes. Outlaw it. Enforce the law with all the determination you can muster. Make the penalties for breaking this law serious deterrents.

Read my story. Read it and believe it, because it happened...in your future. Hundreds of thousands of years into your future.

Entropy increases with time—it cannot fail to—because that is one of the basic characteristics of any and all universes. So, in your Time, if I have made my calculations successfully, nearby universes to your own look very, very similar to yours. This was my goal: to find the correct Time to send this story. I target a Time when the infinite copies of the Earth look very, very much the same. I target the Time before the parallel universes began to fray...to branch and bend.

In my Time, and to a large part due to actions that I myself have taken, the paths humanity treads have exponentially splintered and diverged, and those parallel universes are parallel in terms of Time only. Humanity's worlds in each universe are very, very different from one another, *and so are the various forms of human society on these worlds.*

Accept that there is science which can breach the barrier between parallel universes. I am telling you right now: it can be done.

But, for the sake of all of future Humanity, don't do it. Strive for peace on Earth above all else. Start working now on a strategy to save humanity from the threat of the dying Sun—one such plan which I much admire is that of building enormous solar sails and moving the planet further out in the system between Jupiter and Saturn, for example. I have included design and deployment instructions for these in this capsule. Many other schemes involve using material from the asteroid belt between Mars and Jupiter to form a new planet for humanity to emigrate to. Be aware—and avoid at all costs—any scheme to alter the Sun itself. These plans do not merit pursuit. They are catastrophically wrong. They will ensure the annihilation of the human race.

Please make widest dissemination of this document. I urge you to unite all of humanity in the effort to save every human being from the dangers of our Sun—and the dangers of our separate Earths, whatever we call them.

I alone have written this record; but I include the names of all of the other people who are part of this story.

Signed,
Arne Wong (Future) on behalf of:
Arne Wong (Laboratory)
Arne Wong (The Empty)
Arne Wong (Original)
Mann Yu (Original)
Amnelia Yu (Original)
Amnelia Yu (Restored)
Amnelia Lee (Earth)
Xanu Lee (Nova Terra)
Xanu Lee (Earth)
Maximillian Lee (Nova Terra)
Maximillian Lee (Earth)
Maxx Lee (Earth)
Cece Wong (Original)
Cece Wong (Earth)
Yi-Tai Feng (Earth)
Cece Feng (Earth)
Nene Wong (Original)
Nobe Chung (Original)
Yutani Amniko (At-sui)
Yutani Myochi (At-sui)
Liu Lee (The Empty)
Liu Lee (Unnamed Parallel Universe)
Joxe Xian (Earth)

One

"This is important, Nene Wong," I repeated. "They're doing a sweep. Birthers gotta go underground. Now."

She didn't acknowledge me...maybe because she couldn't. Even though their containers had evaporated, there were at least six tell-tale rings of oily liquid on the table attesting to just how much the girl had had to drink that morning.

I touched her. Just a poke of my index finger, but it provoked a response.

"Get off me, Spiker-scum!" she screamed, recoiling from my finger like it was a loaded trasher.

"Nene Wong," I repeated for the third time in as many minutes. "The Authority is sweeping. This morning. Now, even. Do you have somewhere safe to go?"

"You first," she snarled. She looked at me then. Her eyes were like portals to somewhere I didn't want to go. "Why aren't *you* running, Arne Wong?" Her snarl morphed from snarky to curious. "What makes you different from the rest of us?"

She knew. She knew I was a Birther, too.

She should have.

We were siblings.

"We go through this every time," I responded. "We don't have time to do it again. You have to leave."

"OK, OK," she acceded drunkenly. "Just how do you propose I do that?"

"Out through the kitchen," I told her, calling up the city's grid on my palm. I continued to scroll through details, finally finding the local area's schema. "Take a right at the exit, count three ground panels, then tap the lower right corner on the fourth. It will spring open briefly. Be quick. Jump down into it—you know the routine. It will close behind you. Wait for me there. I will issue the 'all clear' when they've gone." I positioned her mask over her mouth and nose and forcibly pulled her to her feet.

She managed to make it to the exit. I trusted her to follow the rest of my instructions. I had to. It was essential that I be here when the Authority showed up.

I put on my regular show. I littered the table with used stim-cups I carried with me for just this kind of occasion; they created the illusion I needed. The crumpled, stained containers said I had been there all morning. I had designed them to evaporate slowly and sequentially.

The files on my workpad provided cause: terraforming plans and projections were displayed across multiple screen tiers. The active model's 3D holo spun suspended in the air in front of me.

They were real. The plans. The projections. They were real, I mean. I was part of the Terraforming Team preparing Nova Terra for the influx of Earth transfers. Hells, I was the team chief.

We weren't ready. We weren't on schedule. OK, we were late, and the expanding red gasbag that used to be friendly, yellow Sol was constantly reminding us of that. Not that any of us now living remembers a little, yellow sun. The sun we knew had been growing larger and redder for hundreds of thousands of years.

But that little yellow sun was in the archives. Children were taught about it. Artists commonly featured it in their fictional landscapes. It appeared in many corporate logos.

The ugly truth was that not all of Earth's emigrants would make it to the relative safety of Nova Terra. Many of the poor and unskilled Earth population would be left behind to die, albeit slowly. Oh, and painfully. Even the robots would stop functioning eventually, their metal and artificial components overheated and under-lubricated.

At least there wouldn't be new generations of people left to suffer and die. All of the birthing laboratories and equipment had long since been transferred off Earth in anticipation of its abandonment.

But we were late. We were not ready. Our atmosphere was too thin, our surface water still poisonous.

Skilled laborers had been on Nova Terra for generations. Their skills ranged from bio-agriculture to protein manufacture to various sciences, chemistry being the dominant one. Me? I am an engineer. A terraforming engineer. That makes me rare. Rare and valuable.

And a nineteenth generation Birther. Something I carefully hide under many complex layers of deception.

Nene Wong could have "outed" me, but she wouldn't. Her survival and that of our birth mother depended on my job and the status it provided.

Yes, birth mother.

Nene Wong and I were born of a woman. She was impregnated by a man, our father, now deceased. Well, "Involuntarily Retired" is the official determination. He was caught by a random, errant bio-scan on public transportation. The Authority discovered he was an illegal. A rebel. A procreator. He had somehow escaped mandatory modification—you know, the in-vitro surgeries and therapies which rendered a man a neuter and a woman womb-less. Our status was achieved outside the laboratories of the official system. We were born, not decanted. We arrived in the world in blood and pain. We suckled at our mother's breasts. We were not modified. We, too, would grow to procreate. It was our duty—our mandate.

There were many of us. Nova Terra had made us possible. Viable, even.

In the early days, back in our original timeline, when Sol was friendly, Earth Authorities accepted almost anyone who was willing to emigrate to the asteroid colonies. For many, many years, fertile men and women were permitted to emigrate without challenge.

Short-sightedness is a genetic trait common to all human beings. The officials who accepted bribes to overlook and even fake bio-scans truly believed they were ridding Earth of its undesirables, in other words, doing their civic duty.

"Engineer." The androgynous voice interrupted my reveries. I found myself grateful.

"Yes?" I responded, faking an annoyance at being interrupted that I did not truly feel. I slowly raised my eyes from my plans and projections to meet the eyes of my interrogator. They were real. The eyes, I mean. The sleek silver and gold metal Authority official had human eyes.

An officer, then.

"What can I do for you, Officer?" I looked at his medallion. "Yu. Officer Yu. How can I assist the Authority today?"

"You are Engineer Wong?" the official asked in response to my question, I hated that. Hybrids never learn any manners. They almost always answer a question with another question. My opinion, but there it is.

I turned my own medallion toward the Authority representative in non-verbal reply to his question. Unlike his, my medallion was affixed to my outer garment, not my metal carapace.

"I hate that." The voice seemed less androgynous now. It carried raw emotion. Nuance. Personality. Individual personality.

"What?" I paused. "What do you hate?" I heard it in my voice. Surprise. I cursed myself under my breath. How was it that I could not maintain a more detached demeanor? Why did I always respond honestly to external stimuli?

"Humans," the Authority representative replied. "They never respond verbally to a question of identity. They must always simply flash their credentials."

"Credentials?" I repeated. I was doing it again, reacting without dissembling. But this was an instance where I felt justified. The hybrid had just used an unusual word. It was a word that was not part of normal hybrid programming.

Officer Yu did not respond. He just continued to look into my eyes with his own. His own human eyes.

"Brain?" blurted from my twice-damned mouth. In my imagination, the word hung in the air between us. I saw the officer reach for something in one of the myriad pouches hanging from his utility belt. Was he going to trash me for my gaffe?

No trasher was produced. Instead, the hybrid authority "man" slammed a holo-disc on the table in front of me. It sat there glimmering, sparking even, on the only table space not occupied by my plans, projections, and empty stim-containers.

"Yes," Yu responded. Wow. I am impressed. We were communicating—I mean having a conversation.

"That is the primary reason that I sought you out," he said, pulling out a chair and seating himself. Oh, so it hadn't been an Authority raid after all. The Authority was only looking for me...

"Because you have a brain?" I asked.

"Because you noticed," he replied.

I took that in for a moment, silently congratulating myself for my self-possession. When I looked at him, Yu was looking back, patiently waiting for me to be ready to continue.

I nodded at him. More non-verbal communication. I quickly remedied this by speaking.

"You want me to look at this?" I asked, gesturing toward the gleaming disc. Oh, and feeling like an idiot. This had been the perfect moment for non-verbal communication and I blew it.

His face crumpled into an expression. Whoa! This was a very expensive model, then. His expression was readable. Amusement.

He nodded his head in response to my totally unnecessary question. He continued to express amusement.

An amusement which disappeared the moment I reached for the disc and plugged it into my wrist-port.

"I wish to hire you," Yu said. "And it's 'Inspector'," he amended. "As in 'Detective Inspector.'" He paused. He seemed to be making a decision. "As in 'Detective Inspector Amnelia Yu'," he said, evidently having made his decision. She. She said, having made her decision.

"I see," I replied, acknowledging the receipt of unsolicited information on Yu's rank, and sexual orientation.

"I begin to hope that you are, as reported, the man for the job," was Yu's response. "You do not waste precious words."

I nodded again, very deliberately not wasting a word at this juncture.

I activated the holo. A detailed image of a normal-looking human male was revealed, spinning to display his every aspect.

"This is my son," Detective Inspector Yu said. "I need you to find him."

I looked at Amnelia Yu and wasted a few words on her. "Your son?" I asked first. "Why do you need a private investigator to find someone—anyone?" There, I said it. I said it without saying it. I am a private investigator. I gave her this nugget knowingly, investing it in the hope of encouraging her to reciprocate. I also introduced one of my major personal attributes: my skepticism. I challenged her first statement. I told her that I doubted the target's status as her son.

She got it.

"He is the product of one of my ova," she said. So, she is super wealthy, then. I filed this information away where it belonged: in my billing subroutine. "He is my son. I raised him, too. I bought him the finest mnemonic education interfaces available.

"I am emotionally invested in him."

That was an admission. She was saying a lot, here. I looked back at the holo. The man revealed looked very normal. He had no obvious modifications. He was tall for a human—almost five feet tall.

I, myself, at 5'2", am a giant among men. His skin was ebony, as were all humans at this point in our million or so years of evolution. His thumbs and index fingers were twice as long as their three fellows, as expected. He wore his hair in a youthful, spiky style, which spoke to his social status, financial priorities, or both. His eyes were amber and flecked with blue, just like his mother's.

"He looks young," I ventured. "Not yet forty?"

"He will be forty next quarter," she acknowledged.

"What is his occupation?"

"He is an astrophysicist."

"Employer?"

"Yu-Lee Laboratories."

"Coincidence?"

"His grandfather is Max Yu. My father."

"Impressive."

"If you say so."

"Why does he need finding?" I turned to look her in the eyes. Her eyes were there waiting for contact with my own. I had to suppress the flinch I felt at the intimacy.

"He is a danger to himself and to others," she stated without emotion. "He plays with dark matter."

"In his laboratory? As part of the work he does for Yu-Lee?"

"No. In secret. On his own."

"That would require a lot of infrastructure," the engineer in me posited.

"Nevertheless," she said. "He is experimenting. I do not know where he performs his experiments."

"How do you know there are experiments?" my skeptic had surfaced.

Detective Inspector Yu slapped another holo-disc down in front of me. This one bore the official seal of the Authority's Criminal Activities Division.

"Here are records going back two-and-a-half quarters, of crimes committed using what I suspect is banned technology," she said. "It is my own personal theory that controlled dark matter shielding has been used in each crime to circumvent normal detection technologies.

"I am no scientist, but I also theorize that this technology is responsible for the transportation of the stolen goods. It is all quite remarkable—astonishing, even—as you will soon see."

I quickly skimmed through the case files on the disc. "Can I assume your theory has met with official resistance?"

She was amused again, briefly. Her face, though, was completely serious when she next spoke. "You could say so," she finally said. Her robotic voice contained perfectly expressed sarcasm. And irony. It was nuanced.

I had a hunch. "Did your son develop your neural interfaces?"

She was looking into my eyes again. She smiled. Smiled. Her eyes danced. "You are as good as they said," she observed aloud. I nodded my acceptance of the compliment.

"But you're wrong," she said. "My father designed all of the software…It is the hardware my son was responsible for. His expertise is in materials. My face is his patented design and his most advanced accomplishment.

"I thought dark matter was intelligent," I challenged. "How does he control it? Dark matter caused the destruction of our race over many, many timelines. It has kept us imprisoned here for billions of years, stranded in this backwater of a timeline, the pariahs of the universe. There is evidence to support the theory that human civilizations have been 'rolled back' by dark matter forces at least ten times in the last four billion years—that is why the Sun is nearly eight billion years old and our own civilization only three hundred million…" I let my rampage peter out and then die as I saw the look in her beautiful eyes. She already knew what I was spouting. She was exercising patience while I grew increasingly excited, angry even. It is a consistent, genetic character trait of those born of women: we have a visceral hatred of imprisonment. We need to be free, both in will and in movement.

It's frustrating.

"Your genes are showing," Amnelia Yu observed knowingly.

Knowingly. She knew, or at least strongly suspected.

"I have no idea what you are talking about."

"I know," she repeated, this time without attitude. "Let's just leave it at that—for now."

"Is that a threat?"

"If it needs to be," she said flatly. All vestige of amusement had evaporated. In its place, I sensed a certain tinge of regret on her part. Was I imagining it?

"You would rather that I take on your case voluntarily. OK, I volunteer. Does that mean you're not paying?"

She seemed relieved. "Don't be obtuse," she said. I put that word in my new file where I had catalogued 'credentials.'

"You will be well paid," she continued. "File your hours and expenses. Tell me where to transfer the credits. All reasonable claims will be paid without challenge."

She rose to depart, leaving both of her holo-discs with me.

"When and where did you last see him?" I asked the back of her gold and silver head.

She didn't turn around but answered as she powered away. "At home. This morning. As he left for work."

She had nearly cleared the doorway when she stopped and turned around to face me once more.

"I should say *when* he left for work," she said. "I believe he plays with the very structure of time, itself. And he seems to have become lost." She hesitated a moment as if deciding whether to say what she next did.

"I fear he cannot find his way back to our timeline." And with this last, she turned and left, the smooth sound of her high-end hydraulics fading with her increasing distance.

I heard it, though. I heard her voice quaver. With raw emotion. She cried without tears.

Two

I had time to go through the Criminal Activities Division's files in detail later that day, after I had retrieved Nene from hiding and returned her safely home.

"She's drunk again," I told our mother as I dumped my sister on the seating unit in the common room.

"Oh dear," mother replied, nonchalantly sidling up to Nene Wong and placing the back of one hand to her forehead.

"She's fine," Mother pronounced, the accuracy of her feathery touch going unchallenged.

Unchallengeable. She always knew when we were seriously ill. She was uncanny like that.

And drunk. She, too, tottered about a bit, assisted by some unctuous liquid much like what Nene had had.

"Why must you two drink so much?" I asked without any expectation of an answer. At some level, I must have understood their need to self-medicate.

Me? I had my work. I had a reputation and excellent credentials. There was that word again. Credentials.

Mine were fake, of course, but fakes of the highest quality. The Guild had ensured that I was issued these rare commodities after my science aptitude test results were posted.

It was the Guild, the Birther's prime and most powerful organization, which obtained not only my identity for me, but also all of the best mnemonic advanced educational instruction available in science and technology.

I was a terraformer because the Guild determined they needed someone in that low-density skill group. But I could just as easily have been an astrophysicist like the man I now sought—I had earned the degree.

Mann Yu. Actually, it was Manfred Maximillian Yu, but he went by Mann, double-n. I was certain he would have been permitted, encouraged even, to take the famous handle which his grandfather used—Max—but his insistence on establishing himself as separate from his grandsire was an obvious attempt to make himself appear independent. Self-made, even.

As if.

Nobody on Nova Terra was self-made. It was impossible. I had The Guild. Mann Yu had Yu-Lee Laboratories. People not associated with corporations or government entities lived well only if they were decent criminals.

I don't mean criminals with hearts of gold. I mean criminals who are very good at committing crimes which netted material goods.

Like my sister. And my mother. They were criminals. They didn't need to be sober to show up for work.

And now, apparently, so was Mann Yu.

A criminal, I meant. I didn't know if he was sober or not.

The files indicated that a very high-tech cloaking device had been deployed on Nova Terra and that it only seemed to "show up" when crimes were being committed.

"Moms," I said, calling to her from across the room. She mumbled something unintelligible, indicating that she was listening to me.

"What's going on in your world of crime?" I asked. I often referred to the societal stratum she and Nene occupied as a world. It was as different from mine as if it occupied its own orbit, after all.

"What do you mean?" She didn't slur her words. Ever. It was really hard to determine her level of inebriation.

She seemed completely sober at the moment.

"New tech?" I prodded.

"Yeah, there's something new out there," she admitted. "I haven't seen it in person, but it's rumored to be very cool."

"'Very cool'," I repeated. "In what way?"

"Sophistication."

"Sophistication?"

"Yeah, it's very cool. High tech. Powerful. Easily deployed. Just as easily retracted. Pocket-sized, if I'm getting good info."

"Who is using it?"

"Someone new," she said. "Someone we don't know. Yet."

"What is it being used for?"

"Completely confounding The Authority," she said, laughing a little, like she was enjoying The Authority's discomfit at being "confounded."

I returned to the files. Detective Inspector Yu had done an excellent job in documenting the apparent disappearance of an industrial borer, twenty tons of construction-grade constrete, and various types and sizes of power sources. I said "disappearance" because in each case, the security system recorded black-outs, and only black-outs. One moment and the goods were sitting where they should have been, and the next there was absolutely nothing, nothing from any angle or monitoring system. Then, after a few seconds, hardly even time for alarms to be activated, the picture returned crystal clear. Sharp. No fuzzy edges or anything.

But the goods which were being monitored?

In each case when the picture returned, there were no longer any goods to monitor.

No forensics of any kind: no prints, no tracks, no dropped hair, skin cells, or fibers of any kind.

"I don't know how these things could have just disappeared like that," I said to my mother, gesturing for her to come and look at the files.

She travelled across the room in seconds, seeming to float across it as if her feet didn't even touch the floor. That was my moms. She was a beautiful lady, graceful and lithe. Her long shiny hair was jet black and moved as she moved—like a river of silk. She always wore her work clothes—skin-tight black garments which would never do her the disservice of snagging or tearing. Or reflecting light.

And Nene Wong looked just like her.

I must have favored my father, that's all I can say for my own looks. At least I'm tall. Moms and Nene are not. Tall. I am at least three inches taller than either of them.

That's right. I have said it before. A giant among men.

"Very cool," she said once again, viewing the files from over my shoulder. "I want."

"Moms, you need to stay low profile!" I admonished her.

She laughed again, her laughter tripping across the room like droplets of water flung from delicate fingertips. "What could be lower profile than that?" she crowed, pointing across the picture array I had constructed. "Poof! Gone! So cool..."

"Yeah, but this guy's going to get caught," I told her. "Without a doubt. He has called too much attention to himself with these huge heists. He will be caught," I repeated for emphasis. She was still ignoring me. "Moms."

She finally looked back at me and smiled. I knew that smile. It spoke clearly, needing no words.

"Moms, do not go looking for this guy. It's too dangerous."

She had grabbed her overgarment and wrapped herself in it. "I will be careful," she said, checking the house security system before unlocking the door. "Don't worry about me." She slipped into her smooth, black boots and adjusted her face mask just before stepping out. "I will be just fine."

I heard her. I just didn't believe her.

Well, I had better get to work. I had to catch Mann Yu, if that's who this new super-thief was, before my mother caught up to him.

That meant I left our shelter mere moments after she did. As I pulled my mask into place, I could detect faint whiffs of the scent she commonly wore when outside—barely detected, thankfully. Most men would assume the essence was perfume. I knew different.

It was my mother's secret weapon. It was a nerve agent she deployed to screw with people's memories. No one ever clearly remembered seeing her after they inhaled her "attar of neuroses."

Both she and I wore our oxygen masks, and we both knew better than to remove them until she deployed the neutralizer. It only took a few moments for her agent to have effect.

Attar of Neuroses. That was her name for her invention. She was a very clever woman, was my mother. More than clever, she had the brain of an inventor...a chemist, even. Her only education had been squeezed from bootleg mnemonics which were poorly organized and not integrated in the least.

What a waste, I thought. Such a brain, and never to be used in the furtherance of humanity's goals.

She was an illegal. A Birther. A rebel. If she were ever caught by The Authority, it would be involuntary retirement for her.

And that meant death. Perhaps a quick one. Perhaps a neat one. But death, nonetheless.

It is the Law.

Three

I visited the scenes of all of the "disappearances." I swear I thought I caught a glimpse of my mother at each scene, leaving as I was entering.

Makes a boy proud to have such a capable moms.

I love her so much that sometimes it physically hurts, especially in a spot to the left and center of my chest.

Someone told me once that this place is where our hearts used to reside. We surgically reposition them further down in the body cavity now, in a protective casing that prevents them from wearing out or experiencing traumatic stoppages.

Lots of room in those cavities now that our intestines and reproduction equipment have been removed. The anus and vagina exist now purely for recreation for those who go for that kind of thing. We have been like this for hundreds of thousands of years, if by "we" you understand that to mean "we legal citizens," those born in artificial womb-structures in laboratories. Not me. I am not legal. I can reproduce. Most of us, though, have opted for the heart and intestine surgeries. It is really hard to hide the output of an active intestine. We call it the "offal truth," ha ha. It was simply too risky to keep them. The intestines.

For some reason, this errant thought brought me back to my then-present, the scene of the industrial borer theft. I took a quick look around to make sure I was not observed, myself. Assured of my own security, I then took a much longer look.

It's a skill of mine. Observation, that is. Back then I was really great—intuitive, even. I walked the scene until I felt it...that little "ping" in my head, signaling me that some illusory residue of the crime was present.

It was tiny, but it was there. After zeroing in on my "ping," I found it. No, not the ping, but the source of it. Nothing. It was nothing.

No, not the passive absence of something, but rather a hole of nothing where something should have been.

I moved my foot and the hole in it disappeared. I moved it back to its previous location and the hole reappeared. It was odd, though. It didn't travel the breadth of my foot like a shadow. It popped into existence when my foot was in one precise position. An inch one way or the other, and it didn't manifest.

I didn't know what to make of it.

I positioned my foot to make...or allow...the hole to appear. I stuck my finger straight through it. I wiggled the finger. I felt something like emptiness surrounding my fingertip. It certainly wasn't anything solid. When I removed my finger it was whole and unchanged. As was the hole.

But my "ping" was really pinging. I moved my foot once more and stared at the floor. There—a tiny little pinprick of nothing! I took out the stylus I carried for lock-picking and stuck it through the hole. It was a tight fit, certainly tighter than when my foot was wearing the hole.

Odd. Odder and odder.

I moved the stylus and the hole moved with it. I did not expect that result. The hole could be moved. I wondered: could it be picked up?

I had evidence bags with me. I always carried them when I was doing detecting work. I also had an extraction tool. It came in handy when inanimate objects needed to be extracted from animate remains. Hey, it happened more than you'd think. And it was very messy work, too.

Suddenly I noticed that the stylus was being squeezed, in fact, it was being ejected from the hole by some kind of pressure.

Then "pop!" the stylus was free of the hole. And the hole was gone.

I looked at the tip of the metal pin, the stylus, and I couldn't see it. I put my free hand up to it and felt for the tip.

I can't describe to you what the area where my intestines used to be was doing while I watched the invisible end of the stylus pass through the index finger and thumb I was using to feel for it. Its metal tip became visible when the flesh it was passing through disappeared.

It crawled. Not the hole. The near-empty cavern that once contained my guts crawled as the barren hair follicles on the top of my head responded in kind.

I threw the stylus into the evidence bag I had extracted from one of the pockets on my utility vest. It actually stayed where I placed it, locked in place by vacuum.

It had to be more than vacuum. I mean, if you think about it, dark matter practically swims in vacuum. What were the other properties of the evidence bags? Well, they were static-free. Frictionless. Antiseptic. Lined with a microscopic form of constrete—wait, constrete! Like the material stolen by the megaton in one of the detective inspector's crimes. Add some odd to the growing collection of odd...

After scouring the facility for evidence of more holes of nothing, I took my prize home. I had found no more of its kind in the massive structure. That didn't mean there weren't others there, but I did a thorough job. If I didn't find them, no one else would either.

~ * ~

"Broke your stylus?" Nene taunted me when I threw the evidence bag on the kitchen counter at home. "How did you do that? Is there a keypad somewhere with a tiny dagger in it?"

Yes, that is how I employed the stylus: to pick locks. I used its sharp end to activate the codes on the tiny chips which controlled the locking devices.

I still call it "picking a lock." I've researched detective lore from our distant past. I like to use terms from Olde Earth when I can make them stretch to fit my world. I also refer to my gravity-boots as my "gumshoes." Yes, it is quite a stretch, that one. But at some level it pleases me.

"Take another look," I told her.

She got closer to the bag and looked hard. "Why does the vacuum avoid the end of it?" she asked. "I can't see it, but the outline of the bag says it is there."

She looked back up at me. "Is that what you wanted me to see?" She crossed the room and threw herself on the seating unit. She sprawled. When her body was comfortable she levered her head back up to direct her eyes toward mine.

"Big deal," she said.

Strangely, it is this posture and look I remember best when I think of Nene. Back then it exasperated me. Everything bored that girl. Everything. And I miss it; I miss her. She might have been bored, but she wasn't boring—those eyes of hers said volumes.

Hope was what I got from her. Not mine, hers. She hoped, constantly and unremittingly, that I would say something to her that would excite her interest.

I tried. Tried and failed mostly. Hells, she wouldn't admit I said something interesting even if I did. This thought makes me chuckle a little.

"It's nothing," I told her, watching that face of hers closely. "The head of that stylus is full of nothing."

There. An expression. Yes, there was a big component of doubt. But there was something else. I think it might have been a much sought for and elusive question mark, but I can't be sure. She flopped back down on the seating unit and toggled a controller which activated her latest, purloined virtual world. In it she flew over mesas and canyons, the sky blue as our dreams of blue, the far horizon turning glorious shades of amber and umber. And pink.

Nene liked pink. I left her to fly toward it, accelerating to reach it before it faded to dark. She soared, flying both around and through peach-tinged clouds on her way. Her expression was pure rapture. I grabbed my evidence bag on the way out. "Tell Moms I won't be home for eats," I told Nene over my shoulder as I left the apartment.

"Whatever," she said, waving me away. Our "eats" were portable, so I pocketed a couple of nutritive tablets. I would eat, just not at home that night.

I needed to consult with Detective Inspector Yu. I had decided to disclose my discovery to her.

I was also strangely excited to be meeting her again. This feeling I buried deep, partly because I couldn't explain it to myself, and partly because I could.

Four

"Thanks for seeing me," I said to Detective Inspector Yu less than an hour later.

"Did I have a choice?" she replied, her facial expression wooden, and well...robotic. "You said it was urgent," she added. She looked at me and it happened. Her face communicated it: curiosity. She was curious. Was she curious about me or just the urgent matter I proposed to discuss with her? Her eyes twinkled. Was she flirting with me or was that just wishful thinking?

No, not thinking. This was beyond thought. It was feeling, but that word was too weak. Connection. That's what it was. We connected at a level that felt compelling...but what were we being compelled to do, exactly? My ping returned as I gazed at her.

"I found something quite remarkable," I told her, keeping my professional veneer in place. She rolled her eyes at me. She didn't believe, not for a moment, that I missed her unspoken communication.

She didn't believe that I wasn't feeling what she was feeling.

I threw the evidence bag on the enormous table that dominated the room. Unlike most corporate business places, the inspector's office was almost bare of furniture or decoration. She had a very tall desk, no chair, and this enormous, pitted, ancient-looking conference table. I brushed my hand on its surface briefly, and then immediately returned the hand to get a better feel.

Wood?

By the gods, I said in shock to myself. I tried to keep my face neutral, but when I lifted my eyes to meet hers, I knew I communicated my real emotions again.

Shock.

"Yes, it's real," she said, answering a question I didn't have to ask. "We have the greenhouses on-line...well, Yu-Lee Laboratories has them on-line. It is one of their new materials. And yes, my son is responsible for engineering these rapid growth forests."

"So Yu-Lee Laboratories will be delivering my terraforming forests?" I asked. I didn't know the source of the procurement, only that delivery was supposed to be imminent.

"And bushes and bracken, I believe," she replied. "I would be astonished to hear that they had any competition on that contract. Is there anyone else working biologics?"

I smirked. It was my self-deprecating tactic. "Well," I said, "the government laboratories were supposed to be in the lead on overall bio-technology. Maybe they didn't prioritize the trees..."

She was hiking an eyebrow at me. Okay, she didn't believe what I was selling any more than I did.

"So what is in your baggie?" she asked, crossing the room to pick it up by one corner. She peered at it closely and then it was her turn to look shocked.

"Is this what I think it is?" she asked. Her voice was quiet. She was awed.

"That is my theory," I told her. "I found this dark matter at the crime scene where the industrial borer was stolen."

"I am not even going to ask you how you found this in that

enormous complex," she said, shaking her head in what I chose to believe was admiration. "I've been there, several times. I have had teams of ten and twenty detectives go over that place with the best forensics equipment available."

She put the bag back on the table and looked me in the eyes once more.

"What is this skill?" she asked. She was completely serious. "How can you do what no one else is capable of?"

"Well shucks, ma'am," I said, purposely dropping my eyes to the tabletop. I stopped short of blushing, but I admit I did sort of bat my eyelashes in her general direction. "Just lucky I guess."

She laughed. Laughed! I joined her after a moment.

"Okay, so don't tell me," she said, once she had control of herself again. "Keep your super-power secret. For now..."

I had to segue. It was urgent that I do so. "I wish to see Mann Yu's office, laboratory, and records."

"Records?"

"Financials."

"Sure. I have already been through them, though."

"As his mother or as the detective inspector?"

"Both."

"When will you see him again?"

"I expect him for dinner tonight, just as every night. But it's not him, you know."

"I am beginning to get a feeling for it," I admit. "When did you notice he wasn't himself?"

"It has been over a week. He went to work one day, and another man returned home that night in his place. He may look just like Mann Yu. He may sound like him. But he is not him. The detective inspector might not realize this, but the mother does without a scintilla of doubt."

I did not try to hold back judgment. "I believe you," I said.

Her eyes filled with tears. Grateful tears. Relieved tears. She finally had an ally.

I nodded my farewell to her, picked up my evidence bag, and turned to leave.

"What will you do next?" she asked, visibly marshalling control over her emotions.

"I am going to visit a friend at Utilities," I replied. "I think local energy consumption is going to be showing some recent anomalies. I'll let you know what I find."

"Good."

I left. I didn't want to. Just being in her company made me feel that the world was new and interesting. Well, truth be told, Nova Terra is new. But my work? My official work? Terraforming a planet takes generations. The work had started four hundred years ago, and I really didn't expect to see completion in my lifetime. As I have already confessed, we were behind goals across the spectrum. Some kind of technological breakthrough would be a boon to the ages. The interminable duration of the project made it not interesting.

Like these forests. They were interesting. Very.

Their imminent delivery excited me, too. I would get my laborers ready for delivery and transplantation. The forests would evolve with Nova Terra's atmosphere. That was the design specification: we contracted for plants that would interact with their environment, producing desired chemical effects and evolving simultaneously to thrive in the resultant atmospheric soup.

Soup for human beings to live in. No more face masks. Blue skies. Red sunsets. Potable water. The works.

Okay, okay. With our giant red sun, we'd probably settle for purple skies and "purpler" sunsets, but that would be a big and welcome chunk of progress.

I practically skipped all the way back to my office; I had work to do, after all. My "day job," as they used to say in the old days. Now most people are paid to be consumers. Consumers of the products that we real working stiffs put out there. The whole system, ostensibly designed to keep the populace diverted from rioting for social justice and a living wage, is a house of cards.

That's another old one: a house of cards. I like it. It is a vivid visual. Plus, we have some really severe winds here on The N-T.

Nova Terra. "The N-T." I don't care for the nickname, but some popular entertainer coined it and it took off. "Resistance is Futile!" shouts the voice in my head.

My super power. My secret.

My bane. My curse.

I have a voice in my head. Even when it's not speaking to me, it's communicating.

It's the source of my "pings," don't you know.

Five

I had friends. One of them worked for the Nova Terra Utilities Authority. Nobe was his name. Nobe Chung. I had several revolutions over him in age, but what with evolution and medical magic, several revolutions really didn't matter much anymore. We will all live hundreds of years, barring accidents or executions, sorry, "involuntary retirements." Nobe and I shared most traits of young men our age. I was taller than Nobe Chung, but I was taller than almost everyone. Nobe Chung was bigger, though. Much.

Back then, Nobe Chung was a technician at the Utilities Authority. He managed the exchange of currency for current, ha ha.

I didn't come up with that. My voice did. I'll take some of his stuff and put it to work when it's funny or clever.

Or both.

We have an uneasy peace, my voice and I. He tries not to criticize my habits and predilections and I try to ignore him entirely.

It almost works.

"So, Nobe Chung, can you help your friendly neighborhood terraformer with some data analysis?" I said as I entered his office.

He was alone. Nobe Chung was usually alone, lost in the swirling clouds of data that he enlarged, shrank, opened, closed, and repositioned using his two bare hands in the area surrounding his head.

His bald, black, etched head. Etched. He had designs embedded in his scalp which he insisted helped his concentration. Only members of the Data Guild wore scalp designs, so either they did assist him or it was guild-mandated folklore he was required to support. And propagate.

"Sure, Arne Wong, just give me a sec," he replied, pulling one column of data with a twist and a flip that changed its appearance. It was now a graph. Another flick and it was a three-dimensional roller coaster of data trends. With a nod of his head and a one-syllable sound of satisfaction, he used both of his hands to encapsulate his model and send it on its way.

"Okay, Terraformer extraordinaire," he said, turning to face me with a smile. "What can the Data King do for you?"

"Your Highness," I replied, bowing deeply. "I am seeking a miscreant."

"So this is not terraforming business?" Nobe Chung said suggestively. He is one of the very few people who know about my second occupation. "So you're saying it will be an interesting analysis this time?" He had pulled up a seat and plopped into it.

Not too many people were fat on The N-T—it was a choice, really. We could choose how much body fat we wanted to carry. Nobe Chung had opted for obesity. With The N-T's low gravity, it was no strain for him to carry it around, after all. And he was convinced he would survive the next famine when the rest of us wasted away. No amount of arguing could get him to agree that our nutrition supply was safe and plentiful.

He said he had the data to prove it. Said he had centuries of data on famine and its sources. He would gladly share his conclusions with anyone who was the least bit interested.

He had no takers.

Well, he was my friend. I would listen to him if he needed me to. But he was also a very kind person. He would not force anyone he cared about to wade through thirty millennia of raw data, analysis, and his own conclusions and projections.

And he cared about me. Besides me, his only close relationship was with his girl. My sister, Nene Wong.

"I am looking for changes in energy usage over the last few weeks," I said. "I think there is something going on, something criminal, that would require the rerouting of massive amounts of energy to accomplish."

"That's too easy," Nobe Chung said, obviously disappointed. "Plus, all of our protocols would automatically detect such a thing and alert us." He was calling up the data anyway, knowing I would want proof. Evidence.

"There are no spikes," he said, gesturing to the graph he had coaxed out of a mass of data. "Just steady growth in the manufacturing sector."

"Which part of the sector?" I asked.

"Yu-Lee Labs," he responded, pointing to a spot on the graph. "But they projected the increase," he added. "Something about a huge government contract..."

"My forest," I said. "They are going to be delivering my forest."

He looked suitably impressed. On Nobe Chung that's an extra chin and another furrow in his massive forehead.

"Well, so there it is," he concluded. "They requested the increase for the production and we set up the parameters they specified."

I got a ping just then, so I asked a follow-up question. "Who requested it?"

"One each Manfred Maximillian Yu," he said, pulling up a virtual communique out of the air. He was showing off a bit, I was thinking.

It was cool, though.

"Users are required to keep consumption records to show the actual energy-to-production efficiencies, aren't they?" I already knew this. Even the Terraforming Authority had to provide the Utilities guys proof that their precious energy was being used responsibly.

"Of course," Nobe Chung replied. "You need me to check Yu-Lee's records?"

"Can you do it from here?"

"Not legally."

"Then, no, Nobe Chung. I won't put you at risk. I have a contact at the Police Authority who can get those records for me. There is no need for you to get involved."

"Okay, but you have got to tell me if those asses over at Yu-Lee are misusing my resource," he said.

"Whoa," I responded, another ping alerting my attention. "'Asses'? Why are they asses?"

"It's that guy," Nobe Chung said, pointing at the communique which still floated in the air not far from his outstretched arm. "Mann Yu. He's been a real pain in the ass the last week or so. He used to be easy to deal with, and now he's become demanding and insulting. Threatening, even. It's like he's not even the same guy," Nobe Chung said. I reassured myself there was no way he could know how close to right he was. "He must be under some kind of unbelievable pressure or something."

He hesitated, another thought taking him over. I could practically see it happening. He had dismissed the ass Mann Yu and was retrieving some other issue from his enormous brain to quiz me on.

"Who is your contact at the Police Authority?" he asked, a little smirk overtaking his mouth and eyes.

"Not sure I should say," I said. "I'm not sure that she would want that information out in the general public."

"Amnelia Yu-Lee," Nobe said. His smirk grew.

"What makes you think that?" I asked.

It's like I confirmed it for him. He openly grinned and there were multiple chin and forehead special effects suddenly at play.

"She was here last week," he said, leaning forward in his chair to where it creaked and groaned ominously. "She wanted the same information you just asked for."

"Did you tell her that her son was an ass?" I threw at him.

"Not in those words," Nobe Chung said. "I got more class than that," he protested, looking hurt. "I just showed her the document," he said, once again pointing to it. "She just glanced at it. She seemed to dismiss it as unimportant."

"What did you make of her?" I asked my friend. I couldn't help myself.

"She is one cold, cunning bitch," Nobe Chung said.

"Explain. How was she cold and cunning?" I could not make myself repeat the third nasty label. It was too ugly.

"Well, she's an android, isn't she?" Nobe Chung answered. I did not fail to notice that he answered my question with a question. I also noticed that I didn't judge him for it like I had judged the detective inspector.

I supposed that meant I had an unconscious bias against our robot—and hybrid—citizens and I didn't like to know that about myself.

"Yeah, so?" I challenged.

"They got no heart," my friend said. "They got no intuition. They operate on programmed logic. They should be our servants, not our masters. Oh, and most importantly, they have no manners."

Well, I had to remind myself that my first exchange of words with Amnelia Yu had led me to that very conclusion: no manners.

I didn't want Nobe Chung knowing more about my interest in Amnelia Yu. I dropped the subject, ignoring the pinging sounds ricocheting around my cranium.

"See you Thursday?" I asked by way of ending the conversation.

"Of course!" Nobe Chung said. "I wouldn't miss it for anything."

I knew he meant that. Thursday evening meals at Chez Wong gave him a chance to be close to Nene Wong. He would not miss it, not for anything. I believe if my sister asked him to lose weight, he would do it for her, despite his convictions.

I feared Nene Wong was all too aware of her power over our fat friend. I also feared that she was capable of taking advantage of that power. I kept an eye on their relationship for this very reason.

You see, I believed Nobe Chung was correct. I, too, foresaw a future where our protein factories failed, or our supply chain collapsed.

I was just too vain to pile on the lard. I would die well before Nobe Chung if our fears proved founded, but I would live handsome in the meantime.

<h1 align="center">Six</h1>

"I think he's handsome," Nene Wong was saying to our moms when I finally got home that night. "I love his round self..."

Oh, she was obviously talking about Nobe Chung, then.

"He is not for you," our mother said flatly. "You are required to reproduce and he is not capable."

"I have plenty of time for reproduction," Nene Wong responded with a casualness I suspected she didn't feel. "I want to have some fun first. I want to have fun with Nobe Chung."

"Is he sexual?" Moms asked next. Okay, then. This was going to get really personal. I drew up a chair and sat to enjoy their conversation.

"Well, no, he isn't," Nene Wong said. "He's typically ASE, but if I wanted him to have sex with me, I am sure I could engender the proper, umm, reaction." She was smug about it, too. This was fun.

So humans have been reengineered—genetically altered—to be asexual. Nene Wong was right, though. Even if most people weren't interested in sexual intercourse, they all enjoyed physical contact and emotional closeness. They were all technically capable of mating.

It simply wasn't what drove their every thought anymore. It was no longer a major factor in relationships.

This change has been monumental in the quantum-leap advancement of humanity in everything from art to zoology. As soon as people's genetic and emotional changes were instituted, eliminating both male and female libido, peace broke out on Earth. Technological advancements in virtually all fields of endeavor took off exponentially.

We figured out how to travel in space, how to construct a new planet, how to create survivable habitats in hostile space.

How to terraform, theoretically. We are still at it. Victory in this one area has not actually been declared.

Delivery of my forests might change that. If the trees behaved as designed, I might just live to declare that terraforming victory after all. I was lost in that dream when the conversation took a loud turn.

"I won't!" Nene Wong screamed at my moms. I had lost track of what they had been saying, so deep was I in my dreams of a planet with breathable atmosphere and drinkable water.

"I am not reproducing with my own brother!" Nene Wong exclaimed. *Oh, yikes, zounds, and egad,* I thought. *Not this again.*

"Moms," I interrupted. "This is totally unnecessary. There are hundreds of eligible men out there for Nene Wong..."

Moms was staring at me with such anger in her eyes that it froze future utterances in my throat. I just waited. Waited for the explanation. We had heard it so many times before. It was coming.

"You don't have to have sex with each other," she hissed at us. We were both sitting on our hands for some reason. It was like if we couldn't move our hands, we'd have been incapable of speech. "We can inseminate. What we cannot do," and she paused to release me from the power of her eyes in order for her to capture Nene Wong's gaze, "is wait for you to go through the hundreds of 'eligible men' to find someone you like. Someone who meets your standards." By the way she said "standards," it was clear that she held Nene Wong's alleged standards in disregard if not disgust.

Moms dropped her eyes and Nene and I both sighed in relief. She wasn't through speaking yet, though. "You are nearly forty years old," she said to Nene Wong. "You should have had multiple children by now. You are letting everyone down. You are not doing your part."

"Let Arne Wong carry the damned child, then," my sister screamed once more. I experienced an involuntary eye-roll.

"I have a job…a career," I said in even tones. I did not want to be responsible for the inevitable escalation of this argument. "The Guild owns me. Look, Nene Wong, if you can get The Guild to agree to it, I will gladly bear our child…"

"I am not having a child with you!" Nene bellowed. "And you are ridiculous! You are not the one with the womb, here. You offer something you could never deliver." I stifled a laugh. "Deliver," she had said. Like in "deliver a baby."

Still, I remember being hurt at the time. She truly did not want my genetic donation.

Now it doesn't matter. I'll never see Nene Wong again, let alone sire a child with her.

"Well," I said, "since I am obviously not wanted here, I will take my leave." I arose and went for the door, pulling my face mask up over my nose and mouth as I went.

When my moms called for me, I did not stop. I had somewhere to be, somewhere important. I had something to do. Something new and exciting.

No, not the trees. Their delivery was still a few days in the future. Mann Yu. I was going to talk to Mann Yu. And moms and Nene Wong had got me in the right mood for it, too. I felt combative.

I still have all my male parts and juices. Hormones. Enzymes. Spermatozoa. Whatever. My crosses to bear. Where altered men lived lives of peace, logic, and reason, I was driven by my gonads to look for adventure, conquest, or even just a good argument. I had to hide my aggression and ambition from everyone. Some days were harder than others, but they were all hard. I accepted the daily doses of pharma The Guild offered to help me cope.

And yes, I looked down on those neutered men. They were all so docile, so reasonable.

So content.

My musings were interrupted by an incoming communique from Nobe Chung.

"You're not going to believe this," he said the moment I activated the connection.

"Shoot," I said, quite sure that I was capable of believing anything he had to say.

"The energy consumption at Yu-Lee Labs has stopped." He paused as if he were going over the data again, as I was sure he was, in fact, doing.

"...and reversed," he picked up after that moment. "They are now feeding energy back into the grid, Arne Wong. A lot of energy..."

It was like being gripped in a vise. I froze, both body and mind. The cycle I rode continued apace, automatically avoiding obstacles and keeping on course.

"I don't believe it," I finally muttered.

"Told you!" my friend crowed. "I told you it was unbelievable!"

"You win, Nobe Chung," I said, trying to keep the emotion from my voice. "You win."

I cut the connection and accelerated in the direction of Yu-Lee Laboratories. As my cycle sped through alleys and around other commuters, my voice sang. I guess that served to illustrate a meeting of the minds, in a matter of speaking.

I was excited, too. Very, very pumped. I pushed the manual override on the speed regulator and triggered the accelerator toward the redline.

Yu-Lee Labs was ahead. I could see the vast complex of laboratories and offices on a horizon that very quickly loomed ever larger. Closer.

I shivered with anticipation. I remember it distinctly. Shivering like what I felt in that moment is usually a symptom of a dangerous and potentially fatal suit malfunction or atmospheric/geologic calamity. But this shiver was different—it was one hundred percent anticipation. It was heady.

Seven

My shiver of anticipation morphed into a scintillating, tingling mixture of dread and delight when I saw Amnelia Yu standing at the main entrance to Yu-Lee Laboratories.

She looked particularly stunning. She had thrown a filmy scarf around her neck and there were rings sparkling on three of her eight fingers.

As I approached her, unsuccessfully willing the smile to let go of my lips, I detected something else. She was wearing a seductive scent of some kind. I can say that. I know it was a seductive scent because I, as opposed to most modern men, can be sexually moved by sensuous scents.

And I was moved. I was fortunately wearing my protective suit and I was pretty sure Detective Inspector Yu was unaware of my arousal.

"Are you carrying a trasher?" she asked coyly, eyeing the crotch of my suit. "Or are you just happy to see me?"

That's right. She knew. At least she had hinted she was aware of my unaltered—and illegal—status.

She did this on purpose. Was it flirtatious or was she torturing me?

Whichever it was, it was very un-robot-like behavior. But then she was not really a robot except for her body. She had her own brain, her own eyes. And her own heart, I was certain. Did it then matter that her body was artificial?

I did not answer my own question, because I already knew what I thought. What I felt.

She was a completely compelling person. As I thought this, I received a soft ping as if in confirmation.

"Good evening," I said, totally ignoring her taunt, playful or not. As I passed her on the approach to the building, I brushed against her arm.

She shivered.

Oh, by the gods, she shivered! Did that mean the material she was made of had sensation?

She detected my reaction to her own. She hesitated just for a moment before deciding to let me in on one more of her secrets.

"The material that my son designed for my body is capable of feeling. He embedded millions of artificial nerves in the external layer of my faux skin. I feel touch. Rain. Wind. Human contact."

She left it there, turning on her pneumatic heels to precede me through the building's entrance.

"Are you here to see anyone in particular?" she asked, pointedly changing the subject.

"Why, yes," I responded. "I am here to see Mann Yu."

"Do you have an appointment?" she asked.

"No."

"Then you are going to need me," she said. "I can get you in to see Mann Yu. You would never get access to him otherwise."

"Thanks."

"You don't sound like you believe me."

"I have my ways of gaining access to inaccessible people," I replied. I had no intention of elaborating on what those ways might be.

"So you don't want my help?"

"Maybe you're 'one of my ways,'" I said, deliberately injecting my words with the tones and inflections of humor.

"Well, I would recommend you don't make a habit of it," she said, matching my pitch and tone.

She was good.

We passed effortlessly through a number of checkpoints where no humor of any kind was in evidence. Goons in elaborate uniforms saluted Amnelia Yu as we passed. As for me, well, they allowed me to draft in behind her without challenge.

It was like being invisible. I tried hard to change that feeling to "invincible" but gave up after the first two checkpoints. It was wasted effort. I was going to need to reserve, no, *marshal*, all of my brainpower for the confrontation that was soon to take place.

We arrived at an enormous laboratory complex somewhere deep in the bowels of the massive compound. There, standing alone surrounded by humming and blinking machines, was a small man in an immaculate white laboratory coat. The facility around him was white on white, floor, walls, and ceiling. It made our blackness all the more stark in comparison.

"Mann Yu?" Amnelia Yu called to him softly. I wondered if he could detect the coolness in her tone, the whiff of distaste his name left in her mouth.

He turned. "Mother," he said. "Who is this you have brought with you?" There wasn't a touch of welcome or sentiment of any kind in his voice. His eyes seemed to be turned inward like he was repeating a script he had memorized.

"Mann Yu, this is Nova Terra's Chief Terraforming Engineer, Arne Wong."

A small spark of interest lit up Mann Yu's eyes. "The planet's architect, eh?" he asked, turning to look me over. The spark came and went like he was trying to suppress it but couldn't.

"I heard that our forests were nearly ready for delivery," I began, giving Amnelia Yu a look intended to communicate a request for her silent complicity. "I was wondering if I might get a tour of the facility and arrange for an inspection of the stock before it's shipped."

Mann Yu frowned. "No one told me this was a requirement," he said. The spark had fizzled out.

"It is not a requirement," I said. "It's a request."

Amnelia Yu was watching the man pretending to be her son with a snarl. She really didn't like this guy.

"Mann Yu, be civil," she spat at him. "Show Engineer Wong around the nursery. Now."

Mann Yu dropped his head to hide the rebellion writ clear in his eyes. "Yes, Mother," he finally choked out. "Right this way, Chief Engineer." He motioned for me to follow.

As we departed, I looked back once more in Amnelia Yu's direction. She caught my eye, gave me an abrupt nod, then turned and left.

Mann Yu and I were alone.

The forest tour was not what I was interested in. I wanted to find out what else was going on in the laboratory.

As I suspected, the vast forest, comprised of adult and young trees and various types of bush and bracken, occupied less than half of the space inside the Yu-Lee Laboratory complex.

But I could not see what else transpired there, because walls had been erected. Windowless walls. White. All white. Nose around as I could, I was unable to discern the slightest kind of activity anywhere else in the facility.

I thanked Mann Yu for the tour. I praised his efforts. I withdrew my request for pre-delivery inspection, which seemed to please him.

Then I asked him. I asked him what other projects were housed in all of the magnificence that was Yu-Lee Laboratories.

"Proprietary," was all he said. His eyes were dead again, but when I didn't pressure him for more information, that tiny spark reappeared.

"May I ask you a question?" he asked.

"Certainly."

"What are your plans for this planet, long term?" he asked. "Are you really going to import its population from Earth?"

He said "Earth" like it was a curse word. It sort of begged an answer of a certain bent.

"That is not my department," I responded. I suddenly saw a means to break the ice between us. "Yet," I added with emphasis.

It worked. He was interested. "You are extending your authority?" he asked.

"Let's say that I am exerting influence in the right places," I hinted.

"And how would a businessman like myself get involved in this exertion of influence?" he asked.

"Let me get back to you on that," I responded.

He seemed pleased. Good, that's what I was after. I had no real intention of influencing any policy that would strand a single human being on our old dying planet. But it seemed apparent from the words he begrudged me that he was one of those few who considered Earth emigrants inferior, or worse. These few were really quite a few, billions of Nova Terrans, and their numbers were growing.

We walked back out of the laboratory area side by side like comrades. It made me feel sick, but I was, and am, capable of this kind of deception if it gets me nearer to my own objectives.

As we were waiting for the lift to arrive to take me back to the street level, and exit, of the complex, I turned to Mann Yu like I had just remembered something minor I had forgotten to ask him. I had his attention.

"Power," I said.

"Excuse me?" he replied.

"How is it that you are feeding power back into the grid?" I clarified. "A lot of power?"

The look on his face was candid. Unshielded. Unpracticed. Honest. I had intended all of this by springing my question on him as I had.

He was afraid. No, he was terrified. He stuttered. "Wh-wh-what do you m-m-m-mean?" he managed to get out.

As I opened my mouth to answer, a terrific force made contact with the back of my head and I struggled mightily to hang on to consciousness as I fell to the pristine linoleum.

The last look I had of Mann Yu confused me, even as I lost sight of him, the laboratory, well, of everything.

He looked relieved. He nodded his approval and his gratitude to whomever it was who stood behind me.

Whoever had just struck me with such force that I was rendered unthinking, unfeeling, unaware.

I have a vague recollection of being dragged somewhere. And then that was all.

Eight

I awoke with a nightmare of a headache. Someone was shaking me and calling me by my name.

"Arne Wong, Arne Wong," a man was saying over and over again. He noticed that my eyes had opened.

"Finally!" he exclaimed, his relief evident. "Are you all right?"

I croaked. That was all I was capable of, my mouth was so dry. He grabbed a water bulb from the floor beside us and held it to my mouth.

Heaven. The water was cool and if there was a chemical aftertaste, I missed it. So, this water was from an exceptional, and rare, source.

I was able to sit up after drinking half of the bulb in what seemed like three or less gulps. My internal water cache replenished, I had to cease adding fluid even though my parched mouth screamed for more.

I blinked my eyes several times, staring at the man who was trying very hard to seem solicitous about my wellbeing.

No amount of blinking would change the appearance of this man. It was Mann Yu.

He supported my back with his forearm and daubed at the back of my head with a cool, wet cloth.

"You really got clobbered, there," he said, examining the back of my head. "You've probably been concussed."

"What happened?" I asked him, grabbing his hand to prevent any further ministrations. For all I knew, he could be cleaning an open wound with nuclear waste. I mean, this is the guy who was responsible for my being attacked, right?

He shrugged. "I found you down here in the labyrinth," he said. "You were lying on the floor, unconscious."

I decided to challenge him, knowing that playing stupid would have been a better tactic. Yes, my temper was part of my inheritance. Unaltered males have hair-trigger tempers.

"You know very well what happened to me and by whom," I spat out, holding his gaze captive in mine. "I was talking to you when I was attacked from behind. I watched you, Mann Yu. You knew my attacker. You were probably behind the whole thing..."

His face did something strange. It might have been the result of bad acting, bad nutrients, or of him having an epiphany of some kind. I didn't know which.

"Evil Mann Yu," he said. Okay, epiphany, then.

"'Evil Mann Yu'?" I echoed.

"It's a long story and an almost unbelievable one," he said in response to my question. "But you have to believe it and I don't have time to tell it more than once. Do you want to hear it, or should I just leave?"

"Spill it," I said, cradling my aching head in both hands.

And so he talked. He told me about a technological breakthrough that he had made using excited helium electrons. He said he had discovered dark matter and how to control it.

"It's not truly sentient," he said. "Not at the molecular level. It can be contained and used...used to reach parallel universes."

Despite my discomfort I sputtered an objection. "If it's not sentient, how is it that it rolls back our planet's timeline to destroy our advancement and keep us trapped here?"

"Oh that," he said. "It shakes its little toe because the fungus which is the human race gives it a nasty twinge. Its size defies our understanding. That is why we assume its attacks are purposeful. The dark matter being is just scratching an itch, probably without conscious thought, when it flings us back to our primitive status where we must begin all over again."

He stopped there and looked at me. The way my head felt, he could have made a claim to have invented time travel and cloned a dinosaur, and I would just have gestured him to go on with his story.

I gestured for him to continue with his story.

"So I acquired materials and equipment and bored through the dark energy which encapsulates the universe we live in. It's the excited electrons, their volatile gamma rays—they're called X17 particles—and the angle, 115 degrees, that made it possible." He was really getting excited. I found myself warming to this Mann Yu. He was genuine. He was forthcoming.

He was a damned genius.

"And so now I have a tunnel lined with dark matter with portals opening to a thousand parallel universes. A thousand. And I'm just getting started. I theorize that there are an infinite number of universes, separated from one another by thin layers of dark matter."

He paused again, seeming to be overwhelmed by his own accomplishment. He looked at me with wide eyes. "The wonder, Arne Wong. The sheer wonder of it all."

"Where is this tunnel of yours?" I managed to ask between clenched teeth. The headache was not improving with time.

"I built it down here. In the labyrinth." He was gesturing around us like he was reminding me of something I never knew.

"The labyrinth," I repeated between heartbeats which thudded in my damaged cranium.

"Oh, that's right," he said thoughtfully. "I forgot. You are not the Arne Wong who helped me build the labyrinth, are you? You must be the Arne Wong from our own original universe."

"Our own original universe?" I repeated. The implications of what Mann Yu had just told me were trying mightily to break through my aching thought barrier. An awesome realization was seeping through and threatening to bloom into full knowledge.

"Where is this 'other' Arne Wong?" I finally asked.

"Oh, he has long since returned to his own Nova Terra," Mann Yu replied. "Which, by the way, is millennia ahead of ours."

"In what way?" Was I imagining it, or was my pain fading? Perhaps I was just distracted by the discussion.

"Their air is breathable. Their water is potable. They have not just terraformed their Nova Terra, but there are massive forests and numerous bodies of water...seas, even. They control their population very carefully. They did not permit immigration from Old Earth. They allowed the old races to die with the birth of the red sun."

"So you think their approach was better than ours?" I challenged him. The thought of us turning our backs on billions of our Earth relatives disgusted me, and I was aware that my disgust was written all over my features.

I looked at him. His expression mirrored mine. "Absolutely not," he stated. "There is no benefit which justifies genocide. And that's why I allowed that Arne Wong to return to his Nova Terra. That's why I sealed the gate to that world. It won't keep us in if we want to go there, but it will keep him and his kind out."

"Your mother is worried about you," I said for some reason. I suppose she was on my mind at some level. That was a lie. She was on my mind almost constantly.

"I should have planned my absences better," Mann Yu responded ruefully.

"But you haven't been absent."

"What?"

"Your 'Evil Mann Yu' has preempted your life."

"He's what?"

"He stepped right into your shoes. He's running your laboratory. He's eating at your mother's table. He comes to work and goes home every day pretending to be you."

"How did he even get in?" Mann Yu asked, almost to himself. Good thing, that. I mean, how would I have known? I was trying my best to catch up as it was.

"You mean because you sealed the gate?"

"Yes, that is exactly what I mean."

"I would suggest that we go to check the security of your seal. I think 'Evil Arne Wong' might have been the one who tried to kill me."

"What makes you say that?"

"My voice is gone."

"Huh?"

"The voice in my head is gone. He must have been able to transfer to another 'me.' 'Evil Arne Wong' has my voice. And I want it back."

That did it. My head still hurt, but the pain no longer predominated. I had control of my thoughts and my ability to generate more of them.

More importantly, I had control of my legs again. I rose on them and held out a hand to help Mann Yu to his feet.

"Show me your tunnel and your gates," I said. "And I'll tell you what I can about my voice."

"Deal," Mann Yu said, upright once more and brushing non-existent dust from his pants and lab coat. "We'll walk while you talk."

"Deal."

Nine

Mann Yu was an exceptional listener. That did not mean he believed the story I told him about my voice, but he didn't scoff or debate.

We were walking down what presented as an endless corridor constructed with what looked like living constrete. By "living" I mean it didn't seem quite solid. It moved, but only within the confines of its own structure.

"That's the dark matter," Mann Yu said.

"What?"

"It's the dark matter that causes the constrete to roil."

"Roil?"

"Move. Roil as in move. Like moving water trapped between two solid invisible barriers."

"Good description. And thanks for the new word. 'Roil.' I'll add that to my lexicon."

"Lexicon is not such a bad word, either," he replied. We walked some more, now in silence. If his brain were as preoccupied as mine, the silence was only external.

We came to a concavity in the corridor. Mann Yu placed his palm against a panel on the wall next to it, and the concavity became a window. We could see through it. What we saw seemed to be a mirror image of the corridor we were standing in—except the corridor on the other side of the window didn't have anyone in it.

"This is the universe closest to our own," Mann Yu told me.

"Have you been there?"

"Oh, yes, many times."

"Is it identical to our own universe?" I was getting used to this multiple and parallel universe concept, I guess.

"Yes and no," he replied. "This is the world where I found Evil Mann Yu. Their terraforming program is far advanced over our own and their atmosphere and surface water are safe for human beings."

"Oh."

"Yeah, 'oh,'" he said, turning to look me in the eyes. "But this is also the world where they blocked the immigration of humans from Olde Earth. The inhabitants of this Nova Terra are humorless. Their world is beautiful and welcoming, but they, the human inhabitants, are neither beautiful nor welcoming

"They are efficient, however, and that is why I asked Evil Arne Wong to assist me in creating the labyrinth. I don't think I could have been successful without his help."

"And Evil Mann Yu?" I asked him. "How did he play in all of this?" I was gesturing to the corridor and its seemingly infinite space around us.

"He was an associate of yours, I mean 'Evil Arne Wong,'" Mann Yu said. "He and the Arne Wong of this universe had already constructed their own labyrinth, you see. What the other Arne Wong and I built in our universe used specifications and materials identical to those used in this other universe."

"This is difficult to comprehend," I said. I had comprehended the words with ease, but I was having many hells' worth of trouble believing their true significance. In a flash of understanding, I realized why I was having such a hard time getting my head around what Mann Yu was telling me.

"Wait a minute," I said, grabbing the other man by the coat sleeve. "If you had not constructed your labyrinth yet, how did the 'evil' you and me get here to help you? You hadn't built any of your gates, your portals, yet…"

I slowly stopped talking while watching Mann Yu's face go through some subtle and not-so-subtle gyrations. I waited for him to speak.

"It's simple, really," he finally said, not looking like what he was thinking was simple in the least. "They found us. They came through a portal that they made on their world. They came walking through the front door of Yu-Lee Laboratories, kept walking through all of the checkpoints, and walked straight into my office down in the basement. The guards recognized them, of course, and allowed them to walk unchallenged. That must be how Evil Mann Yu returned after I sealed my own gate. They must still maintain the original gate. While I was visiting their world I thought I had blocked their access to ours." He looked up at me, his expression rueful. "Obviously I was wrong," he said.

He lapsed into thought. He looked disturbed and something else. He looked like a man who had just realized he had done something extremely stupid.

And potentially fatal.

"Can we go through?" I asked him some moments later. I had decided to give him time to indulge in his regret and guilt. Not much, but when he looked like he needed an interruption, I did.

I interrupted.

"What?" he asked, shaking himself out of his reverie. "Did you ask if we can go through this gate?" he asked, pointing at the window.

I nodded, watching his reaction very carefully.

"We could. We certainly could…" He seemed to be having a debate with himself.

"But let's return to my laboratory. Please. I want to confirm that the other Mann Yu is there. I must remedy this situation."

"I understand. I will go with you."

He sighed in relief. "I appreciate that," he said. "Thank you."

Like I've said: nice guy. This Mann Yu was extremely likeable. I detected no arrogance, no attitude, no ego.

"So do you think the 'other' Mann Yu and Arne Wong will attack us again?" I asked casually as we returned the way we had just come.

"If they attacked you before, I can think of no reason why they would not attack again," he replied.

"So don't you think we should arm ourselves? You know, pick up some weapons, or even defensive equipment?"

"I am a thirty-second level black belt," Mann Yu told me without hubris. "I can defend myself."

"OK," I acquiesced. I was no slouch myself in the martial arts, but that didn't keep me from getting sandbagged by someone approaching stealthily from behind.

"I will be more vigilant," was my contribution to our plan.

"Shouldn't be hard to do that," he replied, using a familiar form of sarcastic nuance.

"You remind me of your mother," I replied. I, too, used a particular nuance—deadpan—to deliver this statement.

He laughed out loud. The sound seemed out of place as it echoed up and down the writhing corridor, but it was genuine. I had surprised him and he responded honestly. You know, without dissembling.

"So I have been told," he said when he gained control over his amusement. "So I have been told."

We both tried to walk as silently as possible as we neared the laboratory. I had thought we were doing a good job just until we pushed through the double doors which shielded the laboratory from the access hallways.

Mann Yu. The evil one. He stood facing the doors, obviously waiting for us. Standing next to him was me. You know, the other Arne Wong. Both of the men held nasty looking black rods with barbs on one end. I could discern a little hum coming from the weapons.

Powered. They hummed with power. So, the rods were super modern and bad ass trashers, I presumed. I also hoped they had settings this side of "lethal."

I have always maintained that hope is not a plan. In this instance, too, I tried to rid myself of any hope whatsoever. I needed to believe these men could and would kill us, given the chance.

With a speed that nearly defied my sense of vision, Mann Yu was flying through the air, his shiny black shoes making simultaneous contact with both of the weapons and causing them to fly several yards in different directions to fall harmlessly onto the laboratory's gleaming floor. They bounced and clanged noisily, finally settling to the floor about twenty yards away in either direction.

The 'others' looked at their hands in disbelief, and immediately started to run in the directions of their weaponry. Evil Mann Yu was cradling one hand. His face said he was in pain, but as of yet not a single sound had come from either of the invaders.

Invaders. That is how I saw them. They had come to our universe with plans to use it somehow.

They looked like us, but they did not think like us.

It was eerie, but I did it. I tackled the other 'me' before he reached his black trasher. Then I jumped back to my feet and used my best move, a flying side kick, to incapacitate him. As my foot contacted with the side of his head, I heard the sound that signified success. His skull was cracked. He wouldn't be doing anything threatening or dangerous for quite some time, if ever.

I turned to assist Mann Yu, but he had already subdued his twin. I had a moment of doubt—how would I know which one was standing a victor and the other one supine, defeated? They looked identical, down to the crease in their black trousers and their immaculate white lab coats.

"I would be the one with a working left hand," the victorious Mann Yu said, turning to flex said hand in evidence of its wellbeing. "It's me, Arne Wong. Now let's secure these two and wait for them to wake up."

We trussed the two men up and secured them to scoop-backed chairs we found in a storage closet.

And then we waited.

After the adrenalin of the battle had had a chance to dissipate, I was overridden with questions and fears.

"What are we going to do with these guys?" I asked. "You know, it's not like we can call the Authority and have them arrested—how could we possibly explain who they are and how they got here?"

"Oh, I've already called the Authority," Mann Yu said flatly.

"What? You called the Authority? Oh, by the gods, what are we going to tell them?"

"Not them," Mann Yu replied. "I called one Authority..."

"Mann Yu!" Her voice full of emotion, Amnelia Yu sped in on humming hydraulics to put her gold and silver arms around her son. "Oh, Mann Yu, I have been so worried about you..."

He hugged her back, his face gleaming with the pleasure of their reunion. "Well, Mother," he said, holding her back a pace in order to see her face, "this man has been absolutely instrumental in my safe return." He gestured with his head in my direction.

She turned to face me. Her smile and her gleaming eyes struck me like spears in that place behind my ribcage.

"Arne Wong. You are a wonder, every bit as good as they said you were. How can I ever repay you for finding my boy and returning him to me?"

"I love you," I heard myself saying. And then again.

"I love you."

Ten

Mann Yu was laughing again. "Mother," he chided her. "There you go again, playing with young men's hearts."

She blushed—*blushed*—and laughed along with him.

Me? I was so astonished and humiliated by what had come out of my mouth I was rendered mute. I couldn't even stammer.

But I wasn't sorry, either. OK, I was sorry I had made the brash admission, but I was not sorry for the way I felt.

I heard myself speak again. I remember being mildly interested in what I was going to say. "So you play with other young men's hearts?"

Her laughter died in her throat and in her eyes. In its place I saw concern, and pity.

Pity. That is the death blow to love.

"So," I started again, projecting a light heartedness which I definitely did not feel. "I have completed my mission, Detective Inspector Yu. I have found and returned your missing son to you.

But I also have a problem. What do I do with these two interlopers from another universe? Have you any experience in this area?"

Well, all right, that last question was a dig. I knew damned well that no one had experience with something like this.

"Interlopers from another universe?" she repeated, her voice hushed by awe. "Is that where the Mann Yu imposter originates? Another universe?" She was looking at her son for the answer. Okay, then, she was surprised, after all.

I guess she thought I didn't know any more than she did about parallel universes.

She wasn't far off. But still, it hurt that her question was not directed in any way toward me.

"Not only that," I preempted Mann Yu, "they have an open portal into our universe. There may be more of their kind here. They may have planned an invasion..."

The fear on her face grew exponentially with every wild supposition I threw at her.

"Enough, Arne Wong," Mann Yu said. "That's enough. You're scaring her."

I could see that. It did not make me feel good. I lapsed into silence. I dropped my head. That place under my ribcage felt bruised.

"Mother," Mann Yu said, turning once again to hold his mother by her shoulders. He spoke directly into her face, which, like mine, was examining the floor without really even seeing it.

"Mother, these interlopers are from a universe which is parallel to our own. They have their own Nova Terra. They have advances in terraforming we have not yet made. They discovered how to capture and manipulate dark matter as a means of bridging universes. They built a gateway to our universe—hells, they have thousands of other gateways as well. They came through one which brought them here to Yu-Lee Laboratories, and they taught me how to build." He paused as if to collect his thoughts – or catch his breath. "With their help, I have constructed a massive corridor lined with dark matter-infused constrete. I have built gateways to other universes. I have visited many of them. It's all simply marvelous, Mother..."

She had lifted her head and was staring at her child like she had never seen him before.

"Why did you not tell me? Why did you tell no one what you were doing?"

"That was the deal," Mann Yu said. Now it was his turn to drop his head. "I had to maintain utmost secrecy in order to share in their technology."

"But they must have wanted something in return," she protested, attempting without success to regain eye contact with her son. "What did they want in return?"

"Power," Mann Yu said, raising his head and squaring his shoulders. "They wanted a share of our power."

"Our power?" Amnelia Yu echoed. "What power?"

"The power, the dark energy, which results from breaching the barrier between universes," Mann Yu said. "Mother, this power is beyond anything we know about energy. They wished to harness this power, to use it to move their planet further out into the solar system. Their giant red sun has grown bigger than ours. Much bigger. They must move their planet or face annihilation."

Evil Mann Yu had regained consciousness. His head bobbled and he was groggy, but he had been listening to Mann Yu and was nodding in agreement.

"There is one other option we can still employ if you do not cooperate with us," he snarled. "We can invade. We can take over your backward planet and fix it. We can send your populace back through the portal to our dying world." He grinned a hideous grin. "And then we can seal the gateway, all of the gateways to other universes. Permanently." He paused to let all of this sink in. "So cooperate and you can save your world and its pitiful people," he concluded. "We only want your power."

~ * ~

We eventually freed our prisoners from the adhesives which stuck them to their chairs like flies in amber. We moved our discussion into one of the laboratory's secure conference facilities.

"Have you got any food?" a visibly suffering Arne Wong asked. "Don't you people eat?" We had slapped a medicinal compress on his shattered skull and he seemed to be returning to himself.

Mann Yu crossed the room and removed a bottle of nutritive tablets from a cabinet. He also retrieved several water bulbs. He placed the tablets and bulbs on the table in front of the others.

"What is this stuff?" the other Arne Wong asked, a look of disgust and disbelief on his face. "I asked for food."

"They don't eat food," the other Mann Yu snapped at him. "If you had stayed here more than a few hours at a time, you would know this."

The other Arne Wong looked abashed at this reproof. I assumed from this that he was Evil Mann Yu's subordinate.

"They take these tablets and about five tablespoons of water four times a day," Evil Mann Yu continued. "They don't have intestines, Arne Wong. They removed them." He leaned in close to his Arne Wong to deliver his next point. "They don't shit."

At this Evil Arne Wong's mouth dropped. "They don't shit?" he repeated.

"That's why their terraforming is so far behind ours," his boss informed him, and us. "They have no organic waste to mix in with the rocks and soil."

I was dumbfounded, as I am sure Amnelia and Mann Yu were.

"So you do?" I asked Evil Mann Yu. "You defecate?"

"Profusely," he replied. "That has been something of a problem during my stay here. I have had to nip back to my own Nova Terra to relieve myself. I was just on the verge of inventing a contained waste system here in your lab when you came bursting in, flailing and kicking at everything in sight."

"You were not holding weapons?" I challenged.

"Well, of course we were prepared to defend ourselves," Evil Mann Yu responded heatedly.

"That worked well," Mann Yu wryly observed.

"Let's return to our negotiations," Amnelia Yu interrupted. "I want to know why you needed to activate dual gateways between our universes to generate this dark energy flow you spoke of."

"Oh, the flow is generated when any gateway breaches space between universes," Evil Mann Yu said. "But to harness it for use, we need throughput. We need dual gateways or the energy just blasts its way out of the solar system and into open space."

"The Utilities Authority reports that this laboratory is feeding energy—and a lot of it—back into our own power grid," I informed the group. "Have you made an error of some sort?"

"The power flowing into your grid is a minute portion of the energy being generated," Evil Mann Yu responded. He came across as smug, but at least it was animation of a sort. The two "others" were mostly without expression. They had not expressed pain when we were hurting them. They never smiled. Or laughed.

Oh wait. Evil Arne Wong was smirking at me.

"What?" I said. "What are you smirking at?"

"I just had an errant thought," he replied. "It made the corners of my mouth turn up like this. I was close to making an almost involuntary noise to express amusement, at least that's the word I heard in my head just now."

"Amusement?" Evil Mann Yu said. "Amusement was bred out of our species millennia ago, you fool."

"I know, I know," Evil Arne Wong said, and then he was laughing. "Something's wrong with me. I can't stop making this noise," and even though he put his hands over his mouth, we could still hear muffled laughter.

"I need to get him to a medical professional," Evil Mann Yu announced, looking around the table for signs that any one of us might cooperate with him.

"No medical professional is going to be able to help him," I said. "It is hopeless. It's my voice. He has it. It's in his head."

The silence which greeted my pronouncement lasted for a long time. Evil Mann Yu had a look on his face which concerned me; Evil Arne Wong continued to chuckle without cease.

"I must return to my world at once," Evil Mann Yu announced through clenched teeth. "I need to shit."

So that explained the look on his face, then. This shitting process must be very unpleasant, then.

"That is impossible," Amnelia Yu said. "You are going nowhere."

"You will be sorry," Evil Mann Yu replied. "As will I. It is a very messy process."

"Arne Wong," Amnelia Yu said to me. "Take him to one of the matter disintegration chambers. He will leave his waste matter there. Once he has exited the chamber, turn on the incinerator."

"I should have thought of that..." Evil Mann Yu said under his breath. "Why didn't I think of that?" He visibly snapped himself out of his reverie and turned to face me. "Let's go. Now." He was up on his feet and heading for the door.

I ran after him. He had already closed the door to the disintegration chamber. I waited outside for ten minutes or so. When he emerged he was sweaty. I closed the door behind him and hit the incinerator button. I had less than zero interest in examining what he had left behind.

"I need to cleanse my hands," Evil Mann Yu told me.

"Gross," I replied, gesturing toward the nearest decontamination station. "I don't know how you people stand having to do that."

"We don't," he said humorlessly. "We sit."

I wasted a moment making an observation to myself. Even when these people make a joke, they're not joking. He was being quite literal.

When we returned to the conference room, Amnelia Yu and Evil Arne Wong were still seated. Arne had stopped laughing, at least, and his usual sneer was back in place. They stared at each other like the adversaries they had become.

"Everything all right?" Amnelia asked. Since it didn't look like she was really interested in an answer, I simply nodded. "So what's going on in here?" I asked, in what I considered a nonchalant manner. "What have you kids been up to? Saving the world or destroying it?" Yes, I was still miffed with her for rejecting my suit.

"Arne Wong here has been telling me about his universe," she replied. She caught the eye of Evil Mann Yu and directed her next statement to him.

"So I understand your mother died when you were a child." There wasn't a question, so Evil Mann Yu didn't respond.

"Is that true?" she said, producing the needed interrogatory.

"Yes," he replied without emotion. "She died when I was four years old." He looked at the robot with something like contempt stamped on his features.

"You disapprove of me?" she asked, a slight hint of amusement in her voice.

"You are an abomination," Evil Mann Yu replied. "We do not allow the sick to survive and we don't construct robots to carry living organs around. Only the strong and human survive and thrive in our universe." He managed to look smug at this point without sacrificing any of his contempt.

Amnelia Yu laughed, but it was a laugh borne from bitterness, not humor. "My son informs me that you left twelve billion human beings on your Olde Earth. You left them to die miserably in the poisonous aura of your giant red star."

"They had not the means to escape their fate, and we merely left them to it," Evil Mann Yu retorted. "Those of us who accepted asteroid and Nova Terra duties—those of us who strived to create Nova Terra—we took the risks and the rewards. It is only just."

"In this universe, justice walks hand in hand with compassion," Mann Yu said as he reentered the conference room. He carried objects in his arms. These he dumped unceremoniously on the room's enormous table. "My mother was saved by our technology. We would never allow a human life, a precious human life, to simply expire. Actually, we have recently upgraded her. I developed her outer layer, her skin, as a quantum leap improvement over the old, now obsolete, metal casing."

Evil Mann Yu seemed outraged by his clone's speech. "Abomination!" he shouted this time. Okay, so they weren't completely without emotion, I observed to myself. They were certainly capable of anger. Oh, and aggression, I amended, seeing as they had already threatened to destroy our Nova Terra in favor of their own survival. But he wasn't done yet. After inhaling a big breath, he continued.

"Amnelia Yu had a genetic abnormality which would inevitably have caused her to die horribly, in pain and humiliation." He paused, I thought for dramatic effect.

"We terminated her according to the laws of our planet." He looked at our Amnelia Yu again, his look of disgust back in place. "I, myself, at the ripe old age of four years, was subjected to many painful procedures in order to purge my own genetic code of her mutation. As a result, I was allowed to be educated in the field of science, and in the *business* of science."

"In your universe, do you reproduce?" I heard myself ask. Of course I would be interested in this. The Guild would be very interested in his answer.

"Not I," he replied. "The procedures I endured as a child have left me sterile."

"But I can reproduce," Evil Arne Wong interrupted. "I can and I have. The harem is producing my offspring in great numbers."

I was stunned. "So you have sexual relations with the females of your kind?" I asked. "You impregnate them and they carry your offspring within their wombs and give birth to them?"

"Just so," he responded, looking like he was doing me a kindness by answering. "It is my responsibility to sire as many offspring as possible, male offspring, primarily, and it is the duty of females to bear the offspring, to birth them, to nurture them until they are weaned, usually at six months. Once weaned from mother's milk, the children are sent away and the mothers returned to the harem." He paused, a look of curiosity overtaking him. "Why? How do you reproduce here?" Another emotion, if you could call it that. That of a superior indulging in curiosity about an inferior.

Inferior. That would be me. I decided immediately that I far preferred my status as rebel and outlaw in our universe to an inferior status in his.

"So you are Evil Mann Yu's inferior?" I asked him next, really leaning on the "inferior."

He flinched and glanced over at Evil Mann Yu using only the corner of his eyes.

He didn't respond, but Evil Mann Yu did. "I own him," he said without a scintilla of emotion. "He is my property. As are his cows. We need to produce more people to populate our planet, our Nova Terra."

He sat up straighter in his chair to deliver his next line. "I understand your people here refer to your planet as 'The N-T,'" he said. He saw me nod in confirmation that his information was correct.

"Well, the nickname of our planet in our universe is 'The M-T,'" he said. "You know, 'M-T,' as in 'empty.' Our population does not even measure in the millions. Not yet, that is." It appeared to be his last word on the subject. He introduced the next one, addressing it to our Mann Yu instead of his robotic mother.

"So what will it be?" he demanded. "What is your answer?"

Mann Yu looked at his mother, who nodded, acquiescing to some unspoken communication.

Mann Yu, once again using that amazing speed I had witnessed once before, sprang into action and had our evil twins handcuffed in mere seconds. As they sputtered in disbelief and outrage, he returned to the pile of things he had dumped on the table and picked up two very sturdy ankle bracelets as well.

"I designed these," he said with pride. "You will not be able to escape."

"Release us at once!" Evil Mann Yu ordered. "I will unleash the power of our planet upon you and yours. You will be annihilated!"

Mann Yu exchanged amused glances with me and his mother, who also wore an enticing grin, her eyes sparkling with excitement and anticipation.

My heart spasmed. And it spasmed again when I heard Mann Yu's next words.

"We will return to your planet, your 'M-T,'" he announced. "I will return as you and infiltrate your laboratory first. Then we will insinuate ourselves into your governmental offices and functions. You see, I discovered something very important in your Nova Terra when I visited it." He paused to allow the tension to build.

"I discovered a strong undercurrent of rebellion. Most of the people on your planet are enslaved to a very few of those of you who consider yourselves elite." He stared at Evil Mann Yu as he spoke these words. "You have powerful and secret guilds on your planet, much like we do on ours." Now he was looking at me. I tried not to react, but I don't think I was successful, because he winked at me at this juncture and grinned.

"I will work with these guilds, with your rebels, and we will overthrow your elite. We will replace them with leaders who will free all of your slaves." He sneered as he delivered the next statement. "Your 'cows' will be elevated to equal status with your males. It's over, Mann Yu." It appeared he was winding up. "We will not be invaded—*you* will be." He prepared to depart, but stopped to address his clone once more. "You will remain here with my mother and The N-T's Arne Wong."

I started to object but was halted by Mann Yu's outstretched palm. He resumed speaking.

"I think I will have allies from within your inner circle," he said insinuatingly. He looked at Evil Arne Wong, who sat unmoving, his rapt attention focused on Mann Yu.

Our Mann Yu, not his.

"Am I right, Arne Wong?" He was not addressing me. He spoke to the "other."

"I will go with you," the "other" Arne Wong said. There was a light in his eyes that had not made an appearance until just then. He stood and squared his shoulders.

"I will go with you," he repeated, "and we will launch a rebellion. We are ready. We have been preparing for generations. If we cannot overthrow our criminal elite, we will die trying."

Mann Yu smiled triumphantly and turned to address me and his mother.

"I need you two to wait here until I call for you. Our initial insertion into their universe must be small, too small for anyone to notice. Once I have a foothold, I will come for you.

"Evil Arne Wong will come with me. He will introduce me to his leaders, not his owners. The guild leaders. They have a fairly large armed militia. If they are as ready as he says they are, we will move fast. Be ready. I will soon need you both. Prepare yourselves."

I looked at Amnelia Yu and she at me. We turned to face Mann Yu and nodded our understanding and readiness.

At least I'd get to twiddle my thumbs in good company. I don't know what she was thinking, but her facial expression did not indicate that she was displeased.

Eleven

We put Evil Mann Yu in the incinerator room and secured it from the outside. His instructions were simple. Stay put. He glared at us but said nothing.

Amnelia Yu and I accompanied Mann Yu and Evil Arne Wong to the portal. We wished them luck. I clasped Mann Yu by his shoulders and whispered in his ear. "I don't trust him," I said.

He pushed back from me so he could gift me with a reassuring look. "They are not all that different from us," he said. "He is you at his foundations. Don't worry, I will be careful. But I think you can trust this Arne Wong." He said it openly and looked at the other. For his part, Arne Wong straightened his spine and pulled his shoulders back after hearing what Mann Yu had said.

He had my voice with him. That reassured me somewhat. I felt my voice would do what it could to minimize any potential harm Evil Arne Wong might inflict on Mann Yu.

Nothing happens by accident. My voice had made its move from me to the other for a reason.

This is the kind of stuff I told myself during the days Mann Yu was gone.

~ * ~

"I'm going in after him," I said to Amnelia Yu for about the fifteenth time in three days. "Something is wrong."

This time, however, she did not respond with her regular "don't be ridiculous." This time she said, "I'm going with you."

"You?" I challenged. "How can you go to a universe without robots and hope to go unnoticed?"

"Oh, I intend to be noticed," the intrepid Authority Detective Inspector said.

"Are we going in hot?" I asked, borrowing once again from my cache of Olde Earth vocabulary.

She looked at me and smiled. My heart was still doing its spasming thing. "If by that you mean are we carrying weapons, then yes, Arne Wong. We will be going in very hot, scorching, even.

"Evil Mann Yu has said their population is small. We have a chance to overwhelm the portion of it in the vicinity of their gateway at least."

She had given me an idea. "Attar of Neuroses," is what I then said.

She hiked one elegant eyebrow, urging me to explain myself.

"My moms," I said. The eyebrow inched further upward. "She has developed a neurotoxin which causes people not to see her. We should obtain some of her potion to bring with us."

Her eyebrow back in place once more, Amnelia Yu looked pensive. When she spoke again she had a sense of urgency which hadn't been present previously.

"Yes, why not?" she said. "Better yet, let's take her with us. And your sister, too."

I gasped my objection. She shared another one of her rare smiles with me and my objection dissipated like smoke. "They have skills," I said instead of reciting the list of reasons why my family should not be put at risk.

"I know," Amnelia Yu replied. "Trust me, Arne Wong. I know exactly what skills your moms and sis have. And we'll need them. Please go immediately and recruit them. Promise any incentive you need to convince them to join our little team."

I rose and turned to leave. Her hand grasped the sleeve of my outer-garment and I turned to face her again.

"Any incentive, Arne Wong. Including full citizenship. Including commutation of sentences for imprisoned and 'retired' Birthers...." Her look said more. I am sure I just gaped at her, my shock and disbelief temporarily incapacitating me. When I was able to regain control over my legs, I nodded to Amnelia Yu to reassure her that I had heard and received her message...and then I ran. I ran to my cycle and sped home. I pushed the limits of the cycle's capabilities and I pushed the limits of the law.

When I burst through the door of our living quarters, moms and Nene Wong were sitting at the dining table quietly consuming their evening nutritive tablets and delicately sipping on small bulbs of water.

"We need you!" I shouted. Their shocked reaction told me to calm down and I tried. "We need you to come with us to a parallel universe," I said in as calm a voice as I could assume. What I said apparently made up for the loss of volume if I gauged the looks on their faces correctly.

My moms took over. "You must have fallen on your head again," she said, rising and approaching me, her fever-diagnosing hand raised to my forehead. I caught her hand before it made contact and held it tight.

"Moms, I don't have the time to explain it right," I said. "Can you trust me? Can the two of you just come with me? Now?"

"That is not gonna happen," my sister said flatly. "No way. Never."

"Amnelia Yu has promised you full unconditional citizenship

and the commutation of father's sentence." I threw this out and let it sink in on them.

"I'll get my kit," Nene Wong told my mother. As for moms, she was already loading her utility belt with tools and vials.

"Bring all the Attar of Neuroses you've got," I told her. "We've got to move fast. Mann Yu has been gone for twelve days. He may have been harmed or even terminated, for all we know. We are going to rescue him."

"Who is 'we'?" Moms asked.

"Me," I responded. "Amnelia Yu, you, and Nene Wong."

"And me," a baritone voice announced in a tone that allowed no room for argument. "I am going, too."

I turned to face the voice. "Nobe Chung," I said. "And Nobe Chung... he's coming, too."

Nobe Chung gave me a look of satisfaction. "You got that right," he said. "And you are the one who is going to convince Amnelia Yu-Lee of it. I am going with Nene Wong. Nothing in any universe can stop that."

I knew, or strongly suspected, that Amnelia Yu was not going to be happy about this development. But when I played the Nobe Chung-Amnelia Yu scenario in my head, I saw the conclusion: Nobe Chung's love for my damaged sister would trump Amnelia Yu's objections without a doubt.

"That would be one of my conditions," Nene Wong added, as if pressure from her would alter the outcome. "If I go, Nobe Chung goes with me." And the two of them exchanged a glance that said it all. I remember thinking, *Is that what love is?* and then *That looks dangerous*, before I realized that what they had together was what only I had in a one-sided relationship with a robot. The pain in my chest confirmed it. Any objection I might have had withered to brittleness, shattered, and then dispersed itself.

"Let's go," I said. "We don't have any more time. We go now."

We filed out of the living quarters and took possession of our cycles.

We flew like legions of grim reapers were chasing us, riding ghostly cycles of their own.

Twelve

We had a plan. It was Nene Wong's idea. We were all a little surprised, including Nene Wong herself, that we had unanimously embraced her idea.

She was left as Evil Mann Yu's only guard while the rest of us secreted ourselves in the security office where all of Yu-Lee Laboratories' monitoring systems were housed. Nene Wong pretended to be distracted by a security claxon we had set off ourselves. This allowed Evil Mann Yu to escape. Like a mouse in a maze, he was herded through every conveniently unlocked door, following an exit route designed to dump him on the street in front of the laboratory complex. We strategically placed oxygen masks at calculated intervals, and he eventually picked one up.

We paid rapt attention as he exited the building, pulling on his mask. He made his way down a dark and narrow alley separating the two office buildings directly across the street from Yu-Lee Laboratories.

We intercepted him the moment he activated the portal, cutting off his escape and acquiring a second means of access for ourselves. Before I toggled the portal to inactive mode, we could see clearly through it. There were heavily armed thugs on the other side. I doubt they could see anything on our side—we had extinguished all nearby lighting systems and wore our own oxygen masks and dark clothing. Amnelia Yu had encased her shiny metal parts with a black hooded robe. It looked amazing on her.

"Okay," Amnelia Yu addressed me. "Obviously we cannot use this portal. Block this gate so that no one else can come through. Then we must return to the labyrinth and unseal the gate there. I know it's risky, but we have to do it. If we did not, we would have no way to get back to our own universe once we complete our mission."

"As to that," my mother said, stepping forward to face the robot. "What exactly is our mission?"

"We have to be ready to improvise, Cece Wong," Amnelia Yu responded. She addressed my mother, my sister, and my fat friend Nobe Chung with respect. Her ability to accept them as equals increased my respect for her. Pound, pound, wounded heart.

"Our mission will depend entirely on my son's status in this other Nova Terra. If he is safe and his plans are intact, we will probably simply retreat back through the gate and resume waiting. If, however, we discover that he has come to harm, we must rescue and recover him...even if he is dead." She paused to allow her statement to have its full effect.

"Arne Wong and I have talked this over many, many times, and we think that Mann Yu may be in trouble," she continued. "Let's be clear on this, though: we have no hard evidence. It's just that he has been in the other Nova Terra for over twelve days without making any contact with us. His plan depended on the support of Evil Arne Wong. If Evil Arne Wong turned on Mann Yu and exposed his identity and purpose, we fear Mann Yu may be in trouble...or worse."

Amnelia Yu straightened her shoulders and stood. "Arne Wong and I will wear oxygen masks which will serve to disguise our faces. The rest of you should carry your masks for use if Cece Wong needs to deploy her neurotoxin. Are we clear on this?" Everyone nodded in the affirmative.

She resumed. "We will go through one at a time. I will lead."

I raised my voice in objection. "I should go first," I told her. "At least I am not an obvious construct. I will be identified as human. I think that should buy us some indecision on the part of any guard posted on the other side of the portal. We can see the parallel labyrinth hallway on the other side of the portal. We can see that it's empty. What we can't know is whether they've posted any of their people further down the corridor.

"I will go through first," Amnelia Yu insisted. "You may come through next. I will permit you to scout further into the alternate labyrinth while I get the rest of our team through the portal." It was like I hadn't spoken up at all. She wasn't going to bend on this. It occurred to me that she was going first in order to protect me. That was probably a complete fantasy, but I decided to accept it as the reason she was so intractable. I liked the feeling it gave me. I was going to hang on to it.

Each of us carried multiple weapons. Most of them were designed to stun and incapacitate, but a few were lethal.

We all arrived at the portal in the labyrinth. The mirror-image on the other side of the portal did not show any occupants, whether human, animal, or insect. No motion of any kind could be discerned.

"Unlock the portal," Amnelia Yu instructed me. I did as she said. She stepped through and stood, completely visible and identifiable, on the other side. She motioned me forward. I followed her and then proceeded to investigate the corridor. It was completely straight, as was ours, so my initial investigation covered both directions in a matter of seconds.

No one. I saw no one. I proceeded toward a set of double doors nearly a quarter of a mile down the hallway, aware of the silent traversal of the portal behind me by the rest of the team.

I held my hand up in a predesignated signal for them to freeze. Having arrived at the doors, I nudged one of them open, very slowly, by using my right hip and steady pressure. It swung open easily, almost too easily. I held a projectile weapon in front of me, my twitchy finger on its trigger.

Empty. The corridor on the other side of the doors was as empty as the previous stretch had been. I used another signal to indicate it was safe for them to progress to my position.

"There will be three more stretches of corridor just like this one between us and the laboratory proper," I told the team. Amnelia Yu was the only one other than me who was intimately aware of the layout of the labyrinthine annex. "I will do exactly as I just did: I will have you stay at these doors until I reconnoiter. I will signal you to proceed or retreat based on my discoveries. I know this is slow and frustrating, but this is how it's going to go. Do you understand?"

They nodded their responses. They understood. I proceeded to the next pair of double doors. No one. I signaled the team to proceed. I was pleased to note that we were moving noiselessly.

We reached the final set of doors. I had been thinking about our next move during the preceding stages of our invasion. I did not think it reasonable that we would be able to travel the labyrinth and enter the laboratory without being observed by someone, machine or human. Surely they had surveillance systems...they simply objected to making robots or androids which mimicked human behavior, right?

I signaled a halt. I addressed them all, altering my eye contact to engage each of them one at a time as I spoke.

"I really don't think this facility is empty. It's just a hunch, a baseless hunch, but I expect for us to encounter significant resistance the moment we breach the next set of doors. I am recommending we go in firing. I would like to roll in at least one percussion grenade before any one of us passes the barrier. Thoughts?"

I wanted their candid feedback. I needed their candid feedback. I was not a military man—hells, we didn't have military men anymore. We had peace. It was just damned lucky I still had normal levels of testosterone. An adjusted male from our world would not be a successful warrior.

The last set of eyes I engaged with my own were the amber eyes with the blue flecks which belonged to Amnelia Yu. They were shimmering, almost brimming with tears, but not quite. I felt there was emotion, strong emotion, behind these tears. In retrospect, I think she was just worried about her son. At the time, however, I thought she was feeling proud of me. She was moved by effectiveness, my acumen, my manliness.

Her tone of voice did not match up with the sentimental motivations I ascribed to her. She was brusque.

"And if there is no one on the other side of these doors, the noise of our weapons will definitely alert the locals to our presence, Arne Wong. Examine the doors. Make sure they are not secured. If they are open, I would like to ask Cece Wong to enter the laboratory with all guns firing, figuratively, of course. I mean for her to deploy her neurotoxin. We will all have our masks on. But first, check the doors. Will they open or must we enter by force?"

Wordlessly, I complied. I holstered my weapon and very cautiously put the palms of both of my hands against the side of the double doors which had been swinging open for me up to this point.

Nothing. It did not budge.

I tried the other side. Same thing. I was not able to move either of the doors.

"They are either locked or blockaded," I reported.

"Check the locks," she instructed.

I extracted my lock pick tool from my vest pocket and inserted it into the lock mechanism.

"It's not locked," I reported.

"Blockaded, then," Amnelia Yu concluded.

"I would assume so," I replied. I was trying mightily to remain detached. I did not want my growing resentment of her treatment of me to affect our interactions. I was also aware that in my unaltered condition, I was extremely sensitive to being bossed around by a woman.

Even if that woman was a robot—an android.

I had years of practice hiding my feelings toward others, men and women alike. What I really lacked at this point was the humor and sarcasm I used to get from my voice. It was usually able to distract me, to defuse my temper.

But I didn't have it anymore. It had abandoned me. This thought did not help. Now my self-pity grew exponentially. The tears which had sprung to my eyes were generated by anger, not any softer emotion like fear, or love.

"All of us will push together," Amnelia Yu said. "Everyone—get your hands against the door, pick a side to concentrate your effort against. When I command it, push together...now!"

We pushed. The door began to move, something heavy on the other side preventing it from opening. We pushed without cease, encouraged by every inch of progress.

"Stop!" Amnelia Yu commanded. We did, sagging and staggering a bit. I noticed Nobe Chung was helping Nene Wong to stay upright, but he wasn't that steady on his feet to begin with. After a few moments, it was Nene Wong who was steadying the obese man. My moms didn't seem to be affected by the effort in the slightest, and of course the robotic Amnelia Yu was entirely unfazed.

"Arne Wong," Amnelia Yu called to me. "Squeeze through that door. Tell us what is blocking it."

I squeezed through, inching a shoulder past first and then following with my head and one leg for balance. I pulled the second shoulder and leg through with strength borne of terror once I saw what was on the other side of the double doors.

If I should live to see one thousand years, I will never be able to erase the memory of that sight. I screamed in horror and began to retch. Because of our alterations, I had neither stomach nor partially digested foodstuffs to add to the pile of rotting meat on the other side of that door.

Bodies. A lot of bodies. Maybe as many as forty bodies, not fresh, all burned and mutilated. From the state of decomposition, I estimated they had been there for over ten days.

"Ten days?" Amnelia Yu repeated. "So this happened after Mann Yu came through." It wasn't a question. She wasn't really talking to us, but rather to herself.

"Well after." She was reassuring herself.

"Explains why he couldn't return through the laboratory portal," Nobe Chung said. One by one, my companions had come through the door after me, making a wide circle around the grisly mound on the other side of it. We had all been wearing our oxygen masks so we could only imagine what the room must have smelled like.

"I have ascertained that his body is not here amongst these others," the detective inspector said. She was examining the corpses, lifting limbs and examining what was left of the dead men's faces.

Because they were men. All of them were men. They appeared to be wearing similar if not identical clothing, although that, too, was difficult to ascertain because of all of the dried blood and scorch marks.

I looked away from the dead men and surveilled the rest of the room.

It was obviously the scene of a violent struggle, holes having been blasted through walls. Evidence of explosions and fire was everywhere.

"I think Mann Yu must have done this—well, he and the men who supported his revolution. These men must have been trying to reach the portal to our universe. They were stopped. Slaughtered. What else explains this?"

"I agree with your assessment," Amnelia Yu said. I allowed myself to enjoy the feeling that engendered in me. Warmth. Fuzziness. Pride. But she wasn't done speaking yet. "And the struggle must be ongoing," she continued. "If this were a single event, the bodies would have been cleared and security forces posted."

"There must be fighting in other parts of this city," my moms added. "This is a city at war with itself," Nene Wong said, stepping forward to stand shoulder to shoulder with our mother. Nobe Chung stood behind them, his arms crossed, a look of determination on his fat face.

"I think we need to retreat," he said. "What can the five of us do against this level of violence? We have no combat experience. Look at the level of destruction around us. This must be only a small example of what is going on around—"

His speech was interrupted by the noise of doors slamming open. They were at the far end of the room we stood in. Some force had caused the double doors to slam open so hard and fast they banged loudly against the surrounding walls.

Part of my lexicon of Olde Earth words and phrases includes this: jackbooted thugs. I used to like this phrase until I actually saw one.

A jackbooted thug strode through the open doors. He was followed by about five more men wearing identical black leather uniforms and sporting those nasty black rods with the hooks on their business ends that Evil Mann Yu and Evil Arne Wong had carried.

"We have been waiting for you," the first thug announced loudly. "It is not safe here—you will all come with us. Now."

He gestured toward the open doors with his nasty trasher. None of his companions said a word. They merely stood behind him, their faces grim, their weapons held ready.

"The general is waiting for you," the man said, like the fact that someone called "the general" was waiting for us was a signal honor and privilege...and that we should be moving out smartly. He used his weapon to gesture toward the door again and his grim look went lethal.

"I think we should probably do as he says," Amnelia Yu said to us in a low voice. "The way I have this figured, Evil Arne Wong stands an excellent chance of being this 'general.' If we can find him, we can discover what has happened to Mann Yu."

I was the first to move in the direction of the door. The others slowly followed me. Amnelia Yu was the last of us to exit. Once she was through the door, our escort of jackbooted thugs fell in behind us. We walked through the damaged and burned remnants of Yu-Lee Laboratories and out onto a street scene from hell.

Thirteen

Our escorts muttered directions to us as we trod carefully across broken pavers and tangled piles of constrete. "Straight." "Right." "Left." It was arduous going and progress was gained grudgingly. The footing was treacherous and we were instructed—ordered, more like it—to make our way surreptitiously. So I thought it a safe assumption that there were opponents out loose in the city who would consider it their duty to capture or kill us.

Our thugs called the opponents The Bigs. That was helpful for me—I like to have words to label groups of common things. So, The Bigs were probably the old elite of this Nova Terra and the thugs were the rebels. The Thugs, by default, became my term for the people who were escorting us to the general. Naturally, I did not share this label of mine with anyone else. I didn't think The Thugs would find it flattering.

They had not bound our hands, nor were we made to surrender our weapons. I decided this was a positive development. I began to think our mission might still stand a chance to be successful.

I thought this for the forty minutes it took us to get to the constrete bunker that apparently served as the headquarters for the general and his troops. I was pretty sure this underground hideout was in the same location as the mass transit system tunnel in our universe. Things between the universes, at least in terms of the principal city's design, seemed to line up. This could prove very useful if I could manage to remember to use it.

We descended into the bunker. After climbing down its inoperative escalator, we reach an enormous room which had been lit with what looked like stage lights. Some were clear, some were muted, and some were colored. The colored lights spun and twirled. Instead of being festive, they served to distract and disorient.

At the end of this room, we discovered a dais upon which two enormous armchairs had been installed. These chairs had been affixed to the wooden platform.

Wood again. Oh, that's right, I realized. They had forests, massive forests, in this universe. Wood just might be the most common of their building materials.

When we saw the chairs, we made for them. At a subconscious level, we all knew these chairs were thrones. We would find the general in one of them, surely.

As we approached, I realized I did not recognize the man who sat in the chair positioned to the right—it was positioned to the right of the other chair, but it occupied the direct center point on the dais surface. This chair was for the guy in charge. That much was clear.

He spoke. The shock that went through me upon hearing his familiar voice passed like it was pure voltage.

I looked back at my team and found Nobe Chung with my eyes. He looked as shocked as I was. His eyes were bulging from his moon of a face. He shook.

It was Nobe Chung. The man on the throne was a very fit, very well-muscled Nobe Chung. The physical differences between the Nobe Chung of this universe and "our" Nobe Chung were such that an independent observer would never realize these men were clones of each other.

When I saw the look on Nene Wong's face, I followed her gaze. She was looking at the person sitting in the lesser position on the dais. I didn't need to look twice. This time the person was perfectly recognizable.

It was my moms. Our moms, mine and Nene Wong's. She, in turn, was looking incuriously at her clone, who stood five feet behind me in our tiny phalanx. Moms stared back at her, curiosity and challenge in her tense stance. She had not removed her oxygen mask. She rested one hand lightly on her weapon, the neurotoxin disperser.

The two people on the thrones stared at each of us in turn. The other Nobe Chung spoke, finally.

"Bring them," he ordered the chief thug from our escort. Without wasting a single word, the thug saluted and left the room, deputizing two of his crew to follow him with a simple hand gesture.

I could feel Amnelia Yu trembling next to me. I managed to make contact with her, moving close so our arms touched. She did not move away.

After what seemed an eternity, the thugs returned with two disheveled men who shuffled into the room on filthy and bare feet. Their hands were bound in front of them.

Mann Yu. Evil Arne Wong. They looked terrible. They were bruised and dirty. There were places on each of them where blood had dried. Their blood. That much was obvious, too.

"Mann Yu!" Amnelia Yu cried. She made a move to go to her son and was stopped in her tracks by one of the burliest of the thugs surrounding the throne.

"I am all right Mother," Mann Yu said with as much strength and confidence as he could muster. "Please don't bring harm upon yourself."

"'Mother'?" Evil Cece Wong echoed. She had a look of such disgust on her face it seemed she might become physically ill. "Your mother is a robot? A-a-a-an abomination? How is that even possible? We know you, Mann Yu. We know your mother died when you were a child."

"It is as I have been trying to tell you," a battered Evil Arne Wong said. "These people, this Mann Yu, they are not from our universe. Our Mann Yu is still captive in their universe." He paused to look me in the eye. I nodded to confirm his statement. He continued. "We have constructed gateways into parallel universes. I have told you this over and over again."

He turned to address the general, Evil Nobe Chung. "You don't realize it, Nobe Chung, but your twin from this other universe stands in front of you."

The general spoke as he looked us over again. "You will not call me Nobe Chung," he said. "I am *General* Nobe Chung. You will address me as such."

He sat back in his enormous chair, clearly frustrated. "I do not see any such a person here in this pathetic little group."

Cece Wong stepped forward and removed her mask. "You might not see your clone," she said, "but I know you recognize *me*."

"And *me*," I said, also removing my oxygen mask and stepping forward.

General Chung bellowed in outrage. "Who are you people? You," he said, pointing to my mother, "how dare you impersonate my mate?"

"Wait, Sire," Evil Cece Wong said, placing a restraining hand on his forearm. "Wait. You," she said, pointing with her free hand at my moms. "Step up. Get your hand off of that weapon." She paused to look at the chief thug. "Master Sergeant Liu Lee, why are these people armed?" He snapped a salute and signed for his troops to start disarming us. "I thought they were with us," he said. "I had orders to leave them unmolested. To escort them here. To keep them safe."

"Who gave these orders?" General Nobe Chung screamed. "Who dares to usurp my command?"

Evil Arne Wong stepped forward, holding his bound hands out to the nearest thug guard. The guard withdrew a knife from its sheath on his belt and cut the bindings from the prisoner. "I gave the orders," Arne Wong cried triumphantly, striding forward to stand in front of the general. "Release Mann Yu," he ordered the master sergeant, who signaled another of his men to comply.

Soon, Mann Yu stood beside Evil Arne Wong. They looked rough, their clothing stained and torn, their faces covered in bruises and dried blood. But victorious. They looked victorious. They stood ramrod straight, their shoulders squared, their chins held high in defiance. Mann Yu spoke. "You are relieved of your position," he informed a sputtering Evil Nobe Chung. "Step down or I will have you hauled down by the scruff of your neck."

But now the general was laughing, as was the other Cece Wong. He threw his head back and roared. "Now!" he shouted. His shout echoed through the enormous room, finally being drowned out by the sounds of many, many booted feet entering the room from virtually every direction.

"You fools!" he shouted at Mann Yu, Evil Arne Wong, and a dumbfounded Master Sergeant Liu Lee. "Do you really think you could plot a coup under my own nose? I have known of your cabal since its inception." He indulged himself in another huge belly laugh. "Lock them up!" he ordered his new troops. "Master Sergeant Wi Wen, take charge of the detail and get all of these fools behind bars."

Fourteen

We were all packed indiscriminately into two constrete cells. Once the doors were secured, I had no means of contacting anyone not stuffed into my own.

Master Sergeant Liu Lee and his men were among my companions. They seemed to know their fate; their eyes all held the identical look: terror and despair.

They weren't wrong. Minutes after our cell door closed, it opened again and a dozen armed men called for them to accompany them. The prisoners mustered what dignity and courage they could and wordlessly followed the execution squad out of the room. The door closed behind them and I heard the locks engage.

That left me, Mann Yu, and Amnelia Yu. Nene Wong, Nobe Chung, and Moms had been shoved into the second cell. I shouted for them by name, one by one, but if they responded I could not hear them.

As for Evil Arne Wong, General Nobe Chung held him back in the throne room while the rest of us were taken away. I shuddered to think what he must be going through. I found myself hoping his mother, that other scary Cece Wong, could manage to protect him in some way. My very next feeling was despair; there had been no indication the two of them had any kind of relationship whatsoever.

It was not the way of The Empty to allow women to raise their offspring, especially not sons. Sons were removed from their birth mothers after weaning. They were sent to the family estates of the powerful, whose retainers raised and trained them.

Amnelia Yu sat on the floor and cradled her son's head in her lap. She stroked his hair and whispered in his ear. I remember hoping I would get a turn after Mann Yu had had his fill.

I joked with myself, of course. I did not really think Amnelia Yu would ever hold me tenderly and whisper anything in my ear.

How wrong I turned out to be.

The armed men eventually returned and hauled Mann Yu from the cell. I assumed our days were numbered because the men made no secret of their destination.

"You're going home, buddy," the soldier in charge of the detachment announced cheerily. "You're going to take us to this gateway of yours. We're doing a prisoner swap: you for the real Mann Yu. Now shake a leg…"

Mann Yu only had time to share a look with each of us. The one he gave me showed determination; the one he shared with his mother looked like longing, but maybe I was projecting my own feelings by that time.

They were gone for days. We were neither fed nor watered, not that this mattered to Amnelia Yu. Her sadness hurt me to witness.

"At least he got to go home," I said in an attempt to cheer her up.

"They will not allow him to live after they have control of the portals. They use him. It makes me believe that they already tried to get the information from the other Arne Wong and failed. They would have tried to leverage one of their own rather than use someone from an alternate Universe.

"And I? When it's my turn? I will be disassembled, Arne Wong. I am sure of it."

I expressed every kind of encouragement I could wring from my brain, and heart. My words were wasted.

"I am an abomination to these people," she said calmly. "They will no doubt make a public spectacle of it."

Days later, when the soldiers returned, they rolled a round object into the cell in front of them.

A human head.

Mann Yu.

Amnelia Yu picked up the head and cradled it in the same way she had when it had been attached to her beloved son's shoulders.

"You next, robot," the detachment leader announced. "Let's go."

Then I heard it. Affirmation of Amnelia Yu's prediction. "It's the Circus Maximus for you," the man said as he led Amnelia Yu out of the cell. "Then the scrap heap." I could hear him and his men laughing wickedly up to the point they closed and locked the cell door again.

~ * ~

More days of despair and depression followed. I tried mightily not to think about the pain and terror Amnelia Yu must have felt. Ironic that she could feel pain. It would be one of the major advantages of being an android, that. You know, not feeling pain.

Mental or physical.

When the men came for me, I should have been weak. Dehydrated. Thoroughly defeated. But it is protocol for everyone on The N-T to carry protein pills and tiny bulbs of water in secret pockets concealed in virtually every piece of clothing.

I was fine, even considering my confinement.

But I dissembled when they came for me. They had to drag me. I made it seem I could barely walk on my own.

I did not expect them to take me further away than the throne room. I was in for more than one major surprise, as it turned out.

"We have to take you by the stockroom," the detachment leader said. "The general wants you to see how we're taking care of your mother and your sister."

"What about Nobe Chung?" I asked. "What have you done with Nobe Chung?"

The wicked laughs returned. I found myself wishing I still had a cell door to slam on the sound of these men enjoying their cruelty.

"Oh, the general finally worked it out. He found out that your fat friend is supposedly his twin. He is having a great time sweating him, working him, starving him."

"He's already lost fifty pounds!" one of his men contributed. "We are starting to see the resemblance. It's unbelievable! How is it that you have such fat people in your universe?"

So everyone accepted it as a fact. Parallel universes had been discovered, gateways created to them by exciting electrons and harnessing their escaping gamma rays at precisely one hundred and fifteen degrees: the magic angle. Within a matter of days, the population of this universe had come to accept a proposition they had previously, and very recently, challenged and reviled.

I returned to the man's question. "We don't," I replied. "Nobe Chung is one of a kind. There is no other like him."

I don't think they understood me or cared to, but they laughed again mockingly in response to my statement.

"We've got to show you something here," the leader said. His laughter had faded, but his nasty smile remained behind, like trace evidence of it. Or a promise of its return.

Oh, by the gods! What I saw that day cannot be obliterated from my mind.

We stopped at a place in the constrete bunker that had doors which had been heavily reinforced. I could tell from the sounds of the locking system's tumblers that its security was state of the art. Even I might not be able to breach it. In my mind, that was saying a lot.

Women. The room on the other side of those heavy doors was jammed full of women, most of them naked. They were penned in one giant cage which nearly filled the enormous room. On one side of the room were shower stalls, some of them in use. Men lead dirty, disheveled women to the stalls and sprayed them down, scrubbing them with foaming brushes on long handles. I had seen images from Olde Earth just like this, but the creatures being sprayed were not human beings.

Elephants. That's what they were called, I think. They were held in human captivity for their entertainment value.

Just like these women.

"Arne Wong!" one of the captive women called. Nene Wong. It was Nene Wong. "Arne Wong, we're here!"

I followed the sound of the voice. There. Nene Wong and Moms. Still clothed, thank the stars and planets.

"We will strip them once you've said your good-byes," the leader said like he was reading my mind. "The general's orders. You get to see them. You get to imagine what the rest of their lives is going to look like. And then, well then, you get deported." He started laughing again. "Get it? 'De-ported'? You know, like thrown out of one of your precious portals?"

I was not going to argue with this animal. The portals had been discovered in his universe, not mine. But I could not be bothered with this minor point when I was trying to figure out how I was going to rescue my family.

Try as I might, I could not think of any possible way I was going to be able to do that.

"Oh, and the general wanted you to see his new line of jewelry," the goon continued. "Look...here, and here." He pointed to some of the filthy women and I did. I looked.

Amnelia Yu. Pieces of her were hanging around the women's necks or braided into their hair.

Something in me broke then. It happened when I located Amnelia Yu's head being worn like a hat by one particularly dirty and wild-looking amazon. Her beautiful eyes still looked at me. They remained amber with blue flecks. I swore I could still see life in them.

And then she blinked. One lone tear rolled down a silver cheek.

She's alive! Oh, by the gods, she is still alive...

I screamed then. It was the only thing I was capable of.

This pleased the men who escorted me. They looked elated as they bodily removed me from the room and secured the great door behind us.

"Now you've seen the general's harem," the leader said. "You've seen that we have your women captured, even the abomination, now in pieces. We can go to the laboratory now and execute your sentence. This way, quickly," he gestured with his weapon to show me which direction to walk.

Walk. I was walking. "Strength borne of horror," my voice pronounced. It was back! It didn't have its usual cocky attitude now.

"Sorry you came back?" I said in my head.

"I am not staying," it answered flatly. "I need to stay with the Arne Wong of The Empty. He needs me more than all you other Arne Wongs. You still haven't figured out who I am, have you?" it asked softly, almost like it didn't want me to hear it.

"I am in no condition to exchange banter with you," I hurled at it. "Moreover, why in the hells would I care to know who you are?"

"I am *you*," my voice announced. "I existed as you in a very distant time. I am a remnant. I purposely failed to recycle when I died in that timeline. My mission was too important....Your death in this timeline is my next challenge. I am not ready...another reason to stay with the other Arne Wong. I must prepare, to concentrate my energy and resolve so I can carry my mission forward to our next incarnation."

We had long-since arrived at the laboratory complex and were traversing the long corridor that led to our portal between universes.

And past it. We walked past the portal. I began to feel even greater dread just imagining what the general had in store for me. We passed many other portals as we walked. Some of them had corridors which looked identical to the one we were in. Others had various versions of a Nova Terra being terraformed. I realized that, at least in theory, there could be an infinite number of gateways into universes parallel to our own.

"Here," the detachment leader finally announced, activating the portal we stood in front of. "Here is your destination."

Nothing. I could see nothing on the other side of the portal's window.

These goons were going to space me?

It seemed the leader sensed the time had come, because without another word, he shoved me through the portal, headfirst into nothingness.

Fifteen

It was dark on the other side of the portal. Dark and not space after all. It was solid. When I was shoved through the dark gateway, I landed face-down, sprawling on something soft and damp.

"Where are we?" I heard. I recognized the voice. It was my own. I had no answer for either of us.

"This stuff is grass," I announced, feeling it with both hands. "I've seen images of it from Olde Earth literature."

Olde Earth? I thought. *Are we on Olde Earth? How is that even possible? Wouldn't it have been eaten up by the sun?*

"It, this Olde Earth, isn't where it's supposed to be," I said out loud, examining the night sky. Now that my eyes had adjusted to the darkness, I could make out distant stars and nearby planets.

"They moved it," I said. I was awed. The peoples of this planet, this Olde Earth, had *moved* their planet. They had not spent generations gathering planetary material from their asteroid belt. They had no need to terraform, at least not on this planet.

As I contemplated this and all that it meant, I saw a glimmering light on the horizon. I watched it. I stared until it came into focus.

A city. A city of glittering lights. A beautiful city of motion and color. I stared for a long time, not a single thought in my mind. I was too amazed. Amazed and astonished.

And hopeful.

I marked the spot where the portal was with a pile of large rocks I found scattered around the grass, and I walked. I walked toward the shining city on the horizon. And as I walked, I watched Saturn rise in the sky.

~ * ~

I am home. I have been accepted and welcomed by the peoples of this planet.

I have skills. I have employment and income. I have a dwelling. I have created nutritive tablets that keep me alive in a world where human beings are not altered. They eat. They shit. They love. They create new human beings as a byproduct of their expressions of love.

I am very short in this world, perhaps half as tall as the average person here. I am purported to be an immigrant from a pygmy village from another continent. These people are revered by the other peoples on this world, and I am constantly greeted, even by strangers, with grace and kindness.

This planet is definitely Olde Earth. The peoples of this universe took care of their world. They kept its air clean and its waters fresh and teeming with life. They do not war with each other. Every person is cared for, both physically and mentally. Every person is respected for their human nature. Here, no deities are worshipped and blindly obeyed, for here it is humanity which is revered and human life cherished.

I have a good life here. I have friends, women friends, even. The peoples here have created a utopia, if such a word can be employed. Yes, they are born and they die, but their lifespans encompass hundreds of years. They do not die of illnesses or disease. They choose when they die, and they understand that their human energies will recycle into another human life.

But I cannot remain here. I often visit the pile of rocks which marks the portal back to the world where my mother, sister, and friend are. I labor in a physics lab, putting in many extra hours. I am given free rein to play with my ideas, to develop the technology which will take me home. Some of my fellow scientists assist me with my research and experimentation, although most of them just humor me. Still, they are kind.

I am getting close. I don't just feel it; I know it.

My ultimate goal is the return of my loved ones to The N-T.

But first things first.

Because it's The M-T—The Empty—that I must return to first. The Empty is my gateway: My gateway *home*. And if my theories prove out, I may be able to control the *time* of my return, too.

I want to save them all. Especially my murdered friend, Mann Yu. And his mother, Amnelia Yu. I hear her voice in my head, a snippet of sound from our very first conversation: *"I believe he plays with the very structure of time itself."*

I have carefully maintained the tiny ball of nothing I found. It is preserved in the evidence bag I originally put it in.

And that bag? It's in one of my many secret pockets.

BOOK TWO: 140 DEGREES

Sixteen

"It's because you can *read*," Arne Wong was explaining to the two angry women. He was using every ounce of his charm, which was considerable, in trying to make allies of his two new "acquisitions."

"You have *skills*," he continued. "Skills which I need in order to succeed here in 'The Empty.'"

She couldn't resist the bait, even though she knew he had thrown the word out just to get a reaction. Nene Wong spoke. "Succeed in what, you shithead?" she spat at him.

"Nene Wong," Cece Wong, her mother, said in a soft voice. "This man is not your brother. Please remember to whom you speak."

"He's just like him," the younger woman complained. "He's always got his little plots and plans cooking. He wants to use us. We'll probably be killed for cooperating with him."

"We will be killed eventually anyway," her mother replied. Cece Wong looked significantly older and more careworn than before she entered this universe through the Yu-Lee Laboratory portal, the portal that linked her Nova Terra, the "N-T" with this Nova Terra, the "M-T."

"At any rate," she continued. "Death would be preferable to even a second more of the abuse we have endured." She was done speaking, at least for the moment. She sagged in her chair, crossed her right ankle over her left knee and just stared at the young man facing her.

"I am the one who told them the women from your universe were infertile," Arne Wong said, angling once again for their favor. "If I hadn't convinced them, you would have been subjected to rape and torture for the entirety of the weeks you have been here. By law, sex must have the potential for pregnancy in this world. That is why you endured such a short time in the harem. I will get you home, back to your Nova Terra, I promise, once I have accomplished what I mean to do."

"And just what is that?" Nene asked, her tone of voice indicating she didn't think her "brother" capable of doing anything worthwhile.

"*Real* revolution," Arne Wong said. "There, just saying that word could get me executed. You could turn me in at your next opportunity and then be freed of me forever. I have given you the power to betray me, but I am begging you not to. Please help me. Help me to find your Arne Wong. Help me to change this world, to save it from the monsters in charge of it. *Please.*"

"Stop begging," his sister said, dropping her attitude and leaning forward to touch his hand with her own. "Just throw Nobe Chung into the deal and I will help you with all the skills at my disposal."

"And I," echoed her mother. "Find and rescue my son and restore Nene's man to her. We will help you any way we can."

~ * ~

"I cannot forgive him for causing so many deaths," Nene Wong whispered to her mother some time later. The pair had been installed in the spacious apartment Arne Wong owned. They had chosen to share a bedroom for mutual protection, not quite trusting the unaltered men of this Nova Terra to leave them unmolested.

"Perhaps something good will come from their sacrifices," her mother replied, deep in thought. "'From great evil comes great good,' or so it is said."

"You're quoting one of your ancient Buddhists again, aren't you?" Nene asked teasingly. "Where do you find this stuff, anyway?"

"There is much Buddhist philosophy, and lore, passed down verbally over the millennia," her mother responded. "I am teaching you, just as my mother taught me. You're just not consciously aware of it," she laughed, playfully swatting her daughter's shoulder. Nene fell into her mother's arms. The women shared a hug.

"We have to get out of here," Nene Wong whispered. "This place is horrible. The lives of all of these women, Mother!" she wailed. "How can men care so little for women? They are nothing more than breeding stock—no education, no culture, no clothing even. It is beyond horrible!"

"But if Arne Wong is successful," her mother answered in a soft voice, "we can be instrumental in changing all of that. We can be part of a revolution which frees all of these women, and the many, many men imprisoned for crimes real and imagined. We can change this world!"

"Why is it that he walks around free when everyone else involved in the plot to overthrow the general was killed?" Nene Wong asked her mother. "Not only does he live, but he has been promoted!"

"That tells you all you need to know," her mother said. "He was a spy for the general. It is obvious."

"But you think he is sincere when he speaks of revolution, true revolution?"

"I have to," her mother said, sighing deeply. "It is the only thing in our entire situation that gives me any hope at all."

"I'd settle for a drink," Nene Wong said. She was changing a subject which had gotten too big to get her head around. She wanted her mother to relax, to enjoy what little newfound freedom they had lucked into.

"He must have a liquor cabinet," her mother replied, already heading for their bedroom door. "You got your lock-pick?"

"You know I don't, and I know you don't need tools, Mother," the younger woman replied.

"That's right, Nene Wong," Cece Wong crowed. "I have *skills!*"

The women left the room together, arm in arm. And like it was a prediction, Cece Wong did not need any tools other than her own nimble fingers to unlock Arne Wong's liquor cabinet.

~ * ~

Back at Yu-Lee Laboratories, Arne Wong was chatting and laughing with one of General Nobe Chung's personal guards.

"So you flung him out into space?" he said to the guard. The two men were sharing a flask of something that caused their conversation to become looser, and friendlier.

"Yeah," the guard said, taking another hearty pull on the flask. "Nothing but space on the other side of the portal. 'Boom!' I just pushed him through it, and 'poof!' he was gone!"

"That's just great," Arne Wong said, throwing a comradely arm around the other man's shoulder. "I don't suppose I could get a peek at it—the portal—can I?"

"There's nothing to see, but I don't know why you shouldn't have a look," the guard replied. "Right this way, Freeman Arne Wong!" He indicated they should enter the labyrinth.

"It's quite a way in," he said, the beginnings of a drunken slur in his voice.

"I don't mind if you don't," the civilian replied.

"Mind? I'd like to relive the moment again, myself!" the military man said. "It's one of the coolest things I've ever done!"

"Cool, huh?" Arne Wong said, a note of admiration in his voice.

"Yeah, cool," the guard replied. "Very, very cool."

~ * ~

Later that night, Arne Wong had a conversation via a telecommunications device.

"Yeah, the ladies are doing fine," he said. "They drank a little too much so they're sleeping it off." He chuckled a bit at this point, sharing a moment of humor with the person on the other end of the line.

"So we need to get the specs for the portal through to the other Arne Wong. Can you prepare a capsule with the technical information in it? I'd like to toss it through the portal as soon as possible. Yes, I am sure that he will be able to interpret and execute the plans. He is both an engineer and an astrophysicist, as are you. Yes. Yes. No, I will take the risk. I have taken precautions with security. No one will think anything of my being at the Laboratory. I work directly for Xanu Lee now. I am temporarily in charge while Mann Yu is missing. Yes. Good. Very good. Meet me at our regular place in two hours."

He listened a moment before speaking again. "Great. Yes, and thanks. Thank you very much."

He toggled the communication device to the off position and crossed the room to pour himself a drink.

"I am going to need to open an account at the liquor emporium," he said to himself, examining the dangerously low level of amber liquid in the decanter. He chuckled again. "Got to keep the ladies happy!" he said, toasting himself in the mirror on the wall. His reflection toasted him back. It wore the same look as its original, a combination of elation and terror.

Seventeen

"Was that him?" Amnelia Yu asked the manservant, who was quietly disconnecting and returning a comms device to its cradle.

"Yes," Yanu Yang replied. He addressed the head, and only the head, of a gold and silver android which had been carefully positioned on a side table in the room. "It was Arne Wong. He found the portal through which his twin was spaced. He needs the portal specifications encapsulated and delivered to him as soon as possible. He says there is a ninety percent likelihood that the other Arne Wong will be monitoring his side of the portal. He said he will take care of putting the capsule through the portal *personally*. He can have the specs delivered to the other Arne Wong on the other side of the portal in just a few hours, Amnelia Yu."

Yanu Yang looked up, his hands clasped in supplication. "It has started. Very soon now we will have a two-way portal to the universe where the other Arne Wong resides. The *power*, Amnelia Yu! It is almost unimaginable!" His eyes gleamed with excitement and he wrung his hands together.

"But imagine it I do," the head on the side table replied. "We must exercise extreme caution," she continued. "We are so close. We cannot risk discovery."

"Please be reassured, Amnelia Yu," the manservant replied. "I have been insinuating increasing amounts of the sedation into Xanu Lee's evening libation. He will not discover us or our plans."

"I certainly hope you're right," the head replied, her worry communicated clearly in her voice. "We cannot fail."

"We will not fail," Yanu Yang said. "We will soon have a two-way portal to the universe where Arne Wong is. Perhaps we will find another Mann Yu there...and we will use the vast stores of unleashed dark energy to change The Empty forever."

"Amen," the head intoned. "Amen." In her head, though, Amnelia Yu was saying something completely different. *'Another Mann Yu'?* she asked herself. *Impossible. My Mann Yu is gone, murdered by the Arne Wong and Nobe Chung of The Empty. This I will never forget...or forgive.*

As Yanu Yang turned to leave the room, he could not help but notice a solitary tear making a shiny track down the battered surface of the robot's head.

He hid his smile from her. *Good,* he thought. *Suffer, you abomination.*

On the other side of the office door, Ingu Yang stood frozen and undetected. She had heard everything her husband and the abomination had said to each other.

She waited several moments before silently retreating into another nearby room. She busied herself in straightening and cleaning the table surface, even though it was spotless in all respects.

"Ingu Yang!" Yanu Yang cried as he entered the antechamber. "What are you doing? I have already prepared this room for tomorrow's workday."

"I found some dust on the conference table," the pretty young woman replied. "I didn't want you to get blamed for it."

"You are so good to me!" the older man responded. "How fortunate I am that the Xanu Lee made you my wife!"

He graced her with a wide grin. She smiled back at him in a much smaller way. It was tentative, her smile. There was not much warmth behind it.

"Don't worry," Yanu Yang reassured the young woman, his new wife. "You will soon relax and learn to enjoy your new status in life!"

"I know," Ingu Yang responded softly. "Just give me a little time to get used to you—to *it*—okay?"

"Of course, my dear!" her husband said. "Take all of the time you need."

"Thank you, husband," the young wife replied. "I think I will now retire for the evening."

"I will join you in a little bit," Yanu Yang said. "I have one more task to complete before I am able to retire."

"Of course," the wife replied. "I am very tired tonight, husband. I need to sleep."

"I will not molest you," he replied in a soft voice. "I will control my urges."

"I do not deserve your consideration," the young woman said, bowing to her husband from the waist up.

"You do deserve it, little flower," said the older man. "I will see that I do not make a pest of myself."

"Good night," she said.

"Good night," he replied.

~ * ~

"Here is the capsule," Yanu Yang said to Arne Wong not two hours later that night. "I acquired it from a comrade in the laboratory. There is nothing anyone can do to discover the theft of the information or tie it to you in any way. It is small enough to pass through the portal without triggering any of the alarms." He handed the small, plain capsule to the other man. "It also contains the amount of dark matter which will suffice to begin the construction of the physical portal. Only a small amount is needed to pierce the 'skin' between universes. More dark matter can then be harvested from the layer which lies between one universe and the other. Are you sure it can be deployed immediately?"

"The guard is drunk," Arne Wong replied, examining the silver cylinder. "I have ensured that no one will be watching the security feeds. Do not worry. I will not fail. "As a cover for any portal activity today, I took a detachment of men back to 'The N-T' and retrieved Mann Yu. He is back on The Empty in the loving arms of his family."

Here, Arne Wong and Yanu Yang shared a grimace and an eye-roll. "Loving family," indeed…

Arne Wong continued, "If anyone noticed any activity in the labyrinth today, Mann Yu's 'rescue' can serve as explanation."

"What about the camera that watches this place?" Yanu Yang asked, gesturing around at their surroundings. The men were in an abandoned shelter, one constructed when the threat of nuclear annihilation was real.

"Disabled," Arne Wong said. "Long ago. We will not be observed."

"Good. Well, I need to get back to my quarters at the Laboratory. I must be on the premises should Xanu Lee require my services."

"Understood," Arne Wong replied. "How is the wife? I heard you were rewarded with a woman sometime in the last month or so."

"She is young and lovely," Yanu Yang replied proudly. "She is not yet twenty-five years old but has already borne six male offspring for The Empty."

"Six? All boys?" Arne Wong was impressed. "Then it is your hope that you will be able to have children of your own?"

"If the gods allow," Yanu Yang replied, bowing his head to those invisible deities in respect…and supplication.

"May the gods allow," Arne Wong responded by rote. The phrase was automatic on The Empty, much like "Good Health," which was what was said automatically when someone sneezed, coughed, or audibly passed gas.

"Thank you, sir," the manservant said, turning to depart. "Be careful. Be *successful*."

"I will do my best," Arne Wong promised.

"May the gods allow," Yanu Yang responded.

"May the gods allow," Arne Wong echoed. This time, there was deliberate inflection in the words. This reply was most certainly not an automatic one. His voice sharply informed him that everything was up to him, Arne Wong. There would be no help from any gods.

"Whatever," Arne Wong replied to the voice. He was in no mood to debate religion, now or ever.

As the manservant made his way back to his workplace at Yu-Lee Laboratories, he spoke to himself. "At last!" he crowed aloud. Hearing his voice echoing in the empty streets, he finished the rest of his thought inside his head. *Mann Yu is finally back in The Empty! At long last we can advance our plans....*

~ * ~

Ingu Yang did not sleep much that night. She struggled mightily with a dilemma: on one hand, she needed to reveal the plots devised by her husband and the abomination to Xanu Lee; on the other, she did not wish to be made widow and returned to the harem where she had already served for ten years. She did not think she could survive any more childbirth. All six of her deliveries had brought her to the brink of death.

She did not love her husband...she didn't care for any of the men she had been forced to be with. She appreciated his thoughtfulness, however. He was the first man who had ever showed the slightest bit of respect for her worth as a human being.

But if he got caught—if someone else discovered his treachery—she would be considered complicit and would be punished severely. It was the Law.

She finally drifted off into fitful sleep as Saturn set for the night. She dreamt of the six babies which had been wrested from her grudging womb. In this dream they manifested as six big, muscular, determined-looking protectors watching over her, caring for her.

Loving her.

Eighteen

"We have found a canister of some kind at your portal site!" the excited physics student cried, running into my laboratory. The young man carried a cylindrical object.

"Finally!" I exclaimed. "Here, give it to me. I must open it immediately!" I held my hands out expectantly, wagging my fingers at the student in impatience.

"Shouldn't we have our protective forces check it out first?" the student replied, holding the canister away from me, his esteemed professor. "It could as easily be something from an enemy on the other side of the portal as something beneficial from a friend..."

I laughed hollowly, without real humor. "Please let me have it," I said, once more gesturing with my outstretched hands. "I will take my chances. You, however, will wait outside this laboratory until I issue an 'all clear.' I will not risk anyone else. Now give me the canister and go."

The student reluctantly handed the silver cylinder to me, turned on his heel, and fled toward safety, or so he hoped. From what he had heard of the world on the other side of the invisible portal, he knew they were capable of violence; they had a disregard for human life and dignity.

Alone then, I examined the cylinder carefully. I knew it was authentic. Its manufacture was crude, military, even. These were characteristics of the other universe. Its peoples had no use for ornamentation or elegance of design. They were purely utilitarian.

The cylinder was not hard to access. After I pried at various seams along the top of the object, it popped open easily, spilling its contents on the tabletop where I had been working.

Plans—specifications, formulae, drawings. I leafed through them quickly, my excitement growing with the turn of every page. I picked up a vacuum-sealed packet which had no visible contents and whistled in appreciation as I twirled the packet around, peering carefully into its depths.

"Joxe!" I cried. "Joxe Xian, it's safe, you can come in now."

My student—more like a lab assistant—returned quickly, no sign of trepidation on his face or in his movements. If anything, he looked excited. "What is it?" he asked. "Is it from the other side?"

"It sure is," I replied, jumping to my feet to face my young apprentice. "Joxe Xian, it is the answer to our prayers! Look—just look! This information will allow us to complete our portal plans *months* ahead of time."

"And this!" I cried, holding the packet of nothing aloft. "It must be dark matter! We can get the physical construction of the gate started with this and about twenty tons of constrete!"

"Do you know who sent them?" Joxe Xian asked. "Is there a note?"

"Just this," I said, aware that I bore a look of astonishment. I held up a strip of glimmering golden fabric. The hand I held it with shook.

"What is that?" Joxe Xian asked, coming closer to inspect the material.

"It's her," I said, my wonder reverberating through my voice. "She lives."

The student stared at the fabric with a puzzled look on his face. "Her *who*?" he finally prompted.

"It's her. Amnelia Yu," I replied. I felt dazed. But joyful. I felt my smile grow wider as I turned from regarding the fabric to once again engage my assistant, my student, face-to-face.

"She lives!" I repeated, grabbing a surprised Joxe Xian by both elbows; our height difference was such that I could only reach that high on the young man. "They have not annihilated her after all!" I released the young man and performed a little dance across the laboratory floor, swinging the little strip of fabric through the air and uttering cries of joy.

I sobered quickly and placed the material back on the table.

"We must not lose a moment. If Amnelia Yu is sending me pieces of herself, she is still in danger. I will rescue her if it's the last thing I do."

"Will it be the last thing *we* do?" Joxe Xian asked me anxiously.

"Is your resolve wavering?" I asked. "It is all right, Joxe Xian. If you wish to abandon the portal project, I would understand completely. I will still provide you with high marks and a strong recommendation for advancement. I will find you a new project team to work with..."

Joxe Xian hastened to reassure me. "No, no, Arne Wong. I am still committed, even more so now that we have received proof that your other universe really exists, and that you have an ally in it. Please, accept my apology for my words. I if I did not fear the possible outcomes of our actions, I would not be human."

"So true," I said, to reassure the worried student. "Courage— true courage—is not the absence of fear. It is the resolve to continue despite being fearful..."

"What's next?" Joxe Xian asked anxiously. "Will we change our formulae to match what we have been given?"

"Not exactly," I replied. "You see, Joxe Xian, we have worked an aspect of this science that they have not. We have posited— theorized—that changing the escape angle of the X17 particle will not only open a portal into physical space. We expect that manipulating the angle to 140 degrees will also allow us to travel in *time.*"

I turned back to examine the cylinder's contents more closely. I did this meticulously, reading and rereading certain formulae, examining diagrams in minute detail, grunting in surprise and then in understanding at several junctures.

"Here—and here," I said to my assistant, pointing to the portions of the documents I had isolated as important. "These are the portions of the formulae we were missing. Do you see?" I turned to watch Joxe Xian's face as the young man studied what I had pointed out to him.

A look of dawning understanding—epiphany—broke across the student's face. "Oh, I see," he said, awestruck. "We were so close," he observed, looking back at me.

"But now we are exactly where we need to be," I exclaimed. "Exactly! We can get started on the experiments right away.

"But keep the angle, Joxe Xian. I want those X17 particles to escape and cycle at 140 degrees. We are going back in time. We will go back to rescue my friends, my colleagues. My family."

"Yes, Arne Wong," the student replied, a look of grim determination on his face. "I will set up the parameters as you have defined them. Do we have any clear idea of how far back in time we will travel?"

"I cannot be sure," I replied thoughtfully, and truthfully. "But I predict that the time difference between our universe and the targeted universe will be proportional to the change in the angle and the length of the X17 trajectory. Velocity is also a factor. I am going to say that we should be able to arrive some hours before I—the Arne Wong of my original timeline—arrive. We must intercept him and his team, and change events in their timeline." I stopped to regard my assistant one more time. A thought struck me, causing me to make a change in strategy.

"Change that, Joxe Xian. There will be no 'we.' I am going in *alone,*" I announced. "You must wait here and monitor the portal. I may need you to reopen it to allow me to escape back to our own time and space. I will assume the identity of the Arne Wong of the other universe. We are indistinguishable from one another; it's the only way to infiltrate and effect the changes we need…"

"But what if you are caught?" Joxe Xian asked.

"Even the more reason to leave you behind," I answered. "If I have not returned within three days, you must organize a team to take over our project."

"Do you mean a rescue team?" an alarmed Joxe Xian asked.

"No. I do not think that is what I mean in the slightest," I replied. "Not at 140 degrees, at any rate. If the team decides on a rescue, please ensure they breach the portal to the other universe at a synchronous timeline. Return the X17 escape angle to the original 115 degrees."

"But you might be dead by then!" the distraught assistant objected.

"I am doing the time travel alone," I insisted. "To put anyone else at risk on this unproven theory of mine is unacceptable…morally, ethically, and physically."

"Physically?" my student asked.

"Yes, physically. We don't know if we will even survive the portal transition. It might be lethal," I said.

I looked at the younger man with almost tangible focus. "This is an order," I added, not breaking eye contact. "Oh, and Joxe Xian," I said, ensuring that I had the young man's full attention before proceeding. "If the project team decides to destroy the portal, you must not oppose them. You must do what is necessary to protect your world from 'The Empty.' Do you understand me?"

"Yes, sir," Joxe Xian finally replied. "I understand you and will comply with your order."

"Good. Now call in our construction team. Let's get started on that gate."

Nineteen

"How do I look?" I was addressing my assistant, Joxe Xian. I was turning around for full visual effect, my arms held out away from my body to maximize my audience's vantage.

"Bloody awful," Joxe Xian said. "Why do you have to go in looking like that?"

"This is how Arne Wong from the other universe was dressed when I last saw him," I replied.

"Where did you even find clothes like that?" Joxe Xian asked, laughing a bit.

"There is a costume shop for children down in Edgemere," I said. "It specializes in old sci-fi franchises. Real old franchises, you know, like Star Wars if you've ever heard of it."

"No, I never have," Joxe Xian said. "So this Star Wars was a game from the distant past?"

"Actually, yes," I admitted, "but it started as a series of movies from 'a long time ago in a galaxy far, far away...'"

"So just who are you supposed to look like, then?" the amused student asked. "What character are you dressed like?"

"Why, Han Solo, of course," I responded, sniffing arrogantly. "Who else?"

"'Who else,' indeed," Joxe Xian replied. "I'll have to look up this Star Wars thing."

"Well, keep in mind that I made some modifications," I cautioned. "I couldn't very well wear the trasher—no, wait—they called it a 'blaster,' you know..."

"The 'blaster'?" a puzzled Joxe Xian asked. "What is a 'blaster'?"

"Watch the movies," I instructed him. "At least the first dozen. Suffice it to say that Han Solo carried a weapon; he had to. He had a price on his head. There were bounty hunters out tracking him down, after all."

"'Bounty hunters'?" echoed a voice from the laboratory's doorway. Arne Wong. It was the Arne Wong from Olde Earth's universe. Fortunately, his name was not Arne Wong here. Here, he was called Yi-Tai Feng. But it was him...it was this universe's version of Arne Wong, without a doubt, even if he was over six and a-half feet tall. "I know what 'bounty hunters' are," the voice continued as its body strode further into the room. "I should. Technically, I am one myself. It's part of my private investigator's license."

The handsome Olde Earther paused to look me over, his facial expression much like the one Joxe Xian wore. "What in the worlds are you up to?" he asked, walking around me. I had stopped turning around, so he had to do the moving in order to get the full impact. "Is this how the peoples of your universe dress? Native garb, so to speak?"

"Yes," I admitted. "In both my universe and in the other one I am about to visit. We wear a little bit more ornamentation in my universe...the peoples of The Empty don't seem to have any appreciation for fashion. Design. Accessories... I just had the costume shop replace the cool buttons and snaps with others of purely utilitarian design. Too bad, too. The original belt was really cool..."

"'Cool'," Yi-Tai Feng repeated. He and Joxe Xian shared a look and a laugh.

Yi-Tai Feng quickly exhausted his humor, however. He soon turned a serious face toward me.

"So, Arne Wong," he said. "You say that you have a clone or a twin or something in this other universe, right?"

"That is correct, Yi-Tai Feng," I replied.

"If that is so, and I do believe you that it is, then do you have a clone or a twin in *this* universe?" It seemed that this was a question Yi-Tai Feng had been worrying with for some time. He was intent on its delivery, and he was intent on getting its answer.

"I do not know," I said, turning away from my friend to fiddle with my costume. I tried feverishly to come up with a way to change the subject—to distract him—but my brain had stopped functioning.

"You are not being truthful with me," Yi-Tai Feng replied. "I am a private investigator here on Earth," he reminded me. "I investigate lots of private matters for lots of people; it is my *career*, Arne Wong. You know, 'Gumshoe Investigations'? Well, I hired myself to look into this. I have been searching for the 'other' you.

"I have not been able to find an Arne Wong," he continued after a small pause. I was still pretending to be occupied with a snap on my belt. "But I have arrived at a conclusion based on all of the evidence I have been able to acquire..."

"Oh yeah?" I said. "Really?" I still could not bring myself to look him in the eye.

Joxe Xian stood by and watched the exchange of words like he was a spectator at a tennis match.

"*I* am *you*," Yi-Tai Feng announced. "My father is the clone of your father. On what you call 'Olde Earth,' 'Wong' has over the years morphed to 'Feng.' I was named after my maternal grandfather, just as you were in your universe."

I did not contradict Yi-Tai Feng. I did not debate. Instead, I asked a question I had been fretting over the entire time I had known my clone—my unlikely twin—Yi-Tai Feng.

"And your mother? Your sister?" I asked.

This brought any activity in the room to a complete standstill. Yi-Tai Feng looked at me like I had physically struck him. He made a strangled noise in his throat before he cleared it and squared his shoulders, preparing to speak. This took him many moments and visible effort.

"My mother does not live here with me and my father," he said curtly, and defensively. "She has her own life in our world's capital."

"And your sister?" I asked. I missed Nene, my own sister, and would have been soothed by being able to converse with her twin here on Olde Earth.

"I don't have a sister—well, I used to have a sister. I mean, well, uhh, she is now my brother, actually," Yi-Tai Feng said with no small trouble.

"She, I mean he, reassigned his sexuality?" I asked.

"Yes, he did," Yi-Tai Feng replied. "Why, do you not do so in your own universe?"

I laughed one of my humorless laughs. "No, Yi-Tai Feng. No, we do not. We are altered while still in the laboratory to have very low libidos." My laugh warmed up a little while I thought about what I was going to say next. "So, no, we don't really care what our physical sex is...most of us are pretty sexless, actually."

"Wow," Joxe Xian and Yi-Tai Feng said as one. "Wait a minute," Yi-Tai Feng said. "You said 'most of us.' What did you mean by that?"

"And 'laboratory,'" Joxe Xian added. "What did you mean about being altered 'while still in the laboratory'?"

I took a moment to consider both questions. "It's complicated," I said.

"Yeah, I guess it must be," Yi-Tai Feng responded, shaking his head and laughing, his previous tension lightening. "Because you've got like six different ladies here on what you call 'Olde Earth' drooling over you at any given time. That doesn't sound 'sexless' to me!"

I made up my mind to be forthright. "I am completely male," I said, holding my arms out from my side as if in illustration of my maleness. "I am a rebel on my world. I am *illegal*. I have not been sexually modified in any way. Nor has my sister, Nene Wong, nor my mother, Cece Wong. My father was caught while out in public by a random body scan and was terminated because of his illegal status. We live below the radar. We have to. If the Authority could have traced my father back to us, we would all have been terminated."

I had a lot of explaining to do. "We are neutered while in utero," I continued. "Well, most of us are. You see, like I said, I was born of a woman."

"Aren't we all?" Joxe Xian asked.

"Not in my universe," I replied. "Female citizens have had their wombs removed. Male citizens are treated by chemical surgeries to eliminate most of their testosterone and all of their active sperm." I saw the shocked looks on my friends' faces. "No, really, it's not that bad. Look, we haven't had a war in centuries because of the adjustments..." I stopped then, realizing I was trying to defend my universe to these denizens of the peaceful Olde Earth of this universe. On this world, a philosophy of ultimate respect for humanity was the only religion. The chanting of the mantra which was the major feature of their religion filled the planet's air at all times. They worshipped no gods. They had overcome. They had arrived at humanity's perfect place.

"Nene Wong and I were born to my mother. Legal citizens are gestated in artificial wombs," I said flatly. "In laboratories, Joxe Xian."

"And what did you mean when you specified that you have not been *sexually* modified?" the young lab assistant persisted. "Are there other modifications made to your peoples?"

I considered these questions carefully before, once again, deciding to be forthcoming. "Yes. We are all surgically modified. Our hearts are fortified and moved to a safer location in our body cavities. We have most of our stomachs and intestines removed. We subsist on protein capsules which are completely absorbed into our systems. They leave no waste behind to be eliminated."

"You don't defecate?" the young man asked. "Seriously? Oh wait...do you urinate?"

"Once a day, usually in the mornings," I told him.

"Unbelievable!" Joxe Xian said.

"Absolutely unbelievable!" echoed an astounded Yi-Tai Feng. "But how have you survived without any of your capsules? You don't look like you are starving to death…"

I was already reaching into a series of pockets in my clothing—they were cleverly designed to be nearly invisible. From each of a dozen pockets I extracted eight-to-ten green capsules.

"I was never without them," I crowed, showing them what amounted to ten days of sustenance just from my pockets. I then opened a drawer in my desk and extracted three large containers which were also full of the green capsules. "Carrying capsules at all times is standard protocol," I informed them. "They don't lose their potency. Plus, the capsules are ruggedized…they are very hard to destroy, and yet easily sublime in the small remnant of stomach we have. I arrived here with some, enough for several weeks, and then I just made more," I told them. "I was never in trouble of starving."

"But you just had this costume of yours made," Yi-Tai Feng protested. "How is it that you have all of these hidden pockets?"

"Standard protocol," I repeated flatly. "We always have the means to sustain ourselves. Especially on Nova Terra. It is not the friendly world Olde Earth is. It is dangerous. Its waters are not potable; its air is still poison." I looked at the two men to see if they were following me. "It is standard protocol. Just like carrying water bulbs and oxygen masks are." As I said this, I removed several small bulbs of liquid—water—and a small black mask from the inside of my vest. "You can't make a mistake on Nova Terra and expect to survive it," I continued. "I have maintained my standard practices here on your planet. I had to…because I am returning to Nova Terra, The N-T," I concluded. "By way of The Empty. I will collect my family and my friends and bring them here. Once we've created a new portal to Nova Terra, I will take them all home."

I rose to my feet and rubbed my hands together in a gesture of readiness. "Now, Joxe Xian and I need to get back to work. That portal isn't going to build itself. We have a lot to do."

Twenty

Xanu Lee shouted his displeasure at his scowling son.

"Mann Yu!" he shouted. "Why are you not up to this task? You must return to the other Nova Terra and get their portal open. We want that dark energy. What is it you do not understand?"

The business tycoon and financial backer of Yu-Lee Laboratories turned to address an object sitting on a table next to him. "Has he been damaged by his journey to your universe?" he sputtered.

The object opened its eyes—amber eyes with blue flecks—and answered the angry man.

"Can you not see it with your own eyes?" the object challenged. "He is damaged beyond hope, but not by any of the peoples of what you call 'my universe.' He was released back to this universe without being harmed in any way. He has had this seed of madness in him for a long time. It is not the result of his time on Nova Terra.

"The Mann Yu of my universe was intelligent, stable and possessed of a good sense of humor. This one," and here she used her eyes to indicate exactly who she was talking about, "doesn't seem to know right from wrong. If he cries, he dissembles; if he laughs, it is inspired by acts of cruelty, usually his own."

The object, a head—and only the head—of an android, paused for a moment before continuing. The young man being discussed by the unlikely pair stood rigidly before them, his hands clenched at his sides, his breast heaving with each tortured breath.

"Father," the young man said between clenched teeth. *"Father."* He waited for permission from Xanu Lee. He *needed* permission to speak.

The android, seeing this, demonstrated its amusement by the ever-so-slight upward curling of the corners of its mouth. Its expression was meant for only Mann Yu, and indeed Mann Yu was the only person in the room who saw it.

He exploded. He made noises which did not sound human as he leapt for the side table which held the head. "It mocks me!" he screamed at his father, who rose to block him. Xanu Lee harmlessly swatted his son back like he was an insect.

"Leave her be," he instructed the younger man. "She is your mother."

"Abomination!" cried Mann Yu, pointing an accusatory index finger at the object. "She is not my mother; she is not even a 'she!' You are the madman in this room, Father. You have been damaged by your perverted association with this, this, this *thing!*"

"You should get your son some help," the head said next. "It may not yet be hopeless. Surely you have some psychiatric facilities on your Nova Terra which can help the people of your world..." She dangled the idea in front of the man—her husband in several universes—and simply waited.

Mann Yu had returned to his heavy breathing, his hard glare focused on the android head.

"Amnelia Yu-Lee," Xanu Lee replied in a soft voice. "That is just the thing. Mann Yu needs a rest, that's all. And I will see that he gets it." He depressed a button on the face of a device sitting on the armrest of his chair.

"Yes, sir?" a voice projected from it.

"Send a summons to Gude Han," Xanu Lee ordered. "Tell him that I have an important patient for him. This is urgent, Yanu Yang. Tell Director Han I require his service immediately. He needs to report to my office with attendants and sedation. As soon as possible."

"Yes sir," Yanu Yang responded. "Right away, sir."

Amnelia Yu and Xanu Lee observed Mann Yu closely after the orders had been given and the communications device toggled off. Rather than flying into another tantrum, Mann Yu slumped his shoulders in resignation. All of the tension left the young man's body and he fell into a nearby chair, a look of despair and fear on his handsome features.

"The sedation will not be necessary," he said in a very low voice. "I will cooperate."

"Nevertheless," his father said, still keeping his son under rapt surveillance.

"Nevertheless."

~ * ~

Less than an hour later, a subdued and sedated Mann Yu had been escorted from Yu-Lee Laboratories and taken away by ambulance to a distant facility where he would receive diagnosis and treatment for a mental malady.

"We will cure him," Director Gude Han told Xanu Lee with confidence. "Please have no doubts about his care. It will be the best available on all of Nova Terra."

"Thank you, Director Gude Han," Xanu Lee responded. He held his hand out and delivered his signature handshake—warm, dry, firm, and protracted. By the time it was over, the harried director was looking distinctly uncomfortable. He had long since broken off eye contact with the powerful scientist and businessman.

He hurried off to join his attendants and his newest patient without looking back. He did not run, but his walk was more of a quick scuttle than any sort of dignified gait.

"Who will take over the operations of the laboratory?" Amnelia Yu asked Xanu Lee once they were alone again.

"I have already appointed Arne Wong to take over on a temporary basis," Xanu Lee responded.

"Arne Wong?" Amnelia Yu challenged, disbelief in her voice. "Surely he was executed by General Nobe Chung after his failed coup?"

"He was our inside agent in that little debacle," Xanu Lee replied, a grim smile on his lips. "Arne Wong has been our agent for years, keeping us informed of everything happening in that military bunker. He is a close friend of the man who has made himself General."

"But what was his incentive?" the android head asked, her curiosity evident in both facial expression and tone of voice.

"He has been freed from bondage," the businessman said, his tone and expression smug, self-satisfied. "I have freed him in reward for his service. He still works for me. But he is no longer a slave. He has been given quarters in the freedman part of the city. He earns a generous salary. He will even have his pick of women; he may even marry if he so wishes."

"Does he have his eye on any particular woman?" the android asked.

"He has actually exhibited a preference," Xanu Lee said, deliberately teasing the android by withholding the information. He waited for her to roll her eyes and grimace, indicating that although she was interested, she wasn't going to beg. "He has requested that the Cece Wong and Nene Wong from your universe be given to him for his use."

"His *use*?" Amnelia repeated. "But you know that women from that universe—my universe—do not have reproductive organs. He will not be able to sire any children with them."

"I suspect his interest is not sexual," the man continued. "Reproduction is not his aim. He wants them because they have value back in their own universe. This is only my opinion, but I know Arne Wong rather well. He wants them for leverage over the people of The N-T. In our universe, women who cannot bear children are made laborers or terminated. Once we discovered they were incapable of carrying children, they were removed from the harem and scheduled for hard labor. It is the Law."

"How did you make this discovery?" the android asked as if simply idly curious.

"Arne Wong informed us of the customs of your universe," Xanu Lee replied. "Women are womb-less and men are made eunuchs." He frowned in disgust. "They breed their children in artificial wombs in laboratories." He shook his head as if to clear these facts from taking up permanent residence in his brain.

"Oh," the android replied. "I see. Yes, Xanu Lee, those are the facts." Her thoughts continued unspoken: "This is a horror," she said to herself. "Evil Arne Wong cannot be trusted. The Wongs *are* complete. They *can* have children. *But they must not have children with someone of their own gene pool...not without the genetic protocols of Nova Terra...*" The metal skin of her forehead was furrowed with worry and her cheeks twitched with her tension. She closed her eyes, the better to hide her rising emotions from Xanu Lee.

After a few moments, Xanu Lee rang for his servant to bring him his evening libation and then he retired to his bedchamber for the night.

There was no rest for Amnelia Yu. There was never any rest for Amnelia Yu.

Twenty-one

Director Gude Han was holding his usual morning staff meeting. He touched the screen of his hand-held device and read out the next subject on his agenda.

"The next patient up is Mann Yu," he announced. "Doctors Jenn Li and Bune Sung...please brief us on this patient's status and prognosis."

Jenn Li nodded to the senior Bune Sung to signal that he would stand by to assist if needed. Bune Sung cleared his throat and began speaking.

"Subject Mann Yu was brought here yesterday under sedation. We brought him out of his artificially induced coma and ran him through the most rigorous battery of tests.

"His diagnosis is complete. We have confirmed that, although his brain is without obvious physical defect, he himself has serious mental conditions which will be difficult at best to treat. We have determined there is no cure for him. He displays clear signs of sociopathy and egomania. There are irrefutable indications that he is extremely intelligent, a trait which actually worsens the first two diagnoses. His intelligence quotient is placed reliably in the 150 range." Bune Sung consulted his hand-held device before continuing. "Doctor Jenn Li and I are recommending," and here he looked at Jenn Li, who nodded his head affirmatively, "that Subject Mann Yu receive an extended course of chemical treatment to isolate and reduce the parts of his brain which cause him to be deviant."

"Are you recommending chemical lobotomy?" a stunned Gude Han interrupted. "We haven't used lobotomy as a treatment protocol for years! What could possibly justify this recommendation?"

"He is potentially *violent*," Bune Sung replied. "We have had to restrain him, both physically and chemically."

"It is the Law," Jenn Li interjected. "He is a danger to himself and to others. The only other recommendation would be to terminate him."

"The results are completely empirical," Bune Sung added. "We used no subjective information in our research at all. The probes do not lie, Director Gude Han, as you well know. The results are unchallengeable and frankly, quite frightening."

"His father is a very powerful man," Gude Han said. "We must be firm, no—*unanimous*—in our diagnosis and prognosis. I will assign a second team to go over your work. Tests will be conducted again. I will want to review those results personally. Is this clear?"

All of the heads around the conference table nodded in the affirmative.

"Sare Teng and Weye Zou," the director said, pointing to each doctor in turn, "you will be the second team. Reassign your other cases to Jenn Li and Bune Sung for now. I will ensure that you have top priority for the use of the diagnostics laboratory and any equipment you need...any equipment, without exception. I want the second set of results on my desk by the end of the day. Questions?" The director looked around the table. There were no questions.

"Dismissed. We will reassemble as usual at 0800 hours tomorrow morning."

As his subordinates cleared the room, Gude Han sat without moving, a look of concern, and fear, on his face.

"This is going to be rough," he said to himself. It was with significant effort that the clinic director was able to rise to his feet and plod from the room.

~ * ~

Mann Yu had come to a decision of his own. He was going to get out of this clinic in one piece. He was not going to allow these hacks—these so-called psycho-surgeons—to get into his brain. Who the hells did they think they were, anyway?

"The first thing I have to do is get control of myself. I will be the perfect patient," he told himself. "I can do this. These idiots are no threat to me. They don't know with whom they deal."

He continued to plot. He used deep-breathing and other arcane but effective methods to calm his racing heart and mind.

"I will show them all," he promised himself.

"And then I am going to show Father a thing or two. But first I will take care of that Abomination. She is my first priority."

~ * ~

"But these test results are completely normal!" Gude Han exclaimed that night in his office. The second team of doctors stood before him, their arms at their sides.

"Subject Mann Yu shows absolutely no signs of abnormal mentality or personality," Sare Teng said confidently.

"Where are the results of the patient interview?" Gude Han asked, swiping at the screen which stood between him and his two subordinates. "Oh wait, here it is." He took several minutes to pore through the data.

He looked up from his reading to catch the two doctors with his eyes. "There are no indications that the patient was dissembling, absolutely none. These results are indisputable. Do you agree?"

"Yes, sir," both doctors responded as one.

"How can you explain two such disparate diagnoses?" the director demanded. "Did you discuss your findings with Bune Sung and Jenn Li?"

"We did," Sare Teng replied. "They are as baffled as you are, sir."

"I am most certainly not baffled," the director replied heatedly. "I am *angry*. You are dismissed. Send in Jenn Li and Bune Sung on your way out."

"They are gone, sir," Weye Zou said.

"They've already left for the day?" Gude Han asked, his frustration and outrage evident.

"No, sir. They're gone. They packed up their personal belongings, logged out of the system, and left." Weye Zou looked at a point on the wall behind the angry director as he delivered this news.

"Good. Saves me the trouble of an exit interview," Gude Han said dismissively. "Good work, you two. Now go on—get out of here. Now."

The two doctors turned on their heels and quickly exited the office, leaving a thoughtful Gude Han sitting alone and unmoving behind his large wooden desk.

"Phew!" he finally exclaimed, slamming both hands on his desktop and then rising to his feet. "Dodged a bullet on that one!"

He was whistling as he ambled down the hallway and out of the clinic exit. He mounted his sleek silver cycle and roared out of the facility parking lot and into the clean, clear evening skies of The Empty.

An unrestrained Mann Yu watched him from the window of his second-floor room. He could hear the man whistling, even through the transparent metal window pane.

He turned away from his vantage point and threw himself lengthwise onto the hospital bed in the center of his room. He crossed his arms behind his head and smiled. This smile was frightening, like it was a promise of dire things to come.

And then he, too, whistled. The sound he made was identical to the sounds Gude Han had made, if those original sounds had been strained through a bucket of blood, that is.

~ * ~

The next morning, Director Gude Han personally oversaw the discharge of Mann Yu from the psychiatric facility.

"I hope you feel rested and well after your short stay at our humble facility," he said to Mann Yu. He descended to street level and opened the limousine door for his departing patient.

"Oh, don't worry, Director Gude Han," Mann Yu said in a kindly tone. "I won't soon forget you and your clinic. I will find a way to recognize you and your fine facility very, very soon." He smiled up at the director as Gude Han closed the vehicle's door.

"That went well," the director said to himself as the limousine soared into the bright morning sky. Saturn had set for the day and Jupiter was high on the horizon. It reflected the red light from their swollen sun, turning the atmosphere of The Empty a light lavender.

High above the director and the shrinking sight of his psychiatric facility, Mann Yu was also talking to himself.

"Oh yes," he whispered. "I will make sure you get the recognition you deserve, Director Gude Han. You and your 'fine' facility are in for some notoriety, I think. And then, maybe fire. Yes, fire. That would be suitable."

Twenty-two

"We are ready," I announced. "I am going through. Wish me luck."

"Luck," Joxe Xian said softly. He seemed to be fighting back tears.

"Luck!" Yi-Tai Feng said with more spirit.

"What is going on here?" asked an approaching young man in a lab coat. He could be seen—and heard—running up the grassy slope which supported a glimmering doorway to another universe.

"Maxx Lee!" I cried. I gave both of my companions a stern look which said, "do not say one word of what we are doing to this man."

They both gave me slight nods to indicate they had understood my unspoken communication.

By this time, Maxx Lee had approached and stood staring at the three of us, and at the shimmering portal standing on the other side of us.

"I knew it!" he cried. "I knew you were going through, Arne Wong!"

"How could you know?" I asked in astonishment. "Only three people knew anything about this project, and we're all present and accounted for!" I gestured to Yi-Tai Feng and Joxe Xian—and myself—as I spoke.

When Maxx Lee responded with only a small smile, I turned to examine my original companions.

Yi-Tai Feng.

He avoided eye contact. He was blushing under his almond complexion.

"You didn't," I said to Yi-Tai Feng. "Tell me you didn't tell Maxx Lee about this."

Maxx Lee answered for the other man. "But he did tell me, Arne Wong! Why shouldn't he? And furthermore, why didn't you say anything to me yourself? This is my father's laboratory, after all..." Maxx Lee tried to adopt a stern look, but simply couldn't hold on to it. "I want to go with you, Arne Wong," Maxx Lee said. "I want to see this other universe, this Empty, and I want to rescue the other me who is being held prisoner there."

"He was killed," I reminded him.

"Yes, but you are travelling to a time before that murder, aren't you?"

I turned what I hoped was a baleful look upon an abashed Yi-Tai Feng. "You didn't leave anything out, did you?" I asked, using all of the sarcasm at my personal disposal...not much, at that, but it was clear that Yi-Tai Feng got the message. He flinched.

"Arne Wong," he began. He hesitated when he saw how angry I was but continued after a brief pause. "Arne Wong, Maxx Lee and I both want to come with you," he insisted. "Please reconsider!"

My attitude softened. "I appreciate your wanting to do that, both of you." I was touched.

"Don't forget me!" Joxe Xian cried. "I have been your partner, your assistant, from the inception of this project. I have always intended to come with you to The Empty!"

"Don't you see you could not possibly enter into The Empty without being detected instantly?" I said. "Each of you is nearly twice the size of the tallest of us, and your skins are brown, not black. The people of The Empty would capture and kill you, and there would be no way for me to protect you."

"We'll go in armed—we'll go in '*hot*'!" Yi-Tai Feng said. I could not help smiling at my twin's use of the same ancient term that I, myself, liked to use. Had used, in fact, in a well-remembered conversation with Amnelia Yu in what seemed an impossible place and time.

"And just how would you arm yourselves?" I asked in return. "Your world has been completely peaceful for millennia. You don't even *have* weapons."

"I thought you could go through first, you know, clandestinely, and acquire some for us," Maxx Lee said, realizing as he spoke that he wasn't making much sense. "Never mind," he said. "Forget it. It was a bad idea."

"This is too dangerous," I said flatly. "I will not permit any of you to put yourself at risk. And not only am I going alone, but I am going now. No more discussion. No. More. Discussion."

I observed their worried faces. "Look, I am not going unarmed," I told them. "I have mixed up a batch of my mother's neurotoxin. I have a sizeable tank of it in my backpack." After I delivered this information, I dropped my eyes to the ground for a moment and decided that no more words were necessary. I looked up again.

I nailed each of them with my most determined look. Maxx Lee merely mouthed a silent "please," which I pointedly ignored. The three Earth men then did nothing else except to step aside to allow me to approach the portal.

"Make sure you watch activity on the other side of this portal," I cautioned Joxe Xian. "If you see anyone other than me approach it, force it shut. Do you understand me, Joxe Xian?"

"Yes, I understand."

"We will stay and help him," Maxx Lee said. "He will need assistance. You can trust us."

"I know I can," I said, looking warmly at my three friends. "Thank you. I sincerely thank you." And with that, I threw myself through the portal and was instantly visible in the dark corridor on the other side of it.

I saluted my friends and jogged away, quickly moving out of sight.

"If he's not back in seventy-two hours, I am going in after him," Yi-Tai Feng declared.

"We will go with you," Maxx Lee said.

"I am going to brief the committee right away," Joxe Xian announced. "You guys watch this portal while I call an emergency meeting."

"Good idea," Maxx Lee said. "I'll call my father and tell him what is going on. Naturally he will wish to convene the committee."

"Thank you, Maxx Lee," said a relieved Joxe Xian. He turned on his heel and ran down the path which led to Yu-Lee Laboratory's remote site. When Maxx Lee and Yi-Tai Feng saw the laboratory's cycle take off for the main facility, Maxx Lee turned to address Yi-Tai Feng.

"I need to go talk to my mother," he said. "Can you watch the portal for a while? I won't be gone long."

"Sure, Maxx Lee," Yi-Tai Feng replied. "You and your mother have been working on a special project, haven't you?" He could not suppress his excitement...he had his own suspicions on what had been going on behind closed doors at the main laboratory. He and Amnelia Lee enjoyed a close physical and emotional relationship and he had been able to tease some secrets from her.

Maxx Lee winked at him. "You know it," he said. "I will convince her to make an appearance at the committee meeting. She will have a big announcement to make."

~ * ~

Amnelia Lee had made her big announcement. In reaction, the room full of men and women in business attire had just broken out in a general clamor. Her bombshell announcement: she and her son, Maxx Lee, had developed weaponry featuring non-lethal force field technology to capture and disable enemy combatants.

"May I have your attention, please?" she shouted over the noise of the crowd. "Please allow me to elaborate." The noise quieted and then stopped completely.

"Thank you," she continued. "I must inform all of you that Yu-Lee Laboratory's Arne Wong has successfully constructed a portal to the parallel universe known as The Empty." A low but menacing hum of conversation greeted her announcement. "Please remain quiet, I beg you.

"He has gone through the portal and has additionally attempted to travel backwards in time in order to accomplish some things I can only describe as of great benefit to himself and to Earth. His actions are necessary...and they are *heroic*.

"He refused to put any of his comrades in danger's way. He has gone to the other universe, The Empty, completely alone.

"He is dressed as the Arne Wong who is native to The Empty. He intends to pose as this Arne Wong in order to infiltrate The Empty and rescue his family and friends. One of those friends is a twin to my own Maxx Lee," she said emotionally. "In Arne Wong's original timeline, the one which runs concurrent with our own, the Maxx Lee twin, a young man who goes by the name of Mann Yu, has been brutally executed by the militant revolutionaries who run that other world. It is Arne Wong's intention to find Mann Yu and Mann Yu's mother, plus Arne Wong's own mother, sister, and best friend, and return them here to our world."

She paused briefly to allow her audience to absorb what she had said before continuing. "They will not remain here. Joxe Xian is already constructing a second gateway which will open between our world, Earth, and the planet of Nova Terra, the world of Arne Wong. His Nova Terra is not The Empty, but in fact is the first parallel universe that has been *invaded* by the villains from The Empty. The Arne Wong whom we have all come to know and love is from a Nova Terra which is still undergoing terraforming in order to prepare for the immigration of the billions of people still struggling to survive on what they call their Olde Earth."

She looked across the room, making eye contact with many of its occupants. "In our own universe, we embraced the religion of Humanity many thousands of years ago," she continued, her voice soft but each word clearly enunciated. "Our arts and sciences are millennia ahead of those of either of the Nova Terras. In fact, I am told the Nova Terra of The Empty is devoid of art of any kind. Our advancement resulted in our development of the solar sails which enabled us to move our planet away from our dying sun and position it here, where humanity continues to thrive. The rulers of the Nova Terra which is called The Empty abandoned the billions of human beings stranded on their version of Olde Earth. They left them all to die."

There were sounds of shock and horror heard across the room as her last statement was received and processed. She raised her voice to continue to be heard over the sounds. "Arne Wong, Mann Yu, Amnelia Yu, Cece Wong, Nene Wong, and Nobe Chung—remember these names, ladies and gentlemen. These are the first brave men and women to use the portal technology to travel to a parallel universe in order to establish and maintain *peace*. We will join in their fight, their struggle, to bring about peace, justice, and equality of all peoples in The Empty. It is the only way to ensure that the poisons of warfare and abuse of power do not spread to other universes...*including our own*. Our very existence is threatened by what is happening in The Empty. That is why, under the Special Defense Act, decree 1102-989, I am requesting the authority to use portable force field technology against the vile aggressors of The Empty—"

The door to the conference room banged open, silencing Amnelia Lee and causing another general outcry throughout the room.

In strode Cece Feng—Cece Wong's Earth-twin—followed by several harried-looking aides.

"I believe you will be needing my signature on that authorization?" she asked as she walked across the room to join Amnelia Lee. She held one hand out for the electronic tablet containing the executive order while holding her other hand out for the stylus which a quick-witted aide nimbly provided.

"Executive Cece Feng," Amnelia Lee said. "How did news of this meeting reach you?"

"I received a call," the Earth's chief executive announced.

"A call?"

"Yes, a call. My son, Yi-Tai Feng, called to alert me of developments. We have scrambled time schedules and assets to be here."

"It is most appreciated," the man sitting at the head of the table said loudly and clearly.

"Xanu Lee," the delighted chief executive gushed, turning to face the man. "What a pleasure to find you here."

"And where else would I be?" Xanu Lee bantered coyly.

"I understand the twin of your own son is the target of this rescue gambit?"

"That is so," the man replied, his smile fading. "Among others."

"And by 'others,' do you intend my own twin and that of my son?"

"Among others," he said, the smile returning.

"Well, I will have two sons participating in this fight," the chief executive announced. "Yi-Tai Feng will take charge of our army. He will lead the foray into The Empty to rescue Arne Wong and the others."

"And the second son?" Xanu Lee asked.

"Arne Wong, himself. Arne Wong is the *twin* of my own Yi-Tai Feng. Their physical differences notwithstanding, they are the same man in two very different but parallel universes."

The crowd buzzed once more before Amnelia Lee called it back to order. "Xanu Lee and I will also have two sons in key roles in what is to come," she said.

Cece Feng raised one eyebrow in silent inquiry.

"Maxx Lee will fight alongside Yi-Tai Feng," Amnelia Lee said. "And they will be rescuing his twin, Mann Yu, from torture and execution."

The crowd could no longer be contained. It exploded in sound and then dissolved into excited groups of from two to ten people. They energetically discussed the information they had just been given, and they began strategizing how their world could best respond to the evil threat posed by The Empty. Initially, the discussions were conducted with those nearest each other. As precious seconds ticked by, however, groups sharing specific interests with each other coalesced and got down to the nitty gritty business of planning, organizing, and executing. The room gradually thinned as decisions were jointly made and roles and responsibilities defined and assigned. This was the way of the people of the Earth: cooperation, efficiency, and effectiveness.

An hour after the committee meeting had concluded, the room was completely empty. Some residual matters were still being discussed in the Yu-Lee Laboratory's hallways. Remote communications supported other conversations. But these were all conducted on-the-move. No one was idle.

Earth had been mobilized.

~ * ~

Back at the portal, Yi-Tai Feng stood, rigid and vigilant. He was pleased that his mother had reacted immediately and effectively—hells, he was happy she had even picked up his call. She often didn't.

As Yi-Tai Feng stood, Joxe Xian climbed the hill behind him and took his place at his right side. Moments later, they were joined by Maxx Lee, who took a place on Yi-Tai Feng's left side.

"Do either of you have anything to eat?" Yi-Tai Feng quietly asked.

Both Joxe Xian and Maxx Lee held out closed fists toward Yi-Tai Feng as if it had been a practiced move. When they simultaneously opened their fists, green capsules glowed dimly in Jupiter's reflected light.

"Really?" Yi-Tai Feng asked in surprise.

"They're really not bad," Maxx Lee said.

"Indeed, they are not," Joxe Xian agreed.

"Any port in a storm," Yi-Tai Feng said, taking a capsule from Joxe Xian's hand.

Maxx Lee held out a small bulb of water for Yi-Tai Feng to wash the capsule down. "Five sips of water," he instructed his hungry friend. "That's the standard on Nova Terra, at any rate."

"What about on The Empty?" Yi-Tai asked.

"Oh, they eat regular food," Joxe Xian replied. "They are not modified as the peoples of Nova Terra have been."

"Are there any other major differences between the two worlds?" Yi-Tai Feng asked.

"Well, for starters the people of The Empty have not been sexually neutered," said Maxx Lee.

Joxe Xian took a turn. "They keep their females caged and uneducated. They are breeding stock only."

Yi-Tai Feng expressed disgust. "Why do they have such a breeding program?" he asked, his horror evident in his expressions, both facial and tonal.

"They are called The Empty because their population is so small. They don't even have a million people on their planet yet," Joxe Xian said.

"What explains that?" Yi-Tai Feng asked. "Where did all of their people go?"

"They left them," Maxx Lee said bluntly.

"They 'left them'?" Yi-Tai Feng repeated.

"They left them to die on their 'Olde Earth,'" Maxx Lee said. "Over twelve billion human beings were abandoned. Left to die miserable deaths."

The three companions fell silent, each one lost in his own contemplation. Together they watched—*guarded*—the portal as Jupiter began its descent to the western horizon and Mars made its first distant appearance of the night.

Twenty-three

"So you have given my position to Arne Wong?" Mann Yu asked his father. "You have actually *freed* him? May I ask why you have done these things?" Mann Yu forced himself to remain calm, at least outwardly.

"He was freed in recognition of his role in infiltrating and exposing the people who attempted to overthrow General Chung's command," his father patiently explained. He was watching his son carefully, waiting for him to self-destruct.

He could not help but be impressed; it seemed that a day or two at Gude Han's facility had done the young man good, a *lot* of good. He had never been an easy child or young man, but when he returned from his long captivity on the other Nova Terra he was, well—*unhinged*—is the word his father chose. Something in him was broken.

"As for your position," his father said, "after you've had a chance to demonstrate that you have completely recovered, you will be restored as head of Yu-Lee Laboratories."

"I see, Father," Mann Yu replied measuredly. "Just out of curiosity, how long do you think that will be?"

"Let's just wait and see, son," Xanu Lee replied. "Take it easy. Take a vacation if you want. You can go anywhere you wish for as long as you wish."

Mann Yu shuddered. He never wanted to go anywhere again. He did not feel safe unless he was somewhere deep inside the giant laboratory facility. After his captivity in the N-T—the other Nova Terra—he had panic attacks every time he had to defecate.

"Why do you tremble so, Mann Yu?" his father asked. "What is it, son?"

"It is nothing, Father," the son replied, banishing his small seizures by sheer force of will. "There was a stray breeze just now. That is all."

"You see, Mann Yu? It is as I was saying: you need to regain your strength, your health."

"Yes, Father. I grow stronger by the minute." He paused and looked around the room. "Father, what has happened to Amnelia Yu? You know, the head of the robot from the other universe?"

"I have had her taken home for reconstruction," Xanu Lee said.

"Home?" a shocked Mann Yu echoed. "Home? Do you mean she has been returned to the N-T?"

"Well, we have no robotics labs here in The Empty, now do we?" his father challenged. "How else can I have her reconstructed?"

Mann Yu simply nodded, averting his eyes so his father could not see the anger his words had engendered. "I see, Father," he said. "I must go rest now. It has been a busy day and I am still recovering from my *long imprisonment in The N-T.*" He brought this up every chance he could. He still seethed at his father's lack of interest in his whereabouts. He had languished for weeks in that other "NT" before Arne Wong had arrived to free him, to return him to The Empty.

"You do that, Mann Yu," his father replied, relieved that the argument he expected to have with his volatile and unpredictable son was apparently not going to happen. He knew to avoid the issue of the length of Mann Yu's incarceration in that other universe: truly,

Xanu Lee had no excuse for abandoning his son. He simply had not cared. "Have a nice rest," he said dismissively. "Will I see you for dinner tonight?"

"No, Father, I am going out. With friends," Mann Yu replied.

"Oh, good," Xanu Lee said. "It will do you a world of good to have a night out on the town."

"Yes, sir. I'll say my goodnights now, Father. I will be out late. Please don't wait up."

"Good-night, son. Be careful tonight, all right?"

"Yes, Father. I will. Good-night."

As Mann Yu put some distance between himself and his father, his anger blossomed. "Oh, yes, Father," he muttered to himself. "I will be careful. I will be very careful.

"But it's everyone else who needs to be careful. They need to watch out for *me*." And with this thought, his grimace softened and his lips turned up ever so slightly at their corners.

His eyes, however—his eyes glowed with rage. They *smoldered* with resentment and hatred, and a desire for vengeance.

~ * ~

Maximillian Yu was tied tightly to his office chair. The bruises and blood on his face and his disheveled appearance bore testimony to the bad treatment he had received from his visitors.

Visitors.

General Nobe Chung and Cece Wong stood in front of the captive. They were armed to the teeth and wore multiple bandoliers of ammunition like sashes around their chests. They were garbed all in black and wore black bandanas around their heads. White face paint adorned their dark, frowning visages.

"Your progress is not satisfactory," the general said gruffly. "It is not our intention to stay here any longer. Get that robot fixed, and get it fixed now." He gestured for one of his men to approach from behind him. "Maybe he needs more incentive," Nobe Chung suggested to the infantryman.

"No, no...please!" begged the captive scientist. "How can I fix her—sorry—I mean 'it' if I am kept here? Don't you understand that

Amnelia Yu was my software design? I am the only one who can restore her—"

The butt of a military-style rifle was used to interrupt Maximillian Yu. At contact, his head snapped back and he appeared to lose consciousness.

General Nobe Chung turned to his partner, his wife, Cece Wong. "Let's go," he said. She nodded her head and turned to leave the room with him.

"But what about the abomination?" she asked as the duo departed. The general barked out laughter. It was a very unpleasant sound. "He has completed the software work," he told his mate. "He is lying about the other work, the hardware. He has done all that he can. The hardware was not his design—I know for a fact that his son, the dearly departed Mann Yu of this universe designed her skin and skeletal structure. Maximillian Yu is no longer of any value to us. We are taking the robot back to Xanu Lee. Now."

"Why are we doing this?" Cece Wong asked. She was one of the few people of The Empty who could speak to her husband in this manner. "It's illegal to make a robot in The Empty, Nobe Chung. You know this very well."

"But we didn't make the robot in The Empty, did we?" Nobe Chung replied, obviously amused by his own logic. He smiled widely. "It is an invader from The N-T!" he cried, throwing his head back to laugh heartily, and threateningly.

"Do you have any idea how much leverage we will have over Xanu Lee when we return his robot-bride to him? Since we brokered our peace contract with The Bigs, they attempt to interfere with us. They try to influence how we treat the citizens, even the *poor* citizens.

"We will have no further opposition from him concerning who we arrest and how we incarcerate and interrogate prisoners. If he says a single word about how we decide to run The Empty, he and his robot will be exposed. The people will not abide having a robot in a position of power, and respect, on The Empty. They will both be torn to shreds."

"But who will take the place of Xanu Lee? His death would cause an enormous power vacuum!" Cece Wong said. "No one has control over the Guilds like he does."

"Oh, the power transition will be seamless," General Chung replied. "And natural. It is only proper that Xanu Lee's son, Mann Yu, now that he is restored to us, takes over as the civilian power broker on The Empty. He will control the Guilds for us."

"But surely you have heard that Mann Yu doesn't even hold his position as the head of Yu-Lee Laboratories any longer?" Cece Wong asked, still pressing her husband for more information about their situation back home. "Xanu Lee has appointed Arne Wong as laboratory chief, my husband. Mann Yu has been institutionalized."

"It is you who are not up on current affairs," her husband replied, stopping to turn and take her chin tenderly into his hand. He stared directly into her large, lustrous eyes.

"Mann Yu has been released from the Gude Han Clinic; Arne Wong will not be in charge of the laboratory's operations for much longer. Can you not trust me by now, my wife? Do you doubt for a moment that I am on top of everything going on in The Empty?"

Cece smiled up at her man. "Forgive me, Nobe Chung. I am clearly wrong. I should have known that you and Mann Yu would have been engineering events to support your position and his advancement. How stupid of me, really..."

"Stupid?" Nobe Chung challenged. "You? Oh, no, Cece Wong, you are anything but stupid." He dropped her chin and the duo resumed their march down the hallway. "But you will discontinue your efforts to learn how to read," he said softly but firmly, his voice brooking no dissension.

Cece Wong's steps faltered ever so slightly, but she did not fall far behind Nobe Chung. Within moments she had resumed her position by his side.

"As you command," she replied.

"I so command," her husband confirmed.

When the duo and a significant number of armed military

escorts entered the robotics lab, they were confronted by two scientists in lab coats and a dusky golden golem, a robot.

It was sexless. Its golden "skin" did not glimmer. It wore no ornamentation of any kind on its matte finish.

"We are taking the robot now," General Nobe Chung informed the scientists, who were visibly quaking in their shoes.

"Yes, sir, General Nobe Chung," one of them responded. "She—I mean 'it'—is ready to go."

Another lab-coated scientist appeared from behind a computer terminal toward the rear of the room.

"Xanu Lee," Nobe Chung acknowledged. "What is your assessment of your success in reconstructing your wife? Your counterpart in The Empty is looking forward to having *his* wife back....You *are* aware, aren't you, that the Amnelia Yu of The Empty was terminated four years after the birth of their son because of her inferior genes?"

Xanu Lee's black face hardened but he maintained control of himself. His words were delivered in a precise, even clipped manner. He gave every impression of repressed emotion...grief. He grieved for Amnelia Yu, his partner and the mother of his dead son, Mann Yu.

Mann Yu: Xanu Lee grieved mightily over the loss of his beloved son and the manner of his death.

"I understand Amnelia Yu has no living counterpart in your universe," he replied. "Her exterior design is far from what it once was," he segued abruptly. "If you could return more of the material from the original, I might be able to provide an improved restoration."

"Oh, this will do just fine," the general said. "Her looks are of no importance. You were able to transfer the head without any complications?"

"Yes, General Nobe Chung. Amnelia Yu's brain and her optics are unharmed and completely functional."

"So other than her exterior, she is exactly as she was before she was unfortunately disassembled in The Empty?" Cece Wong asked with a nasty smirk. She knew very well how the robot's 'disassembly' in The Empty had been accomplished—she was instrumental in it, after all.

"No," Xanu Lee replied, his eyes welling with unshed tears.

"You cry?" Cece Wong demanded roughly. "You cry for this robot? Impossible! What is it you cry about?"

His answer was soft, hard to hear. But they all heard it.

"Her heart," he said. "You did not return her heart. She has purely robotic parts where her enormous heart used to be..." And a single tear rolled down his left cheek.

The robot, Amnelia Yu, stood stone-faced in the empty space between the two parties. She showed no emotion. If anything, her eyes showed distaste—but distaste for whom? Her erstwhile husband in The N-T? Or her captors from The Empty?

She said not a word as she was led to the portal which would take her back to that other Xanu Lee.

And back to the monster who was Mann Yu in The Empty.

Her metal body did not allow her shudders of revulsion to show. But they were there. They were in her brain.

She paused to think about the emptiness that occupied the region of her chest which once held a beating heart.

She missed it. But its lack did not change her at all. She still loved, hated, liked, disliked and thought complex thoughts in her brain. The heart had been a nice touch, but it was really quite unnecessary. She experienced a touch of amusement as she considered whether or not her heart would have gotten in the way of what she needed to do next.

Twenty-four

I halted at the first sound I heard. I quickly hid behind a convenient door. The room it shielded from the corridor was fortunately empty.

The sound I heard was a footfall. It was not stealthy. It became clearer as the man creating it drew nearer to my location.

A soldier! Heavily armed, even, I observed. I had a need for those weapons and ammunition. Sliding my hand down inside of my utility vest, I removed a syringe which I uncapped.

As the soldier passed by the doorway, I silently entered the hallway behind him and plunged the syringe's contents into his back. I caught the falling man from behind and dragged him into the formerly empty room.

I made quick work of removing the weapons, both a pistol of some kind and a matte black deadly-looking automatic rifle. I helped myself to several full magazines of ammunition for both. I took the soldier's face mask and examined it.

"Good," I said to myself. "It dispenses oxygen." I took some minutes to fit the mask to my face.

I then removed a roll of shiny tape from a pocket in my vest and used it to bind the soldier's feet and hands together. I wrapped a good length of the tape around the man's head to cover his mouth.

Now fully armed, and with redundant protection against my own neurotoxin, I resumed my way down the corridor and into the center of the enormous Yu-Lee Laboratory complex.

I looked exactly like The Empty's Arne Wong now. There was no need for stealth. The only real problem would result from my running into myself here in these hallways. It was a risk I had to take. If my calculations were correct, Evil Arne Wong was already imprisoned somewhere in the army bunker along with Mann Yu, *my* Mann Yu, the good Mann Yu from The N-T.

There. There was the thing I could not predict: what would happen when the two of us Arne Wongs from The N-T met each other? Could we both continue to exist? If I was successful in rescuing myself and the others, would I disappear from the timeline of Olde Earth? If that happened, could the rescue have even taken place?

I blocked this line of thought and conjecture from my mind. I had to concentrate on what I was doing. I could not afford to have my thoughts twisted and my resolve compromised.

I ran into no one who challenged my right to be where I was. I exited the building and made my way to the military bunker where, if my time travel had worked correctly, I would wait for the arrival of my family and friends—and self.

~ * ~

Soon. Very soon now.

Arne Wong and Mann Yu had been arrested on the authority of General Nobe Chung within days of their arrival on The Empty. After a series of conversations with Mann Yu over the course of those few days, the general had declared him an imposter and ordered him imprisoned. General Nobe Chung then accused Arne Wong of being an accessory to the fake Mann Yu and had him taken to the same cell. Despite their successes in mobilizing and leading his own troops against the forces of The Bigs, General Nobe Chung decided they posed too great a risk to his own personal security.

"You haven't been the same since you came back from that other Nova Terra," he hurled at Arne Wong as his military escort muscled him from the throne room. "Maybe you're an imposter, too!"

"Nobe Chung—excuse me—*General* Nobe Chung, you have known me since we were boys. Don't you know me anymore?"

"No, I do not. Not anymore. You are not the same."

"Does my victory over the military might of Yu-Lee Laboratories mean nothing to you?"

"No. That battle is done. I now look to the future. The future I look to does not have you in it."

As Arne Wong was roughly muscled back to his cell, he passed a smirking Yanu Yang making his own way to the general's command center.

"What are you doing here?" Arne Wong asked the other man.

Yanu Yang's smirk got bigger and he sneered an answer. "You would be surprised at the secrets one can unearth when one tries..." He let his sentence dangle until it started looking like a threat.

Master Sergeant Liu Lee prodded his prisoner. "Keep moving," he grunted. The contact between Arne Wong and Yanu Yang was broken.

As soon as Liu Lee and Arne Wong passed the doorway and were out of earshot of Yanu Yang, Arne Wong stopped again and grabbed the other man by his shirtsleeve.

"I've got a bad feeling about this, Liu Lee," he said, his forehead creased with concern, and fear. "Yanu Yang knows. He knows and he's going to tell General Nobe Chung. We have to go to Plan B," he whispered fiercely. "Get the word out to the men. Plan B is effective immediately. After you've locked me back up, return to General Nobe Chung and tell him I have something of vital importance to tell him. Tell him it is life and death—and that it is *imminent.*"

~ * ~

Both Arne Wong and Mann Yu were to be held "indefinitely."

"I am sorry that your ruse did not succeed," Arne Wong said to

Mann Yu. "I did not anticipate having so many audiences with the general so soon after our return.

"I know very well that you are not like our Mann Yu. I should have prepared you better."

"Yes, I think you should have," Mann Yu replied with emotion. "I believe you are the author of my failure. You set me up, didn't you?

"The irony in this situation is that you got caught in your own trap. I don't suppose you intended to be placed under arrest, did you?"

"No, I certainly did not," Arne Wong replied. "I have always been a loyal supporter to Mann Yu and to the general. If he thinks you are a spy, or worse, and I am the one who brought you here, then what choice did he have? Our years of close association with one another would mean nothing in that scenario."

"So you admit that you positioned me to fail?"

"I did."

Mann Yu removed a green capsule from a hidden pocket in his jacket. He also retrieved a small bulb of liquid and used it to wash down the pill.

"I wouldn't let anyone see you doing that," Arne Wong cautioned. "Don't worry too much about sustenance. I am certain we will be fed while here."

"I cannot eat food," Mann Yu replied. "I no longer have the innards to process food."

"Why in the worlds did you people do that to yourselves?" Arne Wong asked in disgust.

"Do you see any dignity in existing as *you* are?" Mann Yu asked. "You must do embarrassing and dirty things all throughout your day, and night. Your women die horribly in the dangerous and disgusting act of giving birth. We are clean. Our women are not burdened with something that men cannot, and will not, do themselves. Our way of life secured peace and prosperity, and equality, for all of our citizens. It gave us back our dignity."

Their conversation, such as it was, was interrupted by the military team which had initially escorted them to their cell.

"Come with us," the Master Sergeant in charge of the detail ordered. He indicated by two nods of his head that he was talking to Mann Yu and Arne Wong. He pointedly ignored the other hungry and disheveled prisoners. The two political prisoners were dragged back out of the cell and thrown into a different cell where they were the sole occupants.

"Thanks, Liu Lee," Arne Wong said to the master sergeant orchestrating the move. "All seems in order, yes?"

"According to plan, Arne Wong," the grim master sergeant responded.

"You know what to do next," Arne Wong said. He stood and faced the two-man detail under MSG Liu Lee's command. He rested both of his arms at his sides and raised his chin.

"Do it," Liu Lee ordered his soldiers.

An astonished Mann Yu watched as both men hit Arne Wong in the face. Arne Wong flew back against the far cell wall from the force of their combined strength.

"Good—make the damage visible," he said, struggling to regain his balance and rubbing a bloody chin. He then turned to Mann Yu. "Sorry, buddy," he said. "But you're next."

After the two prisoners had both received some abuse to visible parts of their faces and bodies, MSG Liu Lee suggested they surrender their belts and shoes.

"It is standard practice," he told Arne Wong. "If we don't take these items from you, it would be suspicious."

"Well, 'suspicious' is exactly what I don't want," Arne Wong replied, removing his shoes and surrendering his belt. "Mann Yu," he said, turning to his battered companion. "Give them your shoes and belt."

A stunned Mann Yu slowly complied. "What is going on here?" he asked Arne Wong.

"Revolution," his companion told him. "We must take the general and his soldiers by surprise."

"You were expecting to be arrested and imprisoned along with me?" Mann Yu asked, his confusion and disbelief evident.

Arne Wong laughed ruefully. "No," he said, shaking his head slowly back and forth. "No, Mann Yu, I was not expecting to be on this side of things. But you—*you*—I was hoping to have out of the way when the fighting broke out. I improvise. It's one of my skills."

"I notice that you laugh now," Mann Yu observed. "You showed a signal lack of any sense of humor when you first visited The N-T." He paused here, waiting for the other man to respond.

"That voice of the other Arne Wong," Arne Wong of The Empty said, "the voice which is now in my head. It makes me different. Once I got used to making that sound and learning what could trigger it, I felt better than before. The Empty seems bigger and more interesting. The people in it seem smaller and less interesting." He paused to laugh some more. "Do you see what it does to me?" he asked Mann Yu, tears springing from his eyes. "I am changed. I am occasionally *happy*, sometimes for no good reason. I am going to teach some of the others about this humor thing. It may catch on."

"How is it that Nobe Chung is your general?" Mann Yu asked, abruptly changing the subject. "And what has become of our struggle against The Bigs?"

Arne Wong sobered immediately. "That is cutting to the heart of the matter..." He sighed. "Nobe Chung has started taking bribes—sorry, 'gifts'—from The Bigs. Our conflict with them fades. Our soldiers become idle. Nobe Chung has made an alliance with the old families, the ones who control the wealth. Xanu Lee is the leader of The Bigs. The old man, Maximillian Yu, although retired, also wields a lot of power, especially with The Guilds."

"And Nobe Chung?" Mann Yu pressed. "How is it that you have made him your leader?"

"That is a good question, Mann Yu," Arne Wong replied thoughtfully. "Well, it seemed a natural progression, really. Nobe Chung always considered himself a 'king' of sorts, not in the dynastic sense, just in ability and strength. He is stronger and faster than almost anyone who serves in any military role. He is extremely intelligent. He is ruthless. He inspires others to follow him."

Here, Arne Wong leaned in to speak to Mann Yu in quieter tones. "And I think he is different in another way, Mann Yu: I think he has always had this germ of 'humor,' what you call 'a sense of humor,' when no one else on The Empty had a scintilla of it. He has always been entertaining. He has a certain way of speaking that mesmerizes his audience. He is original. I am learning that he is amusing. But he is also brutal. Let's not forget that. If anyone opposes him in any manner, that person either disappears or faces trial, torture, and execution in very fast order. Nobe Chung says justice must be swift. He often carries out the sentence himself. 'Keeping his hand in' is what he calls it."

"That is not at all like the Nobe Chung of The N-T," Mann Yu replied. "Our Nobe Chung is kind."

"Oh?" Arne Wong said, his brow puckering like he doubted what Mann Yu had just said. "So your Nobe Chung is not a 'king'?"

Mann Yu stuttered somewhat when replying. "Well, yes. He is. He is our 'Data King'."

"So—you see? They rule in their own separate ways." Arne Wong looked pleased with himself and satisfied with the conversation. "We should rest. You need to partake of your rations," he said to Mann Yu.

"And you?" Mann Yu asked.

"Oh, don't worry about me," Arne Wong said, laughing once more. "My protein steak and fries should be along any minute. That's part of the reason we had to be separated from the other prisoners," he explained. "I will receive the treatment that a rebel leader should expect from his loyal soldiers. I will be fed, and fed well." He sighed in contentment.

Mann Yu had to admire the other man. He appreciated how hard it must be to attain contentment in their dire situation. He paused to consider further and concluded it must be difficult to find contentment anywhere here in The Empty. It wasn't just empty of population. It was empty of beauty. It was empty of art and music. It was empty of normal human interaction between men and women.

It was empty of any trace of respect for humanity. He shuddered with revulsion and despair.

How was he going to escape the mess he'd gotten himself into?

The men sat on opposite ends of the constrete bench that served as the sole raised surface in the cell. Mann Yu swallowed his protein capsule and five sips of liquid from his water bulb. He then curled up in as small a ball as he could make of himself and tried to sleep.

No one was more surprised than he to discover he had slept. He discovered this when he was rousted out of that shallow and disturbed slumber by soldiers who roughly hauled him and Arne Wong out of the cell and down the long corridor which led to General Nobe Chung's "throne room."

Mann Yu was relieved to see that their escort was led by Master Sergeant Liu Lee. He felt that this afforded the two prisoners some level of protection. He looked over at his fellow prisoner as they walked. To his astonishment, Arne Wong's bruises and contusions looked fresh. They bled as if they had just been administered. His clothes looked different, too. And something else: Arne Wong and Liu Lee exchanged a short, and very odd, communication.

"Plan C?" Arne Wong said to the master sergeant out of the corner of his battered mouth.

"Plan C," Liu Lee confirmed. That was the entire conversation.

Odd, that. And interesting—encouraging, even. Arne Wong noticed the look Mann Yu now shared with him.

Arne Wong winked at him. *Winked!*

Mann Yu reminded himself that he had a bad habit: he often found optimism where logic and observation didn't justify it. Nevertheless, *he now hoped.*

Twenty-five

Arne Wong and his group from Nova Terra had breached the doors of The Empty's Yu-Lee Laboratories. They had found the mound of dead soldiers which blocked the doorway they had forced open.

They were now being escorted through the bombed and strafed streets of The Empty's principal city.

"What is this city called?" Cece Wong asked the "escort" nearest to her.

"What do you mean?" the man replied, clearly puzzled, and annoyed.

"Do you have a name for this city? You know, the one we're in right now?" Cece Wong asked again, matching the man's annoyance with some of her own.

"It's just 'The City'," the man said gruffly. "That's what we call it, 'The City'."

"Oh," a deflated Cece Wong said. "Okay. Thanks." She returned her attention to maneuvering over and around the twisted pavement.

The war-torn city had been nearly destroyed by bombings, incendiary devices, and automatic weapons fire. Every few steps pools of dried, and drying, blood testified to the human cost in the class conflict. The war was waged between "The Rebs" and "The Bigs," they had been informed, and it had only been initiated a few days ago. The Arne Wong of The Empty had returned then from The N-T, Nova Terra, to initiate the armed conflict. He had found his rebel brothers ready—he needed only to light their fuses.

This he did. Briefly. The group from The N-T was stunned to discover that all of this damage had been done in under a week's time.

The N-T team: Cece Wong, her son, Arne Wong, her daughter, Nene Wong, her daughter's boyfriend, Nobe Chung, and the robot, Amnelia Yu, were all striving to keep up with their armed escort.

They finally reached a constrete bunker. "Isn't this where the metro station is?" Arne Wong asked his mother. When she didn't answer, he turned to Amnelia Yu and asked her the same question.

"It is very near where the main underground station is in our universe," the robot tersely informed him. "Very close, but not exact."

Cece Wong had not answered her son because she was in shock. When she recognized what the bunker was, she looked around to discover familiar buildings and other landmarks from her own world – but most of them, here in this world, were shattered and torn. Scorched. Some destroyed beyond any hope of repair. She was more than shocked: she was devastated. Her world hadn't had a war or even a conflict of any kind in millennia. The government had essentially taken libido out of the list of possible aggression-motivators for humanity. Both men and women had been chemically and surgically neutered. The tubular nucleus in the brain's hypothalamus which regulates hunger was modified, as were most of the internal organs which supported digestion. People were freed from the enslavement of appetites, whether sexual or epicurean.

War disappeared overnight. Food production became streamlined: protein capsules were all that were needed to sustain the new and improved population. Domesticated herd and flock animals were not bred for food or eggs any longer; their numbers were carefully regulated to control the need for feed, and to keep methane byproducts at minimum levels. Art, literature, and science blossomed. Where here there were the charred remains of what seemed to be blocky, utilitarian structures, back home in her city, *Nova York*, the buildings were themselves works of art, and art itself was scattered between those buildings in abundance. Their air wasn't breathable yet and their water was poison, but their manmade structures were meticulously planned and built to express humanity's hope for a bright future.

The air and the water would come: her son, Arne Wong, was the Chief Terraformer of Nova Terra. He worked tirelessly to prepare the new world for the huge population emigrating from Olde Earth.

The population of Nova Terra was already in the billions. Twelve billion more people would be moved from Olde Earth to The N-T over the next eight-hundred years, just before their old planet was made completely uninhabitable by their bloated and still expanding red giant of a sun.

She followed her fellows and their escort into the heavily guarded bunker and down the inactive escalator stairs in a daze.

They descended into the bunker. It was a long way down. They descended the frozen escalator stairs to make their way to where the train platform was.

The enormous room they were ushered into was obviously a headquarters, perhaps "the headquarters" was a more accurate designation for it.

But there was something off—something not quite military—about the atmosphere: there was a raised dais toward the far end of the room. There were two chairs bolted to its floor. One was centered. The other was just to the right of the first.

There were swirling lights strobing throughout the cavernous room. *That's it*, Cece Wong thought to herself. *This feels more like carnival than army.*

There was a collective gasp of shock when the occupant of the center chair—the throne—stood to fully reveal himself.

"Who is that?" Cece Wong whispered.

"It is me," a stunned Nobe Chung whispered to his companions. "That is what I looked like before I chose obesity." Arne Wong knew this, too. He was well ahead of the others on identifying the man on the throne.

The group stared at the fat Nobe Chung—*their* Nobe Chung—in silence until Nene made a small noise, causing them to turn back to look where she was looking. She gazed raptly at the dais again.

Cece Wong. Armed to the teeth. It was she who was seated next to the man, the general, now in charge of the military forces of The Empty.

"Keep your masks on," Cece Wong whispered. She was cautiously loosening the straps which secured her canisters of neurotoxin.

"Bring them," General Nobe Chung ordered his master sergeant. MSG Liu Lee signaled for two other soldiers to accompany him. They saluted and exited, moving with haste and purpose.

"Hold," Cece Wong said quietly but firmly to her group from The N-T. "Hold."

They held. One by one, they all nodded in acceptance of her right to give them orders. They recognized that Cece Wong had taken on the role of their commander. She was a natural. None of them objected to her issuing commands and deciding tactics, or strategy. Even Amnelia Yu deferred to her.

Arne Wong stood next to Amnelia Yu, touching her arm lightly with his own. She trembled. She did not withdraw from Arne Wong's touch. She actually leaned into it ever so slightly.

And then they came. The military detachment dispatched by the general returned.

In their grasps were two prisoners: shoeless, beltless, and bound. The captives appeared to be too weak to resist their captors. They were bruised and bloody. Mann Yu and I—for it was me, not the Arne Wong of The Empty—were led into the room and made to stand in front of the general and his mate. I wiped fresh blood from a nose which had been recently broken. My bruises were fresh, too, giving the clear impression that Mann Yu had been beaten first, and then me only afterwards.

"Mann Yu!" Amnelia Yu cried. She struggled to go to her son but was restrained by a large and determined thug.

"I am all right, Mother," the battered prisoner said. "Please do not bring harm upon yourself."

"'Mother'?" a disgusted Cece Wong echoed from her place on the dais. "Your mother is a robot? A-a-a-an abomination? How is that even possible? We know you, Mann Yu. We know that your mother died when you were a child."

"It is as I have been trying to tell you" I said through battered and swollen lips. It was not yet time to reveal my true identity. "These people are not from our universe. Our Mann Yu is still captive in their universe." I paused to look the other Arne Wong in the eye. He nodded, affirming to me that this status was still current. I continued. "We have constructed gateways into parallel universes. I have told you this over and over again."

I turned to address General Nobe Chung. "You don't realize it, Nobe Chung, but your twin from this other universe stands in front of you."

The general spoke as he looked the newcomers over again. "You will not call me Nobe Chung," he said. "I am *General* Nobe Chung. You will address me as such."

He sat back in his enormous chair, clearly frustrated. "I do not see any such a person here in this pathetic little group."

Cece Wong stepped forward and removed her mask. "You might not see your clone," she said, "but I know you recognize me."

"And me," Arne Wong said, also removing his oxygen mask and stepping forward.

General Chung bellowed in outrage. "Who are you people? How dare you impersonate my people?" He looked back and forth at the two Arne Wongs as he screamed his challenges.

"Wait, Nobe Chung," his mate said, placing a restraining hand on his forearm. "Wait. You," she said, pointing with her free hand at my moms. "Step up. Get your hand off of that weapon." She paused to look at the chief thug. "Master Sergeant Liu Lee, why are these people armed?" The NCO snapped a salute and signaled for his troops to start disarming the visitors. "I thought they were with us," he said. "I had orders to leave them unmolested. To escort them here. To keep them safe."

"Who gave these orders?" General Chung screamed. "Who dares to usurp my authority?"

This was the moment. I stepped forward, holding my bound hands out to the nearest guard. The guard withdrew a knife from its sheath on his belt and cut the bindings from my wrists. "I gave the orders," I lied, striding forward to stand in front of the general. "Release Mann Yu," I ordered the master sergeant, who signaled another of his men to comply.

Soon, Mann Yu stood beside me. We looked rough, our clothing stained and torn, our faces covered in bruises and dried blood. But we were victorious. I am certain we looked victorious. We stood ramrod straight, our shoulders squared, our chins held high in defiance. Mann Yu spoke. "You are relieved of your position," he informed a sputtering General Nobe Chung. "Step down or I will have you hauled down by the scruff of your neck."

But now the general was laughing, as was the other Cece Wong. He threw his head back and roared. "Now!" he shouted. His shout echoed through the enormous room, finally being drowned out by the sounds of many, many booted feet entering the room from virtually every direction.

Leading the largest phalanx was another Arne Wong, his bruises older and yellower than my own, the blood on his chin and cheeks dried and flaking off. The troops following him were all wearing masks over their noses and mouths.

"Put your oxygen masks on!" he bellowed to the newcomers, holding up a large canister while pulling his own mask up over his face. He withdrew a second mask from his outer garment and threw it to me, still standing next to Mann Yu near the dais.

Amnelia Yu retrieved a mask from a compartment within her carapace and swiftly approached her son. "Mann Yu," she said, "I brought this for you." Mann Yu gave his mother a quick hug and secured his mask. "Thank you, Mother," his muffled voice could be heard saying. She did not need to reply. Her beautiful and expressive eyes told her son everything that needed to be said.

Arne Wong held the deploying mechanism for the canister contents in his hand. "Ready? Deployment commencing!" he shouted to be heard.

Cece Wong's Attar of Neuroses was deployed. The general, his mate, and their loyal troops were disoriented in seconds and disarmed in minutes.

Arne Wong's troops secured the headquarters room and then the entire bunker. There were no troops out on patrol since General Nobe Chung's truce with The Bigs.

"*Sergeant Major* Liu Lee," he said. "You are in charge of the prisoners. Please see they are securely incarcerated." He stopped the newly promoted NCO with a hand to his chest. "And thanks, Liu Lee. Thanks for everything."

The sergeant major grunted his acceptance of the thanks and then turned away to discharge his orders. He barked instructions to his men who hastened to execute them with efficiency and *pride*.

The general and his forces were all incarcerated even though that did not appear to be necessary. They were confused and amnesiac. They staggered around as if they did not know who or where they were.

"I think you may have gone a little overboard," Cece Wong said teasingly to her son's twin, the Arne Wong native to The Empty. "They may never recover from the dosage you gave them." She stood next to her own Arne Wong who was unharmed, not a scratch or a bruise on him.

The three of them, Cece Wong and Arne Wong from The N-T, and Arne Wong of The Empty turned to face me as I approached them from my place near the dais.

"And just who might you be?" the unscathed Arne Wong asked. He stared at me, his duplicate—or would that be triplicate?

I put my arm around the shoulder of The Empty's Arne Wong and he put one of his arms around mine. "Meet yourself," the Arne Wong with the older injuries said, handing me a clean cloth to staunch my fresher wounds. "That was a stroke of genius, getting Liu Lee to take you to me—switching places was, well, it was just—just *genius!*"

"Well, I was in no position to lead your troops, was I?" I said to my bruised other. I then turned to complete the introduction of me to me.

Now that the moment had arrived, I felt a sense of unreality. I think I must have been in shock. When I spoke, I felt my words confirmed this diagnosis.

"I really am you," I said, sounding stunned to be saying so. "I came here as you. I escaped—well, to be perfectly honest, I was executed. Spaced. Through a portal to nowhere…I am babbling. Sorry. How to explain this? We both exist. You are from our original timeline and I travelled back in time from my future timeline to change the events which would have happened—did happen, actually—I mean, I was there, wasn't I?" I stopped and looked at my audience and then paused when I once more met the other Arne Wong's eyes with my own. "I didn't know what would happen when we met each other. When we ended up occupying the same time and place—"

The recently arrived Arne Wong interrupted me; it was really a charitable thing to do, after all. I was obviously under a lot of stress. "So let me get this straight," he said. "You are me. You were killed. Then you came back in time to save me—I mean *yourself*."

"Well, I wasn't killed," I corrected him. "Obviously. But they thought they had thrown me through a portal to empty space. It wasn't. Empty, I mean. It was Olde Earth, but in orbit right where we are. The people of that universe invented solar sails. They moved Earth to safety."

"You created and travelled through a new portal, and went back in *time*?" Amnelia Yu challenged me. "How did you do this?"

"Someone here from your future—my original timeline—sent the information through the portal to Earth. It would have taken me much longer to make the breakthrough if I had not been sent those plans...

"As for the time-travel?" I looked the robot in her eyes, something that nearly unnerved me—they were so beautiful, so *alive*. "It was something you said about Mann Yu *playing with time* that gave me the idea. It was a gamble. It was my own theory, my own programming design. I took the risk. I needed to get here before you did so I could disrupt the original events."

"What happened in this timeline, Arne Wong? In this *original* timeline?" Nobe Chung asked. He looked distressed.

"Horrible things," I said. "Things you are much better off not knowing."

"Did you stop those things from happening?" Nobe Chung persisted, obviously straining for understanding. "If they happened to you before, and you came here to stop them from happening, do you still remember those events?"

"I do."

"Wow. Just wow," Nobe Chung said, holding his head like it might explode. "Could those things still happen? Do people and events just reset?" Nene Wong smacked Nobe Chung on his massive chest with her tiny fist. "Dry up, silly man!" she said. "Shake it off, Nobe Chung! We are all here and we are safe. You should be satisfied with that."

She flung her arms around him, well, as much of him as she could. His expression softened and he was soon smiling happily once again. He stopped asking his unanswerable questions, distracted by his beautiful Nene Wong.

"So what is next?" Cece Wong asked us, her *sons*.

"We are going to take you safely back to Olde Earth," I informed her. "Then to home. We will build a portal to The N-T."

"Oh, that sounds good," she said, smiling at me while hugging the original Arne Wong.

I found myself wondering how I could possibly be so jealous of myself. It was complicated.

Amnelia Yu silently approached me and nudged me gently with one arm. "Jealous?" she asked, laughing softly. I turned to face her, taking one of her golden hands into my own. "Not anymore, I'm not," I replied, raising her delicate golden hand to my lips.

Amnelia Yu looked troubled. "Oh, dear," she said. "I find myself wondering exactly what happened to me in the original timeline. You look like you never expected to see me again."

"You might say that," I said, holding her eyes—and hand—with mine for a long second. "You just might say that."

That is when it happened. Amnelia Yu tenderly reached her supple metallic hands around my head and drew it to her chest. She massaged my throbbing head with her hands and whispered in my ear.

For my part, I quickly abolished the memory of her doing exactly the same thing with her dead son's head. That was the timeline I had come to negate. I forced myself back to my new timeline. I wanted to enjoy what was happening to me.

"Thank you, Arne Wong. Thank you for saving us. I can imagine what you went through to accomplish this. Your motivation is clear. Our fates must have been horrendous. You saved us. Thank you."

"I'll give you precisely one hour to knock that off," I responded, my eyes closed and a deliberate expression of bliss on my face.

We both laughed at this. After a few moments, we regretfully separated and went in pursuit of the others.

There was much to do.

~ * ~

At that precise moment, Xanu Lee was deciding to hire a manservant. He had fired the previous one some weeks earlier for dereliction; the man simply did not maintain his uniform properly. Xanu Lee was feeling every year of his age and wanted—*needed*—a little pampering.

"You're hired," he told the tidy little man standing in front of him. "Welcome to Yu-Lee Industries, Yanu Yang," the wealthy and powerful executive said.

"Along with your new position, we are awarding you with a woman," Xanu Lee continued. "She has been a productive member of the harem for some years now. Ingu Wing her name is, well, now it's Ingu Yang," he amended, chuckling a little. "She has borne six sons for The Empty and is deserving of a little reward herself.

"I think you will both be happy here. Your duties will be light. Please go to the indoctrination center on the fourth floor to receive your instructional interfaces. When you return, prepare me my evening nightcap. Its preparation instructions are part of the interface you will receive. That is all for now, Yanu Yang. Take care of the in-processing and then return as quickly as you can."

"Yes sir," the newly employed manservant replied.

"Oh, and Yanu Yang?" Xanu Lee said, interrupting his departure. "What have you heard about the goings-on down at the military headquarters? I heard there was something of a stir earlier today?"

"Oh, sir," Yanu Yang replied. "I would have no idea of events in that sector. I do not have those kinds of contacts, sir."

"I see," his employer replied in a noncommittal manner. "Very well, then, off you go."

Yanu Yang turned once more to leave. *Was he disappointed or relieved that I said that?* he asked himself. He reminded himself of the orders he had received from his real master: "Be discreet. Be vigilant. *Stay in character at all times.*"

Twenty-six

Yi-Tai Feng had assembled his task force and stood at its head at the portal entrance. "Activate the portal!" he called to Joxe Xian via remote comms.

Almost immediately, the material surrounding the black portal began to dance and shimmer and a corridor became visible on the other side of the gate's opening.

I had briefed Yi-Tai Feng thoroughly concerning what little I knew about The Empty. Due to this, he knew how the laboratory in the parallel universe was laid out...it was in most ways very similar to the Yu-Lee Laboratory facility on his side of the portal, and nearly a duplicate of the laboratory on my native The N-T.

"Are we ready?" he called to the forty-one "troops" he was to lead. He looked them over carefully, and proudly. There were no real troops on Earth, his Earth, that is, and so forty-one of the bravest scientists and administrators, including Maxx Lee, had armed themselves and had pledged allegiance to Yi-Tai Feng as their leader, their *commander*. They stood before him in stances representing each individual's understanding of what "attention" was. There were no hands or voices raised in response to his question. They were ready, then.

There had been no time to research military disciplines. They barely had time to learn how to effectively use their new weaponry, after all.

"Time is something you can create for yourself," Joxe Xian had told Yi-Tai Feng over and over. "I need only adjust the angle of the X17 particle stream and you can travel backwards in time."

"That is one thing I promised Arne Wong I intend to honor," Yi-Tai Feng replied. "No time travel. We will go to The Empty in our own timeline."

Joxe Xian finally gave up and agreed to use 115 Degrees as the escape angle for the particles. In other words, he would send the task force to The Empty in the timeline contemporary to their own.

Joxe Xian harbored a bad feeling about this. But he could do nothing to convince Yi-Tai Feng to change his mind. The task force would arrive a full month after Arne Wong's estimate of the original The N-T's team's arrival: what would they find? Surely by now I, and other Arne Wongs, would have returned if my, or *our*, situation had allowed it.

Joxe Xian tried to shake off his feeling of doom. After all, the task force was equipped with state-of-the art weaponry. Plus, he had received a second capsule of specifications which corrected deficiencies contained in the first. So the team had powerful weapons and improved portal support. This must give them an advantage, right?

"We will be all right, Joxe Xian," Yi-Tai Feng shouted over the comms. "Stop worrying yourself to death already!" He barked a laugh and then shouted, "Tight formation...entering portal—*now!*" and then he led those brave men and women under his command through the portal and into The Empty.

The task force met no resistance. The laboratory complex appeared to be deserted.

"Where are they, sir?" one of his troops asked.

"I do not know," Yi-Tai Feng responded. The task force was equipped with new communications equipment. As long as they wore the headgear Amnelia Lee had designed for them, they could speak to one another freely. "Maintain comms silence for now, please," he added.

They continued through the laboratory and out onto the street.

Still no one. Not a person could be discerned on the street. Everything was eerily quiet. A gentle breeze stirred the collars of their overgarments. A flag flapped somewhere in the distance. Yi-Tai Feng could just make out the design the flag bore: it was a giant red sun on a field of white.

They reached the bunker location and cautiously and silently descended the metal staircase. They eventually reached the command room. It was empty.

"Gian Chen, Ciao Xi," he ordered. "Take four more of the team with you and check the area behind that wall. Stay in touch. I want you to tell me what you see. What you smell. Anything you sense in any way."

He was disturbed. He could come up with no good reason that the military encampment would be empty. He could, however, imagine several *bad* reasons for it. He suppressed his troubling thoughts and focused on his immediate surroundings. He was leading the rest of his troops through two huge metal doors and down a wide corridor.

Cells. What looked to be jail cells lined the end of the corridor on both sides. The jail cells were empty. Not a scrap of anything littered the constrete floors.

The small team he had dispatched to investigate in the other direction had been continuously reporting, and now they rejoined their teammates. Nothing. They had found nothing.

"Sir!" one of his men shouted. "Sir! There is someone descending the metal staircase!"

Yi-Tai Feng leapt into action. "Maxx Lee, Senn Jo, Fung Fun, Li Lyu—you four come with me. The rest of you remain back here at the ready. You must come in haste should I call for you."

He looked his four-person detachment one by one in their terrified eyes and said, "Let's go." He found himself hoping his own eyes had communicated something other than terror, but he could not convince himself it was true. "Have your weapons out and primed," he instructed. They complied instantly.

A pair of diminutive men descended the long staircase. One of them appeared to be in charge; the other, an underling of some kind. The man in charge looked confident and fearless; the other looked terrified. His eyes grew large as Yi-Tai Feng and his four-man detachment came into sight.

"Just who are you *giants*?" the superior asked. "Where have you come from?" Yi-tai Feng could hear his Universal Translator converting the man's words so he understood them perfectly.

"We come from Earth, what you may call 'Olde Earth'," Yi-Tai Feng said. "I am called Yi-Tai Feng."

"You have a strange way of speaking," the small man said, "but I can understand your meaning." The translator had no problem interpreting this speech to Yi-Tai Feng and his men. "What sorts of beings are you? And just how did you get here? Just so that you are aware, we have been tracking you since you arrived at my laboratory."

"We used the portal technology you originally developed," Yi-Tai Feng responded. "We arrived at Yu-Lee Laboratories and walked here. We expected to find more of our people here."

"You call yourselves 'people'?" the man asked. He seemed to be surprised by this revelation. "And what is this 'Yu-Lee Laboratory' you speak of?"

"Yes, yes, I forgot. I should have said," Yi-Tai Feng replied, "we are people just like you. In our universe, we moved Earth out into your orbit. We did not suffer the hundreds of thousands of years of exposure to the expanding sun that you did. As a result, we did not evolve as you did. We have our own evolutionary path. We share a timeline with you, however. We come from a universe which parallels yours. As for 'Yu-Lee Laboratories'," he continued, "that's what we call the complex which houses the portals."

"Oh, I see," the man said, his face communicating his dawning understanding. "Here, the laboratory complex is called 'Yutani-Ri Laboratories. The portals are there, but most of the complex is dedicated to housing our archives. I am Yutani Myoto, the founder and chief executive of the laboratories."

"What have you done with our people?" Yi-Tai Feng asked in what he hoped was a non-confrontational tone. "For that matter, what have you done with *your* people, the military force which should be headquartered in this bunker?"

"Bunker?" the small man said, looking around himself to make sure this strange 'man' was seeing what he, himself, saw. "This is no bunker," he continued. "This is an abandoned transportation center."

His servant whispered fiercely in his superior's ear: "Remember the other? He said he sought some kind of military headquarters..."

The superior nodded to indicate he had received and understood the communication. "Say no more of this for now," he commanded the other man. The underling bowed deeply without verbal reply.

"As for 'your people,' I can assure you that I have no idea what you are talking about."

Yi-Tai Feng struggled to process this information. "I should have worded my question differently," he finally said. "The people I am talking about look more like you than they do me. They are people from another universe more like your own than mine. They are small—short—like you. Their skin is ebony, just as yours is." He lapsed into silence, still thinking furiously about what could have happened. Had they come to the wrong universe?

"Do you refer to Arne Wong?" the man's underling asked in a quavering voice. He was silenced by the look his superior gave him. "Do not speak again, Yanumura," the man said in a voice which carried significantly more threat than the words he used. Yanumura ducked his head and did not speak again other than to whisper, "Yes, Yutani-sama."

"Arne Wong is one of the men I seek," Yi-Tai Feng confirmed. He spoke to the superior. He felt that was the correct protocol. He ignored the subordinate and even bowed slightly to "Yutani-sama."

"The man who calls himself 'Arne Wong' is a guest of ours. He researches something in our archives," the man replied, softening his stance and facial expression.

"He came through the same portal you used. It has never been used before. We thought it a dead end."

"How long has he been here?" Yi-Tai Feng asked.

"Oh, just a few days," the man said. "I can take you to him if you like. You will be safe here. We have no crime. I would prefer that you surrender your weapons, however. It is against the laws of our world for citizens to carry lethality."

"Our weapons are not lethal," Yi-Tai Feng was quick to point out. "We are a non-violent population, Mr. Yutani. Our weapons fire force field nets to incapacitate our foes. We do not believe in killing other human beings. We revere human life. It is our highest credo."

"I see," Yutani-san said with a wary expression. "As long as you holster your weapons, you will be allowed to keep them...for now."

"Thank you, sir," Yi-Tai Feng said with another bow. He did not know why he was bowing. He instinctively felt it was appropriate. But he laughed at himself without showing any exterior signs of humor. *You are ridiculous,* he said to himself.

"Your manners are impeccable," Yutani Myoto told a surprised Yi-Tai Feng as he gestured for the tall young man to follow him up the flight of metal stairs. "Your father must be proud of you."

"My father?" Yi-Tai Feng echoed. "Yes, sir, I guess he is. But it is my mother's pride that motivates me. One day I hope to earn it."

"Oh, your *mother* do you say?" Yutani Myoto asked, turning to face the taller and younger man. They stopped their forward progress for the moment. "That is something we all seek: the approbation of our mothers. Here we worship all women, but most particularly our blessed mothers."

They turned and resumed their march up the numerous stairs.

"Excuse me, sir," Yi-Tai Feng said after climbing perhaps fifty of the stairs. "What do you call your planet?"

"We call it 'Atarashiki tsuchi'," the elder man said. "It means 'New Earth.' We built it from matter we harvested in the asteroid belt. It is home to fourteen billion human beings. Our 'Earth' as you call it, is extinct. All worthies were brought here many, many years ago. We peppered the Earth with nuclear explosive devices and propelled it into our sun."

This statement brought Yi-Tai Feng to a complete halt. "You nuked the sun?" he asked, dumbfounded.

"We did indeed," the other man said. He had kept climbing, unaware of the impact his statement had on his guest.

"What happened to your sun?" Yi-Tai Feng finally choked out. "What was the outcome of your experiment?"

"We will know that in just a few days," Yutani Myoto replied. "It has taken nine hundred years for the Earth to complete its spiral into the sun. It should arrive there at seventeen hundred hours three days from now. We predict that the explosion will retard the growth of the sun...it will keep it from becoming a red giant. It should collapse back into a warm, yellow sun once more. It is our hope that we can save this solar system."

"And if you're wrong?"

"You talk like one of our scientists," Yutani-san said, laughing lightly. "Where's your faith?"

"My faith?"

"This is a religious matter," the man said. "Three thousand years ago, Kenjin Kobayashi received a message from the Sun God. The god gave him explicit instructions for how many nuclear devices were to be used and where they were to be placed. The god provided the physics, the formulae, for propelling the Earth into the sun."

"The Sun God?" Yi-Tai Feng asked incredulously.

"The Sun God," the other man confirmed. "He came to Kobayashi-sama in a vision which lasted exactly fourteen days. The Sun God told him what to do. He brought the message to the people of the Earth. It was voted on. We began immediate plans to create 'Atsui'—sorry, that is the nickname that has developed over time from 'Atarashiki tsuchi.' 'Atsui' is what most people here call our new world."

"And what does that mean?" Yi-Tai Feng inquired. "What does 'Atsui' mean?"

"Warm," Yutani-san said. "It means *warm.*"

Yi-Tai Feng reeled from the irony of what his host had just told him. Warm. Yes, he told himself. Warm. It was about to get very warm here on 'Atsui.'

He had no doubt.

Twenty-seven

I led my group back through the portal to Olde Earth. I left myself—or rather, the Arne Wong native to The Empty—in charge of the bunker, its soldiers, and its prisoners.

"I will be back after I see to their safety," I told my twin. "From Olde Earth I will take them back to Nova Terra, The N-T. We just have to locate, build, and activate the right portal."

"Why do you not simply return to The N-T from here?" Arne Wong asked.

"Well, for one, I am not sure who remains in charge of the portals on The N-T," I said. "And for two, I have allies and friends on Earth. I promised them I would return so our grand experiment could be validated. Documented. *Celebrated.*" I paused for a moment, deep in thought. "And finally," I concluded, "We want to establish a relationship, a partnership, between our worlds, our peoples. To do that, we need a two-way portal."

"I guess I see," the Arne Wong of The Empty replied, still looking a bit puzzled. "Well, don't worry about us, we have everything well in hand."

"Are you all ready?" I asked my companions. Each of them nodded their assent grimly. I signaled for them to cross the active portal in the same order in which we arrived. I transited last.

The moment we were all safely on Olde Earth, I retrieved my communications device from an inside pocket in my utility vest. I toggled it on and contacted Joxe Xian.

"We're back!" I announced.

"Who is this?" a voice clearly belonging to Joxe Xian asked.

"It's me, Arne Wong. I have brought the team from The N-T back through the portal. We are approaching the remote laboratory complex now. Are you there?"

A choking sound was coming from the communications device. "Come in, Joxe Xian, are you there?" I repeated.

A voice not belonging to Joxe Xian provided an answer. "Arne Wong, this is Arne Wong. You are back before I have even left! Please don't approach the laboratory building. I don't know if we both can exist in the same timeline."

He and Joxe Xian were dumbfounded to hear laughter greeting his astonishing announcement.

"Don't worry," I said, trying to control my laughter. "I have already met the original Arne Wong—that would be the Arne Wong from The N-T's original timeline. He is here with me, as are Cece Wong, Nene Wong, Nobe Chung, Mann Yu, and Amnelia Yu."

"So you and the original Arne Wong coexist in this timeline?" Joxe Xian had taken the communications device back from his stunned mentor. "Nothing happened to either of you?"

"Nothing whatsoever," I replied. "We are coming in. You will see."

"Fascinating..." the Arne Wong back at the laboratory was heard saying. I cut him off and pocketed the comms unit. "Let's go!" I told the group from The N-T. I did not fail to notice that original Arne Wong was smiling. It was a nervous and tentative smile, but it was a smile, nonetheless.

A few minutes later, all of the people rescued from The Empty were standing in the laboratory. We stood not three feet from two very surprised men in lab coats.

We stared back and forth at them wordlessly. We stared at Joxe Xian because of his height, mostly. He was also remarkable for the lightness of his skin and the azure color of his eyes. His hair was a shade of red which did not exist in either The Empty or The N-T.

Then we stared at the three Arne Wong's, one after another—well, I could only stare at my two twins.

"We have just answered a question for the ages," Laboratory Arne Wong announced. "We can meet ourselves in parallel universes and in *timelines* both parallel and past. Amazing!"

"Don't publish yet," I said with a smirk. "We really don't know what we've done to those timelines, do we? I mean, just think about it. I went back in time and rescued Mann Yu and original Arne Wong's team. But I remember those horrific events that happened on their original timeline. I think by going back, I only created a *new* timeline, or a knot in the original. Will those events still take place, or did I really prevent them from happening? And if I prevented them from happening, how is it that I remember every grisly detail? What's more, how is it that this Arne Wong," and here I gestured toward the "me" wearing the lab coat, "is still here when I was never thrown through that portal?"

"You are hurting my head," Joxe Xian replied, clutching that head with both hands as if to illustrate.

"I want to know what happened in that original timeline," Amnelia Yu said, looking to me for the answer. "You can consider that an order from The Authority," she added.

I turned to face the team I had just rescued. "Yes, I think you all need to know what happened. You need to know because we have to figure out how to find you and fix you in the alternative timeline where you were not rescued, because I am certain it continues unaltered.

"Mann Yu, you were executed. Beheaded." Mann Yu reacted with an appropriate expression of shock. He put his hands around his neck as if to reassure himself that his head was still connected to it. "I am afraid there is nothing we can do for you in that other timeline...you are no longer in it."

"Nobe Chung, the last I saw of you, you were being starved and beaten. They wanted to melt the fat off of you just for amusement. You had already lost fifty pounds when I was spaced—thrown through the portal which turned out to be the one to Olde Earth.

"Moms, you and Nene were in the harem. Your future was going to be hell. Women are not people on The Empty. They were going to use you for breeding purposes." I plowed ahead, ignoring the stunned looks on the faces of my four dearest friends and relatives. I turned to face Amnelia Yu. I felt my expression soften, then harden into a mask—a mask of horror.

"You, Amnelia Yu. You were taken to something called The Circus Maximus where you were publicly humiliated, battered, and dismantled. The last time I saw any part of you was in the harem. You had been torn to pieces. Various of the barbaric women wore pieces of you as jewelry. One gigantic specimen wore your head as some kind of headdress, but you—your head—opened your eyes and looked at me! You looked at me with those beautiful eyes of yours, and a single tear rolled down one of your cheeks..." I was overcome with emotion; I had to stop for a moment to regain any semblance of composure. "Then the guards dragged me away. They took me to a portal they thought led to space. They threw me through it, laughing and jeering." I paused for effect. "But it was Olde Earth on the other side of that portal. I landed on grass—*grass*, Amnelia Yu! I saw the shining city on the horizon, framed by a rising Saturn. I walked there and found people who took me in, people who listened to me. They assigned me space here at this facility and have allowed me access to their science and their scientists."

At this point, laboratory Arne Wong stepped up. "I can take it from here, Future Arne Wong," he said. "Everything he has said is absolutely true," he told the enrapt group standing in front of him. "But Joxe Xian and I were making slow progress. Then someone managed to get a cylinder of information and data through the portal.

This cylinder contained advanced portal technology which allowed us to complete the construction of the two-way portal capability months ahead of our original schedule.

"But the time travel...that discovery was mine. Joxe Xian and I incorporated my untested theories on travelling back in time into the portal technology.

"My theory, which worked, by the way, was that changing the escape angle of the X17 particle stream would allow someone from our timeline to travel to past timelines, in worlds parallel to our own.

"Your arrival here," at this juncture he turned to me and put a hand on my shoulder, "proves that my science worked. You, who are really *me*, travelled back to the original timeline of our team from The N-T to rescue them from their fates.

"It worked. It works. It really works! You just got back a little early, that's all." He paused and looked down at his feet, his thoughts swirling through his head. "We have tested the method of travelling to the *past*," he said, almost as if to himself. "But you would have had to travel to the *future* to have arrived back here *after* you left. That is why you are back here before you even left. I think." He laughed ruefully.

"You're not really me," he corrected himself. "You have memories, experiences, which I do not." He then looked at original Arne Wong, who stood stock-still in front of his two twins. He looked dazed. "And you," Laboratory Arne Wong continued. "You haven't had either of our experiences. You were rescued before these events could happen. We are not the same people, if our experiences—our memories—define who we are."

"You don't really even look like each other that much," Mann Yu interjected. "You," he said pointing to Laboratory Arne Wong, "you have furrows in your brow that your twins do not. And you," and here he pointed to Original Arne Wong, "you look younger than both of these other Arne Wongs." He pointed to me and laughed. "And you, Future Arne Wong...you look like some kind of old bounty hunter from the rec-vids or something."

"'Bounty hunter'?" echoed a voice from the laboratory's doorway. Yi-Tai Feng, the Arne Wong of Olde Earth, was striding through the laboratory, a look of astonishment blossoming across his handsome features.

"I am the bounty hunter here," he said, turning to look each of us Arne Wongs over. His puzzlement was clear. He shook his head as if to clear it of cobwebs. "But I gotta admit," he finally said, "*this* bounty hunter is lost. Completely and utterly confounded." He fell silent. His face communicated his confusion.

"You are also Arne Wong," I announced, stepping forward to grab Yi-Tai Feng by his—well, his belt loops. The Olde Earth human was nearly twice the height of any of the Arne Wongs. He was a warm light brown color, not ebony as we were. His hair was a lustrous brown and streaked with blond highlights, where the men from The N-T had black hair—well, except for me and Nobe Chung who sported a pate swirling with intricate and colorful etchings. Mann Yu, being younger than the others, had let his hair grow and wore a popular spiky youthful style. Yi-Tai Feng's almond-shaped eyes were a startling blue. All of the people from Nova Terra had pitch-black or yellow-brown —amber—eyes, except for the robot, Amnelia Yu and her son, Mann Yu. Mann Yu had his mother's magnificent amber eyes, flecked with specks of turquoise blue.

Yi-Tai Feng stuttered his response. "Y-y-yes," he said with apparent difficulty. "Yes, I am. That is why I came here today. I meant to confront you," and here he pointed to Laboratory Arne Wong, "and get you to admit it. I have been looking for this world's Arne Wong for a long time now," he added. "I put all of the resources of Gumshoe Investigations on the case. All of my research pointed to me. I am the Arne Wong of Earth."

"Just who the hells are you people?" he asked, addressing me and Original Arne Wong. He gently pried my fingers from his belt loops and held me out at arm's length. "Do I know you?" he asked.

I laughed. "Yes, Yi-Tai Feng, you know me. I am him," I said, gesturing toward Laboratory Arne Wong. "I went to The Empty on a trajectory that took me back in time. When I returned, I discovered I hadn't even left yet! It's all quite astonishing."

Yi-Tai Feng then said something that reinforced the proposition that he was Earth's Arne Wong: he accepted the facts in front of him and moved on.

"What's next?" he asked, looking at each of us Arne Wongs in turn. "What do we do next?"

Twenty-eight

"...and that is why we are asking for your assistance."

Laboratory Arne Wong was addressing an executive session of Earth's governing body. At the front of the enormous conference room sat Cece Feng, the Earth's chief executive. To her right sat the elder Maxx—*Maximillian*—Lee. To her left, his wife and fellow scientist, Amnelia Lee.

Behind Laboratory Arne Wong sat his team: me, Mann Yu, Yi-Tai Feng, Amnelia Yu, Cece Wong, Nene Wong, Nobe Chung, and Original Arne Wong.

It had been difficult to bring the room to silence once this team entered.

"Mother!" cried a young man from the gallery. Laboratory Arne Wong recognized him as Maxx Lee, the son of the two scientists co-chairing the meeting.

"Mother," Maxx Lee repeated. "Our research! It is time—we must reveal our invention!"

Amnelia Lee tried to silence her son with a glance, but soon softened. "May I speak?" she asked Cece Feng. The chief executive nodded her permission. "It is about time you told the committee what you and Maxx Lee have been doing with the Laboratory's resources," she added in a chiding tone.

"We have not used any public funding for our work," Amnelia Lee responded defensively. "We used our own resources."

"Please continue," Cece Feng instructed impatiently. "The suspense is killing us." She rolled her eyes and drummed her fingers on the table in front of her.

Amnelia Lee turned to face the room. The tension in her body communicated itself as clearly as words: she and the chief executive were not presently on good terms.

"We have invented weapons," she said. The room exploded with exclamations, questions, and objections. Cece Feng used a large brass bell which sat in front of her to call the session back to order.

"Order! Order!" she called, eventually succeeding in restoring some semblance of calm to the room. "Please take your seats. Give Amnelia Lee a chance to explain."

Amnelia Lee shot the executive a grateful glance, but Cece Feng refused to meet her eyes with her own.

"My son, Maxx Lee, and I have been working for months to develop non-lethal technology for defensive purposes," she announced. "Once we had a visitor arrive here through the portal from The Empty, we knew we needed to prepare for future visitors, invaders, even.

"Arne Wong has told us repeatedly about The Empty and its militaristic and acquisitive nature. It is only logical, sensible, even, to make plans to defend ourselves against them.

"We have developed the technology; only prototypes of the weapon were made. We have harnessed force field technology to create weapons which capture, and capture only. The technology will not be used to harm any human beings, whether they be from Earth, from Arne Wong's universe, or from The Empty.

"If this committee decides to go forward with our project, we are ready to set up production facilities and acquire materials. Our workforce would be created by borrowing skilled scientists and technicians from other teams within Yu-Lee Laboratories," she continued. "We expect and accept that there will be significant government oversight. We think it is time. It is time to ask for permission to proceed." She sat next to a stone-faced chief executive. Her own husband looked at her from the far side of the executive with a smile of pride.

Phew, she told herself, after processing the look he shared with her. *One hurdle taken. At least Maximillian is not angry with us!*

"We are going to need a lot more detail than that," a senior scientist from the government oversight department grumbled. "We certainly cannot approve, or disapprove, your project on the scanty information you have provided here today."

"Of course," Amnelia Lee responded. "My son will schedule a briefing at your convenience. He and I are prepared to discuss and even demonstrate the new technology...at your *earliest* convenience," she added emphatically.

Cece Feng rang the bronze bell again. "Tomorrow," she said forcefully. "Zero eight hundred hours. Here. In this room. We will have the full committee in attendance."

Heads around the table and in the surrounding gallery nodded. Complete silence held until the executive rang the bell indicating the session had ended.

Then pandemonium broke out. In the confusion, Cece Feng grabbed Amnelia Lee by her shirt sleeve. "You are right," she said. "The time is now. Good job."

Amnelia Lee sputtered. "Are you saying you are aware of our research?" she asked. Her eyes were wide with surprise, and more. Scientists on Earth were not accustomed to being spied upon. She was just a little indignant.

"You don't think you could come up with something this big without my knowing, do you?" the executive asked, smirking knowingly. She rose, turned on her heel and left the meeting, leading a trail of aides and other cabinet members behind her. She waggled her fingers playfully at Maximillian Lee as she passed him. He gestured flirtatiously back at her.

"Maximillian," Amnelia Lee said to her husband, choosing to ignore the silent exchange between her husband and her boss. "We are going to need help setting this room up for the briefing tomorrow. We have to move equipment, prepare a demonstration, rearrange seating—"

"Anything you need, my dear," Maximillian Lee interrupted. "Anything. Just tell me what you want done and I will see to it."

"Thanks, Maximillian," Amnelia gushed. "Thanks so much.

"You know," she added, looking around the room for someone—or something. "I need to meet my twin, the robot. Amnelia Yu. Do you see where she might be?"

The room was chaos. The taller Earth people blocked the sight of the visitors just by virtue of their height and numbers. "There, there it—I mean 'she'—is!" Amnelia Lee exclaimed. She grabbed her son and drew him close to her and his father. "Maxx Lee," she said. "Make a list of everything we need for the demonstration tomorrow and give it to your father. He will see that things get moved here. Be specific, Maxx, but be quick."

Maxx Lee was struggling with the same issue as his mother. He was trying to meet Mann Yu, his "twin." Amnelia Lee saw him craning his neck in an effort to get a glimpse of his "other" and relented. "I get it. I know what you're feeling," she said. "Me, too. I want to meet that other 'me.'

"Let's do it, but quickly. We'll just introduce ourselves and then go immediately back to the lab to prepare for tomorrow. I think we will have future opportunities to get to know them, and to make sure they have a chance to get to know us."

Maxx Lee was already in motion. Amnelia Lee drafted in behind him as the pair pushed through the crowd to get closer to their guests.

~ * ~

The demonstration the next day was successful. Yu-Lee Laboratories was given the go-ahead for production of non-lethal force field weaponry.

Earth's resources were approved for the manufacturing of the weapons themselves; scientists and programmers were reallocated to the project to ensure the technology was tested and validated before production was initiated.

The peoples of the Earth were long accustomed to working together for a common goal. Within two weeks, the first weapons were produced, tested, and accepted. Mass production was approved.

But those first weapons? Well, they were to be put to immediate use. There were forty-one of them. That was the number of people to be assigned to the task force which would travel through the portal to rejoin and reinforce Arne Wong, or rescue him if necessary. Its mission: a preemptive strike against The Empty. Yi-Tai Feng was appointed as the task force leader.

"I would like you to come with me," he asked me. "I need your intelligence, your experience."

I readily agreed. I also understood that the tall Earthling had not just complimented me on being smart: by "intelligence" he meant "information." I knew more than any of the other travelers about the dangers of The Empty.

Laboratory Arne Wong bowed to me. "I defer to you," he said. "You are the right Arne Wong for the job of leadership."

"And what will you be doing while I am gone?" I then asked Laboratory Arne Wong. Original Arne Wong stood close by, observing if not participating in our conversation.

"I need to locate and open a portal to Nova Terra—The N-T," he replied. "We will eventually need to go home."

"I will assist," Original Arne Wong said, speaking up for the first time. "As the Arne Wong who put all of this misadventure into action, it is only right that I be the Arne Wong to test the success of the new portal."

"Agreed," all of us Arne Wongs said at the same time. Silence fell and lasted for long moments.

"Well, let's get to work, then," Original Arne Wong said, spurring the other two of us into action. "Let's get to work."

Twenty-nine

"I found a glitch in our new portal software," Joxe Xian announced to two Arne Wongs. The young lab assistant—a student, really—approached his mentor at a run. "It's a good thing we did not deploy the Earth task force before this was found!" he continued.

"This irregularity could have resulted in their transitioning the portal to the wrong world."

"What happened?" Laboratory Arne Wong asked. "What caused the error? And how is it remedied?"

Joxe Xian brought an object out from behind his back. It was an ornate silver cylinder. "I found this outside the portal, Arne Wong," he said. "I opened it. I read its contents. They are new formulae and diagrams of the portal technology. They differ significantly from the second set of designs we received in several critical areas," he continued, ignoring the astonished looks on the faces of both Arne Wongs. "We can correct our calculations fairly easily, but here's the deal, Arne Wong and Arne Wong: the new specs are completely in agreement with those from the *first* capsule. We thought the second capsule contained updated information, but it appears it contained *false* information. If we reverse the alleged corrections we made because of the *second* capsule, the portal will be safe to use and our task force will arrive at The Empty on a timeline completely consistent with our own."

"You should have brought this cylinder directly to me," Laboratory Arne Wong said sternly. He turned the silver capsule around in his hands, awestruck by its sheer beauty. "This did not come from The Empty," he said. "This kind of beauty is unknown to them."

"I wanted to make sure it was safe," Joxe Xian protested. "It could have been a weapon!"

"That risk should have been mine," Laboratory Arne Wong replied, putting the new cylinder on the work table alongside the other two cylinders they had received previously. "I do not wish for you to take such chances. You are technically a student, Joxe Xian. Please remember this in the future."

"Yes, Arne Wong," the student replied, not cowed in the least. "Should another cylinder fly through the portal, I will bring it straight to you."

Both Arne Wongs shared an identical look with the student. Their facial expressions said, "I know you are being a smart ass." Laboratory Arne Wong's wry expression was suddenly replaced with a look of horror.

"Get on your comms to Yi-Tai Feng!" he instructed Joxe Xian. "Tell him not to go through the portal with his task force—tell him the truth. He must delay using the portal until we get this programming corrected!"

"You are right!" the young man responded. "I should have thought of that first!" He grabbed the communications device from a nearby table and toggled it on.

"Yi-Tai Feng, Yi-Tai Feng, this is the remote laboratory calling," he intoned into the device. "Yi-Tai Feng, come in."

"Is that you, Joxe Xian," Yi-Tai Feng's voice responded.

The three men in the laboratory exhaled a collective sigh of relief.

"Yes, it is Joxe Xian," the student confirmed. "Yi-Tai Feng, there is a programming error in our portal technology. Do not—I repeat—do *not* go through the portal to The Empty. We need to make some adjustments to our formula. Do you read me, Yi-Tai Feng?"

"I read you," the task force leader replied. "But Future Arne Wong has already gone through the portal. He left a few minutes ago, to 'reconnoiter,' he said. He said he had adjusted the X17 particle stream to travel to the recent past. He said he wished to ensure that he did not lead us into an ambush. What's the problem? Shall I go to retrieve him?"

"Negative, Yi-Tai Feng," Laboratory Arne Wong interrupted, grabbing the communicator from Joxe Xian. "No one else is to go through that portal. We will have to trust Arne Wong to find his way back to us."

As Yi-Tai Feng was confirming receipt of Laboratory Arne Wong's instruction, Original Arne Wong and Joxe Xian were powering down the portal. In seconds, the shimmering gate went dark.

Now Yi-Tai Feng could not go through and Future Arne Wong could not return.

~ * ~

I had not made it out of the laboratory complex on the other side of the portal.

"Halt!" someone shouted at me.

"Do not touch your weapon. Leave it holstered," another voice commanded, also in a shout.

Hands up in the air in a universal symbol of harmlessness, I turned around slowly. I had not drawn my force field weapon before braving the portal. Now I was chiding myself.

"I will do you no harm," I called out to the pair of people who came into my view. They were dressed strangely—archaically—in split-legged skirts; they wore broad sashes around their waists. They carried very long swords. Cylindrical sticks attached to one another by metallic chains hung from their sashes. Their faces were hidden behind black masks: only their glittering black eyes were visible.

"Who are you?" a man in normal garb asked as he silently entered the hallway to join the armed duo. He was accompanied by a subordinate who walked slightly behind him, his eyes averted, his hands folded in front of him. When the armed people saw the first man, they immediately bowed deeply, almost to the floor, and backed away. "Yutani-sama," they both whispered reverentially. They did not sheath their swords but continued to hold them at the ready.

"I am called Arne Wong," I announced. "I have come to The Empty to talk to your Arne Wong at the military headquarters."

"You talk nonsense," the man named Yutani replied. "Why must I use my translator to understand you?"

"I, myself, am confused on that issue," I replied. "I did not need to use the translation technology the last time I found myself here." I did not mention I had been to this place *twice* before. I did not wish to divulge my time travelling discovery.

"We do not have 'military headquarters,' and we do not have a citizen called Arne Wong," the man responded. "Explain your presence here."

"Is this the world known as The Empty?" I asked. I was starting to grasp that this world was very different from the one I remembered.

"It is not," the man replied. "You are on 'Atarashiki tsuchi,' or 'Atsui' as we natives call it. I am called Yutani. Yutani Myoto. This is my laboratory."

"This world was not my destination," I said. "I apologize profusely, Mr. Yutani," I continued. "I have trespassed on your world. I will immediately return to my own."

"We will escort you back to your portal and will make sure to secure it behind you," Yutani Myoto said, gesturing for me to precede him down the hallway. His henchmen fell in behind us, their swords still deployed and ready.

We arrived at the portal just minutes later. "It is secured from the other side," one of the guards announced after attempting to activate the gate. "Actually, Yutani-sama, it has been switched completely off."

"If they see me standing here, they will reactivate it," I said confidently. A moment later, I realized my flawed logic: I was in the past. My fellows back on Olde Earth would not be able to see me. I decided not to mention the time disparity to my new hosts. I could not be sure what their reaction would be.

"This is not working," Yutani Myoto finally announced after many minutes had passed with no activity at the gate. "This portal has never been used. Are you certain this is the one you came through?"

"Yutani-sama," the guard interrupted. "I checked the security records just prior to our coming here. This is the portal this man exited."

"I do not understand what has happened to me," I confessed. "I have arrived in the wrong universe and the way back to my world is no longer operative." I slumped to the floor next to the inactive gate. "I need to think," I said.

Yutani Myoto laughed lightly. "Well, I can offer you a more comfortable place to do that," he said. "I will allow you access to our archives. You may do all of the research you like there. Perhaps you will be able to figure out what happened—and how to remedy it."

"That is most kind of you," I replied, rising to my feet and bowing deeply. I asked myself, *What are you doing, bowing like an idiot?* but instinctively I knew I was doing the right thing in this place.

"Your manners are very good," Yutani Myoto noted. "Your father must be very proud of you."

"My father is unfortunately deceased," I said. "I hope he would have been proud of how I turned out, though."

Yutani Myoto made a shallow bow to me. "My sincere condolences on the passing of your father," he said.

"Thank you, Mr. Yutani," I returned. "My mother still lives," I continued, "but I don't think she would say that she is proud of me."

Yutani Myoto smiled back at me. "Mothers can carry many secrets behind their stoic facades, Arne Wong. We strive our whole lives to hear their praises, do we not?"

"Oh we do, Mr. Yutani," I said with a tight smile. "We do indeed."

I surrendered my force field weapons to Yutani Myoto's men. I had been provided a large, well lit working space in their voluminous archive complex.

"You have free access to any materials stored here," Yutani Myoto told me. "Use the automated interface to make your searches. If there is a solution to your dilemma, you will find it here, I am certain. Please use the sleeping and relief cubicles found at the rear of this facility. Now, let us discuss your diet. How may I see that you are nourished?"

I reached into a small, nearly invisible pocket in my overgarment and removed a glowing green capsule from it. From another pocket, I retrieved a small bulb of liquid. "This is all I will need," I said. "I have enough protein capsules to last me for several weeks. The most I might need would be some water."

"You will have all the water you need," Yutani Myoto replied. "I will see to it. Please, begin your research. I bid you good luck."

"Thank you for your kindness," I said, executing another of my deep bows. Yutani Myoto smiled his acceptance of the bow's tribute and turned to leave.

"I feel I need to direct your attention to the files on our Sun," he said softly, his back to me. "Start there, please. There is an imminent event you need to be aware of. It will occur well before your 'several weeks' transpire." After delivering this mysterious guidance, Yutani Myoto, his manservant and both guards left the archives.

I was left alone to begin my research. I discovered a terminal on the workstation I had been given and stroked the screen. It spoke a welcome followed by a statement of its desire to be of service. My translation technology interpreted the words from the computer; I spoke commands and queries which were also instantly, and correctly, interpreted. The dialog was successfully negotiated.

It was in this way that I found and accessed the files concerning what this universe had done to its Earth.

And its Sun.

Two days later, Yi-Tai Feng and three members of his task force were brought to me, again by Yutani Myoto and his manservant.

"I did not know you were related to one another," Yutani Myoto was explaining to Yi-Tai Feng as they entered the complex. "You do not look like you belong to the same species."

Yi-Tai Feng smiled. He understood fully what the man was saying. "Well, how could you?" he responded. "We are from different universes, after all. Our evolutions differ enormously from one another."

I had risen to my feet and rushed to greet the Earthmen. "I knew you'd come for me!" I said.

"How in the worlds did you get *here*?" Yi-Tai Feng asked. "We transited the portal for The Empty to join you there....You are the Arne Wong of Nova Terra, The N-T, and not the Arne Wong of The Empty, aren't you?"

"Yes, you are correct, although I don't know how you can tell us apart," I replied.

"I have not yet met the other Arne Wong," Yi-Tai Feng said. "But you? I know you well."

"Well, of course you do!" I exclaimed. "I am your task force scout, after all. I came through the portal to reconnoiter, but I ended up here instead of The Empty. I have found many interesting things here in the archives. Things that indicate that Joxe Xian and Laboratory Arne Wong have a significant glitch in their portal program that needs to be fixed. I have all of the diagrams and formulae right here..." My speech tapered off slowly into silence when I saw the look on Yi-Tai Feng's face. "What is it?" I asked the tall Earthman. "Why are you looking at me like that?"

Yi-Tai Feng had blanched. He stuttered his reply. "Wh-wh-who is 'La-la-laboratory' Arne Wong?" he asked. "And what do you mean, you're 'part of my task force'? How can you be when it is *you* we came to rescue?"

"Rescue?" I echoed. "I admit I got stuck here for a few days, but that's because someone on the Earth side of the portal inactivated it."

"I find that hard to accept," Yi-Tai Feng replied. "We had a very rigorous plan to come to The Empty to assist you and the other Arne Wong to complete your tasks and return to Earth. We were prepared to find you in trouble and to rescue you if needed. We developed and manufactured *arms*."

"Yi-Tai-Feng, I am well aware of your weapons development! I had returned to Earth many days ago with Mann Yu, the original Arne Wong, Cece Wong, Nene Wong, Nobe Chung, and Amnelia Yu," I said in a daze. "I rescued them from their horrible fate and returned them to the Earth."

"That did not happen," an equally dazed Yi-Tai Feng said woodenly. "You had gone through the portal—alone—two weeks ago and we had not heard anything from you. We rushed production of our force field weaponry and came after you."

I was lost in thought for some moments. "Our timelines are crossed," I concluded. "I came here as part of your task force—well, I was supposed to go back to The Empty. But I arrived here instead. And now I know why." I held up sheets of files—diagrams, formulae, instructions—to back up my next statement. "We are victims of this glitch. I must get this information back to Laboratory Arne Wong. This data will enable him and Joxe Xian—and original Arne Wong— to correct the errors. But the portal is closed from Earth-side," I continued quietly. "How can I communicate with the Earth when we cannot go through the portal?"

Yutani Myoto then spoke up. "I think I can help you there." He held out small metal cylinder. "If you can put the essential data in this cylinder, it has magnetic properties which will allow it to transition through even a closed gate."

"Do you have a larger capsule?" Yi-Tai Feng asked, eyeing the small metallic object with something like suspicion.

"A larger object cannot pass," Yutani Myoto replied. "This is the largest size which can successfully transition."

I accepted the cylinder with another deep bow. "You have saved us," I said gratefully.

~ * ~

Yanumura Yanu brought his master his evening's libation much later that evening.

"Will there be anything else, master?" he asked, bowing deeply.

"Yes, Yanumura," Yutani Myoto replied. "Please ask my son and my wife to join me here in my study. Tell them it is just an informal visit. They have no need to change into formal garb."

"Yes, master," Yanumura Yanu replied, again bowing deeply before departing to execute his orders.

Within moments, a much younger version of Yutani Myoto entered the room, accompanied by a stunning white globe which soundlessly accelerated through the air without any apparent means of propulsion.

"Father, you called for us?" the younger man asked, bowing deeply. The glowing white globe bobbed in place, emitting a single golden greeting which seemed to hang in the air between them: "husband."

"We reach the time of Ultimate Transformation," Yutani Myoto said, a beatific expression on his face. "Within two days, the Earth will reach the Sun and the honored instructions of the Sun God will finally be executed. Release the order to all of the peoples of the world, Yutani Myochi. We should ensure that all of humanity stand on the surface of our planet, facing the Sun, at the appointed hour and day. Arrange transport and housing for all of those peoples from the dark reaches so our entire populace can witness the miracle to come."

"Yes, Father," the young man replied, executing another respectful bow. "All of the releases have long been prepared. They will be sent. Transportation and housing services are all arranged and are already underway. Everything will be as you wish, Father."

"Excellent," Yutani Myoto replied. "That is all. You may go now." He picked up his glass and took a long drink from it.

His eyes were already growing tired and dull.

Thirty

Mann Yu stood in front of the burning clinic, a wide smile on his soot-smudged face. His eyes reflected the brightness, the violence, of the flames which too soon ran out of fuel and slowly, slowly, stopped flickering and then died.

Gude Han lay on the ground directly in front of Mann Yu. Incendiary devices and fuel containers lay around him. His right hand had been molded around an undetonated grenade.

He was dead.

Mann Yu mounted his shiny silver cycle and took off up into the pink and lavender skies of The Empty. If anyone had been close enough, they would have heard that he whistled a familiar tune as he soared up into the atmosphere and out of sight.

As he rode, he toggled his communications device to active status.

"Yanu Yang," he spoke through the device. "Go to secure mode and inform me when you have done so."

"Ready, sir," the attentive manservant acknowledged seconds later.

"How go our plans?"

"Oh, very well, sir. I continue to incapacitate your father on a nightly basis. The abomination trusts me completely now. I work with her to provide portal technologies—flawed technologies, of course—to Arne Wong, who remains clueless to my deception. Everything is going right to plan."

"Excellent," Mann Yu replied. "I will be back at the laboratory in under twenty minutes. Meet me at the Earth portal then."

"Yes, sir," Yanu Yang acknowledged. "Will do, sir."

Mann Yu closed communications and made the rest of his return trip in silence. Well, verbal silence at any rate. He continued to whistle and cackle evilly as he flew.

He was as happy as he knew how to be.

~ * ~

Yutani Myochi and his mother—the beautiful white orb which carried the living brain of Yutani Amniko—were alone in the young man's quarters.

"Mother, I have found them. The hidden controls which can inactivate the nuclear devices on Earth. All of the controls are centralized on a single device buried behind a dual layer of security. Men—guards—provide the security. There are no automated safeguards at all. I chatted up one of the guards. It is because of the sanctity of the commands of the Sun God that only human guards have been mounted.

"It is very heavily guarded, but I have had many discussions with the foreigner Arne Wong about our situation. He tells me of an invention of his mother's which I think we can use to overpower security and abort this Ultimate Transformation catastrophe."

"Please tell me more," came the golden words.

The young man shivered in delight. "Mother, are you as pleased with the vocal software I developed for you as I am? Your voice is like liquid magic."

"Yes, Myochi-chan," the voice replied. "It is indeed lovely. Please, though, tell me about this discovery of yours."

"It is a neural toxin, as far as I can tell," the son told the mother. "It is rumored to cause amnesia. Arne Wong told me that his mother invented it on a world parallel to our own. She called it her Attar of Neuroses."

"Clever," his mother observed.

"Anyway, Arne Wong said that if he can solve the portal problem—if he can get back to the world he calls The Empty—there are canisters of this toxin which we can use to disable the guards, and access the nuclear detonator controls.

"Mother, I think this might be our only chance to save the human race from certain annihilation."

"You give me hope, my son," the orb replied in its magical voice. "What can I do to assist you?"

"Mother—you have used portals before, right?"

"Oh yes, son, before your father put a ban on their use, I travelled abundantly through many parallel universes."

"I don't suppose you know of a way to get to the world called The Empty?"

"No, son, I do not," the orb replied, her golden tones communicating her disappointment. "There are almost an infinite number of parallel universes, and the number of them increase exponentially with every use of the portal technology.

"But still..." She let her words hang.

"But still?" Yutani Myochi echoed hopefully.

"Let me work with Arne Wong," his mother proposed. "I can help him to zero in on the right portal. He can bring me up on his research so far, and I can complete the analysis for him."

"Mother, I am so proud of you!" the young man exclaimed. "You are our only hope!"

"I know," she replied. "It's a lot of pressure." And she punctuated the mock arrogance of her message with a glissade of tinkling laughter. It was a beautiful sound.

"Let's go," she instructed her son. "I have been wanting to visit this guest of ours for some days now. His very existence excites me in some way I have never felt before."

"Yes, Mother," Yutani Myochi replied. "Indeed. Let us go."

~ * ~

Yanumura Yanu and his wife, Yanumura Inago, were having a hushed conversation in their quarters.

"The son plots with his robot mother," the husband told the wife. "I can't be sure, but I think they try to undermine the commands of the Sun God."

"How can we be certain?" the wife replied.

"We will need to get close to them," her husband said. "We must be very cautious, though. Yutani-sama would have us executed if he thought we dishonored his wife or his son."

"We have to find proof," Yanumura Inago replied. "By any means possible. We must become spies, husband. I can put listening devices in their quarters."

"And I will follow them when my duties permit," her husband replied. "It will not be suspicious. I am often out and about on the orders of Yutani-sama, after all."

"Let it be done."

~ * ~

In The Empty's original timeline, Mann Yu met Yanu Yang at the portal through which Arne Wong had been banished. He carried a metal canister. This he handed to the manservant.

"I am going to activate this portal," Mann Yu said to Yanu Yang. "When it reaches its highest pitch, throw the canister through and signal me. I will close the portal after the canister has been deployed."

"Why wait for the high pitch, Mann Yu?" Yanu Yang asked. "What does pitch signify?"

"I alter the angle of escape of the X17 particle stream," Mann Yu said. "It is a theory of mine: if we adjust the escape angle from 115 degrees to 140 degrees, it is my theory that anything passing through the portal will actually travel backwards in time. I have also adjusted the stream velocity to target a time approximately two weeks prior to now.

"It is just a theory, Yanu Yang, but I did a lot of work on it while I was on The N-T and I think I have perfected a formula.

"It is untested, so I use this canister as my 'guinea pig'."

"Very good, sir. I stand ready to deploy the metal container. May I ask what is in it?"

"Instruments," Mann Yu replied without embellishment.

"I see," the manservant acknowledged skeptically. "Very well. I will do as you ask."

"As soon as the canister transits the portal, I will power the portal down and then adjust the X17 particle stream back to 115 degrees," Mann Yu said. "I will then re-activate the portal and signal the capsule to return here. Its equipment will have sampled approximately two weeks' worth of environmental and societal data concerning what is on the other side."

"I thought there was only vacuum on the other side of this portal," Yanu Yang said in surprise. "What societal data do you expect?"

Mann Yu chortled. It was not a nice sound coming from him. There was certainly no humor in it. "I suspect we are in for a big surprise," is all he would share with the other man.

"Are you sure this is wise?" the manservant asked.

"Wise?" Mann Yu repeated. "No, it is not wise, Yanu Yang, but it is necessary."

"Very well, sir," Yanu Yang responded. "I stand ready to assist you in this *unwise* experiment."

"Good man," Mann Yu said, slapping the other man on his back. "Good man."

~ * ~

Also back in The Empty's original timeline, Arne Wong walked from the portal control room to the portal itself. He held the canister which had been prepared for him by Yanu Yang, his undercover man in the Yu-Lee Laboratory. He also propelled a magnetic-levitator upon which were stacked nearly a hundred boxes of goods labelled "RATIONS."

He quickly walked up to the shimmering portal, the one that the guards had expelled me through. He threw the canister through it, and then used the portal's controls to power the gate back down.

He pushed the mag-lev much further down the corridor and pushed it, boxes and all, through another humming portal.

"Mission Accomplished!" he crowed to himself. He returned to the control room and erased all evidence of the portal's use.

On his way out of Yu-Lee Laboratories, Arne Wong stuck his head into the room which housed the security surveillance systems for the lab.

The guard was sprawled across the desk, unconscious. Drool accumulated under his gaping mouth.

Satisfied that everything he had done had gone unmonitored, Arne Wong returned to his new apartment.

He was looking forward to talking with his mother and sister. Cece Wong and Nene Wong would be there waiting.

He just hoped they were sober enough to hold a meaningful conversation with him. This thought made him smile.

He was as happy as he knew how to be. He had his freedom. He had received a significant promotion and a family had been provided for him as well. *And he had a mission:* Arne Wong had a reason to live. He felt proud—he had transformed himself and soon he would transform his world.

"Pride cometh before a fall," he heard in his head. Arne Wong knew the voice which tutored him in humor continued to train him in other matters. What it meant with this abstruse aphorism was beyond him for now. It made him feel vaguely uneasy, but he would study the words later and try to discern their meaning.

He could not understand why the voice had not returned to me. It had originally belonged to me, after all.

"Space abhors a vacuum," the voice interrupted his thoughts again. "I fill the empty spaces in your head with my wit and wisdom."

Now Arne Wong knew to laugh. The voice was just deploying more humor.

Or was it?

"I'm home!" he called out as he reset the security system after entering his spacious apartment. "Is anyone here?" he asked. He paused to listen. Yes, there they were. He could hear them in the back room they shared with one another.

Snoring. They were snoring.

"I guess I have to let them sleep another binge off," he told himself. "It's just as well, I guess. Nene Wong will only harangue me about Nobe Chung and I haven't been able to figure out how to free him yet. The general has made him his pet. They are rarely out of each other's sight."

"Why don't you join your women?" his voice prodded.

"What, invade their bedroom?" a shocked Arne Wong asked.

"No, you numbskull. Drink. Have a drink."

"Good idea," Arne Wong replied. "I think I will. Thanks!"

"Welcome," the voice intoned lugubriously. "Just remember this when you wake up tomorrow."

"What do you mean by that?" Arne Wong asked, pouring himself a very healthy portion of amber liquid in a plain multi-purpose drinking vessel. He congratulated himself on procuring a resupply of liquor earlier in the day – the ladies had already put a respectable dent in it.

"You might not be thanking me in the morning," the voice replied, not changing its tone.

"You joke," Arne Wong said. "You are always joking."

"One can only hope," the voice said. "One can only hope."

~ * ~

In The Empty's alternate timeline, Arne Wong crossed the throne room, seeking something of an alcoholic nature to drink.

After the victorious overthrow of General Nobe Chung's regime and the departure of our group back through the Earth portal, he felt he deserved a drink.

"To the victors go the spoils," his voice prompted him.

He was surprised. Arne Wong thought the voice in his head would have returned to me—or even Original Arne Wong—before we left The Empty.

Sergeant Major Liu Lee entered the room. "If you are looking for the liquor," he said, "It's in that cabinet in the far corner."

Arne Wong walked to the cabinet in the far corner of the room and removed a large bottle of amber liquid. He pulled the cork from it and sniffed the contents.

"Phew!" he exclaimed, holding the bottle out from his nose. "Potent!" he told the other man.

He held the bottle out in invitation to the sergeant major, who nodded his grateful acceptance of the unspoken offer. Arne Wong poured the liquor into two glasses nearly to their rims and gestured for his sergeant major to help himself.

"Sergeant Major," he said after his first gulp, "I am going to have to make this place my home for a while. "If I return to my room at Yu-Lee Laboratories, I am sure to be detained by Xanu Lee. Detained and most probably executed. Tomorrow we will complete our coup. We will capture the civilian authority and force them to come to terms."

Sergeant Major Liu Lee was nodding his acceptance of Arne Wong's strategy. "Yes, sir, Arne Wong," he said between healthy slugs of drink.

"Let's get some rest," Arne Wong said, polishing off the last of the liquid in his glass. "We have a big day tomorrow."

"Yes sir," the sergeant major said. "The men will be ready to deploy by 0600 hours."

"Excellent," his commander said. "So will I. We will catch those fat cats napping."

Arne Wong made a makeshift bed on a bench against one of the walls of the throne room. He managed to sleep for several dreamless hours.

His dreams arrived after he had awakened. There were still two hours left before the next campaign started. And so his waking dreams had time to play out before him.

He saw in his mind a Nova Terra, an Empty, abuzz with people freely pursuing their own dreams, a world not "empty" any longer. Men and women were walking, talking, and laughing with each other; they carried their children in their arms or they held them by their hands. There were outdoor recreation areas where these families could relax and enjoy nature and each other.

He borrowed some visions from what he had observed while on The N-T, that other Nova Terra where he and Mann Yu bartered portal technology in return for mass quantities of dark energy. These memories evoked visions of inspirational architecture and art works. He wanted these things for his world. He wanted so much for The Empty.

Including the twelve billion human beings that The Empty had stranded on a dying Earth.

He wanted them, too. What he did not want was the return of Mann Yu. His continued imprisonment on The N-T would be kept a close-held secret. Mann Yu's return to The Empty would not further the causes of The Rebs; on the contrary, his position of wealth and power would definitely place him, and his influence, with The Bigs.

0600 hours arrived quickly. He arose, picked up his weapon, and left to join, and command, his troops.

The Bigs were going to be forced to become better human beings. The poor people—slaves and women in particular—were going to be elevated. Today, they would truly become human beings in every sense of those words.

"I swear it on the memory of my sister," he promised himself. "Nene Wong will not have died in the harem for nothing."

If not happy, at least Arne Wong had purpose. Sometimes that has to suffice.

~ * ~

Amnelia Yu regarded her new body with distaste. "So clunky," she observed to herself.

Well, at least she was mobile again. Being a metal head had real disadvantages if one were accustomed to being in control of oneself, which she was.

Playing along with the fool, Yanu Yang, had been trying. She comforted herself with the thought that she no longer needed his services. She could help herself again.

She hid her illegal robot form from view by donning an enormous black cape.

"I must exercise my hydraulics," she told her "husband," Xanu Lee. He had just finished his evening nightcap and was feeling generous. "I need to go out. To walk vigorously. To run, even."

"Very well, my dear, but be careful...very careful," he cautioned.

"Do not worry, Xanu Lee," she responded. "I do not wish to receive any more abuse from the citizens of The Empty. I will be extremely cautious."

She found Arne Wong at his apartment.

"It is my belief that Yanu Yang works for Mann Yu," she continued, "and that can't be a good thing. That young man is seriously unbalanced, and he hates my, well, my *guts*. Don't let on that you know," she told Arne Wong. "He will still have his uses."

"I will not say anything to either of those men," Arne Wong reassured her. "I will maintain our relationships as if nothing had happened."

"I am certain the portal specifications he obtained for you are not legitimate, Arne Wong. Can we correct this by sending another cylinder with legitimate specifications and formulae?"

"I believe I can," Arne Wong responded. "I have access to the system which houses them, and I have created a one-time situation where I can access the system without being observed. We have to go now or we will lose this opportunity."

Amnelia Yu thought Arne Wong's behavior was unusual. He was unsteady on his feet and his speech was slightly slurred.

"What is wrong with you?" she asked him. He flinched.

"That voice of yours is harsh," he slurred.

"That is of no matter," Amnelia Yu responded. She was very aware that she had lost her most valued interfaces: her voice, her beautiful and efficient exterior, and the nervous system that once allowed her to feel contact throughout that silver and gold gleaming body.

"I need you to retrieve the data and activate the portal. I need you to alter the security recordings so no one knows what we have done. We need to do this immediately. The false data has already been there—wherever 'there' is—for far too long."

"Let's go," Arne Wong replied gamely. He staggered a bit as they were leaving the apartment but seemed to gain better control of himself before the duo entered the dark and quiet of Yu-Lee Labs.

Arne Wong was relieved to find things unchanged at the laboratory. His guard still snoozed. The portal control room was empty, as was the terminal at his workstation which accessed the portal technology he needed to retrieve.

This effort took many sweaty minutes, and his waning inebriation didn't help him one bit, but Arne Wong finally had what he needed.

"I used a back door to the data," he informed Amnelia Yu. "No one will know I was accessing these records."

"Good," Amnelia Yu replied. "Were you able to acquire another of those cylinders?"

"Yes," he replied. "And I altered the inventory records so no discrepancy will be noticed there as well."

"Well done," the robot responded with her robotic voice. She was unable to put any of the nuance into her speech she had been so adept at before her dismantling. "Let's go," she added, mourning her lost communication skills.

At the gate, Amnelia Yu asked Arne Wong to wait. "Open the cylinder," she instructed.

He did so. He stood in front of her with the open cylinder in his hands, trying to repress any anxiety or even curiosity.

She removed a sparkling piece of metallic fabric from a compartment in the chest of her body.

"Xanu Lee built this compartment for me," she explained. "He said I needed somewhere to carry my things," she added.

"And just what is that thing, that scrap?" Arne Wong asked as she placed the shiny ribbon of fabric into the open capsule.

"It is part of the old me, my delicate nervous network that my brilliant Mann Yu designed for me," she responded. "The Arne Wong on the other side of this portal will know what it is. That is what is important. This will signal him that the contents of this cylinder can be trusted."

"If you say so," Arne Wong said with a shrug. "OK to send it through now?" he asked her.

"Yes."

"Here goes," Arne Wong announced before throwing the second cylinder of the night through the portal. "Let us trust Arne Wong to be monitoring this portal from his side."

"I trust him to do so," the robot said.

"Yeah," Arne Wong said, "I guess I do too."

Neither of the pair had enough experience with the portal technology to realize the significance of the high pitch the gate made when activated.

Arne Wong did not realize that Mann Yu had been using the portal just minutes earlier. The controls for the gate were still set for 140 degrees.

The cylinder that Arne Wong and Amnelia Yu had just sent through the one-way portal to The N-T's Arne Wong would arrive two weeks before the one Arne Wong had sent just a few hours earlier.

As Arne Wong and Amnelia Yu left the laboratory's labyrinth of gates, there was stealthy motion further down the dark tunnel. Arne Wong's muddled senses prevented him from detecting the sound and movement.

Mann Yu and Yanu Yang tiptoed down the corridor, craning their necks and listening hard to make sure it was clear.

"Get the portals set back to 115 degrees," Mann Yu told the manservant and spy. "I will activate the gate and signal my capsule to return. Be quick, man! We cannot risk being caught!"

"Yes, Mann Yu," Yanu Yang said, already rushing toward the control room. "It shall be done."

Minutes later, and the second set of clandestine portal users departed, one of them carrying a dull silver canister and the other the entire storage system, complete with the full disc tray, of the laboratory's security recordings.

"Don't you think that's a bit much?" Mann Yu asked the older gentleman. He looked at the stolen security device as he spoke.

"I think it's just enough," Yanu Yang replied mysteriously. "Xanu Lee will be suspicious of everyone when he is informed of this theft. His robot will be suspect number one; I will see to that."

"I like it," Mann Yu replied. "And I don't like much, you know."

"Yes," Yanu Yang replied. "I know."

~ * ~

"You have got to open that portal," Amnelia Yu was saying to Laboratory Arne Wong. "Arne Wong is trapped in The Empty! We have to get him out of there!"

"Actually, Amnelia Yu," Laboratory Arne Wong replied, the expression on his face troubled. "We are pretty sure Arne Wong—Future Arne Wong as we call him—is elsewhere. The error we had in our programming almost certainly resulted in his transitioning to another parallel universe."

"Can you duplicate the error?"

"What?"

"Can you duplicate the error?"

"Well, yes, certainly we can…"

"Then do so. I am going through. I will rescue Future Arne Wong. Get that portal open, now!"

"I am going with you," Original Arne Wong interjected. "I'll not let you go alone."

"Very well," the sleek golden robot replied, already engaging her hydraulics and exiting the remote laboratory. "Let's go." She paused at the exit to face Laboratory Arne Wong. "Get that portal open," she commanded as she turned and powered away.

"Whoa, *bossy*," Joxe Xian observed for Laboratory Arne Wong's benefit.

Arne Wong sighed and looked longingly at the space where the robot had stood just moments before.

"I know," he said. "Isn't she wonderful?"

~ * ~

Yutani Amniko hovered in the air mere centimeters from my left ear.

"I am so happy we have been able to solve your portal dilemma," she said, creating trills of delicate nuance with her golden voice. I assumed she did this deliberately.

"I could not have done it without you," I said, admiring the beautiful floating orb.

"Let's get the programming corrections into this cylinder," I said, holding the ornate silver cylinder up to illustrate. "Are you sure that this will pass through the closed portal to Earth?"

"My husband designed the interface himself," the white orb replied musically. "It will work."

"Fabulous," I replied. "Let's go transmit these specifications as soon as possible. Can we go now?"

"Yes, Arne Wong," the orb replied. There were depressed tones evident in her voice. "I will be very sad to see you leave here," she said.

"Amnoki-chan," I said, lowering my voice to emphasize what I wanted to say next. "You must come with me or risk being destroyed by the Sun. We only have two days left before the Earth reaches the Sun and sets off a nuclear holocaust. You must come with me. If we cannot gain access to the controls and disable the nuclear devices, you and your son must both come with me back to Earth."

"We must not fail," the orb responded. "Let us go transmit this cylinder. We need access to The Empty to retrieve the canisters of neurotoxin. We have no time to waste."

"I know a way to buy us more time if we need it," I told the orb as we walked to the labyrinth containing Atsui's portals. "It's my invention, or perhaps 'discovery' is a better word. One hundred and forty degrees," I said. "That is the angle for time travel. We can have all the time we need."

"You play with the very structure of time?" the orb asked. Her voice communicated something. Horror. She was horrified. "I do not believe this will be permitted."

"Then I won't be asking for permission," I replied. I once again changed my tone, intending my voice to communicate something very specific. Determination. I needed her to understand that I was determined.

"I will do what I can to conceal your efforts," Yutani Amnoki said with a sigh.

"Appreciate it," I acknowledged. "Thank you."

"You are welcome, Arne Wong."

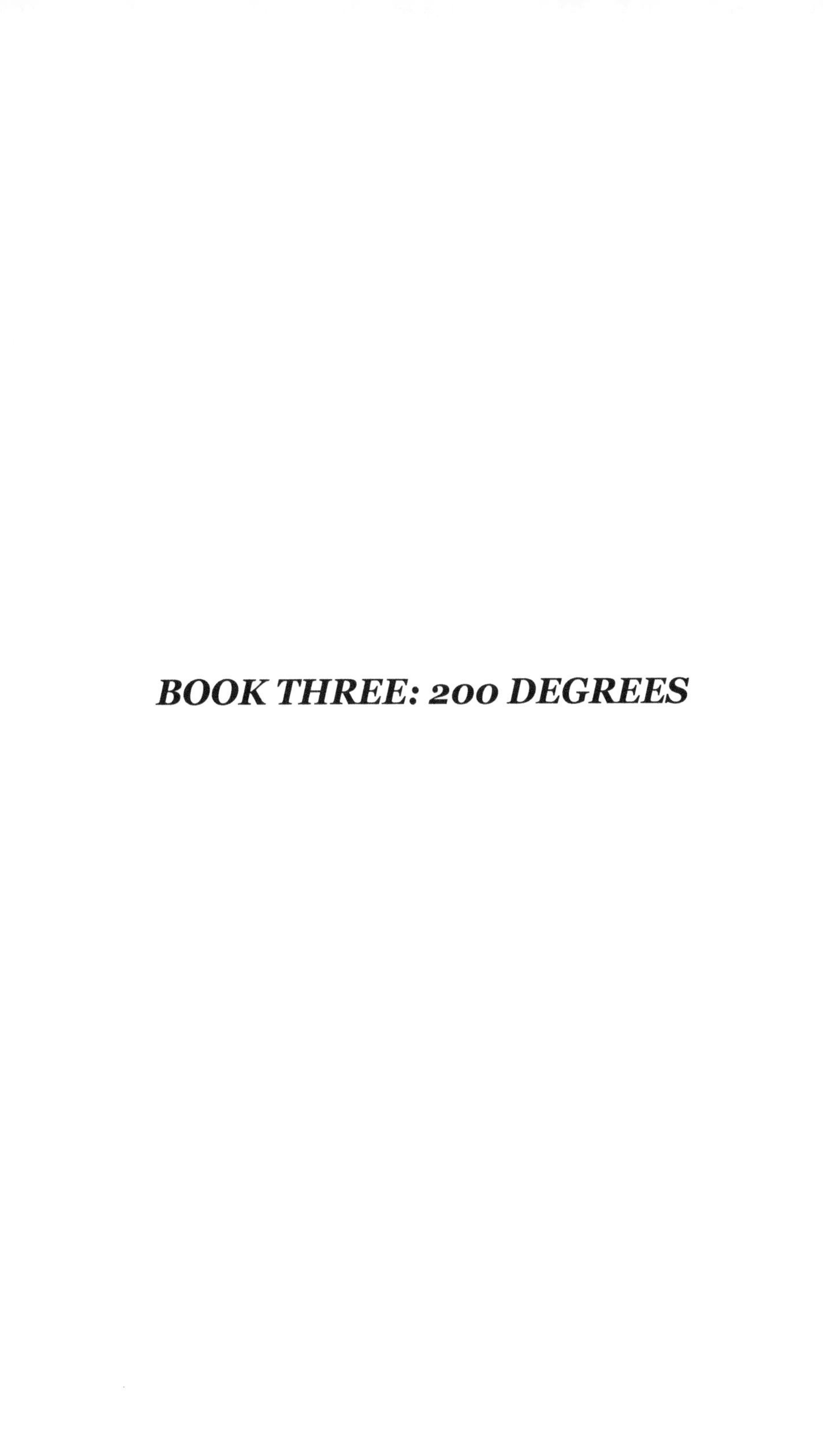

BOOK THREE: 200 DEGREES

Thirty-one

Mann Yu had managed to free himself a few hours after Arne Wong and his ragtag team of heroes transited the portal to The Empty to rescue *their* Mann Yu.

It was simple, really. No one left behind in the massive Yu-Lee Laboratory complex knew anything about The Empty and its doppelgangers: they all thought he was the one and only Mann Yu, native to The N-T—Nova Terra. He pretended to be embarrassed when he was found trapped in one of the lab's decontamination rooms. "The door locked behind me," he explained with a liberal dash of "aw shucks". Once free, he reassumed the job, home, and lifestyle of the Mann Yu who belonged here on The N-T. Now there was no Amnelia Yu to hover over him suspiciously, no Arne Wong to stalk and pry, and no Mann Yu of the deadly flying back-kick and just really unbelievable speed to incapacitate and imprison. He was free and he intended to enjoy it.

It almost made him cheerful, had he been able to become so. But cheerful was not in his chemistry, or inclination. Instead, he cultivated one of his go-to moods: evil with an unhealthy splash of devious. Oh, and angry. Throw in a pinch of paranoia, and there you had his recipe.

"There is no one here to stop me," he said to himself. "I can steal as much dark energy as I wish and there is no one to know I'm doing it. I have created a storage grid between universes and I conceal my purloined power there. If the portal in The N-T should ever become incapacitated, I can reach my energy grid through the remaining portal in The Empty."

He had but one worry: he needed to make sure he extricated himself from this backwater planet before the two-way portal between the parallel universes disappeared.

It kept him up nights. The fear did. But the promise of huge profits kept him going. "They even took their local energy guru with them!" he crowed after viewing the security system's records. These digitized images clearly showed that Arne Wong had taken his mother, sister, her fat boyfriend and Amnelia Yu with him to The Empty. That fat boyfriend, Nobe Chung, was the only person on The N-T who would have been able to figure out the source, and secret destination, of all of that dark energy.

He experienced a sweaty few days early on when General Nobe Chung had brought the head of Amnelia Yu back to Nova Terra for reconstruction. He hid in the dark recesses of the laboratory, monitoring the general through the security system.

He did not know why the general's troops did not look for him. Was it possible the general did not even know Mann Yu had been abandoned here? Whatever the answer, he watched with giddy relief as Nobe Chung, his woman, his troops, and a matte gold robot made the transit back to The Empty. It almost hurt his feelings. This thought made him laugh. Sort of. There was not much humor in it, this laugh.

As the days stretched to weeks, and then to a month, he experienced a growing curiosity as to why the Arne Wong from his own world had not returned for him. The Arne Wong of The

Empty was his property, his slave. Perhaps he simply did not want his master to return—was that possible?

"I'll make him pay dearly for his neglect," Mann Yu promised himself. "In the meantime, I trust dear old Dad is seeing that Arne Wong is hard at work at the laboratory." He banished this line of thinking from his mind and concentrated on the business at hand: shepherding billions upon billions of terawatts of energy into the narrow, but infinite, space between the universe of The N-T—Nova Terra—and the Universe of The M-T—*The Empty*.

He continued to use the decontamination chamber to destroy evidence of his physical nature, eventually putting one entire wing of the laboratory off-limits to everyone but himself. His physical nature was basically human: he had not had the surgeries and genetic manipulation the natives had. He still needed to defecate, for example. And he had all of his working parts. He had not been chemically castrated.

He had lost weight, but not excessively so. He only had the protein capsules of The N-T for sustenance, after all. But those glowing green pills were chock full of goodness, even if they had no flavor and did nothing to fill the void in his belly.

"Just tighten the old belt, Mann Yu," he told himself. "Once you've harvested enough power, you will go back to your home planet and gorge yourself on wine, women, and song. OK, skip the song. Make it steak. Rare. With all the trimmings."

He wiped the drool from his mouth with a spotless white handkerchief which he then threw into the decontamination room along with a container of his own meager droppings. He hit the "incinerate" button and let the room destroy evidence while he counted the seconds—it only took *seconds* for the powerful incinerator to render the room's contents ash—and his secret was safe.

~ * ~

Mann Yu's "property," the Arne Wong native to The Empty, had acquired his freedom from Mann Yu's father, Xanu Lee, at the insistence of a grateful General Nobe Chung. It was in Arne Wong's best interest to keep his former master away and ignorant of his own status change.

The general continued to collect graft from the rich business owners and The Guilds. This motivated him to maintain peace. Unfortunately, it also caused his men to become restless and bored. He would eventually need to distract them with action of some kind. In the meantime, he tried to keep them entertained. He used Nobe Chung for this, but the man was becoming thin and nowhere near as much fun to mock and deride as before.

"I think it's time for Mann Yu to return," he told Arne Wong. "Let's see what he's been up to on The N-T all this time. You don't think he's been idle, do you?"

"Oh, I don't think there's any danger of that," Arne Wong replied. "He won't be happy to find out I have been freed and promoted."

"His happiness is not my concern," General Nobe Chung replied. "But *my* happiness should be *your* concern, Arne Wong. Take a detachment of my men on a field trip to The N-T. Fetch back Mann Yu for me. There's a good man."

And so it was that Mann Yu's lengthy stay on The N-T was finally interrupted.

Arne Wong brought a detachment from General Nobe Chung's forces with him to Nova Terra. He had Mann Yu placed under arrest and taken back—by force—to The M-T.

"House arrest is good enough," General Nobe Chung told the detachment commander upon his return. "Give him back to his father."

Arne Wong spoke up. "I had a look at the data at the laboratory," he said. "Mann Yu has been tapping the dark energy between the universes. I think he has invented some way to store it, to hide it."

The general was impressed. "Interesting," he said to Arne Wong. He then turned back to his man. "Sergeant, make sure his father knows Mann Yu has been quietly siphoning dark energy from the stream. Ask Xanu Lee to find out from Mann Yu where he has been storing—*hiding*—all that energy."

Mann Yu was sputtering in protest. "What are you talking about?" he demanded of Arne Wong. "How could I steal dark energy without anyone noticing? You are being ridiculous!"

"Am I?" Arne Wong asked defiantly. "Am I indeed? You remember that I am an engineer, Mann Yu? Do you think I cannot interpret the data on this massive energy transfer? Do you really think I cannot do the *math?*"

Arne Wong turned to face the hardened veteran in charge of the detachment. "Please tell Xanu Lee that I calculate that four billion terawatts of dark energy are missing—no, belay that. Not 'missing.' *Stolen.* By his own son."

General Nobe Chung interrupted Arne Wong to address the detachment commander himself. "Xanu Lee needs to convince his son to tell us where he has stored all of this energy. I am certain he will be able to persuade Mann Yu to be forthcoming. He can take his time. Tell him he has one week. After that, I will take over the interrogation. Personally."

"Yes, sir!" the soldier said, delivering a snappy salute and manhandling Mann Yu out of the bunker. Mann Yu sagged in the soldier's grasp.

If Arne Wong weren't so familiar with his former master, he might have thought Mann Yu had surrendered.

But he knew him well, and he knew surrender was not in Mann Yu's nature. Well, not at first. A little intimidation and physical force would go a long way, though. He knew this, too. Mann Yu was not a man with deep reserves of courage.

Thirty-two

"You grow on one," General Nobe Chung said to the captive. "Just as you grow more handsome by the day." The general laughed mightily at his own wit.

Nobe Chung—the civilian data analyst, not the military leader—stared balefully at his captor. He said not a word.

"Release him from his bonds!" the general ordered his nearby henchmen. Two men fought each other over the honor of obeying the general's command. The loser of this fight was rendered unconscious and lay supine on the ground without being attended to in any way whatsoever. Cece Wong sat in her chair next to the general, watching the fight with a distinct lack of interest.

The winner quickly cut Nobe Chung loose from the light but strong fibers which bound him. Nobe Chung rubbed his wrists and bent to rub his ankles.

He still had not uttered a word.

"So now we finally look like one another," the general continued congenially. "How much weight have you lost over the last few months? Over two hundred pounds, I am guessing."

He got no response from his prisoner.

"Well, at any rate, I am giving you a choice, Nobe Chung of The N-T: you can get spaced like your friend Arne Wong, or you can join my armed forces as a grunt, a 'thug' as you used to call them before you were rehabilitated."

The general waited while the grubby civilian standing unsteadily in front of him considered his options.

"What have you done with Nene Wong?" the captive croaked.

"Ah!" the general crowed. "He speaks! What was that you said, Nobe Chung?"

"Nene Wong," the man answered, still having difficulty in finding his voice. "What have you done with Nene Wong?"

"Do you mean that girl and her mother who came here with you and your Arne Wong?" the general asked teasingly. "That girl we put in the harem until it was disclosed that she was barren?"

A spasm of anger washed over Nobe Chung's face. It was fast. But not fast enough to escape the notice of the general. The general also noticed that the look of anger was immediately replaced with one of fear.

He laughed.

"Oh, don't worry, Nobe Chung," he said. "We have not harmed your woman—your *women*. They have been given as booty to one of my best men."

Nobe Chung relapsed into silence. He continued to glare at the man who had tortured and starved him for weeks in his constrete bunker with the lurid lights and seemingly endless streams of amber liquor.

These people were always drunk. That was Nobe Chung's observation, at any rate.

His clothes hung in tatters on his emaciated form. He was dirty and bruised; so dirty, in fact, that it was hard to distinguish the dirt from the bruises.

"If you are saying Nene Wong is still here on this World and in this universe, then I will stay. I will be a thug for you," Nobe Chung said. The emotions playing over his features were complicated and hard to decipher.

He wasn't happy. That much was evident.

"Take him to the showers and find him a uniform," the general shouted. Once again, men fought each other for the honor of carrying out his wishes.

Cece Wong, dressed as usual all in black leather and headdress, filed her long nails and yawned.

"It's about time you moved on," she told her mate. "It's like this other Nobe Chung was an obsession with you."

She put her nail file away in a black leather pouch she wore slung over one shoulder and arose. She approached General Nobe Chung with a suggestive swagger and stopped to stand mere centimeters from his leering face.

"I used to be the object of that obsession," she said in a sultry tone. "And I want that back."

The general grabbed Cece Wong by her generous hips and pulled her close. "I cannot believe you think I could ever stop wanting you," he said, his eyes gleaming with his lust.

"I've kept track, you know," his mate said insinuatingly. "It has been many days since you showed me any real attention at all..."

"Well, let's fix that right now," General Nobe Chung replied with enthusiasm. He rose from his chair, his throne, and grabbed her by both of her wrists.

"Come with me now," he ordered her. "I will make up for the lack of attention you complain of. I will make it up to you until you beg me to stop."

"What makes you think I can be placated so easily?" Cece Wong asked teasingly. "What makes you think I'd take you back so readily?"

"You don't have to allow it," the general said, his playful features now congealing into a leer. "I take what I want, Cece Wong. You know this."

She sighed and allowed him to pull her from the room. She put up some token resistance, but it was without serious effort or intent. "Yes, General Nobe Chung. I *do* know this."

~ * ~

Once the showered and uniformed Nobe Chung was returned to the "throne room," it was apparent he had been dirtier than he had been bruised.

His resemblance to his counterpart here in The Empty was awe inspiring, especially since the general had returned from his hour-long dalliance with Cece Wong sporting some new scratches and a blooming black eye.

He smiled, however. He smiled smugly and practically purred with satisfaction as he sat in his throne and regarded his new soldier.

"You will not be issued a weapon," the general informed his conscript. "You will begin your duties working with our medical team. There are still bodies to be collected and disposed of. The whole planet reeks with the stench of death."

"Where is Nene Wong?" Private Nobe Chung asked. "Who is this hero you have given her to?"

"Why, it is Arne Wong himself!" the general announced.

"Arne Wong?" Nobe Chung echoed in disbelief. "The Arne Wong from this place? The Arne Wong who worked to overthrow you?"

The general laughed again. "He was my man from the beginning," he said. "He helped me to identify who of my men were willing to attempt an overthrow, a military coup, and in reward I had him freed from slavery, acquired freemen quarters for him, arranged a plum job for him at the Yu-Lee Laboratories...*and* rewarded him with those women. Oh, and I permitted him the honor of disposing of the coup participants. He personally saw that Liu Lee and his traitors were spaced." He stopped speaking then, waiting for Nobe Chung's response.

"You really think you can trust such a man?" Nobe Chung asked the general.

"Trust him?" the general repeated. "He is my *most* trusted man, Private Nobe Chung, as I am his. I trust him with my life. As should *you,*" he continued. "It is he who has interceded with me on your behalf. He says you could be useful to us. Apparently you're some kind of genius or something. At least that's what the younger of the women told him."

Nobe Chung decided silence was once more the best tactic. To himself, however, he made a wish: *let's hope it comes down to just that—your life.*

"May I see the women?" he asked plaintively. "I don't need to talk to them. I just want to see them."

"No," the general replied. "This grows tiresome. You are dismissed. Join the cadaver recovery team immediately. Now. One of my men will take you to their location."

The fight that ensued after this statement took three men down. The fourth man, the only one left standing, took Nobe Chung by the elbow and steered him from the room. The thug was limping but proud and determined.

~ * ~

"He wanted what?" a stunned Arne Wong said some time later that same day.

"He wants to see those women, the ones you picked from the harem," General Nobe Chung replied.

The men were seated next to each other in the thrones which were the central feature of the cavernous room. They each held metal cups which they refilled periodically from a huge bottle of amber liquid.

"I don't mind," Arne Wong said. When he saw the look on his general's face he was quick to elaborate. "I mean, it'll keep him in line, won't it? If he sees they are still alive and under my thumb, won't he be quicker to assimilate? You can use them to motivate him, can't you?" He smiled suggestively. "He would be very useful in the search for Mann Yu's hidden power reserves."

The general sighed, shaking his head as if this were a matter he would never be able to understand. "Do as you wish, Arne Wong," he relented. "It is of no matter to me."

The men drank a while longer in silence.

"Where did you assign him?" Arne Wong asked, breaking the silence.

"He is on cadaver duty," the general replied. "Over at the lab, I believe."

"I'll just take the ladies for a walk over that way," Arne Wong said casually. "It will look like a complete coincidence."

"Whatever," the general said, already having dismissed the issue from his busy mind. "Do you want another drink?"

"Yeah, I have to get it here," Arne Wong replied, laughing lightly. "Those women don't leave much liquor for me at home. They have a truly uncanny tolerance, and love, of alcohol."

"That is interesting," the general said. "Something else that they have in common with us, eh?"

"I think you refer to the sense of humor we have, you and I?" Arne Wong asked. "Yes, the women have that, too, although there has been little opportunity for it to expose itself."

"I don't know where you got yours," the general responded, "but I hope you don't lose it. I hated being the only one on this planet who saw the world a certain way."

The two men laughed and clinked their cups, toasting each other. They drank deep into the night.

Thirty-three

"Let's just go out and get some fresh air," Arne Wong pressed. Nene Wong and Cece Wong looked at him with eyes which, if not bleary, were at least unfocused. "It'll do us all some good," he insisted.

Cece Wong shrugged and went to where she had thrown her hooded cloak. She put it on with panache, swirling it around her like a matador with a cape; she was so very graceful. It was a beautifully executed motion.

It served to inspire Nene Wong, who also crossed the room to pick up her short leather jacket. She gave it a deliberate swirl before slipping her arms into its sleeves.

"Well?" she asked her "brother. "Let's go, then."

"That was a lot easier than I thought it would be," he said, holding the door open for the ladies and securing it again behind them. "I thought we'd walk toward Yu-Lee Laboratories," he continued. "There's something there I want you to see."

"How mysterious," Nene Wong said. "Lead on, Arne Wong."

The walk was not a far one. Within twenty minutes or so, they had reached the enormous laboratory complex.

"So what are we here to see?" Nene Wong asked. "I don't see anything but this hideous building—why don't you people build anything that is not just functional? I mean, would it kill you to put some ornamentation on your structures, or maybe plant some shrubbery, for crying out loud?"

They had been walking and talking, but at that moment Nene Wong froze mid-stride. "Oh the gods," she said, exhaling like she had just taken a hit to the gut. "Oh, Arne Wong," she said, turning to face him with tears in her eyes. "Is that him? That really skinny man with the brilliant tracery on his head—is that Nobe Chung?"

For his part, Nobe Chung had been watching the trio approach, his wonderment increasing exponentially as they neared his location. He, too, stood stock still, staring at them—well, staring at one of them at any rate.

Arne Wong looked at Cece Wong and smiled. He and she both had tears in their eyes, too.

"We can approach a little closer," Arne Wong said quietly in Nene Wong's ear. "Just please don't run to him. Don't touch him. Don't..." His words died as he realized he no longer had an audience.

Nene Wong was running. Nobe Chung was running, ignoring the orders being shouted to him by the soldier in charge of the cadaver detail.

They met with a smack. An audible thud. Their arms went around each other and they kissed passionately.

The man who had been yelling at Nobe Chung stopped yelling and began to slowly applaud. "Way to go, Private!" he called out. "Go get her!" The rest of the detail, looking up from their grisly work and seeing what was happening, also began to applaud and cry out encouragement.

"You are so skinny!" Nene Wong cried in dismay. "We need to fatten you back up."

"Don't worry about that," Nobe Chung reassured her. "Starvation is the least of my problems. They imprisoned me, Nene Wong. They bound me and starved me and beat me and tormented me. None of that mattered. I don't care if I starve to death. It's you, Nene Wong. I needed you. I *need* you. I love you."

"Oh, Nobe Chung," Nene Wong cried. "I love you, too! But what can we do? Why are you here? Have you been released?"

"I was given a choice to join General Nobe Chung's army or be spaced," the thin man replied. "I had to stay, Nene Wong. I had heard that you were still here, still alive..."

The pair simply stared at each other, wordlessly, tears streaming down their faces.

"Enough of that already, soldier!" the detail commander yelled. "Get back to work now, son." He said it in a kindly tone.

"When can I see you again?" Nobe Chung asked the young woman.

Arne Wong had approached by this time. "Are you confined to your quarters?" he asked Nobe Chung.

"I have no idea," Nobe Chung responded. "How would I know?"

"Here," Arne Wong said, smacking a tiny adhesive microchip to the other man's forearm. "This is where we live. If you can leave the barracks, come here. General Nobe Chung and I are friends," he continued. "I will see what I can do to secure your freedom."

"Thank you, Evil Arne Wong," Nobe Chung said. Arne Wong was trying to extricate Nobe Chung from Nene Wong's embrace.

"You have to get back to work or we'll all be in trouble," Arne Wong told Nobe Chung. "Nene Wong, let go of him if you want him to stay out of trouble."

"He is no longer 'Evil Arne Wong'," said Cece Wong, approaching to help disentangle her daughter from her boyfriend. "He is just 'Arne Wong,' Nobe Chung. Our Arne Wong was spaced. He is no more."

Nobe Chung, at last and reluctantly freed from his girlfriend's embrace, returned to the cadaver detail, looking back over his shoulder the entire way.

"Get to work, soldier!" the detail commander ordered.

"Let's go," Arne Wong prompted the women. "We have been here too long. If any of these men know who you are, I have put you in danger's way. I just wanted you to see what I have done to get Nobe Chung some relative freedom."

"You?" Nene Wong sneered. "What *you* have done? What could *you* do?" She still did not think this twin of her real brother had any authority, or competence.

"Nene Wong, you are ungrateful," Cece Wong interrupted. "You should be thanking this man. Gratitude is the hallmark of a good human being."

"Oh, Moms, just spare me more of your Buddhist bullshit propaganda," Nene Wong replied. She slumped, exhausted. Arne Wong took her by one arm, and her mother took her by the other one. They carried her away, walking back toward the apartment they now called home.

~ * ~

Amnelia Yu heard about the encounter between the newly released prisoner and the Wong women. She congratulated Arne Wong in her head. *Good one!* she silently communicated to him.

She actually felt a connection: she sensed that Arne Wong had also somehow sensed her approval. She shrugged the feeling off. "I will tell him directly the moment I see him," she promised herself.

She had been examining the room as she pondered. Bending from the waist, she grasped and removed a tiny metallic object from underneath a side table's surface.

"Ahah!" she crowed, crushing the object between her powerful metal fingers. It dissolved into microscopic bits which she wiped from her hands onto the room's floor.

"That makes six devices today alone," she told herself. "Yanu Yang becomes bold. I will need to do something about that."

Her hydraulics powered her from the room, nearly silent in their efficiency.

That little wife of his is going to crack any moment now, she continued in her head. *I allow her to overhear conversations which will eventually push her to make a decision. Is she on our side, or Xanu Lee's side? It must be one or the other, because it can never be both.*

In her room on the same floor, Ingu Yang contemplated a sharp narrow object: a knife. She tested its blade's sharpness on the inside of her arm. A sliver of blood rewarded her effort. The knife was sharp. Very. She heard a noise from the next room and quickly slid the blade back into its leather sheath. This she secured up her sleeve.

"My husband," she said as Yanu Yang entered the room. "You are home early. Is everything all right?"

Yanu Yang was distracted. "What?" he asked, having not heard a single word his wife had said.

"Are you all right, husband?" the young wife repeated. She waited in silence, not really caring if he were all right or not.

"Yes, yes. I am fine," Yanu Yang repeated, searching through his desk for something.

He found what he was searching for and shoved it, a small box, into the pocket of his serving apron.

"Xanu Lee is still awake," he said, preparing to leave the room again. "I must see to him now. I will return once he sleeps."

"Yes, husband," his wife responded.

Once he had left the room, Ingu Yang approached the desk and opened the same drawer her husband had just been rifling through. She found more boxes like the one he had pocketed but could not identify the tiny metallic objects they contained.

"What is he up to now?" she asked herself. "Does he conspire with the abomination to do harm to our master?"

She heard conversation just on the other side of her door. It was the robot! The abomination! She crossed the room and put her ear to the door.

"So, Yanu Yang," she heard the robot say clearly. "How has Mann Yu's return to The Empty affected our plans? Will he resume control of our revolution?"

"Mann Yu?" the young wife repeated, holding her hand up to cover her mouth. She knew the little gasp that she had involuntarily emitted could not possibly have been heard through the door; her reaction to hearing *his* name had been reflex, that's all.

She crossed the room once more and sat. She slid the leather sheath out of her sleeve and resumed contemplating the blade within, drawing it out and then returning it, drawing it out and returning it. Her face looked anguished.

"Mann Yu," she moaned softly. "How could he be alive? I am sure he was dead—his head was completely severed."

She collapsed in tears, sobbing loudly and beating her chest with both of her clenched fists.

"*Not Mann Yu*," she repeated. "*Oh, no...*"

Out in the hallway, Amnelia Yu, all alone, heard the gasp clearly and left satisfied that her message had been successfully delivered. She had not stayed long enough to hear the sobbing and moaning.

Thirty-four

"So here's what I think." Laboratory Arne Wong was speaking to a group which included his original self, Cece Wong, Nene Wong, Nobe Chung, Mann Yu and his mother, the robot, Amnelia Yu. Yi-Tai Feng, Joxe Xian, and Maxx Lee stood at the back of the crowd, towering over everyone else. "I think it's important we think this through before we permit any more portal usage, especially with time travel." Although he spoke to the whole group, his eyes were on Amnelia Yu.

As for Amnelia Yu, she managed to look anxious. Impatient. She was armed and ready to traverse the portal to the time and place where I had been sent. Laboratory Arne Wong thought he saw tendrils of steam escaping through some of her seams.

"Just hear me out," he almost begged. "Here is what I think: I think every time we travel using X17 particle streams over 140 degrees, we create another parallel universe. We fracture the original into two. What's more, I think that concurrent portal travel does the same damage if we use it to interfere—to change—events in the parallel universe we travel to."

A general hubbub erupted over this pronouncement. "Listen!" Laboratory Arne Wong enjoined his companions. "When Future Arne Wong went back to rescue our original team from The Empty, he did not erase the timeline where everyone was captured or killed and I was mistakenly sent here to Earth. That timeline most certainly continued. Those events happened. He didn't prevent them from happening. That universe still exists. Its events continue to unfold. In it, Cece Wong and Nene Wong are slaves. Nobe Chung is made the general's freak show. Amnelia Yu is destroyed. Mann Yu is dead—decapitated—and Evil Arne Wong wins some kind of significant reward for betraying his co-conspirators. We can only guess what his reward is. I think, at a minimum, he has been freed from Evil Mann Yu's ownership and remains a close ally to General Nobe Chung. I propose we accept this premise as a basis for what follows. All right with everybody?"

A low grumble met his question, but it seemed to be very generally an assent.

"So in the other universe, where you have been rescued before being captured or killed, General Nobe Chung and his people have all been sidelined, gassed with Cece Wong's Attar of Neuroses, and Evil Arne Wong has taken over command of the revolutionaries, The Rebs. They will fight 'The Bigs' for the freedom and human rights of the slaves—women and men—of The Empty."

"So are you saying that Evil Arne Wong is not really evil?" Joxe Xian asked.

"Joxe Xian," Laboratory Arne Wong replied. "I am forced to assume that Arne Wong is not evil in either of those two timelines. As hard as that is to accept, he is the same person in both scenarios. So if he takes the high road in the second universe, his character would dictate that he would take it in the first, as well." He paused until he was satisfied everyone had time to absorb what he had said.

"But he had all of his men captured and killed, surely?" Amnelia Yu asked, her anxiety on hold for the moment.

"Do we really know that?" Laboratory Arne Wong replied. "If he was able to save them in the second universe, why wouldn't he figure out a way to do that in the first?"

Mann Yu piped up. "I saw that he and Liu Lee were very close. I have always found it hard to believe Arne Wong would sacrifice Liu Lee, or any of his men, for that matter."

Arne Wong nodded his appreciation for Mann Yu's contribution. He was not the Arne Wong who had participated in the "rescue" timeline, after all. He needed some eyewitness corroboration. He continued.

"So there are timelines one and two. They cannot be happening in the same physical world, so I propose that these are also *alternate parallel universes* for these two versions of The Empty. Still with me?"

More grumbling. Laboratory Arne Wong appeared satisfied with the response.

"So the next time we travel, Future Arne Wong returns here with all of you *before he has even left*. Since I—he—am still here, he continues as Future Arne Wong while I become Laboratory Arne Wong. We co-exist in our original universe here on Earth because time travel was not employed—or do we? Is it not possible that the timeline where only one of us exists still continues? What is to say that we have not splintered the Earth universe with our use of the portal travel to change events, like our rescue?

"But, hold on, because this is important: I believe our Earth timeline *was* changed by other events outside of our control." He paused to make sure he had his audience's full attention.

"I strongly suspect that the capsules—or at least one of them— were sent from The Empty using time travel," he continued.

"Here is what I think: the capsule we received first had valid specifications and formulae for the construction of the two-way portal to The Empty from Earth. We assumed the second capsule contained corrections, but it was actually the *original* capsule. It contained flawed designs, intended to sabotage our travel. That is how we have sent Future Arne Wong to the wrong universe. That is why we are going to allow Amnelia Yu to go to the same universe to rescue him. Original Arne Wong will accompany her. But I have to propose that the use of time travel to send that second capsule to us from The Empty definitely created a parallel Earth, with all or most of us in it. But we cannot be sure that each and every use of the portal, with or without time travel, created another Earth with the capsules in it, and left the original world without the capsules as well. My own arrival here doubtless created a new timeline for Earth...." He paused again. He knew he was telling a complicated tale.

He continued, "We cannot accurately guess what might have happened, but I have given this a lot of thought. What if, in this alternate Earth, Yi-Tai Feng's task force was sent through to the wrong place? What if they never made it to The Empty, but rather are in the same wrong universe as Future Arne Wong? I tell you this, Amnelia Yu, to prepare you for the eventuality. You may find different versions of some of us on the other side of this portal."

"Do I bring them back here?" the robot asked. "Or do I try to send them back to the alternate Earth universe they came from?"

"The answer to that question relies fully on the society and the status and availability of portals in the other universe," Arne Wong said slowly and carefully. "You will need to be prepared for a wide range of options."

"I am ready," the robot replied.

"And I, too," original Arne Wong said, stepping up to join Amnelia Yu. "I am ready."

"Well, let's send you through," Arne Wong said, signaling Joxe Xian to take his position at the portal controls. "At 115 degrees. Current timeline. Faulty settings."

He turned to face Amnelia Yu and original Arne Wong once more. "Be careful. Please attempt to return on our concurrent timeline. Do everything in your power to keep universes intact. Please. I fear that a weakening of the dark matter structure may result. Too much of that kind of erosion could have catastrophic effects on this universe—*and all of the others.*"

~ * ~

A puzzled Joxe Xian approached Laboratory Arne Wong later that day after Amnelia Yu and original Arne Wong had been sent through the Earth portal to their mystery destination. He was joined by two other Earthmen: Yi-Tai Feng and Maxx Lee.

"What about *your* home, Arne Wong?" Joxe Xian asked. "We spoke at length today about The Empty, but what about The N-T? How is it involved in this parallel universe scenario?"

Arne Wong sighed deeply. "We left Mann Yu—Evil Mann Yu—at our Yu-Lee Laboratories," he said. "He does not have a very elevated life condition. He is not noble like Evil Arne Wong. I do not like to speculate about what he has been up to. He may still be there for all we know. As soon as we have completed reconstruction of our two-way portal to The Empty, we will discover how one of those alternate N-Ts fares."

"And the other?" Yi-Tai Feng asked. "What of the other N-T? Does it even exist?"

"I am very much afraid it does," Arne Wong replied. "We have the N-T matched to The Empty where Arne Wong wins freedom for the people of his world. This is The Empty that Future Arne Wong went to and rescued our comrades. I firmly believe that The Empty's Arne Wong will protect this N-T. But then we have the second scenario where we are captured and killed. In this universe, people like General Nobe Chung and Mann Yu are free to do whatever they wish to our peaceful populace."

"What can be done?" a concerned Maxx Lee asked.

"Arne Wong, the Arne Wong of The Empty," Arne Wong replied. "He must save them. He must save them all."

~ * ~

Amnelia Yu and original Arne Wong stealthily entered the gleaming white labyrinth on the other side of the Earth portal. They were armed with force field technology.

They had only traveled a few steps when they heard a familiar voice calling Amnelia Yu's name. The voice—it was mine—

originated far from their location, up the long, white corridor. I was not yet in sight.

"So what am I, chopped liver?" a disgruntled original Arne Wong mumbled under his breath.

"Shush," Amnelia Yu said. "Be quiet, Arne Wong. We must listen."

It hurt. As close as Arne Wong felt to the beautiful robot, she seemed to prefer the more experienced versions of himself to his original.

It stung. It really did.

I continued calling, and soon they could see me running down the long corridor. "Amnelia Yu! Amnelia Yu! I am coming!" I shouted.

I arrived out of breath. I was elated to see her. I barely gave original Arne Wong a glance. A brilliant white and silver orb hovered near my head.

"Have you managed it?" I asked the orb.

"Yes, Arne Wong," it replied mellifluously. "I have inactivated the sensors. Your friends' arrival has not alerted the security services."

"Thank you, Yutani Amniko," I said, bowing deeply.

A young man could be discerned approaching us at a run from up the winding corridor.

"Mother! Arne Wong!" he cried. "Wait for me!"

"Yutani Myochi," chided the orb. "Did I not tell you to stay put?"

"Oh Mother," the young man laughed. "You certainly knew I could not obey that instruction!"

The orb emitted a cascading series of chimes that very obviously represented laughter. "You are a scamp!" she told the young man.

Amnelia Yu made a sound, too. It was like a human clearing his throat. She accompanied this sound by hiking one delicate metal eyebrow while establishing eye contact with me. I felt locked in her gaze like a startled deer.

"And just who might this be?" she asked. She jerked her head toward the white orb to illustrate who her question targeted.

"Oh, forgive me, Amnelia Yu," I stuttered. "May I introduce you to Yutani Amniko, the wife of the owner of this laboratory, and her son, Yutani Myochi."

I said, "Yutani Amniko and Yutani Myochi, please meet my friend, Amnelia Yu. Oh, and me. Meet me. I believe this is 'original' Arne Wong." I got a grudging nod of assent from the other me.

Yutani Amniko bobbed and rolled in the air while her son bowed deeply. "The pleasure is ours," she chirped.

Amnelia Yu and original Arne Wong nodded respectfully. "And ours," Arne Wong said.

Pleasantries out of the way, I approached even closer to Amnelia Yu. "You are a sight for sore eyes!" I said, grinning from ear to ear. The floating orb drew nearer as well, hovering protectively near my head. It seemed to bother Amnelia Yu at some level. I know this makes no sense, but I felt her *bristle* in response to the orb's proximity.

"I have come for you," Amnelia Yu replied. "You have been gone for days. You obviously haven't been sent to The Empty. What is this place?"

"This is another universe!" I announced. "This is Atarashiki tsuchi – or Atsui as its inhabitants call it for short. You arrive at a most propitious time!" I continued. "In two days, the Earth of this universe will reach the sun and detonate many, many thousands of thermo-nuclear devices!"

"You jest," Amnelia Yu said in a flat voice. "I do not find the humor in it, but you do jest...don't you?"

"No, I do not jest," I said grimly. "We were just about to adjust the X17 particle escape and travel back in time a few days. You know, to buy more time for us to disable the nuclear devices."

"You must not use time travel, Future Arne Wong," the robot replied in an urgent tone. "You—Laboratory Arne Wong—have established that universes are split, timelines are conserved *and also changed* every time someone, or something, travels through our portals at particle escape angles greater than 115 degrees. He speculates that *any* usage of the portals may have the same effect if we use them to change events in the parallel worlds."

She went on, "If you three travel back in time, you will meet yourselves, also in the past, creating multiple timelines for people and events in this universe, fraying it. Causing it to split and unravel. Laboratory Arne Wong believes that each additional branch we create undermines—stretches out—that dark matter which separates one universe from another. He says that we may create a situation where the dark energy can no longer be contained by the weaker dark matter structure. If he is right, it means the end of us."

She added ominously, "The end of all of us. All people. All worlds. All universes. It will be a cataclysmic event of unprecedented proportions."

"That is confusing," Yutani Myochi said. "But serious. Mother, we must consider this warning. I imagine that a large thermonuclear blast could trigger the cataclysm Amnelia Yu speaks of."

"Attar of Neuroses," I said. The others looked at me like I had spoken gibberish. I explained myself. "We need to knock the guards out, disable them completely. I need my mother's nerve gas. Yutani Myochi is right: the thin fabric of dark matter between universes most likely will not withstand an explosion like that which is imminent."

"Arne Wong," Amnelia Yu interrupted, addressing me. "Are there any more of us here? Yi-Tai Feng, for example. Maxx Lee. A task force from Earth. Are any of these people here?"

"How did you know?" I asked. "They are here, but they are not from our timeline."

"I know," the robot responded. "We do not have time to travel to The Empty for your mother's gas. Why can you not use the troops' force field weapons to overpower these guards of yours?" she asked.

"They are sequestered," I explained. "They have been separated from their weapons and have been housed far from here. The local authority considered it too dangerous to allow us to conspire."

"Conspire?" Original Arne Wong echoed. "Do you conspire?" He looked confused.

"We would if given the chance," I replied. "As it is, I conspire with Yutani Amniko and her son. If we were discovered planning to disable a nuclear holocaust nine hundred years in the making, I am certain that no time would be lost in destroying us—*executing us*—with prejudice I might add. These people are religious fanatics. They are convinced they received the instructions to use the Earth to nuke the sun from the Sun God, himself."

I paused to mentally review the security situation. "There are eight heavily armed guards protecting the detonation controls in a room in this complex," I explained next to original Arne Wong, who immediately assumed a look of understanding. He nodded his thanks to me and I nodded back.

"Eight of them and five of us?" Amnelia Yu asked. "I like those odds. Plus, as you can see," she continued, holding up the force field deployer she carried to illustrate, "we came in 'hot'." As she said this, she shared a bright smile with me.

I returned it. We continued to stare into each others' eyes until it apparently became uncomfortable for our companions to watch.

"Does someone need to get a room?" Original Arne Wong asked gruffly. I thought he sounded jealous.

"Seriously," seconded the dulcet tones of the shining white orb. Seemed that she was jealous, also.

"Mother, you still have the ability to shock, don't you?" Yutani Myochi interrupted, breaking the mounting tension.

"Why yes, I do," his mother responded. She directed her comment elsewhere, however. When she confirmed her lethality, she was looking at Amnelia Yu.

Amnelia Yu was oblivious to the other robot's glare. She still stared deeply into my eyes.

"I think I can free up Arne Wong's weapons," the young man continued. "Father had them secured in his own armory. They are not guarded and I happen to have the security codes. We have to wait for Father to retire for the evening," he continued. "Then I will retrieve the weapons and we can attempt to overpower the guards."

"Who understands enough about the controls to disable those nuclear devices?" Amnelia Yu asked, finally breaking the look she shared with me. The change was like the sun retreating behind a cloud. I sighed.

The resulting silence was finally broken by Yutani Amniko. This time her musical voice was low and solemn.

"You, Arne Wongs. You must save us." She looked from me to original Arne Wong and back to me again. "You must save us all."

Thirty-five

Liu Lee had not been idle, nor had he allowed his men to become bored or inactive…they planned. They organized. The moment they had been escorted through the one-way portal to the world they now inhabited, they started.

"The constrete will arrive in two-ton loads," he informed his troops. "We will need to store the bags somewhere out of the weather until we have the twenty tons we need to construct the gateway. Let us begin to reconnoiter around a ten-mile perimeter. Work in teams of two. Look for raw material; look for caves. Look for ground water. Watch out for wildlife. It is possible there are escaped zoo animals on the loose. Arnie Wong has assured me the people who terraformed this planet were all wiped out by a plague of some sort. We should be alone here. That said, keep your eyes open, people."

He paused to look at each of his troops in turn. "Report back here in four hours," he continued. "I will take each team's report in the order of its return—the last team back will be first to report. Be thorough but be careful. That is all. Go now."

While his men were out reconnoitering, Liu Lee took stock of the boxes of rations which still sat on the now inoperative magnetic levitator. "This world must not have a magnetic core," he observed to himself. "The mag-lev would have been useful but it doesn't work here....Arne Wong was as good as his word," the master sergeant said aloud to himself. "These rations will last three months. Maybe we can supplement them with some native provisions."

He noticed something lying on top of the cartons of rations. Tarps! He felt another surge of appreciation for his leader and friend, the Arne Wong of The Empty.

He covered the small mountain of boxes with the tarps, securing them at the corners with large rocks.

And then he waited.

Three hours later, two of his men returned at a run. "Liu Lee!" they cried. "We have found a city! There are people here!"

"I know I said that the last team back would report first, but this intelligence trumps that order," an excited and frightened Liu Lee said. "Take me there, now." His men reversed their direction, preparing to return to where they had found the city.

"No, wait," he said, halting. "One of you must remain here to tell the others where I have gone and why. You, Chen Chen, you stay here. Xio Xien will take me to the city."

Chen Chen saluted and stepped back to the area where the rations stood covered by shiny black tarps. Xio Xien and Liu Lee sped away wordlessly.

The teams straggled in over the next hour. Chen Chen informed each of the men that Liu Lee had gone with Xio Xien to investigate a sighting.

"We found a city," he told them. "Xio Xien and I. We returned here to report it immediately, and Master Sergeant Liu Lee went to see it for himself."

"A city?" one of the other men exclaimed. "There aren't supposed to be any people here, are there?"

"Not as far as we knew," another man confirmed. "But, you know, it's hard to really discover what might be on these parallel worlds when the portal is only one-way. How could anyone check and report back?"

"Right," his comrade said. "No one could get back to make a report. They would be stuck here with their precious knowledge. Like us."

~ * ~

Liu Lee and Xio Xien approached the city boldly. It was not overlarge, but it was modern and exhibited taste in its design.

Fountains ran. Parks with grass and shrubs were found on most major street corners. There were residential towers and business buildings. There were public buildings and gathering places.

But there were no people.

"Find the local Authority," Liu Lee instructed his companion. "There have to be records there about the whereabouts of the people who live here."

"*Lived here* is more like it," Xio Xien responded, standing over a pile of old and dusty clothing. Bones and a skull were protruding from sleeves and collar. "This person has been dead for a very long time."

Liu Lee approached and rifled through the body's clothing, extracting an identity chip. This he put in the reader in his own wrist.

As soon as the tiny disc entered the reader, a sharp hologram of a small black man sprung from Liu Lee's wrist. The hologram began speaking immediately, the small figure of a man starting out as a very old man, growing back to young adulthood, and then returning to ancient.

"I am the last of our kind," the hologram—now an old man again—spoke. I am called Arne Wong. I built this planet and this beautiful city that you stand in. We had plans to bring all of humanity here to start a new life. The sun had already grown too hot to live on Earth in comfort. We moved all of the birthing laboratories here and had a long-range plan to transport everyone from Earth over a period of eight hundred years." He paused as if he were steeling himself to make a pronouncement. "Then it happened," he continued. "The asteroid—one we had chosen not to harvest to build our New Earth—

was struck by another in close orbit, causing it, in turn, to impact with our new world."

He drew a deep breath and spoke again. "The air was full of choking dust and soon grew cold, too cold to live in without protective clothing. It was not breathable for many years. The energy grid was directly impacted by the asteroid and was completely wiped out. The laboratories, our future, died within days without power. Our entire reserves of ova and sperm spoiled. I and my friend Nobe Chung restored power to the city eventually, but it was too late for the laboratories. They were gone, and with them went our future. We are sterile. We cannot bear children. Without the laboratories there would be no more children." He shook his head in sorrow.

"I can only assume you come from elsewhere. I hope your world is a peaceful one, a beautiful one like ours," and here, the hologram swept his hand across the cityscape the two visitors could see even if the speaker could not, "and a fruitful one. I am the last human being on New Earth," he then announced. "And if you are reading my identity chip, then I am most certainly dead. Should you need a place to live, I invite you to help yourself to anything we have left of value. I would like to think that our beautiful city, our lovely New London, would one day be a bustling metropolis once more. Welcome." And with this last word, the hologram popped out of existence.

"I will bring the chip with us," Liu Lee said to Xio Xien, "but first, let us collect what is left of this Arne Wong and see that his remains find a decent resting place."

It was a solemn task. The pair of military men took care of it efficiently and effectively before they returned to the portal location where the rest of their comrades waited.

"It is early days yet," Liu Lee was telling his soldiers. "We cannot expect any communication from The Empty for some considerable time.

"Therefore, I say we send the bulk of our force to the city, New London, and do a thorough examination of its facilities. It is a two-hour march from our portal location. That is far, but not so far as to be completely unreasonable. Assess what you find. I want you to give me your best analysis of what New London has to offer us. Inventory living spaces, manufacturing capabilities, energy capacity and food. Look for transport—we need to eliminate that two-hour commute."

He gestured towards the tarp-protected stores. "We have three months of rations here thanks to Arne Wong," he continued. "But I would feel more secure if we could supplement what we have with renewable resources from this world. I will go with you. We leave four men behind to watch the portal and our supplies. I will accept four volunteers for this mission."

Four men stepped forward, clearly aiming only to demonstrate their loyalty to their leader. To a person, everyone in the unit wanted to go to the city.

"Your sacrifice has not gone unnoticed," Liu Lee told the men. They stood taller and prouder after hearing his praise.

"Yes, Master Sergeant," they replied. "Thank you, Master Sergeant."

In the end, Liu Lee and his people decided to make New London their main base. They found construction materials to erect a large building—a barn, really—at the portal site. They found solar-powered flying cycles much like they used in their own world, reducing transit time from the city to the portal from hours to minutes.

Men were rotated into and out of "barn duty." There could be no activity at the portal which went undetected by them. There was always someone on duty to monitor portal activity.

So how a group of fifteen women got through the gate without being caught was an event without an explanation.

The women were all outfitted in military uniforms and carried weapons. They were well organized and coordinated.

When they marched into New London, the women quite literally stopped traffic.

"We are here to speak with Master Sergeant Liu Lee," a woman acting as unit leader told the first man she encountered in the city. The poor man needed more than a moment to collect his wits. A woman? Dressed like a soldier? Speaking to a man as if she were his equal?

"You women need to give us those weapons," he stuttered. "They can be dangerous in untrained hands. And your clothes. You must surrender them. These are the clothes of warriors."

"We are trained in all matters military," the woman replied in a loud and steady voice. "I am the unit's marksman, actually," she added, a grim smile appearing on her lips. "I can demonstrate my knowledge of weapons use if you like." She was looking into the man's eyes with unmistakable menace.

"I will take you to Master Sergeant Liu Lee," he said, averting his eyes and turning on his heel. "He will sort you out."

"Well, let's get to it," the woman said, shouldering her weapon and preparing for movement. She used hand signals to communicate with her troops. The unit moved out as one: smoothly and silently.

"We are volunteers in a manner of speaking," the woman told Liu Lee several minutes later.

They had been led to a large public building with skylights and topiary. It was breathtakingly beautiful. Their admiration for the facility was evident in the women's facial expressions. This was not lost on Liu Lee.

"My headquarters," he said proudly. "Is it not inspiring?" He did not wait for an answer for the battle-hardened master sergeant had questions of his own.

"Who are you and what are you doing here? How did you get here?" He had already picked the unit leader out. Her behavior had given her away.

"Arne Wong rescued us from the harem," the woman said. "We had all been selected for forced retirement. You know, Master Sergeant, forced labor and *death*. Arne Wong hid us from the general. He trained us in secret. He clothed us and armed us. He has done this at considerable risk to himself."

She made inclusive gestures with her arms to indicate that she spoke not just for herself, but for all of the women in her unit. "Some of us have even learned to read, although there is still much work to be done before we can be considered proficient. We volunteered to travel through the one-way portal to join forces with you. The oldest among us is thirty-five years old. The youngest is but twenty. We are all fertile. We are all willing to be assigned to one man each and this a man of our choosing."

She squared her shoulders and raised her chin to deliver her conclusion. "Arne Wong has instructed us to build a society here on this New Earth," she concluded. "We are each of us sworn to do our best to begin this effort. It is our mission."

Liu Lee listened without interruption. After the woman's final admission, he gave her a small smile and repeated a question that she had not yet answered.

"And how did you get here without being caught by our sentries?" he asked.

"Arne Wong has armed each of us with defensive weaponry against men," the woman replied, her chin held out in defiance. "We carry redundant supplies of the Attar of Neuroses developed by the woman Cece Wong of The N-T. We used that to cause your sentry to forget he saw us. So you see, Master Sergeant, you caught us. You just *forgot* you caught us." A small smile played on the woman's lips.

"Arne Wong," Liu Lee said to himself. "He thinks of everything, does he not?"

Although he had not addressed the woman, she responded to him. "He is out to save us, Master Sergeant Liu Lee," she said. "He will save us all."

The women were assigned a residential building of their own. Liu Lee immediately launched instructions for the men under his command: they were not accustomed to women having rights, after all. They needed to thoroughly understand the new rules. The New Earth Law.

But they were also members of Liu Lee's band of rebels. That meant they shared a common belief in basic human rights for all citizens, at least that was their platform. Their coup had been planned as the first step in freeing the many prisoners of The Empty. Freeing and educating the women of their world was very definitely in their plans. *Eventually.* Putting those beliefs into action could not be left to chance.

"If any of you feel inclined to treat these women as subservient, or worse—as slaves—let me tell you that they have the means to resist you, and I have authorized them to use those means to protect themselves. If your behavior toward these women—fellow citizens of this New Earth—does not meet with their standards—sorry, *our* standards—you will be severely disciplined. By me. *Personally.* Do you understand?"

The men grumbled. One put his hand up. "Liu Lee?" he called out. "How will these women be integrated into our unit? Will their weapons be redistributed?"

"I will begin by assigning women to each of our work teams," Liu Lee replied, actually pleased to be asked this particular question. "That way, men and women can begin to know each other. The women will retain their weapons. Men will need to understand that any weapons work will be done by the women of their units. Weapons will be the exclusive domain of women from here on out. These women are here to stay. Let us make sure that they feel welcomed. Appreciated. Valued."

Much to his surprise, his men broke into cheers after his last words. They roared their approval—their commitment to the new future they could now start to visualize. They could make it a reality. Their return to imprisonment and death in The Empty was no longer a given.

Liu Lee was thinking about that future. He had forty men and only fifteen women. This would be the source of trouble. He knew this as a certainty.

Well, at least Chen Chen and Xio Xien would be all right. They were already in love with each other. So make that thirty-eight men and fifteen women.

Liu Lee did not count himself in the numbers. He would maintain his celibacy in the interest of keeping order and discipline.

And maybe Arne Wong would send reinforcements. That was not an impossible dream. Unlikely, perhaps. But not impossible.

Thirty-six

Mann Yu could not help himself. He cackled.

"This is very undignified," he told himself. This only served to make him cackle harder and louder.

He was viewing the results of the "spying" he had performed on the world of the portal through which Arne Wong had been dispatched.

It was Olde Earth, but one from many thousands of years in the past. He could not be certain, but it was possible those years could be numbered in the hundreds of thousands.

No, that was not funny. But what Mann Yu had sent with the instrumentation was. Funny. And he knew it had been found by a person from Olde Earth in that distant past, because the event was recorded.

There was a man recorded. He was tall and tan. His hair was the color of tree bark. As Mann Yu watched, he saw the man approach the cylinder. He picked it up. He fumbled with it and it opened, surprising him into dropping it.

As soon as the cylinder touched the ground, it happened: Mann Yu's hologram was deployed.

"Greetings, people of Earth," he said. "I am the Sun God."

The man—for it was a man, a single man, and not a group of people who had found his capsule—fell to the ground and covered his eyes. He was obviously terrified.

Mann Yu had prepared for this eventuality.

"Do not be frightened," the prerecorded hologram continued. "For I am here to save humanity from being devoured by its angry sun. The sun is my domain, after all.

"And I hunger in my domain," he continued. "I starve for fuel, for energy.

"In order for you to placate me, I need humanity to leave this Earth. You will find construction material in the asteroid belt between Mars and Jupiter. Build yourselves a new world. Create a new society. Then you will arm your old world with nuclear explosives as I have described in the documentation in this capsule. Remove these documents now, for I will be recalling this capsule to me in a matter of days

Mann Yu saw the Earth man collect himself and once more pick up the capsule. He removed its documents, leaving the instrumentation untouched. The documents detailed the position and explosive power of thousands of nuclear devices. It instructed the people of this world on how to propel their planet on a gradual trajectory directly into their sun.

"If you do not follow my instructions to the letter, your world will be destroyed—eaten—by its angry red sun. You can save humanity from annihilation. Only you. You are my emissary."

There were a full two weeks of recordings which followed his contact with the man of Olde Earth. He had enough data to measure the potential impact this visitation by the Sun God would have in this world.

It was perfect. The man who found his hologram, the man in possession of the detailed instructions for his world's destruction, this man was made an instant celebrity. A religious cult quickly developed around him and spread across his world.

It was enough. Even if his plan lost momentum, his "emissary" had the support of his own nation—a nuclear power in its own right—and its vast military resources to force the rest of the world to embrace its new paranoia, its new religion.

Mann Yu laughed and laughed. He howled with his merriment. For he was the image of the Sun God. He had recorded the hologram himself.

He was the face replicated in statues across the world. Its peoples burnt incense and in many cases sacrificed animals and even each other to him.

It just simply could not be any funnier. Finally weakened by his own hilarity, Mann Yu retired for the evening, very satisfied with himself.

The Sun God.

~ * ~

Yanu Yang spoke with his young wife. She trembled with obvious emotion.

"You work for Mann Yu again?" she asked her husband, her voice weak and fearful.

"Woman," Yanu Yang responded with kindness. "You must not concern yourself with what I do and who I do it for. It is not your place."

"But the robot said you both were working for Mann Yu now!" she cried, immediately abashed when she realized that she had disclosed a secret, that she had overheard a conversation between her husband and the robot.

"When did she say that?" Yanu Yang cried. "Mann Yu would never work with the abomination. He despises her and everything she stands for!"

"Do you work with her?" the anxious woman asked.

"No," he responded firmly. "I do not."

The woman was wracked with confusion. Her mind swirled with doubt and fear. She knew what she had heard. The robot and her husband most certainly worked together! Then why had he just lied to her about it?

"Ingu Yang," her husband said to her softly but firmly. "You must not worry about these matters. They are of no concern to you whatsoever."

"But Mann Yu?" she cried, throwing herself to the floor in front of her husband. "He is *evil*, Yanu Yang! He cannot be trusted. Please, I beg you, distance yourself from him at all costs!"

Yanu Yang bent to help his wife back up to her feet. "Well, of course he is evil," he said. "He is the only one on this entire planet with enough ill will to overthrow his father and his cronies. He is well connected with the military. He has everything he needs to stage an overthrow. A *revolution*, Ingu Yang."

"But wouldn't that leave him in charge?" she protested. "Wouldn't that mean he could do as he pleased to whomever he pleased?" She shuddered with fear and revulsion.

"Interesting," Yanu Yang said more to himself that to her. He addressed her again, more audibly. "You seem to know him well, my wife. We must speak of this one day. But as for Mann Yu, please do not concern yourself. As soon as he has overthrown the government, he will be disposed of. It is all part of the grand scheme. And I, as his most trusted henchman, will be ready to lead our fractured world back to civilization."

"As you say," Ingu Yang capitulated, too weak and confused to continue the dialog.

To herself, she did continue, however. *Why does he lie about the robot?* she asked herself. *I know what I heard. He does work with her. Why would he lie about it?*

Amnelia Yu's plan had succeeded. She had planted a serious seed of doubt in the mind of the young wife, Ingu Yang. It would grow into something that would create a rift between husband and wife: trust had been broken.

Ingu Yang resolved to do something more. She would speak to the abomination about what it and her husband were conspiring to do. And Xanu Lee. She would talk to Xanu Lee. Her master must be informed of any threat to him from inside his own abode.

That would resolve the issues which burned in her heart like live embers.

~ * ~

Mann Yu remained imprisoned by his father. He had been bullied and beaten, but not severely.

He believed his father thought him a coward. Well, he intended to show him that he was made of sterner stuff.

The door crashed open and two of his father's aides, bulky and muscular young men, stood just outside silhouetted by the hall light behind them.

"Your father wishes to speak with you," the taller of the two said. He was a giant of a man, taller yet than Arne Wong, who towered over most men.

"I am at his disposal," Mann Yu responded, a feeling of dismay and a shiver of fear running through him. Would this be the encounter that would break him? Resolved as he was to stand up to Xanu Lee, Mann Yu was terrified by physical intimidation. Pain.

Still, resistance is futile, he told himself. *I will ask for Yanu Yang and his lovely wife to be standing by afterwards with their miracle lotions and salves.*

He threw his shoulders back and lifted his chin. He did not need the escort; he knew where he was to go. He walked in front of his father's strongmen, trying his best to show no fear.

"At last, Mann Yu!" Xanu Lee cried. "Please, come in, my boy! Come in and take a seat!"

Startled and suspicious, Mann Yu walked cautiously further into the room and perched on the edge of the nearest chair.

"Yanu Yang has offered to find your hidden energy for me," his father announced, still smiling and exuding good will. Camaraderie, even. "Before entering into my personal service, he was employed as an energy specialist. He assures me that he will be able to find your cache, if in fact it exists."

Yanu Yang stood beside his employer, solemn and unblinking. He did not look directly at Mann Yu.

"I have told you over and over, Father," Mann Yu snarled. "There is no hidden energy."

"Then there's no harm in letting him have a look, is there?" his father retorted, smile in place.

"What does he want for it?" Mann Yu challenged. "He must want something. What is he even doing here? I thought he was your *valet*?"

"He only wants to please me. He wishes to demonstrate the depth of his loyalty, something you should be taking notes on."

Mann Yu stared at his father slack jawed. He stared balefully at Yanu Yang. What was the man up to? Surely they still enjoyed their partnership? Then it hit him: the invaluable Yanu Yang was proving his worth once more. He would put together a sham investigation and extinguish Xanu Lee's suspicions concerning the theft of dark energy. Brilliant! Mann Yu could not suppress the smile these thoughts engendered. This small, nasty smile did not fail to excite his father's attention.

"Of all of the things I see wrong in you," his father replied, his smile disappearing like smoke, "your belief in your own intelligence is by far the least attractive. Of course I have known of the relationship between you and Yanu Yang. I am aware that you plot together to assume my position of power and authority with the Guilds. I would have to be deaf and blind not to know it. Why, just today I received direct testimony of your conspiracy from a source very close to Yanu Yang, himself."

Xanu Lee turned to face his servant. "Your wife came to see me today," was all he said.

Yanu Yang lost his aplomb. He began to stammer denials. He sweated. His tidy appearance disappeared in moments. He became wild and disheveled.

"Since you bring it up," Xanu Lee continued, "I have just now sent for the armed guards which will take our very same Yanu Yang to the general. He is to receive a trial by the military tribunal for treason. I expect him to be executed within the hour. It would be no trouble at all to name a co-conspirator, you know…" Xanu Lee let this threat dangle.

He was interrupted by the arrival of the guard, a force of two burly men. They handcuffed the terror-stricken servant and muscled him out of the room.

These events and their potential implications to himself seemed to paralyze Mann Yu. He stood stock still in front of his father, his eyes on the decorative rug beneath his feet.

Slowly, slowly, he lifted his chin and raised his eyes to look into those of his father. He allowed a small grin—a very nasty looking thing—to capture his lips.

"What are you going to do with his wife?" he asked, drool collecting at the corners of his sneering mouth. His amber eyes were flecked with not only blue, but also red.

"We can certainly work something out," Xanu Lee said. "Just cooperate with me. Surrender your secrets."

Mann Yu knew there were still elements of his plot which had not been uncovered. His strategy was not as dead as the man he had recruited to assist him in it. He simply needed to acquire his freedom in order to set the "final solution" in motion.

"I think I can do that," he said to his father. "I will need your terms in writing. I want a Guild witness to attest to the contract's validity as well."

"Done," his father said, ringing the bell on the side table which would summon a servant.

A slave.

~ * ~

Later that day, Xanu Lee's guards knocked on the door of Ingu Yang's apartment. She opened the door cautiously, only to see two uniformed, and armed, guards standing in the hallway.

"You will need to come with us," the taller of the two guards said

"Where are you taking me?" the young woman asked. She was shaking.

"Just grab some of your things," the man said without inflection. "We are going to relocate you for your own safety."

"My own safety?" the woman repeated. "Why am I unsafe? I spoke with Xanu Lee just this afternoon. Does he approve of what you are doing?"

"The Law is clear, ma'am," the shorter man said. "Your husband has committed treason. You, therefore, should share his fate."

"But it was I who disclosed his treachery!" the woman protested.

"You can thank Mann Yu for saving you. Mann Yu has commuted your sentence, your death sentence, to life without parole. He has done this with the full and written approval and permission of Xanu Lee.

"You will be imprisoned in Mann Yu's quarters, the sumptuous apartments of the son and heir to The Empty's most powerful civilian position."

Ingu Yang's dark face took on an ashen aspect. She dithered and stuttered her reply.

"How marvelous," she said dully. "I'll just get some of my things and we can be on our way..."

The two young guards smirked at each other. They were getting some vicarious thrill from their roles in the drama which was unfolding.

"Hurry about it," the taller man urged her. "Mann Yu is impatient."

"I'll just be a moment," Ingu Yang said quietly. She retired to her inner chamber, retrieved the sheath she had hidden up her sleeve and took the knife from it. She sliced the veins running up both arms from wrist to elbow. The blade was sharp. Her flesh parted smoothly; the cuts were deep.

"This should be you, Mann Yu," she hissed as she lay dying, her blood jetting in hot streams in time with her heartbeat. "It is you who should be wallowing in a pool of his own blood. You are not a man. You are an animal..."

Thirty-seven

"We don't want your damned mansions and belongings," Arne Wong announced at the beginning of the negotiations between his Rebs and the old, rich business owners and Guildsmen who constituted the controlling power on The Empty. A grim General Liu Lee stood rigidly to his right, a bright-eyed and manic Mann Yu to his left.

"We don't want your money. We want our freedom. We want women to be elevated to the same status as men, and we want all men, all people, to be equal to one another under the Law of this world."

Initially, the rich business owners and guild leaders laughed at Arne Wong. To them, his proposals were so ridiculous as to be insane.

His persistence wore them down. He peppered his persistence with demonstrations in which a carefully selected representative or two from their number were publicly tortured and executed while their peers watched, frozen with horror and unable—or unwilling—to lift a finger to help them.

After the second such demonstration, family and guild seals were applied to the document which detailed the rights of all human beings on The Empty—simply called by its proper name, Nova Terra, in the concord. Penalties for transgressions against former slaves were spelled out in great bloody detail: this revolution had been won with blood and violence. Blood and violence would continue to enforce these new provisions until they became ingrained in their new society.

"And we will immediately start arrangements for the evacuation of the remaining citizens of Olde Earth," Arne Wong told the entire planet via audio and video comms.

"Prepare for the reception of twelve billion more inhabitants to this world—we will no longer be The Empty!

"Your wealth and authority will be affected," he continued, turning to address the men sitting on the right side of the assembly room. "But you will also be allowed to profit from your businesses and industries, within reason.

"Your free labor is gone. You will pay your employees a living wage. You will abide by the terms of our concord in creating a fund for the education and rehabilitation of women. These conditions are non-negotiable. In one year—one Nova Terra year—seven hundred and eighty-nine days, we will hold elections for representatives who will form a legislative body for our world. We will elect a team of two people who will form an Executive Branch and we will appoint a judiciary.

"In the year preceding these elections, I, Arne Wong, will rule. Mann Yu, once one of you, will serve as my civilian deputy. General Liu Lee will continue to arm and train an army to keep order and enforce the new laws. General Nobe Chung has been disabled. He will no longer be able to accept your bribery in trade for your safety. His entire command structure has been dismantled.

"We mutually engage in a complex and difficult process. A long process. We will move as deliberately as we can, but we will delay none of the human rights provisions of our new contract.

"I am sure that you have questions and comments, but I will not allow them at this point. You may consider yourselves under military lockdown until elections are successfully and fairly conducted and office-holders sworn in. That is all. You are all free to return to your residences and places of employment. You will all need to develop the means to begin paying your employees and taking care of their medical and childcare needs in accordance with the contract you have all just signed.

"All women will be freed from slavery and from employment for the period of four years during which they will receive training, education, and psychiatric services. All of which you will pay for – in their entirety."

Arne Wong paused and smiled grimly. "Good day. Welcome to a new and free Nova Terra!"

The left side of the room rose to its feet and burst into cheers while the right side filed out of the room slowly and silently.

"We are going to rearrange the seating next time," General Liu Lee said to Arne Wong. "No more house of poor people on one side and house of rich people on the other."

"It says more than you know about human beings," Arne Wong observed. "The right side of this room is tiered; the left is completely level. The Bigs went for the 'thrones' while the poor—sorry, The Rebs—made for the humble, equal seating. It's a mindset we have to change, General Liu Lee."

"I understand, Arne Wong. But I will begin with revising the seating arrangements," the general said quietly but firmly. "We must start somewhere."

~ * ~

"You know you can increase your profits by using your military might to take over the government," Arne Wong said.

"You're drunk," the also drunk General Nobe Chung said, slugging the other man's arm with a meaty fist.

"Maybe I am, but I know I speak a truth, here," Arne Wong replied, rubbing his shoulder. "They have no real security forces—they have servants. Servants, who, by the way, would support our revolution since they are really slaves."

"You are serious, aren't you?" General Nobe Chung asked, his eyebrows hiked in surprise.

"I am."

"That's a lot of risk, Arne Wong. I am doing just fine taking the free money that The Bigs and the Guilds pay me for keeping the peace."

"Throw the next payment back in their faces," Arne Wong suggested. "And then attack. I know for a fact that you will have the backing of Mann Yu, as well.

"No one need die, but we must be prepared to kill in order to overturn this world's order. Your men grow restless, General Nobe Chung. They joined you to change things. Now they sit idle, drinking and gambling, and grumbling.

"We need a new order, General Nobe Chung. We need to free the slaves. We need to educate the women. We need to allow your troops to carry out the mission they volunteered for. And we need a system of laws, General Nobe Chung. Laws which will defend the human rights of every citizen. Laws which will enforce the emigration of those billions we left behind on Earth."

The general grew thoughtful. "I had family left behind," he said softly. "And I know in my heart that Cece Wong is as intelligent—even more so—than any man. But that abomination, Arne Wong. I cannot accept that...that...that *thing* as a person! It goes too far!"

"Then reward her to me and allow me to take her back to her world, her Nova Terra."

"That I could do," the general allowed grudgingly. "Can you ensure that she or any other robot they may have created there can never come through the portals again? That we can maintain at least this one aspect of our society?"

"We can block portal access, General Nobe Chung," Arne Wong reassured his friend. "You need not ever see a robot again—that is, unless you wish to vacation on The N-T sometime in the future." And now Arne Wong punched his friend in the arm.

He did not pull it. His punch was so hard General Nobe Chung was knocked from his seating.

The general lumbered to his feet and swung back. Arne Wong suddenly leapt through the air separating them and tackled the general to the ground. They rolled around exchanging punches and laughing wildly.

"OK, OK," General Nobe Chung said, pushing himself shakily back up onto his feet. "If we still believe in what you have said by the time this alcohol wears off, then we have a deal."

"A deal?"

"I will lead the troops. We will overthrow the government of The Empty. You will make me rich. I will give you your precious abomination. I will look the other way about the women."

"The women?"

"It seems, Arne Wong, that fifteen of our retiring breed stock have gone missing. Inventories of rations, weapons, ammunition and uniforms have come up short."

"I was hoping you wouldn't notice," Arne Wong said. It was a confession and he knew it. He tensed for the justifiable repercussion he expected from his volatile friend.

"Notice what?" the general asked with an innocent expression on his face. He nudged the other man with an elbow and whispered an aside: "This is me looking the other way..."

Arne Wong's expression said it all. He was surprised. Flabbergasted, actually. And relieved. "Thank you," he said in sincere gratitude.

The general was already walking away toward his quarters.

"You solved a huge problem for me. Cece Wong's best friend was part of that group. She has been haranguing me night and day to save her. I could not afford to set that precedent. Thank you, Arne Wong. You are a good man. Good night. I will see you in the morning."

"Good night, sir," Arne Wong said, turning to leave the bunker by way of the metal stairs. He knew better than to return the compliment to the other man.

Because Nobe Chung was not really a good man. He was greedy. He had an enormous ego. He could be brutal.

But he loved his woman. He could be reasoned with. He was funny, something quite rare in The Empty. And Arne Wong thought he saw something else: he thought that he saw the general growing. His thoughts seemed deeper. His paranoias shallower. His rigidity loosened.

Oh, there was that feeling again. Arne Wong put his finger on it this time: hope. It was hope.

~ * ~

Sobriety, as it happened, did not affect the agreement the two inebriated men had come to the prior evening.

"As long as you can guarantee that my position as supreme military commander is safe, I bow to you as my civil authority, Arne Wong." the general said. "Should you fail me, be assured I will overturn your new world structure."

"I understand the conditions of our partnership," Arne Wong replied. "Are we ready? Are your men prepared for what comes next?"

"They wait only for my signal."

"Then give it and let's go," Arne Wong said, straightening his own gear and weaponry in preparation.

"Remember your promise, General Nobe Chung. The moment that we have secured The Empty, I will take possession of the robot, Amnelia Yu."

"You can have her and good riddance with only one condition: you take her back to her Nova Terra the moment we have secured the city."

"Deal."

The two men—friends and allies, both—clasped each other's hands and shook them in the universal symbol of mutual contract. "Deal," General Nobe Chung repeated. "We have a deal."

Thirty-eight

"You're better than new!" Xanu Lee exclaimed. "My lovely wife is restored to her former splendor!"

Amnelia Yu held her arms out from her sides and executed several graceful turns as the scientists and engineers of Yu-Lee Laboratories admired her. They applauded.

"This sensory interface material," she said, fingering the "skin" on her forearm. "It seems thinner and yet more responsive than before."

"Yes, Amnelia Yu," Xanu Lee replied. "We have made some improvements since we last built you a body. You are now truly state of the art!"

"Well, let me take it on a road trip," she said coyly, approaching her husband and putting her silver and gold arms around him. "Thank you, Xanu Lee," she whispered in his ear. She kissed him lightly on the lips.

The scientist laughed as he gently pushed her away. "Amnelia

Yu, you scamp!" he said. "Save your affections for someone you truly care for." He looked at Arne Wong as he spoke.

Amnelia Yu cupped Xanu Lee's chin in one of her lovely hands, redirecting his gaze into her own. "Not *that* Arne Wong," she said. "He is not the right Arne Wong."

Arne Wong stood by, trying to ignore the entire exchange.

"Are you pleased with your adjustments?" he asked the robot.

"They are a delight," she replied. "I don't know what motivated you to do this for me, but I am eternally grateful, and that's hardly a figure of speech for a robot." She laughed lightly, the sound cascading like a liquid.

"You look lovely," he said. As soon as the words fell from his lips, he clamped them tightly shut, a look of panic washing over his face. "For a machine, I mean," he amended lamely.

Amnelia Yu hiked both of her finely arched metal eyebrows and looked intently at the man from The Empty.

"You have changed, Arne Wong," she said, approaching him and peering into his eyes. "There is now more to you than there once was. I think I'll need to keep an eye on you. I look forward to future 'developments' in your character."

"Speaking of which," Arne Wong said, recognizing a good place for a change of subject, "you can reach me at any time over the trans-portal communications device I have invented for this purpose. But it is critically important that you never—never, Amnelia Yu—*never* come through the portal again. General Nobe Chung has promised your complete annihilation if you should ever return to The Empty."

"Rest assured," the robot replied, her voice quiet but determined. "I have no desire to ever step foot on The Empty again." She shuddered.

"Farewell, Arne Wong," she said. "Good luck."

"Farewell, Amnelia Yu," Arne Wong replied. "I am confident your Arne Wong will find a way back to you."

"He was spaced," she said flatly.

"Well, now, you see," Arne Wong said, "that may not be exactly true."

He paused when he saw the looks of astonishment on the faces in front of him.

"I should have said earlier," he stammered. "You see, I sent instructions for portal construction through the same portal Arne Wong was ejected through. I am fairly certain he lives. I am also fairly certain he received my instructions. I hope that we will see him one day."

"We?" the robot challenged.

"Yes, 'we'," Arne Wong said. "He'll need to come through The Empty to get back to The N-T. The portal he was sent through connects only the world he is on and The Empty." He stopped speaking for several moments and seemed to be having an internal argument with himself. He looked conflicted.

"And listen," he finally added. "This part is a little out there, so just listen. I believe Arne Wong may play with *time* in planning his return. He will want to rescue you. All of you: his mother and sister, his best friend Nobe Chung, Mann Yu, and you, Amnelia Yu. You most of all. And to do this, he would have to return to The Empty before you even went there."

The others stood stunned for many moments before Amnelia Yu responded.

"Yes, that sounds like Arne Wong," she said. "You are not wrong. He would try to do this."

"Yes, I know," Arne Wong replied. "Because that is exactly what I would try to do."

"Evil Mann Yu played with Time," the robot reminded him. "Do you remember when we first met, Arne Wong? Your Mann Yu was impersonating my Mann Yu, my son. It was my suspicion your Mann Yu was experimenting with the manipulation of Time."

"He was," Arne Wong replied. "But it was the only thing in his life he didn't talk to me about. There was no shutting him up on everything else he said or thought or did; this was the only subject he kept to himself. But I know that you are right. It is one of the reasons why I keep Mann Yu close. He has dangerous secrets. I don't trust him, you see. I know he is dangerous. He is nothing like your Mann Yu, an honorable man. Our Mann Yu has no honor." At this point, Arne Wong looked directly into Amnelia Yu's beautiful eyes. "But then, he had no mother, either. Your Mann Yu benefitted from having you in his life. I think this is likeliest to explain their innate differences."

"Thank you, Arne Wong," Amnelia Yu said, tears brimming in her very human eyes. "I appreciate what you have said."

"I'd better go now before I say something else I would wish to unsay," Arne Wong said, turning to leave.

"That, too, is like my Arne Wong," Amnelia Yu called out as he strolled down the labyrinth to the portal to The Empty. The look the robot gave the man's departing back was a thoughtful one. Wistful, even.

After Arne Wong had finally disappeared from her sight, she turned away with a soft sigh to rejoin the team responsible for her resurrection.

"Thank you," she told them once again.

"Thank Arne Wong," Xanu Lee responded. "He has saved us all."

"What do you mean by that?" the robot asked.

"That general of his – the Nobe Chung of The Empty," one of the other scientists said. "Arne Wong has promised us that the general will no longer visit The N-T. He said they have struck an agreement. You will stay here with us and General Nobe Chung will stay on The Empty. Arne Wong did not tell us any more than that, but my guess is that this bargain did not come cheaply for him."

"No," Amnelia Yu replied. "No, I believe he must have paid dearly for it. *Or will do so.*"

~ * ~

"So how did it go?" General Nobe Chung asked Arne Wong upon the other man's return to The Empty.

"Fine," Arne Wong responded without embellishment. He busied himself reviewing some holographic projections, avoiding making eye contact with the general.

"Did you install the remote device?" the general asked.

Arne Wong sighed. "Yes," he said, now making eye contact. "Yes, I installed the remote device." He did not seem to be very happy about his own admission, however.

"Good," the general said with an unpleasant smile and two thumbs up. "Good man, Arne Wong."

"That's what you say," Arne Wong replied. "That is not how I feel, though..." He looked worried. Anxious. Sweaty. "You have promised not to use it, General Nobe Chung. Should I mistrust your promise?"

General Nobe Chung threw his head back and laughed heartily. "It's just insurance, Arne Wong," he said. "You deliver the wealth you promised and the device will never be activated. I promise."

Arne Wong looked at the general with distrust. "I intend to hold you to that," he said. "You must keep that promise."

The general simply walked away, still laughing loudly. Arne Wong sat heavily in a nearby chair and dropped his head into his hands, the very image of a man driven to do something completely against his own nature.

~ * ~

"Did he do it?" Mann Yu entered the general's chamber later that night already speaking.

He was always doing that. Entering rooms already a sentence into a paragraph. It was a feature of his mania. He was always a step ahead of himself.

"Yes, he did it," the general responded. He remained seated and waited for the other man to approach closer.

"Get this straight, Mann Yu," he said, pointing his finger at Mann Yu's chest. "This device can only be activated by me. A direct order from me. You will not use it to exact revenge on the people of The N-T. It is too valuable a weapon for that."

"What if I could prove to you that detonating the device would result in your acquiring wealth beyond your wildest dreams?" Mann Yu countered.

The general hesitated and finally rewarded Mann Yu with a conciliatory smile.

"I'm listening," he said.

Mann Yu sidled up beside General Nobe Chung. "General," he said. "I have a winning proposition for an ambitious man...

"...are *you* that man?"

General Nobe Chung did not respond but raised his hand and motioned one of his men to approach closer.

"Arne Wong warned me about you," the general said to Mann Yu. "Sergeant Ulon Zou," he said, addressing his soldier, "take Mann Yu to one of our *finest* cells. Make sure he is alone. He cannot be trusted not to coerce or bribe any of the other criminals we keep back there."

"Yes, sir," Ulon Zou said, saluting smartly. He grabbed Mann Yu roughly by one arm and dragged him from the room. The sounds of the man's protests grew louder the further he was dragged until finally a clanging door blocked all sound entirely.

General Nobe Chung removed his comm device from his utility vest and toggled it on. "Arne Wong," he said. "Arne Wong, he did just as you said he would. Mann Yu is in custody. Do you still intend to charge him with treason against the state?"

Arne Wong's voice could be heard through the device. "Yes, General Nobe Chung. But first we must extract the details of his plot from him. Use your best men and try not to kill him under interrogation. But interrogate. Be thorough. I am on my way back. Be there in an hour. Out."

General Nobe Chung toggled the device off and put it back in its pocket. After a moment, he took it back out again and reactivated it.

"Ulon Zou," he said into the device.

"Yes, General Nobe Chung," came the prompt response from his man.

"I will handle the interrogation of our new prisoner personally. Immediately. Please have him placed in restraints. I will be there in two minutes."

"Yes, sir!" the sergeant could be heard saying as Nobe Chung cut off the comms.

I wonder what this proposition of his was? the general asked himself. *And I wonder who else he may have approached about it?* He pondered these questions as he walked out of the room and into the hallway holding the cells.

He had one more question for himself. *And just how ambitious am I, anyway?*

Thirty-nine

Yi-Tai Feng grew desperate. He and his team had been held in comfortable lock-down for days with absolutely no communication from Arne Wong, or anyone else, for that matter.

"We have got to find a way out of here," he commented to the Human Resources Administrator, Sen-yat Sung. Yi-Tai Feng often found the other man in close proximity. Once eye contact was made, often accidentally, Sen-yat Sung would begin peppering him with questions. Yi-tai Feng often had to ask the curious team member to hold his questions until a more appropriate time. After it became clear that their current circumstances did not contain an appropriate time, the sheer volume of questions decreased and then nearly dried up altogether.

"There are five guards," the administrator—and head-counter— replied. "And forty of us. I don't know if I told you this or not, Yi-Tai Feng, but I have a very mean flying back kick..." He hiked his eyebrows insinuatingly at his commander.

"What a coincidence!" a voice said from behind them. They both turned to discover Maxx Lee standing not two feet from them. He smiled and continued, "The flying back kick is my signature move as well."

"So you are a martial artist?" Sen-yat Sung asked the bigger and beefier man.

"He has won many prizes for his skills," Yi-Tai Feng interrupted, knowing Maxx Lee was not the sort to brag about himself. "He is famous back on Earth. Infamous, even." Yi-Tai Feng smiled to take the sting out of his words. "You know," he added, "with the ladies?"

Maxx Lee dropped his eyes to the ground and actually blushed.

"Yeah, well, I don't do too badly myself," Sen-yat Sung said, hands on his narrow hips and weak chin raised high. "Getting back to my original proposal," the administrator resumed. "I think we can overcome five lousy guards." He puffed his scrawny chest out in a display of bravado.

"They, too, practice martial arts," Maxx Lee cautioned, looking like he was fighting to keep a straight face. "And we are the only two out of our group who have the same level of skill."

Yi-Tai Feng made a decision. "We wait for Arne Wong," he told the other two men. "Arne Wong will come for us. He will save us."

"And if he doesn't?" Sen-yat Sung challenged.

"This planet has only days left," Yi-Tai Feng said bluntly. "If he doesn't free us before the Earth of this universe reaches its sun, none of us will continue to exist.

"This entire planet and all of the people on it will be destroyed, utterly and finally."

~ * ~

Yutani Myochi walked boldly into his father's office. He knew better than to appear surreptitious. That would just arouse suspicions. There was nothing suspicious about the young man visiting his father's rooms, after all. Well, it might be suspicious that he carried a satchel, a bag, but he had made a trip with that bag to the exercising hall just moments earlier. He simply had not taken the bag full of sweaty clothes back to the clothing recycler yet.

He rehearsed this explanation in his head, readying himself for questioning by his father's efficient security staff.

His father lay in bed in a back room, snoring softly. His evening cocktail, laced as it was with narcotics, ensured that he slept deeply. Yutani Myochi's knowledge of his father's self-sedation made him bold.

He went to his father's safe and deftly twisted the dials that served to lock it.

He retrieved two force field weapons from the safe, closed its doors and twisted the dials randomly to re-engage the locking device.

He opened his satchel and put the weapons in it, shuffling the bag's contents around so the weapons sank to the bottom. Should he be searched for some reason, his dirty exercise kit should serve to distract and, well, repel. He smiled grimly.

"Good night, Father!" he called out as he left. It was a ruse, of course. His father had not stirred in the slightest and he certainly had not heard what his son had called out. Yutani Myochi played his part for the guards, should any of them be watching the entrance to their master's quarters, as they most certainly would be.

Closing the door softly behind him, the young man returned unmolested to the labyrinth where his mother and the other-worlders waited.

"I've got them!" he called out as he closed the gap between himself and us.

"Let me show you how these work," I told the young man. "Here, take this smaller one…" In about three minutes, the training was complete.

"That was simple," the young man said.

"Just as designed," I replied. "They don't have soldiers on Earth—they don't even have weapons. These were designed specifically for our rescue mission. Our 'troops' are untrained scientists and administrators." I anticipated the young man's next question. "But they are *armed*," I answered preemptively. "Each of them has two force field deployers, just as we did." This seemed to satisfy the younger man's concerns.

"So what's next?" Yutani Myochi asked.

"I have decided to find and free Yi-Tai Feng and his troops," I announced.

"Do we have the time for that?" Amnelia Yu asked, her concern evident in her tone of voice.

"You have just told me that we don't have time to go to The Empty for the Attar of Neuroses," I replied. "Plus, I need Maxx Lee. We need the extra fire power."

"Maxx Lee?" Amnelia Yu asked. "Why Maxx Lee?"

"His martial arts skills are a match to any of the guards here," I said, glancing quickly at Yutani Myochi. "No offense intended," I added.

"None taken," the young man responded with a slight bow. "Do not underestimate our training, however."

"'Our'?" I repeated.

"Yes, 'our,'" Yutani Myochi replied. "I have received exactly the same training as the men in our security force. You will find me an asset if your intention is to fight instead of disable."

"I am certain we will need to do both," I responded. "I am glad we'll have you with us."

"Mother is no slouch, either," Yutani Myochi added, winking and grinning at the hovering orb which lit up in response to his words.

"So how do we go about finding our task force?" Amnelia Yu asked, sparing a withering glance at the flashing orb.

"I know exactly where they are," Yutani Myochi promptly replied. "I just don't know how to get us there without attracting notice—the bad kind."

"Do your religious people, priests or whatever, wear robes by any chance?" I asked.

The young man's face brightened. "Yes, they do. Hooded ones, at that!"

He thought a moment, just a moment before speaking again. "We do their clothing recycling for them in this complex. There are bound to be hundreds of reconstituted—*clean*—robes waiting for pick-up. I will take you all there now. There is a short-cut through the laboratories we can make without exciting any alarms."

The operation went smoothly and in a few minutes we were all covered head to foot in saffron robes, except for the orb, Yutani Amniko, who decided to go directly to our destination alone at hypersonic speed.

"I will await you all there," she said before departing. "Be careful. If you are caught impersonating a priest on our world, you will be executed without even the semblance of a trial."

"Good to know," original Arne Wong muttered, pulling his hood further over his face.

~ * ~

The site where the Earth task force had been incarcerated was a large temple.

"They are held in the inner sanctum," Yutani Amniko whispered to me as our group of "priests" arrived. When she got no response, she spoke again. "Arne Wong, did you hear me?"

I was staring, my jaw agape, at the huge golden statue which was the central feature of the temple. There were hundreds of people in this part of the temple, kneeling, bowing, intoning mantras and burning incense.

I pointed at the great statue and stuttered a question. "Wh-wh-who is th-th-that?" I managed to get out. I stared, confounded and stunned, unblinking.

"Stop pointing!" the floating orb commanded. "Put your hand down, Arne Wong!"

I complied, moving more robotically than the robot.

"Why do you stare so?" Yutani Myochi had approached to find out what his mother was so excited about.

"What—or who—is that statue?" I asked, keeping my voice down to a harsh whisper.

"That is the Sun God," the young man calmly responded. "This image was fashioned from the hologram from which our world religion originates. Why?" the young man asked. "Why do you ask?"

"That is Mann Yu," I said, still staring at the golden image. "From The Empty. 'Evil Mann Yu' as we used to call him."

I looked Yutani Myochi in the eyes and delivered a message truly horrible in nature and scope.

"If Mann Yu is behind your world religion, you can be sure that you are doomed," I said. "Mann Yu is morally bankrupt and certifiably insane. He is a psychopath who only enjoys watching others suffer."

I stopped speaking suddenly, a thought bursting into my mind.

"Does he watch you, I wonder?" I asked, more to myself than to the others.

"What was that?" Original Arne Wong asked. "What did you just say?" He, too, stared at the statue with a look of disbelief.

Amnelia Yu had been dumbstruck by the golden image, too, and only now recovered her ability to speak. "That is definitely the Mann Yu from The Empty," she confirmed. "And in answer to your last question, I think it is inevitable that he has designed some method to watch the developments here on Atsui. His nature would not allow him to let it go unmonitored."

"But how?" Yutani Myochi asked. "Our portals are strictly controlled. He can't have come through, we would know it."

"He is a brilliant scientist," the silver and gold robot replied. "He is sure to have monitoring devices here, and he could have sent them here at any time."

In response to the look on Yutani Myochi's face, Amnelia Yu continued. "He manipulates time," she said simply and finally. "He can pick any time he wishes to send something through."

"He wouldn't come himself?" the young man wanted to know.

"I don't think the portal is two-way," she responded. "They have hundreds of one-way portals in the labyrinth of Yu-Lee Laboratories in The Empty. But he could get small devices through. It's just my guess, but my gut tells me that I'm right."

"Your gut?" Yutani Amniko asked, mockery in her tone of voice.

"My human instincts," Amnelia Yu responded calmly. "You have them, too, don't you?"

"I am a human brain," the orb announced proudly. "Of course I have instincts."

"Well, so am I," Amnelia Yu responded, this time with heat. "I hate to say this, but I am certain we are each other from parallel universes. You are me. I am you."

The other robot paused many seconds before responding. When she did, it was with a voice full of wonder. "Yes, I see it now. I also see why you would hate it."

The two robots stopped speaking to each other at that juncture. Amnelia Yu swung around to address me. "What now?" she asked.

"Let's go get Yi-Tai Feng and Maxx Lee," I said. "Stay in formation behind me. Heads down. Hoods up. Fingers on triggers."

~ * ~

It was a strange-looking battle. The guards responsible for incarcerating the task force from a world of giants had gotten friendly with them and were not really on alert.

Plus, what they saw as we approached was a small column of priests, hands folded in front and heads bowed in respect, a sight only too normal for the temple.

"Now!" I said loudly. At my command, all of the other priests removed their hands from their robes to reveal weapons which they fired immediately and repeatedly.

All five guards were bound with force fields within moments. There was no barrier to the prisoners' freedom now.

"I knew you would come!" Yi-Tai Feng said to me. The Earthman hesitated, but also nodded appreciation to Original Arne Wong, who acknowledged him with a nod in return. The usually glum Original Arne Wong actually smiled. For the first time since the portal travelling adventures had begun, he truly felt engaged—and needed.

"Our weapons are in that container over there," Maxx Lee said, pointing to a large metal box in the corner of the interior room.

"I can have those locks open in seconds," Amnelia Yu said, crossing the room with a determined stride. "Me, too," said the orb, speeding to catch up with the other robot.

"Work on the other side," Amnelia Yu commanded the other robot brusquely.

"I was headed that way any way," the orb replied coldly. "You do not command me, Amnelia Yu."

"Nor you I, Yutani Amniko."

They both went to work breaking chains and disabling locking devices until the container was open. It took mere seconds.

I sidled up to Original Arne Wong. "Makes me miss Moms," I said, tongue in cheek. Original Arne Wong laughed out loud. "She would have had them open sooner, though," he observed. I gave my original self a friendly slap on the back and left to approach the people of the task force.

"All right," I told Yi-Tai Feng. "Have your people reclaim their weapons. We must plan our escape."

"Where do we escape to?" Yi-Tai Feng asked.

"Back to Yutani-Ri Laboratories," I said. "We have a world to save."

"We are ready, Arne Wong."

"We will wait for nightfall. It is less than an hour away. Have you all eaten?"

"We have been well fed. You?"

"I have my capsules. I am fine."

"Let us put our heads together with the locals and plan our route."

Yutani Myochi proved a very helpful guide when the sizeable group of people—most of whom were giants by this world's standards—silently filed out of the temple after nightfall.

"Walk single file and maintain complete silence," he instructed them. "The security system will not alert on slow, steady movement. If anyone speaks, coughs, sneezes, makes any human noise at all, all hells will break loose."

To many of us, it seemed like it took hours to wend our way back to The Yutani-Ri Laboratory complex. I was astonished when I checked the elapsed time to discover we had made the return trip in under an hour.

"Really well done," I congratulated everyone. "Now comes the difficult part. Yutani Amniko has disabled the internal sensors so we can move about without setting off alarms. That does not make us invisible, however. Yutani Myochi informs me there are banks of monitors inside the secure room we are going to breach. The guards inside will know of our approach. They will be prepared." I paused to gather my thoughts. "We have a big advantage, however," I continued. "They cannot call for reinforcements. We have disabled their communications. By our best estimate, there will be eight armed guards inside the room which is our target. It contains the detonation controls for thousands of nuclear weapons which are nearing the sun as we speak. We have less than one full day to figure out the controls and disable the nuclear warheads."

"Wouldn't the heat from the sun be enough to trigger detonation?" Original Arne Wong asked.

"Not the way these warheads are constructed," I responded. "I had time to pore over the design of these devices in the laboratory's archives. We can actually de-construct the warheads, rendering them harmless. There will be no chain reaction triggered. If we do this right, that is."

"But the heat...." Original Arne Wong was not satisfied with the answer he had been given.

"Yes, technically, the heat would eventually be enough to cause spontaneous detonation," I said. "But the warhead controls will be activated many hours before this can happen. The resulting explosions were designed to catapult the Earth deep into the heart of the sun in order to maximize the effects of the nuclear blasts."

Original Arne Wong nodded his head to indicate he understood, and accepted, my explanation. He had long since lost his smile. He looked grim again.

We all did. We were all grim. And determined.

"Let's go," I said. "The Earth people will take the first shots from their higher ground, so to speak."

Yi-Tai Feng held his weapon up to show that his hands were

steady and that the safety was off. "Ready," he said for himself and the other members of his task force. "We are ready."

The forty-three people and two robots ran the entire distance to the secure room, making as little noise as possible. They ran to reduce the amount of time they would be visible on the security monitors.

It was even possible—remotely—that the monitors were not being watched, many of us very likely told ourselves.

But we were. We were watched.

Forty

"We are ready," Laboratory Arne Wong told Yi-Tai Feng. "It is safe for you and your task force to cross through the portal to The Empty.

"I have tested the transit with a remote device. Here," and he motioned the tall Earthman to join him in front of a large monitor, "here is the hallway on the other side...wait! Someone is approaching..."

The pair watched as a man pushed a magnetic-levitator full of huge bags of something—the labelling could just now be made out—it was constrete, past the remote device. The man and the mag-lev proceeded further up the labyrinth and eventually out of sight.

"It seems peaceful enough," Arne Wong continued, "and the detector confirms it exists in time consistent with our own. Are you ready go?"

"More than ready, Arne Wong," Yi-Tai Feng confirmed. "Itching to go, actually." He restrained his urge to accompany his message with some scratching—some moments are just too solemn for horseplay, he thought to himself.

"Yeah, well an occasional shower might help with that," Arne Wong replied, not held back by any sense of propriety.

Yi-Tai Feng's hearty laughter was a clear indicator of his tension.

"It wasn't that funny," Arne Wong pointed out.

"I know—it was totally lame," the other man said, holding his side and laughing loudly, "but so unexpected it snuck under my defenses." He got himself under control with obvious effort.

"I will walk you to the gate," Arne Wong said next. "Joxe Xian will be at the portal controls back here. He will not need my assistance."

Joxe Xian simply nodded his head respectfully at the departing men. He appreciated the trust Arne Wong placed in him.

The entire task force—minus Future Arne Wong who would have been its scout but for a portal mishap—was gathered at the gate, waiting for their leader.

"Everyone ready?" Yi-Tai Feng asked, addressing the assembly of forty Earth men and women, and one short, black man from The N-T. Mann Yu was going through with them, replacing Future Arne Wong as scout.

"I should go through first. If anyone should see me, at least I will look like them. You people are hard to hide." He smiled brightly at his comrades as he spoke. "On your command," he said to Yi-Tai Feng.

"You have it," the Earth man told him. "Proceed, Mann Yu."

Mann Yu turned to face the portal and stepped through it.

They could see him clearly on the other side. He quickly surveilled up and down the hallway and then motioned for them to come through.

In less than two minutes, the entire task force was on the other side, on The Empty. They proceeded down the labyrinth on the other side as Laboratory Arne Wong switched the portal to inactive mode.

He removed his communications device from his lab coat and toggled it on.

"They are through, Joxe Xian," he said into it. "Please turn the remote sensors on. I have put the portal in sleep mode."

Joxe Xian acknowledged receipt of Arne Wong's instructions and the men logged off.

"Out."

"Wilco, Arne Wong. Out."

~ * ~

Mann Yu led the task force directly to General Nobe Chung's command center.

There, they confronted the general, himself, and disabled him by throwing force field nets around his shoulders and legs.

General Nobe Chung shouted for his men, and they came staggering through four different entrances in various stages of sleepiness or drunkenness...or both.

They were no match for the Earth men and their weapons. One man who arrived late to the fray managed to get off a shot before he was disabled. The shot winged one of the task force's women in her shoulder.

"Take her back to the portal and send her back for medical care," Yi-Tai Feng instructed Mann Yu. "Then you get back here as quickly as you can."

"Can you walk?" Mann Yu asked the female scientist. She nodded affirmatively and the unmatched pair took off at a run back to the Yu-Lee laboratory complex.

"Why did you send Mann Yu on this task?" another of the task force members—this one an administrator from Human Resources—asked.

"He should be able to make it back here without exciting any attention," Yi-Tai Feng patiently explained. "Not for nothing, people, but if you stop to challenge every one of my decisions, we are going to fail. Please save your questions and opinions for another more suitable time. I will hear you out. You have my promise."

"Sorry, Yi-Tai Feng," the administrator said sheepishly.

"Later," Yi-Tai Feng admonished.

He turned to face a sputtering General Nobe Chung.

"Who are you giants?" the general gasped. Yi-Tai Feng dialed the controls on the force field to loosen it somewhat. It wouldn't do to strangle the military leader, after all. "What do you want?"

Yi-Tai Feng had to admire the other man's self-possession. There were many other questions that could have been asked, but in his opinion, the general had asked the most important ones.

"I am Yi-Tai Feng," he replied. "These men and women are volunteers from our World—we call it 'Earth'—who have accompanied me here to rescue our people."

"Your people?" the general echoed with a sneer. "You are the very first giants to arrive here on The Empty. If we have any of 'your people' here, I know nothing about it."

Yi-Tai Feng smiled. "You are correct, of course," he said. "May I confirm that I am speaking to General Nobe Chung, the military leader of the world known as The Empty?"

"You do," the general said.

"I apologize for misspeaking," Yi-Tai Feng continued, his smile disappearing in a flash. "We come to rescue Arne Wong's people, people from a World known as The N-T to its own citizens."

"Arne Wong?" the general repeated. "The Arne Wong from The N-T? I had him spaced—" General Nobe Chung allowed his words to fade out, a look of comprehension washing over his face.

"Not spaced?" he guessed.

Yi-Tai Feng nodded grimly. "Not spaced. Landed softly on a nice bed of grass, actually. On Earth."

"Earth?" the general exclaimed. "Earth isn't in position to be reached from our orbit! Impossible!"

"We moved it," Yi-Tai Feng explained. He was speaking patiently to his captive, but it was becoming difficult for him to maintain. "Our Earth is in an orbit consistent with your own."

"You moved a planet?" the general asked. He looked impressed. "I'm impressed," he said.

"Where are Cece Wong and Nene Wong?" Yi-Tai Feng demanded. He was done explaining anything more to the general. "Where is Nobe Chung? And any remains, any parts, belonging to Amnelia Yu. We want those as well."

"You don't ask for much," the general replied sarcastically. "What makes you think I have them?"

"Arne Wong has told us everything about what you did to the people from The N-T," Yi-Tai Feng said. "Everything. We know they were your prisoners and their fates were entirely in your hands."

"Well, I have released them," the general replied, assuming an innocent expression that really didn't work for him. "They are free citizens of The Empty now."

"'Free citizens?'" Yi-Tai Feng repeated. "I did not know there was any such thing on this World."

"We have changed."

"Changed? How?"

"We just established a new government with a new constitution. We abolished slavery," the general stated as if those things were easy to do. "Even freed the women."

"'We'?" Yi-Tai Feng once more challenged.

"Arne Wong, me, and my men. Mann Yu—*our* Mann Yu, of course. As a matter of fact, your women—Nene Wong and Cece Wong—now live with our Arne Wong. Who, by the way, is president of our new government for the next solar year, by which time we will hold free elections." He said this casually as if the accomplishments he recounted were something easily had.

"A lot has happened here," Yi-Tai Feng acknowledged. "And what of Nobe Chung? And Amnelia Yu?"

"Oh, your abomination has been returned to The N-T," the general said dismissively. "Arne Wong took her back to be reconstructed. And as for your Nobe Chung? Well, he has joined my Army, completely voluntarily, mind you." The general laughed. "You won't even recognize him," he chortled. "We have completely rehabilitated him."

"Starved him and beat him, you mean?"

"Tough love." The general was amused by his response.

"Was it tough love you showed our Mann Yu?" Yi-Tai Feng's anger flared. He knew how Amnelia Yu mourned the death of her son, and the brutal way the execution had been carried out.

General Nobe Chung flinched when this question—an accusation, actually—hit him.

"That was an unfortunate accident," he said, looking genuinely repentant.

"Accident?"

"Well, it was an accident which caused him to be left alone with someone who thought him to be *our* Mann Yu. Someone with a grudge..."

"Then he did not receive a military execution?"

"He did not. Even in our formerly lawless society, what happened to your Mann Yu was murder."

"And what you did to his mother?"

"We will not discuss the abomination as if it were human."

"But it—she—is human. She has a human brain. Human vision. She even had a human heart."

"Suffice it to say the abomination enjoyed no rights in The Empty."

"Who is the murderer?" Yi-Tai Feng pressed. "Who murdered Mann Yu?"

"Oh, you know, we rounded up the usual suspects," General Nobe Chung said, adopting a bored tone. "We interrogated many of our soldiers and slaves, especially those, both men and women, who were known to have had shall we say 'unpleasant' encounters with Mann Yu in the past? Some of them did not survive their interrogations. We never found the culprit."

"And how was the murder done?"

"Knife. A very long, very sharp knife."

"Murder weapon never recovered?"

"Never."

"Our mission does not include exacting satisfaction from you, personally, for what you did to our friends," Yi-Tai Feng said. "We are here to recover—rescue—them and return them to our World."

"Why not return them to The N-T?" the general asked.

"Is the portal open and safe?"

"It is."

"Then I will consider that as an option. Tell me, where can I find your Arne Wong?"

"He is in and out of here several times every day," the general replied. "If you free me, I can ask him to report here."

"No need!" the familiar voice of Mann Yu interrupted the conversation. "I have him with me now!"

Mann Yu pushed a magnetic levitator which had something that looked like a large pupa on its bed. The pupa wriggled as if its butterfly were striving to release itself.

Mann Yu flipped a brown tarp away to reveal what was under it. It was a very angry Arne Wong, bound arms and legs in a force field net. His mouth was covered with a piece of shiny silver. This Mann Yu removed in one smooth, and painful, move.

"Mann Yu, release me this moment!" Arne Wong demanded.

"Gee, how did Mann Yu overcome you?" a snide General Nobe Chung asked. His eyes twinkled.

"I believe it's called a 'flying back kick,'" Arne Wong said, a strange look overtaking him as he answered. "And just *incredible* speed..." He turned to face Mann Yu. "By the gods, are you the Mann Yu from The N-T?" he asked in amazement. "No need to answer. I can see now that you are." And Arne Wong began to laugh. His laugh expressed more than humor. It rang with appreciation. Admiration, even.

"Who are the rest of your friends?" he asked Mann Yu when he could speak again. "These giant people. Where do they come from?"

"We come from the world you spaced Arne Wong to," Yi-Tai Feng responded. "We call it 'Earth'."

A look of understanding lit up Arne Wong's face. "Oh, I see," he said, looking the group over more closely. "Well, of course I had hoped he landed somewhere safe, but I didn't really think the world was Earth. How did you get the Earth out in asteroid belt orbit?"

"Solar sails," Yi-Tai Feng responded. "Have you sent anything else through the portal since you spaced Arne Wong through it?"

"Actually, yes," Arne Wong admitted, watching the look on General Nobe Chung's face as he spoke. The general, for his part, looked flabbergasted. He looked at Arne Wong as if he had never seen him before.

"I threw a canister—two of them, actually—with diagrams and construction specs for a two-way portal. Oh, also a gram of dark matter. It was just enough to 'salt' the constrete for portal construction..."

General Nobe Chung was nearly foaming at the mouth. "You traitor!" he screamed, struggling against his force field bonds. "I will have you arrested and executed for treason!"

"Do you think you could keep my general under wraps until he calms down?" Arne Wong asked Yi-Tai Feng. "If he kills me now, it will undermine all of the progress we have made." His tone was light-hearted. In truth, he was glad his secrets were finally out in the open...and that his general could not react as he'd have liked.

"General Nobe Chung," Arne Wong began as Yi-Tai Feng started loosening the force field bonds which entrapped him. "This was for the good of us all," he continued. "You did not actually command that The N-T's Arne Wong be killed. You merely said to space him through one of the dark portals...that is exactly what we did." Arne Wong stopped to gauge how his explanation was being received. It sounded a little thin even to his own ears.

The general obviously agreed. He struggled against his bonds with even more desperation and sputtered horrible epithets at his erstwhile partner.

"I beg your pardon," Arne Wong interrupted at one point. "But my father was a human being like you and me."

That stopped the general for a moment. It was enough. He regained his sense of humor even though it was apparent he had been enjoying his rageful rant.

"Arne Wong, you are a son of a something," he sputtered between gales of laughter. "You know very well I wanted rid of that other Arne Wong. I don't care that you didn't murder him. I care that you *tricked me.*"

"Sometimes you need to be tricked for your own good," Arne Wong told the general like a mother scolding a child. "Your temper is a force of nature. It needs *tempering.*"

Yi-Tai Feng completely released the force fields around Arne Wong and assisted the smaller man to his feet. Mann Yu kept his force field weapon at the ready, pointed at the newly freed man just in case he threatened any of their number, especially Yi-Tai Feng. The two men had become very close over the short time they had known each other. Mann Yu felt as protective of Yi-Tai Feng as he felt for Arne Wong—*any* of the Arne Wongs, he now realized. He lowered his weapon.

Mann Yu had confided his feelings to Cece Wong and she seemed ready with an answer.

"It's karma," she said confidently. "You have known each other over many, many incarnations and reincarnations."

"Don't get her started with her Buddhist crap," Nene Wong interrupted. "You won't be able to shut her up."

"Disrespectful girl," Cece Wong hurled at her daughter. The smile on her face took all of the sting out of it, however.

Mann Yu forcibly dismissed these thoughts and focused on what was happening in his here and now.

"Dare I release the general?" Yi-Tai Feng was asking Arne Wong.

"As long as his men are all secured elsewhere, there is very little he can do to us by himself," Arne Wong replied. "There are a number of newly emptied cells. The general released all of the political prisoners when we won our little war of independence."

"Why don't we release him after we have Cece Wong, Nene Wong, and Nobe Chung in our safe possession?" Mann Yu suggested.

"Yes, Mann Yu," Arne Wong said. "I like that option.

"And while you're at it, you might want to find out where his Cece Wong is, his woman. I don't see her here among the other captives."

"You go too far," General Nobe Chung snarled, once more losing his sense of humor. "Leave her be."

"I have to make sure that she does not try to masquerade as the other Cece Wong," Arne Wong explained. "That is all. We need not lay a finger on her. We just want to see her."

"And have her see me like this?" the general objected. "She will not be happy to see me trussed up like some bird for the oven."

"Nevertheless..." Arne Wong shrugged. "Call her to you. I have toggled the comms device on. She will hear you if you speak up. She will probably hear you even if you whisper..."

"I hear him now," Cece Wong said, stepping out of one of the shadowy recesses which littered the bunker. "And I would never try on the persona of that other woman. She has no *style*."

"I am certain that her current 'style' is due to your handling of her," Mann Yu said heatedly. "That lady had plenty of 'style' before you took her captive, let me tell you."

Cece Wong smiled cruelly. "I say the same thing about you and our Mann Yu," she spat out. "You lack a certain something our Mann Yu has in spades."

"I am going to thank you for that compliment," Mann Yu replied with a small bow. "Because your Mann Yu is batshit crazy from what I have seen and heard."

Cece Wong looked over at General Nobe Chung, and he at her. They both burst out laughing at the same moment.

"Touché, Touché!" Cece Wong cried. "I cannot contradict you on that assessment." She continued to look at General Nobe Chung, who had become somber and watchful.

"Please make him more comfortable at least," Cece Wong asked. "He looks just terrible."

"That we can do," Yi-Tai Feng replied, once more fiddling with the force field controls.

He turned to address his task force. "See that his men are placed in the cells, and then inactivate their force fields. Make sure we are in complete control of the security back there. There must be no opportunity for the general to regain the power these men represent."

"Why does the general's army only have men in it?" the HR specialist asked.

"Later, Sen-yat Sung," Yi-Tai Feng said between clenched teeth.

"Sorry, Yi-Tai Feng," the man muttered. He lapsed into an embarrassed silence and got busy helping his teammates in shepherding the captives back into the complex of cells.

The general was released from his force field bonds and taken to a private cell. Cece Wong was housed in the cell next to his.

"You will be released as soon as the people from The N-T are safe," Arne Wong reassured him.

"What is going to ensure that *you* are safe?" the general spat back at him through the bars of his cell.

"Just remember who is in charge here," Arne Wong told the sputtering captive. "Remember who is making it possible for you to grow rich. I will hold up my side of our bargain. If you should harm me in any way, the entire house of cards we've constructed will be blown to the winds."

The general appeared to think this over. He shrugged. "I will consider a truce. You did not tie me up nor did you put me in this cell. But you will let me out. As soon as these people have left, you will free me and my men. You will restore me to my command."

"I will," Arne Wong promised.

Arne Wong was allowed to leave. His mission: to bring Cece Wong, Nene Wong, and Nobe Chung back to the labyrinth housing the portals.

"Meet us at the Earth portal," Yi-Tai Feng said. "We need to discuss the merits of taking them straight to The N-T instead of home to Earth."

"You should be safe using the direct route," Arne Wong said. "I have abstracted a promise of non-interference from General Nobe Chung.

"As long as you don't try to come back to The Empty, you will be safe."

"There are still people from The N-T on Earth," Mann Yu pointed out. "Cece Wong and Nene Wong also need to get back to their own world...The N-T."

"I will negotiate their transfer with the general," Arne Wong promised. He seemed distracted by something that could not be sensed by the others.

"Is there something you are not telling us?" a suspicious Mann Yu asked. He was watching Arne Wong carefully. It seemed to him that Arne Wong was holding something back.

"You know me—I mean the Arne Wongs—too well, Mann Yu. There is one other thing about The N-T that you really need to know. I designed a communications device. It allows Amnelia Yu to contact me if she needs to." Arne Wong paused so that his next statement would get the emphasis it deserved. "And it allows General Nobe Chung to set off a nuclear explosion if he needs to. We will need to disable that device before freeing General Nobe Chung. We also need to locate and neutralize our Mann Yu. You see the communications device is my design—but the nuclear explosive is his."

Forty-one

I need to leave some marks," General Nobe Chung told Mann Yu. "Otherwise it will not look like I put my all into your interrogation."

Mann Yu was bloody. Contused. His eyes were bloodshot and his hair and clothes were in disarray.

"I understand completely," Mann Yu replied, smiling broadly to reveal blood-stained teeth.

"How will you deliver on your promise?" the general asked, holding a cup of water to the prisoner's lips. He gulped it greedily.

"It seems to me that I am taking all of the risks," General Nobe Chung said. "You are just going to sit back and collect half of the profits."

"There would be no profits at all if it were not for all of my planning," Mann Yu replied angrily. "The device that gives us our leverage would not even exist if it were not for me.

"I simply cannot be associated openly with this plot," he continued. "I will naturally be the prime suspect, but I will have a solid alibi for the time of the invasion.

"That is the only way I will evade arrest—and execution. I will be at the family estate with my new woman. There will be records kept. Witnesses will be plentiful."

"New woman?" the general echoed. "Do you think that is wise?"

"I hate it when people ask me that question," Mann Yu said. "The answer is always the same: 'no, it is probably not wise, but I am going to do it anyway.' This is a special woman. I have just recently acquired her from my father. We have history. We were not able to have children, but that is not to say that we did not try." He sighed, an evil light in his eyes. "They returned her to the harem where I hear she proved very productive indeed."

"I have no interest in any of this," General Nobe Chung replied brusquely. "Allow me to recap what you have just asked of me and get your agreement—or correction—to my understanding of your plot.

"You have an explosive device hidden within the portal to The N-T."

"A *nuclear* explosive device," Mann Yu emended. "Very powerful."

"You have four billion terawatts of dark energy stored in a grid in the space between universes."

Mann Yu nodded.

"You will use the 'leverage' provided you by the explosive device to take over the Yu-Lee Laboratory complexes on both sides of the portal."

Another nod—and a correction. "No, General Nobe Chung. Not I. *You.*"

The general nodded his agreement to the correction.

"You will then sell this dark energy to the highest bidder."

"Correct. Funds to be untraceable."

"The successful buyer will be provided with the secret location of the storage grid and that will end your—our—gambit." After receiving the confirmatory nod to this last, the general spoke again. "I have a question for you, Mann Yu," he said. "How do I escape prosecution for my part in this scheme?"

"I will protect you and your men," Mann Yu said. "Or you can pick another world upon which to enjoy your profits. You can start looking now."

"What happens to the bomb—sorry, the 'explosive device'?"

"I think I will explode it," Mann Yu said, a mad sneer on his face. "I will permanently destroy the gateway to The N-T."

"But that's your only two-way portal!" General Nobe Chung exclaimed. "Isn't it the source of the dark energy you have stolen?"

"Exactly," Mann Yu replied. "I am pleased to see you understand."

"Understand what?"

"You understand that our energy will triple in value when its source is destroyed."

"But your grid is in the space between universes," the general challenged. "Won't it be destroyed in the explosion?"

"Oh, I will have moved it by then."

"Moved it? Where?"

"I was thinking Earth," Mann Yu said, pretending to be deep in thought. "They ought to be finishing work on their side of the portal by now."

"And just how do you know this?"

"Oh, I know lots of things that others don't. I have recording devices. I have spies. I have the kind of wealth that buys a lot of information."

"I see."

"So do we have a deal?"

General Nobe Chung took on the aspect of the deep thinker. He picked up his communications device and toggled it on.

"Arne Wong," he spoke through the device. "It is done. You should come in now." And then the general sat down and enjoyed the look on Mann Yu's face.

"You are without honor," General Nobe Chung said bluntly.

"I will get you for this!" Mann Yu screamed. "You will die a miserable death—in poverty. I will see to it."

"Oh, I don't think you're going to have time to do much of anything," the general replied blandly.

Arne Wong burst into the room with four of the general's troops. "Take Mann Yu to the conference room in the Yu-Lee Laboratory building. Make sure he is securely bound."

Arne Wong turned and placed a hand on General Nobe Chung's shoulder. "Thank you, Nobe Chung," he said. "That couldn't have been easy."

"Well administering the beating was fun," the general replied with a cold smile.

The four soldiers had successfully forced Mann Yu to his feet and out of the cell. He could be heard sputtering and protesting all the way down the hall, out into the corridor, and up the frozen metal steps to the street.

"Well, we'd better catch up with them," Arne Wong told the general. "We don't want to be late to the trial—you are the star witness, after all."

"Proud to serve," General Nobe Chung responded, giving Arne Wong a proper salute.

~ * ~

General Nobe Chung had given Arne Wong wide latitude in handling the case against Mann Yu. Arne Wong had created a courtroom in the huge conference facility at Yu-Lee Laboratories.

He had appointed a judge; he had seated a jury which represented a broad swath of the small but diverse population of The Empty. There were no women on the jury or even in the room, for that matter. Their rehabilitation had just started, after all.

Arne Wong had even appointed a lawyer to represent The State—that would be him. He was The State. The State would be prosecuting the case. And he had appointed a lawyer to represent Mann Yu.

Mann Yu's father, Xanu Lee, sat at the defense lawyer's side, fiddling with a handheld device of some kind. He did not look up at his son when he was hauled into the room.

When Mann Yu saw the setting, he recognized what was at stake. He stopped protesting. He attempted to straighten out his attire and his hair. He sat in the chair provided for him.

Arne Wong and Nobe Chung were the last men to enter. Once they crossed the threshold, the room's massive doors were swung shut. The sound of bolts could be heard clearly throughout the room—they were all sequestered and secured.

"Your Honor, distinguished members of the jury, I am Tran Han representing the government of this Nova Terra—known familiarly as The Empty—in a capital case we bring against Mann Yu." The lawyer walked up to the judge's dais and deposited a sheaf of documents before continuing.

"Mann Yu is accused of high treason against the State. He has proposed using nuclear explosives to threaten and extort not only our own world, but the world known as The N-T which exists on the other side of our only two-way portal between universes. We have elected to designate the charge against him as high treason in that it is the only charge which can possibly result in the death penalty we seek. I will bring forward the case very simply: I have one exhibit and I have one witness."

This statement was met with muted mumbling throughout the courtroom. The judge employed his gavel to bring the room to order.

"If you cannot maintain silence, I will bar you from this court," he told the trial attendees. "One more such outburst and I will have this courtroom cleared."

While he was speaking, Xanu Lee had slid the handheld device he had been fussing with across the table to his son. Mann Yu looked at the device in horror, then looked directly at his father.

"Use it, son," Xanu Lee said. There was no obvious emotion in his voice or expression. "Do the right thing for once."

Mann Yu looked at the device again. He picked it up and brought it up to his forehead in one swift movement. He depressed a button on its surface.

A jolt of power leapt from the device and surrounded Mann Yu's head with a halo of blue and bright, bright white. The arc of energy was almost too bright to look at.

It had all happened so suddenly that no one in the courtroom had had time to react.

When the people crowded into the room registered what had happened, shouts rang out as Mann Yu slumped to the table, his eyes and mouth wide open. A pool of drool formed below his gaping mouth. He twitched.

The judge was gaveling again even though no one paid him any attention.

"Get the medical team in here immediately!" he yelled to his sergeant-at-arms. This man was already unlocking the huge doors which kept them all prisoners, or trying to. His nervous haste had rendered him clumsy. After many sweaty moments, the tumbling of the locks could be discerned.

The doors flew open and the medics ran in, two of them muscling a gurney through the narrow spaces between rows of spectators.

They soon had Mann Yu strapped down. He continued to flop and twitch as they raised the gurney and wheeled it from the room.

"Clear this courtroom!" the judge cried. "Only legal teams and Xanu Lee are to remain. *Now*, people. I want this room cleared in under two minutes!" He once again signaled to his sergeant-at-arms who deployed his men to assist in getting the stunned spectators to their feet and exiting the room. Once the men got a person through the doorway, they turned to assist the next. Not too many people were seriously harmed in the process and the judge's two-minute deadline wasn't missed by more than forty seconds.

"Xanu Lee, step forward!" the judge intoned.

A subdued Xanu Lee stood, stepped around the table he sat at, and approached the judge.

"What was that device you gave to your son?" the judge inquired. He said it softly, but his words had a sharp edge to them.

"It was a medical device," Xanu Lee responded woodenly. "He uses it to control his migraine headaches."

"Are you saying the device malfunctioned?" the judge demanded, his doubt flaring.

"I have no idea what happened," Xanu Lee said, still not looking at the judge, or anyone else. "I suspect someone may have tampered with it."

"Are you not concerned about your son's condition?" This time, the judge sounded like he was struggling with disbelief.

"Of course I am!" Xanu Lee finally looked up and into the eyes of his inquisitor. "I am in shock, Your Honor. I am stunned by what has happened here."

The judge looked at his sergeant-at-arms, who stood by his side, at the ready.

"Take custody of that device," the judge ordered. "Do not touch it. Bag it. Tag it. You know the routine."

"Yes, sir!" the man was already in motion, removing what looked like an evidence bag from his pants pocket.

"Call Arne Wong back into the room, please." The judge was no longer expressing any emotion at all. He was calm and in control. He also tapped one finger on the desktop in front of him as he waited for his order to be executed.

Within minutes, Arne Wong and General Nobe Chung had re-entered the room.

"Thank you, Arne Wong," the judge said, after the door had been secured behind the two newcomers. "I know you are incredibly busy, but I was wondering if you still ran your private investigation business. I have a need for an immediate and *private* investigation."

Arne Wong stood forward. "I would be very interested in helping if it has anything to do with what has just happened in this room."

"It does."

"Does the prosecution agree with this action?"

"We do," affirmed the head lawyer at the prosecution's table.

"Objection!" called a lawyer from the defense table.

"Over-ruled," the judge said severely. The lawyer sat back down with an audible "plop." The judge seemed to think better of his actions. "Well, explain the grounds for your objection, and be quick about it," he said impatiently.

"We have detectives in our police force," the man said, stammering slightly. "This is a matter for them."

"And if they are implicated in this matter?" the judge challenged.

"Implicated, Your Honor?" the man replied, his confusion written all over his face.

"Our so-called police force is The Authority empowered by General Nobe Chung for his wife's use. It's her little hobby. Do you disagree with my definition?"

"N-n-no," the man stuttered. "I cannot disagree with your definition of The Authority, Your Honor."

"Do you still stand behind The Authority's impartiality—or even capability—in investigating the events surrounding the wounding— *the maiming*—of Mann Yu in this courtroom today?" The judge's voice was approaching strident. His dander was up.

"I see what you mean," the lawyer said, lowering his eyes which now regarded the table in front of him. "Mann Yu and General Nobe Chung had many dealings..."

"Yes, and most of them were of questionable legality." The judge waited for the man's response.

"I withdraw my objection," the lawyer said, resuming his seat.

"Can I object, Your Honor?" an affronted General Nobe Chung asked.

The judge simply ignored him. An eye roll did his speaking.

Xanu Lee didn't appear to be listening to this exchange. He didn't appear to know what was happening around him at all. He suddenly addressed the judge, however, a look of epiphany on his face.

"Your Honor, did the prosecutor announce that he was Tran Han?" he asked, strength and vigor back in his voice.

"He did."

"Does his brother, Doctor Gude Han, operate the Nova Terra Mental Health Hospital and Research Center here in this very city?"

"He did, Xanu Lee. But his facility was destroyed and the director himself killed. It is a suspicious fire and is under active investigation."

Xanu Lee appeared to be shaken by this development. He trembled as he continued to pursue his line of thought.

"Is there a facility that has the ability to safely and humanely incarcerate criminals with mental conditions?"

"There is. The Northrup Health System is just such an institution. Ironically, it is operated and managed by Sune Han, Gude Han's cousin."

"Your Honor," Xanu Lee said. "Could you see that Mann Yu is transferred to Doctor Sune Han's care? He needs immediate intervention. Once the hospital has stabilized his condition, they have no capability to treat a trauma like the one we just witnessed."

"I will take it under consideration."

"Thank you, Your Honor."

"You may go now, Xanu Lee, with my sincere condolences," the judge said, motioning Arne Wong to approach the bench.

As Xanu Lee was escorted from the room, Judge Gen Bo leaned over to speak to Arne Wong.

"I must maintain my impartiality," he said. "I cannot show any prejudice toward any aspect of this case."

"I understand, Your Honor."

"But I smell a rat, Arne Wong. A big one. A formerly invincible pillar of our business community."

"I understand, Your Honor."

"Turn this case inside out. And do not ignore the possible connection of this case with the destruction of the Nova Terra Mental Health Hospital and Research Center. *And* the suspected murder of director Gude Han. No one is outside the scope of your investigation. No one."

"I understand, Your Honor. May I have possession of the device Mann Yu used to harm himself?"

The judge looked at his sergeant-at-arms. "Is the evidence catalogued and scanned?" he asked. The man nodded his head as he removed the evidence bag containing the device from his inside jacket pocket.

He held it out to Arne Wong. The judge nodded his assent. Arne Wong took the bag and briefly surveilled its contents.

"I need to use some of Yu-Lee Laboratory's equipment to analyze this device," he told the judge.

"I will issue the order. They will comply," the judge promptly responded.

"Very well, then, Your Honor," Arne Wong said. "I'll be off then. Gumshoe Enterprises has reopened for business!"

~ * ~

"General Nobe Chung," Arne Wong called. His general crossed the room to take a look at the object Arne Wong had disassembled on the laboratory workstation. It was now in hundreds of pieces.

"Do you see this, here?" Arne Wong asked the general. He pointed at a magnifying device instead of the miniature component, itself. It could barely be seen with the naked eye.

"Yes, Arne Wong," General Nobe Chung responded. "I see it. But I don't know what it is."

"Neither do I," Arne Wong admitted. "Not completely. But it is definitely the culprit. And it's custom made. Made by someone with access to design and manufacturing capability."

"Like Yu-Lee Laboratories?"

"Exactly like that."

"I see."

"This tiny part was designed to convert very low level power into a one-time arc of extreme power. It is burnt out. Its purpose is fulfilled."

"So this is no accident."

"It is not."

"Is there any way to discover who is responsible for its construction?"

"Just one," Arne Wong replied. "We will need to go through hours of security footage. We will need to comb through logs of materiel usage."

"Materiel?"

"This tiny, burnt-out component?" Arne Wong said. "It was powered by the tiniest molecule of dark energy."

"Dark energy?" Nobe Chung repeated. "Who has access to that controlled commodity?"

"Two people, as far as I know," Arne Wong replied. "Xanu Lee. And Mann Yu."

"You don't think Mann Yu did this to himself?" Nobe Chung challenged.

"No. No, I don't," Arne Wong replied. "I think his father had simply reached the limit of what he was prepared to take. Mann Yu had simply gone too far this time."

"I have already sent men to the security control room," Nobe Chung informed his friend. "It has been completely gutted. All storage and recording devices have been removed, and without finesse, I might add."

"The plot thickens," Arne Wong said, almost to himself.

"I like that," Nobe Chung replied admiringly. "'The plot thickens.'"

"Yeah, it's old-speak," Arne Wong explained. "I love that old language. That's where 'gumshoe' came from."

"I see," the general replied. He segued. "But what do we do next?"

"Simple," Arne Wong was quick to reply. "Nobody would think of the logistics records. We'll just go to Yu-Lee Laboratory's Supply Division and look through their asset records. There we will find our molecule of dark matter – and who signed it out. We've got them!"

"I believe you are right," the general said.

"Take whichever of my men who are suited to the task. Go there now. Don't warn anyone. Let's surprise them, shall we?"

"Good idea."

"I get them occasionally."

"I've noticed."

~ * ~

Xanu Lee was on his comms device.

"So you can reverse the damage just as we discussed?"

He listened for a few seconds and spoke again.

"We have an agreement. I will live up to my side of it. How long before Mann Yu will recover?" He listened again. "Good. That's very good, Sune Han.

"You will be pleased with your reward. I will not let you down."

Xanu Lee toggled his communications device to its "off" mode and put it back in its cradle on the table in his den. He sighed with contentment.

Yanu Yang appeared with the tray which held Xanu Lee's nightly cocktail.

"It is done," Xanu Lee told the servant. "It is in Sune Han's hands now.

"That idiot judge has appointed Arne Wong of all people to investigate our little 'accident.' He'll get as far as the security room and hit a dead end. That was a genius idea, Yanu Yang. I know I did not thank you at the time, but destroying that evidence has made all of this possible."

"You are welcome, sir," Yanu Yang said with a bow. "I occasionally experience good ideas."

"I've noticed," Xanu Lee said with appreciation. He drank deeply from the large but ugly drinking glass. "Your contributions have not gone unnoticed."

Forty-two

I led the charge. Original Arne Wong was directly on my right. Yutani Amniko whizzed over our heads, firing bolts of energy at the guards inside of the chamber.

Sen-yat Sung and Maxx Lee also leapt to the front of the vanguard and began hand-to-hand combat with the four nearest guards. They were joined by Yutani Myochi who took on a guard of his own. He quickly disabled the man and pivoted to engage one of the two men fighting Sen-yat Sung, who was visibly struggling to contain his opponents.

The rest of the detachment had no choice but to leave them to their personal battles—hurling force fields about in such a situation would most certainly end up disabling unintended combatants.

"Follow me!" Yi-Tai Feng ordered his "troops."

"We will use our weapons on the men inside, weapons only! We go in 'hot!'" He smiled grimly.

The inner door was locked.

"Amnelia Yu!" Yi-Tai Feng called. "Can you unlock this door?"

"Allow me!" Yutani Amniko cried, once more zooming across the room to arrive at the door before Amnelia Yu could respond.

The orb began extruding devices which she then inserted into the locking mechanisms. She seemed to be having difficulty. The locks had not disengaged before Amnelia Yu reached the scene.

"Stand aside!" the robot cried, throwing herself feet-first against the metal door.

The door exploded inward, pieces of it flying around like shrapnel. Yutani Amniko was also thrown, but soon recovered her orientation. She moved quickly to rejoin the other robot.

"Are you all right?" she asked a shaken Amnelia Yu. "That was very reckless, you know."

"I am fine," Amnelia Yu said, performing an internal, and external, equipment check. "Yes, it was reckless. You make me thus."

"We don't have time to talk about this now," the orb replied softly. "Later, okay?"

"Yes, certainly," Amnelia Yu replied.

The detachment had already bypassed them and had entered the room. When the seriously unmatched robot pair breached the door jamb, they saw that the battle was pretty much over.

All but one of the guards had been disabled by the force fields. The last one had taken refuge under a workstation and was being surrounded by a determined group of armed giants.

"Let's go see how Maxx Lee is doing," Yutani Amniko suggested.

"Yes, and Yutani Myochi," Amnelia Yu responded. "Let us make sure our sons are safe."

The sounds of the hand-to-hand combatants were muted compared to those in the next room. Loud and differing kihaps— the call of the martial artist—punctuated an otherwise silent battle.

There were still three guards on their feet although they all looked much worse for wear. The three taskforce members were also still on their feet, launching one fierce attack after another.

"You take the one on the right, and I'll zap the one on the left," Yutani Amniko whispered to Amnelia Yu.

"Got it," the golden android replied.

They deployed. A single downward chop of Amnelia Yu's right hand to her man's collarbone was enough to fell him. There was an audible crack as she made contact. He was not conscious when he hit the floor.

Yutani Amniko extruded another long metallic pole and touched her man with it. He collapsed, lifeless.

The robots' involvement in the battle changed the dynamic completely and within minutes all of the guards had been immobilized by their attackers. They were all breathless and bruised, all except Maxx Lee, that is. His giant status had given him an edge—he was every bit as fast as the smaller men and had much more mass to utilize.

"Gather the Arne Wongs," Amnelia Yu called out. "Maxx Lee, you, too. Help Future Arne Wong—whatever he says, do it."

Maxx Lee ran from the room to join the group of myself, Original Arne Wong, and Yi-Tai Feng. We were soon joined by Yutani Myochi and a frazzled Sen-yat Sung.

Maxx Lee was dragging the last conscious guard along with him like a rag doll. "He will tell us what the access codes are," he told the group with confidence. "Let's get him trussed up a little first to encourage him to fulfill his word."

Yi-Tai Feng fired a small tendril of force field around the man's shoulders and deadly feet.

"That enough?" he asked Maxx Lee.

"Should be," Maxx Lee responded. "Future Arne Wong, we stand by for your instructions."

"What is the meaning of this?" a voice called out. We turned as one to see who intruded.

Yutani Myoto stood quivering in rage in the shattered doorway. He held a katana—a very long, very sharp sword—and had it pointed directly at me.

"How dare you—my guests—violate the relationship between us in this manner, and on the very eve of our greatest moment!" he cried. He approached closer, his blade catching the room's lights and throwing off glints of silver with each movement.

He raised his hand and started a powerful downward sweep of the mighty sword. I stood frozen, directly in the path of the deadly blade.

With a strangled cry, Yutani Myoto halted his arm. A strange and wondering look took over his face. The sword dropped from his now lifeless fingers and clattered across the floor.

He fell, sprawling across the bright white marble, a large pool of blood forming under him.

Yanumura, the loyal but abused and disrespected servant, stood behind him, a short wide dagger in his right hand. He wiped it carefully and restored it to its sheath.

"Please continue with your work," he said. He turned on his heel and left the room.

I was the first to speak. I turned to face Yutani Myochi and his mother.

"I am sorry for your loss," I said. "I did not mean for this to happen."

"Arne Wong," the orb spoke. "We will all be annihilated in a very short time if you do not take advantage of the opportunity which Yanumura has provided. If we survive past tomorrow, we will grieve my husband."

"Yes," Yutani Myochi echoed. "We must get to work. I can sign us into the system, but we will need the codes for each of the nuclear devices in order to disable them."

"How many are there?" Mann Yu asked.

"Three thousand," Yutani Myochi replied. "Three thousand that are big enough to worry about. There are thousands of smaller ones, but they will not have enough effect to destroy the sun."

"So we have around seven hours to defuse three thousand bombs," Yi-Tai Feng summarized.

"That is approximately correct."

"Well then, we had better get to work."

I had been talking quietly but intently with our prisoner. After our discussion, I crossed the room and stood in front of a large and solidly constructed safe.

"They are here," I announced.

Amnelia Yu and Yutani Amniko were at my side seconds after I had spoken.

"What are in there?" both robots asked simultaneously. I hiked an eyebrow and regarded them with as much humor as I could muster.

"The codes," I said. "The codes are all in a book in this safe."

"Shall we open it?" Amnelia Yu asked.

"Please. The sooner the better," I replied, feigning patience for effect. "Now!" I shouted. "Please." I stood aside.

The two robots jockeyed for position, appearing each to defer to the expertise of the other. Precious moments ticked by.

"Amnelia Yu," I interjected. "You try it first. It looks pretty conventional as far as locking mechanisms go."

The golden robot nodded to me and to Yutani Amniko and approached the safe, already touching the locking device and listening intently. She removed a small tool kit from a compartment hidden in her carapace.

It took a minute. No more. After she applied two different tools to the mechanism, she stepped back and twisted the safe's handle.

It opened smoothly and noiselessly.

"Very nice job," Yutani Amniko acknowledged.

"Thank you," Amnelia Yu replied.

I had already stepped inside the enormous vault behind the door and was searching its shelves.

"They are here," I announced, brandishing a large white binder. "These are the digitized codes.

"Yutani Myochi, get us logged into as many computer stations that can connect to the Earth devices. I will divide these codes up and we will all take turns scanning in the inactivation sequences.

Each code will have to verified manually—that is the failsafe system in place.

"We must be careful. We will only work for two hours each before taking a break and letting someone else take over our terminals.

"We must be accurate—no mistakes, people. One wrong digit can trigger a premature detonation.

"If you don't feel that you are up to these demands, admit it, and admit it openly. There is no shame. In fact, there is great honor in honesty. Think now for a moment. Are any of you afraid? Dyslexic? Bad with numbers?" I tried to lighten the moment and it worked. The tension in the room palpably lessened.

The Human Resources administrator had a hand up. "Yi-tai Feng?" he asked. "May I ask a question now?"

Yi-Tai Feng laughed out loud, thawing the room further. He responded to the administrator's request.

"Sen-yat Sung," he said, grinning at the fussy administrator. "You may now ask a question. It needs to be a short one."

"What is the white robot doing?" the man asked.

We all turned as one to see that Yutani Amniko had connected another long metal rod which she extruded from her shell to the central computer unit. She was either extracting information or feeding data into it, but which was unclear. The people simply watched her. Many of them held their breaths.

I approached her, not wanting to disturb her, but needing to satisfy my curiosity.

After just a few minutes, the orb disconnected and retracted its metal rod and spun around to face me.

"It is done," she announced.

"What is done?" I asked.

"They are disabled."

"They are disabled?" I was just repeating her words like a moron. I was stunned.

"Yes, three thousand large nuclear devices and four thousand three hundred and sixty small ones. Disabled. All of them."

"How did you accomplish this?" I asked, still stupefied.

"The binder you retrieved from the vault contained the location where the codes existed in the main computer. I memorized this location, found the codes exactly where they were supposed to be and activated the disabling protocols."

"You are amazing." This time it was I and Amnelia Yu who spoke simultaneously. The white orb spun and chattered brightly, clearly pleased by our praise, and amused that we had spoken as one.

"Arne Wong," the orb said next. "Is there not another mission you wish to accomplish?"

"Yes. Yes, there is. I left the records in the archives."

"Please go update them while I make an announcement to our people," Yutani Amniko instructed. "Bring the records and meet me in the labyrinth." She turned to her son. "Yutani Myochi," she said. "Please report to the portal control room. Arne Wong will give you instructions on which portal we will utilize.

"You will adjust the trajectory of the escaping X17 particle to 200 degrees, Yutani Myochi. This is critically important."

"But we have never used a reflex angle before, Mother," the young man replied, eyes wide with fear. "What will happen?"

"We don't know. Maybe nothing," the orb replied. "But then again, maybe everything. Go now. Prepare."

~ * ~

"Some of the people were very angry," Yutani Amniko told me later that day. "The priests rent their garments and crawled across broken glass on their hands and knees.

"But most of the people cheered, and cheered excessively. I have opened my husband's wine cellars to the public and I am sure the celebrations will go on for days."

"You realize we might not have many more days?" I asked her softly. "If my predictions are right, sending these records through to the distant past might mean that none of our Worlds, our universes, would now exist. We would not exist. And it would happen immediately after deploying the capsule. We would have no time to prepare or react.

"We will simply cease to be. To *exist*. To never have been."

"I understand, Future Arne Wong," the orb replied. "But the peoples of the past need to be warned about their future, the futures our Worlds have created. They need to be warned about time travel in order to preserve the fabric of space and time. It is too late for us. Our fabric is rent—*torn*. It has become weak and dangerous.

"We must do this. If we fail to educate them, it will mean the end of everything—and everywhere, and everywhen.

"Do you begin to doubt? Does your resolve faulter?"

"No, not really," I said. I sighed deeply. "It's just that I was hoping to have more time with someone special."

Now it was the orb's turn to emit a sound like a sigh. "I understand," she replied. "I, too, have developed a strong interest in that Original version of you..." She dangled that little tidbit of information to divert my regret—to *share* it, human to human.

I was not surprised. "I thought I detected a connection there," he said. "It wasn't blatant or anything, but I felt something..."

"What are you feeling and where are you feeling it?" a familiar voice asked. Amnelia Yu was approaching, walking down the labyrinth's corridor like a golden dream.

I swung around to face the robot, my face undoubtedly shining with pure pleasure.

"Oh, I was just telling Yutani Amniko that I thought I detected her interest in Original Arne Wong," I said, moving to meet her. I escorted her to where Yutani Amniko floated, humming and bouncing.

"What are you so excited about?" the golden robot asked the white orb.

"Future Arne Wong must tell you that," the orb replied mysteriously. "It is his story. He must tell it."

"Does it have anything to do with what is in the cylinder he holds?" Amnelia Yu persisted. She was teasing us, or delaying me from telling her something she suspected but did not wish confirmed.

"It does," I said, stepping between the two robots and effectively taking command of the conversation. "I must tell you something. It won't be easy to hear."

Amnelia Yu sagged a little, stepping back one small step to create space between us.

I stepped forward to eliminate the space and took one of her gold and silver hands in my free hand: the other clutched a bright silver cylinder like it contained my soul...which it did.

"I have made a history—complete with dire warnings and sure predictions—and had it translated into something a human several hundreds of thousands of years in our past could 'read'—that's their word. They used to 'read' marks on flat sheets to learn things.

"We are preparing to send this cylinder to that distant past."

I stopped there. I knew how intelligent and even intuitive Amnelia Yu was. I had given her enough information. She could surmise the rest.

"You are trying to teach our predecessors?" she asked. "You think that by educating them about the dangers of traversing portals to parallel universes and the ravages of time travel, you will cause them to prohibit such things?"

"I am. And I do," I replied.

"And if they take these steps, everything we know and are will disappear." She was not asking a question. She was stating the reality. "You are going to use time travel to accomplish this."

"Yes."

"You aim for a time so far in the past that the fabric and structure of the universes will be strong and unaltered."

"Yes."

"Bur Earth will already be in the proper orbit?"

"I have found a portal where that is true."

"Okay," the robot said. "Let's go."

"Really?"

"Really, Arne Wong. It must be done."

"Thank you."

"You are welcome. Thank you for creating the record. How did you do it?"

"Oh, there's a lot of guess work in it," I said, smiling broadly. "Like this very conversation, in fact." Now I laughed. "But I got it almost perfectly right. It's in here, too. This very conversation." He held up the cylinder as if to illustrate.

"Almost perfectly?"

"Yes. I put in another sentence that didn't actually happen."

"I am going back to the secure room," Yutani Amniko said in a rush. "I need to talk to Original Arne Wong." And with that announcement, the white orb sped off.

"There," I said, once again grinning widely.

"There, what?" Amnelia Yu asked.

"There was the missing sentence," I replied. "Now my history is completely correct."

"You're amazing," the robot replied.

"No," I said. "You are."

We gave ourselves a moment more, our arms wrapped around each other.

"I have one more thing to say to you," Amnelia Yu whispered in my ear.

"I'm all ears," I said, snuggling one of them closer to her mouth.

"Your citizenship—and that of your mother and sister—have been documented in the annals of The Authority. Your father's crime has been forgiven and expunged from all criminal records."

"Somehow, that still matters," I said, looking her in her gorgeous eyes once more. "Thank you, Detective Inspector Amnelia Yu."

"I lied," she replied. "I have one more thing to say: I love you."

"I love you, too," I said, sharing one last kiss with her. "But I must go now."

I pushed her from me and drew my arm back to throw the cylinder through the humming gateway. At the last possible moment, I withdrew my arm and threw my entire body through the portal.

I felt her. I felt Amnelia Yu entering the portal fractions of a second after I did.

Then nothing.

No sights, no sounds, no scents. No light, no dark.

Nothing.

Forty-three

Arne Wong returned to the bunker with his mother and sister... well, not *his* mother and sister, but those of other Arne Wongs: the Original, Laboratory, and me, Future Arne Wong.

"But where is Nobe Chung?" Mann Yu asked. "Why isn't he with you?"

"It would seem that our general has lent him to Xanu Lee," Arne Wong responded. "I thought I had better bring the ladies to you before heading over to Yu-Lee Laboratories. That is where I expect to find both Nobe Chung and Mann Yu. *Evil* Mann Yu," he explained to a confused-looking Mann Yu.

"Oh, I see," Mann Yu replied. "But what do you want with Evil Mann Yu?"

"I need him to disable that nuclear device he designed," Arne Wong explained. "As I said before, he designed it and inserted it into the communications console I left for Amnelia Yu."

At that moment, as if summoned by the mention of her name,

Amnelia Yu's voice projected from the communications device in Arne Wong's vest pocket.

The communication was short.

"Arne Wong," she said. That was all.

The sound of a massive explosion followed her third syllable. And then it, too, went immediately silent.

"By the gods," Arne Wong said. He did not need to say more; his face said it all. Shock. Horror. Grief.

And anger. Anger as big as the explosion they had all just briefly heard.

"I am going to the laboratory!" he shouted, pivoting and running up the frozen metal stairs. "Wait here, all of you!"

Mann Yu refused the order and ran after him up the stairs and out onto the street. His speed allowed him to catch up with his friend—or The Empty's version of him.

"I told you to stay in the bunker!" Arne Wong shouted.

"She is my mother," Mann Yu replied. "I am coming with you!"

Arne Wong didn't waste a word in response. He was already breathing hard from running. Mann Yu had not yet broken a sweat and was breathing easily.

The pair entered the laboratory complex and immediately turned to run up the labyrinthine corridor to the portals. They knew from experience where the portal to The N-T was. There was no hesitation.

They simultaneously came to a halt in front of the portal.

Dead.

Nothing could be seen on the other side.

Nothing. No debris, no explosive remnants. Nothing. The portal was as lifeless as if it had never existed.

"Mann Yu," Arne Wong said. "Go to the portal control room and activate this gateway. Set the particle escape trajectory at 140 degrees."

"Yes!" Mann Yu said, a realization of what the other man was proposing blooming over his face. "Yes! We will travel back in time prior to the explosion and rescue my mother and grandfathers. Genius, Arne Wong—just *genius!*"

Arne Wong was too distracted to reply to the younger man's praise.

"We need to get Evil Mann Yu and Nobe Chung first," he emended. "Don't activate the portal yet. Come with me. We will send Nobe Chung back to the bunker and will make Mann Yu our prisoner. He will travel with us to un-do the evil he has done."

"Good idea," Mann Yu replied. The two men ran back down the corridor and re-entered the enormous lobby. They accessed the magnetic lift chamber and went directly to the offices of the chief executive of Yu-Lee Laboratories: Xanu Lee on the top floor of the building.

They did not bother announcing their arrival, but rather pushed the administrative assistant in the front office out of their way. They crashed through the double doors—wood, Mann Yu noted—and trained their weapons on the men they found inside.

"Nobe Chung," Arne Wong said, addressing the man from The N-T. "Return to General Nobe Chung. A team from Earth has taken him captive. They wait to return you, Cece Wong and Nene Wong to Earth."

"Why not go to The N-T?" Nobe Chung challenged.

"That was the original plan, but it is no longer an option now available to us," Arne Wong replied, glaring balefully at Evil Mann Yu.

When Evil Mann Yu saw the look on Arne Wong's face, he broke into a wide smile.

"She used the communicator?" he guessed, his grin growing wider and his eyes gaining twinkles of merriment.

"Shut up, Mann Yu," Arne Wong said. "You are coming with me. To the past. We are going to defuse that bomb of yours before it has a chance to go off."

"Too late, isn't it?" Mann Yu sneered. "The timeline has been created. You can't un-create it."

"No, but I can rescue the people there in a new timeline," Arne Wong said. "And that is the only option that makes any sense to me at all."

"Sounds like fun!" Evil Mann Yu crowed. "Let's go! Good-bye, Father," he said, turning to face Xanu Lee. "I will be back and we can resume our strategizing—sorry you will lose your new pet," and here he nodded toward Nobe Chung - "but I am really liking our agreement. I won't betray you. And the woman. I am going to *love* having that woman back!"

Yanu Yang had been standing silently in the room's corner amidst shadows. The lifeless bodies of the guards who had been manhandling him to General Nobe Chung's bunker had been secreted in a little-used conference room twenty paces down the outside corridor. He strode forward and drove a dagger into Evil Mann Yu's back. Mann Yu fell forward, dead before he hit the floor.

They all stood there stunned for a moment. Arne Wong was the first to react.

"Yanu Yang! No!" he cried. "I needed Mann Yu. I needed him to inactivate that explosive device he created and planted in The N-T."

"I can do that for you," the serving man replied calmly, wiping his knife clean on Mann Yu's shirt and putting it back in its sheath. "I helped him design it. I can disarm it. I can go at any time, at once if you wish."

Xanu Lee was on his feet. "Yanu Yang, you will be punished for this!" he cried. "You have murdered my son in front of multiple witnesses! New government or not, murder is still a crime punishable by death."

Yanu Yang remained calm. Undisturbed. He turned to face his employer.

"Xanu Lee," he said, with all of the gravity of a judge. "Your witnesses, including yourself, all know of Mann Yu's crime. The use of nuclear fuel has been forbidden on The Empty for centuries. This crime—your son's crime—is also punishable by death. I have merely accelerated the course of justice. Don't worry. I will come back and face charges. These men will bring me back." He turned to address Arne Wong and Mann Yu. "You will, won't you?" he asked them.

"If you wish," Arne Wong replied. "I think you should consider the option of remaining on The N-T, however."

Yanu Yang was already shaking his head. "My wife is here in this World. I will return to her, even if only for the short time I am allowed to live. Whether General Nobe Chung executes me for treason or a civil tribunal sentences me to death for the murder of Mann Yu, I will return here. The abomination is in that other World. I cannot live in a world where she exists."

"There is nothing more to do here," Mann Yu pointed out. "Let's get going."

"One more thing," Yanu Yang said. He turned back to Xanu Lee.

"All of the security equipment and records," he said. He waited for Xanu Lee to nod in understanding. "They are all in a very safe place. They will serve to document your son's involvement in the theft and use of a number of prohibited items. There are a significant number of other questionable enterprises undertaken by yourself and your subordinates captured in these records as well. Only I know where the records are. Only me. But if something should happen to me, I have left instructions for the records to be disclosed to the public."

He turned back toward his new companions. "That is all," he said. "We can go now."

They left as they had entered...at a run. Mann Yu stopped at the portal control room while the other two men proceeded up the corridor toward the gateway to The N-T.

Mann Yu had learned a lot about portal technology from Joxe Xian. He knew how to open the portal and establish the trajectory angle.

He also knew what 140 degrees meant, and also how to set the parameters on a small time delay which would allow him to join Arne Wong and Yanu Yang at the gate before it opened.

He was careful. Opening the portal without establishing the timeline would transport them all to a nuclear nowhere. He would confirm the physical presence of the corridor from the past through the transparent portal *before* they went through it.

He knew intellectually—from Laboratory Arne Wong—what further use of time travel would mean to their local fabric of space. But he felt he could not possibly know just how thin the dark energy barrier between universes was stretched near this particular portal. He accepted the risk—he had to: his mother's life was at stake.

Adding to the potential for catastrophe was the fact that Evil Mann Yu had been siphoning off dark energy from the same coordinates for months.

Their three-man team would make it to The N-T in the past, in time to save his mother and grandfathers...but would they be able to make it back? Mann Yu didn't even know enough to ask himself this question. He only knew he needed to save his mother.

He ran up the corridor to confront a puzzled Arne Wong. "Mann Yu," Arne Wong said. "Why are you not in the control room?"

"Everything is set," Mann Yu reassured the other man. "I just put the execution on time delay so that I could go through with you."

"I see," Arne Wong replied resignedly. "I understand. We will all go together."

As he spoke, the controls began to whir and the corridor from The N-T from the past materialized. Mann Yu reached forward and activated the local portal controls.

"Let's go," he said, indicating that Arne Wong and Yanu Yang could precede him transiting the portal.

They went.

"Amnelia Yu!" Arne Wong shouted. As he and his two companions ran the length of the labyrinth, he caught sight of the spectacular robot at the end of the corridor. She was holding the controls of his comm device in one hand, preparing to toggle it to its "on" position.

"Do not use that device!" Arne Wong screamed. "It is a trap! Evil Mann Yu has booby-trapped it!"

She heard him. As if in human reflex, she dropped the device onto the gleaming white tile of the labyrinth's floor. It clattered harmlessly away where she allowed it to lie.

Arne Wong ran to her first, taking her arms in his hands and looking into her eyes. They were so beautiful, those eyes. A shock of emotion caused him to shiver. "Are you all right?" he asked her. As if just noticing that he was touching her, he held his hands up and backed away a step.

"Of course I am all right," she replied, laughing. "You're back to save me from myself again, I see." She paused, then took a step toward him and put her hands on his arms in a very deliberate and intimate gesture. "What would have happened if I had turned that device on?" she asked.

"Oh, nothing much, Mother," Mann Yu interrupted, running to the robot and throwing his arms around her. "Just a nuclear explosion. You look just glorious, Mother!" he cried. "So beautiful! Even more so than before!"

"Thank you, my precious son," Amnelia Yu said, removing her hands from Arne Wong and enveloping Mann Yu in a tender hug. "Thank the gods you are all right!" A tear rolled down her golden face. Mann Yu carefully wiped it away with his sleeve.

"Don't cry, Mother," he said. "Arne Wong has brought us back in time to inactivate the explosive device." He gestured toward a Yanu Yang who stood apart from their happy group with a look of distaste on his face. "Yanu Yang is here to disable the bomb," he explained.

"You traveled back in time?" Amnelia Yu asked her son. "So that means the device has already exploded?"

"Afraid so," a tight-lipped Yanu Yang answered. "Now please take me to the device so I may do what I came here to do. I don't want to stay here a second longer than absolutely necessary." He refused to so much as look at the robot.

"Follow me, Yanu Yang," Arne Wong said. "I will take you to the device. I installed it. It's back near the portal. Come." And Arne Wong led the other man back up the corridor they had just come down.

"You knew we were cutting it close, didn't you?" Yanu Yang asked Arne Wong. "How did you know we needed to intercept the abomina—the robot—so quickly?"

Arne Wong took a minute to think this over. "A voice in my head told me," he said.

"A what?"

"Never mind," Arne Wong said dismissively. "It is of no importance."

"Sounds important enough to me," the other man said, clearly shocked by the admission. "Voices in one's head are a gift from the gods. My revered mother used to tell me that."

"Here," Arne Wong cut the man short. His voice was chuckling loudly, irritating him no end. "I put the communications device behind this panel." He pointed to what looked to be a ventilation duct. He bent and quickly pulled the cover off, revealing an object which looked like nothing more than a plain metal box.

"Utilitarian design...obviously from our World," the erstwhile servant observed, removing a small tool kit from his utility belt. He had the box open in just a few seconds.

"Why did you plant this bomb here?" Yanu Yang asked Arne Wong. "It is clear that you have feelings for that...that...that *thing* back there. Why did you try to blow her up?"

"I was coerced...well, I allowed myself to be coerced by General Nobe Chung," Arne Wong confessed. "It was a loyalty test of sorts. But as soon as I discovered Mann Yu was back and exerting influence over the general, I began to doubt. And fear. The general claimed the bomb was leverage over The N-T. He needed a buyer for all of the dark power that Mann Yu had stolen, and he needed to get as much for the sale as possible.

"He hungers and thirsts for wealth, does General Nobe Chung."

While Arne Wong talked, Yanu Yang painstakingly disassembled part of the device. He held a tiny component out for Arne Wong's inspection. "We need to get rid of this," Yanu Yang told the other man. "*Now.*"

"There are several portals to nowhere nearby," Arne Wong suggested. "We can just throw it through one of those."

"Good. Let us do so," Yanu Yang agreed. "*Now*, Arne Wong."

The men took several steps up the corridor and Arne Wong selected a portal and keyed in several digits of code. "Throw it through," he instructed Yanu Yang.

Yanu Yang heaved the small component through the transparent portal. He could see nothing but distant stars on the other side of it. As Arne Wong disabled the portal, a very bright flash of light burst out briefly before the portal went dark again.

"Just in time," Yanu Yang said. "*Again*. Only this time, it was my instinct that told me to hurry."

"Is that what you think the voice in my head is—instinct?" Arne Wong asked.

"No, I don't think so. My instinct does not speak in words," Yanu Yang replied. "It just jangles my nerves like it's tapping out a message, an *urgent* message."

"Shall I send you back through to The Empty now?" Arne Wong asked. "You will go in concurrent time, so you may meet yourself on the other side. It is undoubtedly going to create another timeline, but I don't see any way to avoid it."

"Meet myself?" an astonished Yanu Yang replied. "Which one of us will be real?"

"That's the beauty of it," Arne Wong said. "Take it from me. There are so many of me around between The Empty, The N-T, and Earth that I don't even know them all. You will both be real. Both of you."

"Weird."

"Yeah, very."

Yanu Yang safely launched onto The Empty, Arne Wong returned to where Amnelia Yu and Mann Yu stood talking intently.

"Do you mind if I stay a while?" he asked the robot.

"I thought you'd never ask," she replied coyly. "I would like that very much."

"And me, Mother," added Mann Yu. "Now that I'm home, I want to stay."

"Of course. I hope we are all where we are meant to be," she replied. "I feel we are. Where we are meant to be, that is."

"Something is coming," Arne Wong said, straightening and stiffening as the feeling washed over him. "Something big. And yet nothing at all."

He crossed the space between himself and the robot and took her in his arms as Mann Yu looked on in surprise, and then in approval.

Arne Wong could sense them: the other Arne Wongs. One in particular. Me: the one they all called Future Arne Wong. I held something in my raised hand. Arne Wong felt his own arm raised, poised to throw something. And then, the movement changed. The arm came down and Arne Wong felt me throw myself head-first at something.

And then it happened.

Nothing.

Where they, the enormous laboratory complex, and a newly terraformed Nova Terra once were, now only the empty vastness of space existed.

Forty-four

Mann Yu had his hands around Dr. Sune Han's throat, squeezing with all of his might.

"You quack!" he screamed and sputtered into the man's face. "You told my father you could fix me. You lied, you fucking fraud.

"I am going to kill you!"

And in the next moment, nothing remained of the two men or their World. The difference between Mann Yu's expectation and Dr. Sune Han's abilities was dust. Less than dust. Totally meaningless.

~ * ~

Back on Earth, Laboratory Arne Wong felt something momentous and yet not of any importance at all. He clutched a small strip of gleaming and supple golden fabric. He had been looking at it longingly, being careful not to be observed by the all-too-observant Wong women—and Joxe Xian.

That was of no matter now—and then, nothing was of any matter.

Earth had disappeared, along with its moon. Nothing stood between Mars and Jupiter.

Or so it seemed.

~ * ~

Original Arne Wong experienced a jolt of emotion when the brilliant white orb which was Yutani Amniko returned to the security room which had just recently been their field of battle.

"You have returned," he lamely observed.

"Can't get one past you," she said, laughing the silvery tinkling liquid cascade of her humor.

"I love you, you know," Original Arne Wong told her.

"I know," she replied. "I, too, have strong emotions for you."

"It's like we've known each other before," Arne Wong said.

"It is exactly like that," she replied.

Less than a fraction of a second later, nothing—not a stray molecule—remained of them or their World.

~ * ~

Liu Lee had been powerless to prevent it from happening: he had fallen in love. At least that's what he concluded it must be: love. It was debilitating.

He had resisted for days, but every time he had to speak to the female task force leader, he became a doddering idiot.

So finally they were alone together.

"Shai Gin," he whispered. "I promised I would remain celibate. Please, you must find a mate in one of my men. I must set an example."

Shai Gin just smiled at her man. She was determined to make him hers, and she saw readily enough that he grew *weak* in her presence.

"Liu Lee," she whispered back. "You are for me, and I for you. There will be no other man for me – ever." She approached him and wrapped her arms around his taut, muscular waist.

His hands came up. He was trembling with the effort to resist her.

She kissed him. It took a moment, but he thawed. His arms went around her slender waist. He kissed her back, groaning with desire—and a contentment he had never known before.

And then—nothing. It took no time at all. They were gone along with their beautiful city and all of the busy people in it.

It was exactly like they had never existed at all.

Because they hadn't.

~ * ~

Yi-Tai Feng was escorting Nene Wong and Cece Wong through the corridor of the labyrinth. Nobe Chung followed close behind them.

"I don't know why we can't go home to The N-T," Nobe Chung was saying.

"Big man, stop your sniveling," Nene Wong teased him. "Don't you want to see the 'Planet of Giants' with Yi-Tai Feng?"

"Has something happened to The N-T?" the now very small Nobe Chung asked worriedly. "Is that why we can't go directly back? Something has happened, hasn't it?"

The trio passed a stunned looking Yanu Yang on their way up the vast hallway. They nodded to each other without speaking.

"Didn't Yanu Yang go with Arne Wong and Mann Yu?" the ever thinking Nobe Chung asked next. "What is he doing back here alone?"

"I am sure all of these mysteries will be solved," Cece Wong admonished her daughter's boyfriend. She grabbed him by the shoulder and kept his eyes oriented to the front so he could not turn around and see that a second Yanu Yang was running up the corridor behind them, accompanied by Mann Yu and Arne Wong. "Please relax and stop resisting what cannot be resisted. At least this trip will allow our escape from this horrible place, and that horrible General Nobe Chung," she continued, shuddering somewhat. She did not relax her grip. She was not sure if Nobe Chung would be disturbed by the sight behind them or not. She just knew it would generate another flurry of questions from the precocious young man…and her nerves would not survive another onslaught.

"What about his girlfriend?" her daughter taunted. "Your twin, Cece Wong? She is totally scary."

Her mother did not disagree with her, at least not in words. The look they exchanged puzzled Nene Wong, however. If she interpreted her mother's expression correctly, she did, indeed, *not* agree with her daughter's assessment of her "evil" clone.

They continued up the corridor, nearing the Earth portal with each step.

Then it happened. Yi-Tai Feng froze and uttered a single strangled sound.

Then: nothing.

Well, were you to be standing where the four of them had been, you would have seen nothing.

Give it a minute and let your perceptions clear. What first looked like nothing is really the dark side of a dead planet. It is about a fifty thousand yards below your dangling feet.

Wait another minute. Not a dead planet—a moon. And there, just on its horizon comes its dawning planet.

The planet's slow appearance on the far side of its moon is awe inspiring. The planet is a brilliant ball of blue, green, and brown. Pure white cloud cover scuds over parts of the surface.

It wears two tiny gold and silver bracelets which rotate around it counter to each other. They are solar collectors.

And then another planet rises: brilliantly roiling and raging Jupiter joins the dance of dawn.

And then Saturn, blue and silver and serene. The blue, green, and brown planet and its single moon sits between the angry behemoth and its serene partner.

Should one have the kind of vision to see beyond the barriers of dark matter and dark energy, one would see exact images of the planets and their moons fanning out in an infinite number, each in its own universe.

Almost simultaneously, huge and gracious crafts appear in space around each planet, blinking into and then out of visual range.

The universal condemnation of humanity has been lifted. On these planets, in each of their own universes, humanity can travel to the stars: it has defeated its own greed and ignorance and has been accepted into the larger family of sentient beings.

And the sound is glorious. Each of the Earths in each of those universes throbs and resounds with the mantra of peace in accord with its Universal Law.

No longer The Empty: now the Full and The Complete.

Forty-five

"Over here, Mortenson!" Max Young was yelling to be heard over the considerable distance separating him from his partner.

"Oh, drat and damn that man," he muttered to himself. He took a handkerchief from his back pocket and wiped the sweat from his brow. It was only nine in the morning and the sun was already incredibly hot. "Hope we don't have to move again," Max Young said. The red sun continued to bloat. It was ballooning, actually, on its way to becoming yet another kind of star altogether.

It was early days. Scientists like Mortenson and Young had calculated that mankind had two hundred thousand years to find a way to escape the sure death sentence that the sun's continuing metamorphosis represented. This after moving their planet painstakingly over six hundred thousand years to its current orbit.

Doctor Phineas Mortenson finally appeared from behind the pyramid wall. "Stop your bellowing, Young," he said dryly. "I am here. On schedule. Ready to return to work."

"Sorry," Doctor Maximillian Young said. "You know how impatient I am for today's work. We are finally going to be able to open that box and survey its contents."

"You still think the box is part of the original design of this complex?" the other man asked. "You don't think it looks of a different era entirely?"

"I admit that its design differs from its surroundings," Dr. Young admitted. "But all other tests indicate it's been here as long—if not longer—than the structures that have protected it all of these years."

"Very well, then," Dr. Mortenson said, juggling his camera and tripod. "Let's go. Let's get started already."

He followed Dr. Young, carting his camera gear. They hadn't far to go, just down a sandy and ill-lit flight of stairs and into the first chamber whose door appeared on their right. They, in turn, were followed by six local men who would be doing the heavy lifting.

The eight men were alone, the entire pyramid complex being barred to the public. So many antiquities stolen, so many priceless tablets and wall murals defaced. The new level of protection almost came too late.

It was a sad commentary on the human race.

Drs. Mortenson and Young were not interlopers. They were scientists—archaeologists—and their years-long investigation of this site was about to culminate in the rarest of discoveries.

They had found a tomb, you see. The funereal casket—the coffin—had not been opened yet. That was about to change.

"Ready?" Dr. Young asked Dr. Mortenson nervously.

"Yes, yes, man. Get on with it," Mortenson answered. "I am all set up here." He placed and lit a large lamp so he could take his photographs of their discovery.

"How is your daughter doing?" Mortenson asked his partner. "Is she still in the hospital?"

"Oh, yes," Young replied somberly. "I despair of her ever leaving the damned place." While he spoke, he very carefully broke the seal that kept the lid sealed to the casket proper.

"It's so plain, isn't it?" Mortenson observed. He also wanted to change the subject. This was no time to drag poor Dr. Young back to the subject of his sick, his *dying* daughter.

"She's hell bent on marrying that boy," Young picked up the previous subject once more. "She bore him a son, you know. She named him Maximillian after me."

"How lovely!" Mortenson murmured. "Uhm, uh, what boy would that be?" He was snapping preliminary pictures as he talked.

"That boy, Arnold Woods," came the distracted answer. "You know, the wunderkind of the new astrophysics set? He's just a mad dreamer if you ask me..."

The lid was loose. The men gave no more thought to their prior remarks: they were all in the moment now.

"Give me a hand with this," Dr. Young called to one of their silent assistants. The young man immediately approached and signaled to one of his companions to go to the other side of the casket to help.

And so the lid was painstakingly removed. Two more young assistants were needed to lower it to the floor of the chamber and lean it again the side of the coffin.

A reverent silence fell.

And was immediately broken.

"Would you look at that!" an obviously amazed Max Young said. He said it to no one in particular—and everyone in the room was already staring, mouths agape, at what had just been revealed.

"Is that a golden statue next to the mummy?" Mortenson finally asked.

"Yes, and the statue is almost as tall as the mummy," Young replied. "But I don't think it's real gold."

"Why do you say that?"

"Too shiny. Polished. Still gleaming after all of its years down here buried in sand and dirt."

"Well, we can test all of that," was Mortenson's reply. "What is in that mummy's hand, can you tell?"

"It's a metal cylinder of some kind," Young replied. "Here, Phineas, move in closer and get some shots of this. We have to have everything inventoried, photographed, and measured before we can remove and examine any of it."

Eventually, Mortenson was satisfied with his work. "That's it, old man," he said, addressing his colleague Max Young. "I must have three thousand pictures. All of the measurements are done and documented. As for the inventory, we have one male mummy, five feet and two inches tall; one gold and silver metal statue, four feet and ten inches tall; and one metal cylinder, silver in color, ornately decorated, twelve and a half inches tall by six inches in diameter.

"Can we open it now?" He looked up at his partner mischievously. "Well?"

"I think we should wait until we are back in laboratory conditions," Max Young replied, although it was apparent that he, too, chafed to find out what the cylinder's contents were.

"Let's take it out carefully and take some more photos of it by itself," he said, using his double-gloved hands to ease the cylinder from the tight grip of the mummy who clutched it.

As careful as he had been, as cautiously as he proceeded, the capsule fell open in his hands the moment he had freed it from its previous owner.

He gasped. "More pictures, Mortenson," he urged. He held his hands out to give Phineas Mortenson more room and better lighting.

"They are documents," Mortenson commented, taking snapshot after snapshot. "There are pages and pages of something written in black on amazingly white and pristine pages...of what, I cannot tell you."

"Yes, we will have to get these back to the laboratory and get our forensic folks on them." Max Young stopped suddenly and gasped. Then groaned.

"Oh no," he moaned.

"What? What is it, Max?"

"There are discs here."

"Discs? What do you mean discs?"

"Compact discs, Phineas. Stored information. On discs."

"Oh dear. Are you thinking this whole site is a sham? A fake? Counterfeit?"

"How could it be?" a distraught Max Young asked. "We vetted it completely before beginning the excavation." He came to a decision.

"I am sealing this capsule back up and we are taking it back to the laboratory. I've had a thought, Phineas." He hesitated.

"What? What is your thought?" Mortenson prodded. "Speak, man. What is it?"

"Aliens," Maximillian Young said. "This could be proof of alien intervention—or at least visitation—during the Golden Age of the Pharaohs of Egypt."

"You've lost it, man," the other man replied dismissively.

"Have I?" Max Young challenged his partner. "Have I, Phineas? Well then, what is your explanation?"

"Well," the man huffed and puffed a bit. "We will have to wait until our analyses are complete. I promise you that I will keep an open mind."

"That is all I can ask and expect," a partially placated Max Young replied. "All I can ask…"

~ * ~

Amelia Young smiled up at her new husband from her hospital bed. "Don't look so glum, Arnie," she gently teased him. "I am so happy today—I am finally Mrs. Arnold Woods!"

"This isn't the honeymoon you wanted," the young man replied. "And Max is worried, too."

"He is too little to be worried," Amelia replied.

"He is not too little to miss his mother," Arnie Woods corrected.

"No, of course not," Amelia said with a deep sigh. "I miss him, too, with all my heart."

"He is nearly five years old, Amelia," Arnie Woods said. "He needs you…he needs *us*."

"Have you heard what my father found in that desert site he's at?" Amelia segued. She needed to change the subject. Their last few conversations had ended in tears. They were getting a head start on their mourning: her of her life, husband, and son, and he of the love of his life.

"No, what?" he asked. He would play along, keeping his emotions on an artificial high.

"He found a real live mummy and a gold and silver statue in that old crypt of his."

"He must be excited," the young man said.

"Excited isn't the right word," Amelia Young-Woods replied. "Puzzled is more like it. Seems that there were some modern artifacts mixed in with the ancient ones."

"Well, that's odd," Arnie observed. "Very odd—and disappointing, I'd imagine," he added.

"That's just it," the young woman said, her feverish eyes brightening even further with her excitement. "They date back to 3500 years before the common era!"

"Phew," Arnie Woods whistled in appreciation. "What are these modern artifacts?"

"Discs."

"Discs?"

"They were data storage devices in the twentieth through twenty-fifth centuries," she said. "Thousands of years later than the pyramid. Oh, and some advanced kind of paper. Reams of it. Covered in writing—and most of the writing can be easily deciphered. It's *English*, Arnie. English. Stilted, unnatural, sometimes garbled English!"

"That is unbelievable," Arnie muttered. "*I don't believe it.*"

"It gets more unbelievable with each passing day," Amelia told him. "The more of the document they read, the more bizarre it gets.

"Apparently it is a cautionary tale from the future," she said. "It contains formulae and instructions for moving Earth away from the Sun for its safety."

"Aren't we already doing that?" Arnie scoffed dismissively.

"Solar sails," Amelia answered. "If we are able to use solar sails instead of controlled nuclear blasts, we will be able to move much more quickly. There are also many prohibitions—that's why I said it was a cautionary tale."

"Prohibitions?"

"Yes, against—now listen to this, Arnie—against time travel. And the construction of gateways called 'portals' to parallel universes."

"Unbelievable." He fell into a stunned silence. They both became lost in their thoughts, she fascinated with thoughts of investigating the mysteries her father had discovered, he in thoughts of parallel universes and gateways between them.

"I ought to let you rest for the night," Arnie finally said, rising from his bedside chair to give her a kiss. She held on to him, transforming the chaste peck on the lips he had offered into a passionate, minutes-long embrace.

"Give Max a kiss from me," Amelia said. "I love you, Arnold Woods. You are my love for all time." She began to cry.

"No matter what happens to me, I believe we will be together forever," she said, sobbing in earnest.

"It's that new cult you've joined," Arnie joked, trying to cheer her up. "Soon they will have you worshipping the Sun or some such."

"Oh, Arnie," she gushed. "It's not a cult. It's a philosophy. And part of the philosophy is a belief in reincarnation. We will be together, again and again throughout time without end. I know it."

"I hope you're right," Arnie said begrudgingly.

"Believe it," she pressed him. "Believe it. Substitute faith for the scientific evidence you need so badly. *Have faith.*"

"I'll try," he promised. "For you—and us, together for eternity—I will try. I love you, Amy. Good-night."

"Good night, my love," she said as she watched his departing back. She sighed. "Good-bye, my darling Arnie Woods. I will see you again in another life. Good-bye."

She silently cried herself to sleep and sometime during the night her disease took her body down, releasing her eternal energy back into its universe.

Meet Jude LaHaye

Jude LaHaye lives in a rustic cabin on Washington State's Whidbey Island. His humble home is very high-tech, however, as LaHaye is an avid gamer and enjoys live-streaming some of the more competitive games he likes to play.

He forces himself to limit his online time by taking walks among the trees and along the beaches of his island home in the Puget Sound.

LaHaye is a student of world religions and likes to interweave themes, particularly from Eastern religions, into his novels. Although he has a Master's Degree from Purdue University in psychology, he prefers to analyze the vagaries of human behaviors with words in his books rather than on couches in his den. His characters are very human. That is, they are complicated and prone to making rash—even bad—decisions at times. They get into trouble...frequently. They can't always get out of that trouble by themselves, though. In this way, LaHaye emphasizes that human relationships are what make living worthwhile, or even possible, in some cases.

LaHaye can often be seen on his walks with his Irish Wolfhound, Judy. Whether just unwinding, exercising, or pondering new characters and plot twists, he and his huge hound are frequently discovered out enjoying nature, and each other, in silence and solitude.

Letter to Our Readers

Enjoy this book?

You can make a difference

As an independent publisher, Wings ePress, Inc. does not have the financial clout of the large New York Publishers. We can't afford large magazine spreads or subway posters to tell people about our quality books.

But, we do have something much more effective and powerful than ads. We have a large base of loyal readers.

Honest Reviews help bring the attention of new readers to our books.

If you enjoyed this book, we would appreciate it if you would spend a few minutes posting a review on the book's Amazon page or on its Wings ePress, Inc. webpage at www.wingsepress.com

Thank You very much.

Visit Our Website

For The Full Inventory
Of Quality Books:

Wings ePress, Inc

Quality trade paperbacks and downloads
in multiple formats,
in genres ranging from light romantic comedy to general fiction
and horror.
Wings has something for every reader's taste.
Visit the website, then bookmark it.
We add new titles each month!

Wings ePress Inc.
3000 N. Rock Road
Newton, KS 67114